A Life
in the Future

Martin Caidin

This book is for a young aviator who soon will be
new to the 21st Century, and the wonders
of flight that await him.
My friend and fellow birdman—

ROB MILFORD

A LIFE IN THE FUTURE

Copyright © 1995 The Dille Family Trust
All Rights Reserved.

Cover art by Larry Elmore.

First Printing: June, 1995
Printed in the United States of America
Library of Congress Catalog Card Number: 94-68141

9 8 7 6 5 4 3 2 1

ISBN: 0-7869-0144-6

TSR, Inc.
201 Sheridan Springs Road
Lake Geneva, WI
U.S.A.

TSR Ltd.
120 Church End
Cherry Hinton
Cambridge CB1 3LB
United Kingdom

Introduction

If I were a poet or possessed of lyrical talent, I might even dismiss this word of introduction and simply title this greeting to the readers of years to come "The Ballad of Buck Rogers." My story actually has the ring of a western saga, and certainly it encompasses many of the characteristics and nature of the heroic figures who tamed America's Wild West.

I refer to you as the readers of years to come, for by the time this incredible record reaches your hands, I shall be dust, returned, as we all must be, to the very substance from which we were created—the detritus and debris of exploded stars. We are, one and all, mighty and minuscule, intelligent and primitive, friend and alien, made of the dust of stars, and we shall all return to it in the end.

I never expected to put these words to paper. That is not to say I didn't expect to record my tale for posterity, but, quite literally, to put the words to paper. At the time I write this, neuronic systems are available that are capable of transferring my thoughts directly from my mind to a computer. Living what amounts to two separate lives, more than four hundred years apart, has revealed many such wonders to me.

However, such a technological aid to storytelling is not for me. I wish to share my story with you, the reader, in a comfortable, almost intimate fashion, and this means setting it down in a manner far more familiar to you than to those of my present day. This is, after all, my own guide, enabling you to sweep with me through unexpected adventures and wonders, to share my journeys through the air in machines both ancient and so technologically advanced as to be incomprehensible to a reader of your present time. Together we shall leap and hurtle through the black, timeless void to nearby worlds and discover aliens from beyond our own galaxy.

It is a tale of the future, of our land, of our nation, and of the universe. It echoes with the sounds of thunder and battle, for there is little surcease from this most ancient indulgence of man.

But I indulge myself in philosophy when I should instead share with you the marvelous people, the men and women who bore me into the future, who became my friends and confidants and fellow warriors, and especially the woman who shares my life with me even now.

This woman is Wilma Deering, whom I would not meet and learn to love until nearly five hundred years from the time I was born. No, there is no mistake in these figures, for my story resembles that of a modern Rip Van Winkle, but without the full beard of that sleepy gentleman of childhood storybooks.

I have now lived for a total of 128 years. Once such longevity would have been something to marvel at, but even at this advanced age, I am hale and hearty, with the enthusiasm and drive of a man a century younger.

Let me not confuse you. From 1996 until the year 2429 A.D., I did not exist, at least not in human form. I was born in a small town near Oshkosh, Wisconsin, in 1962. Oshkosh is a teeming aviation center famed throughout the world, and I moved smoothly into that world. At the age of sixteen, I soloed my first aircraft. Less than ten years later, I had been an Air Force fighter pilot, bomber and transport pilot, and had gone on to become an airline captain. I flew everything from ancient First World War biplanes to heavy bombers of the Second World War at air shows throughout the country.

I was what other pilots called a "natural" behind the controls of an airplane. I flew in small wars throughout Africa and Central and South America—wherever my country needed me. I lived for flying, and when I entered stunt competition, I fell wildly in love with a stunning Italian girl, who was also a pilot. Shortly before we were to marry, she saw me crash in a mock combat during an air show. My plane exploded in flames while she watched, helpless and horrified, as the blazing engine tore loose and smashed directly into my chest.

For the public record, I was officially, medically, legally dead. The proper forms and papers proclaimed it so. According to the wishes expressed in my will, my body was cremated.

But in truth, I was not dead. Not quite, although in medical terms, I clung to life only by the slimmest of all possible margins, and it required a massive program involving the most advanced medical science to keep me alive. Had I had any say in the matter, I would have pulled the plug myself. One eye was ripped out of my skull. I had very few bones that had not been broken; my skin was slashed, scraped, mangled, and burned. My muscles were little more than limp rags; unassisted breathing was impossible and the pain unbearable.

At the time, I was aware of none of this. By some fantastic stroke of fortune, my tragic accident took place just when a government-funded medical program was seeking a once-healthy human who had been dumped at the doorstep of death.

I had nothing to do with events except to be barely alive, though this qualified me as a valuable research animal, unable to protest what was going on. Everything in life is a matter of timing. Many times in my long lifetime a split second spelled the difference between life and death. This was no different.

I lay there, mangled, unconscious, a travesty of a living human being. The best medical treatment in the world was barely able to keep me alive. Even they knew I would never recover. The details of the incredible program that sustained my life will not be told here and now, for they constitute a major element of my story. Suffice it to say that I was the unwitting player in a drama that continues to this very moment, and will continue to do so until the day I finally, actually die.

As I composed the remarkable narration that follows, I became increasingly aware that I could not hope to tell the whole story without assistance from certain individuals who were directly involved. Obviously I could not repeat conversations in which I did not participate, nor could I know the feelings or sensations or the attitudes of others. These people, named and unnamed, have helped to fill in the spaces, flesh out the events, and give meaning to the days, weeks, months, and years of my labor.

*   *   *   *   *

I departed the world of the living in 1996, near the close of the twentieth century. I was returned, willingly or unwillingly, back to pain and consciousness in the year 2429. It was now 433 years since I had been officially declared dead.

I need not now detail the modern miracles that restored me to life. Do not look for a statement to the effect that "they remade me better than new." It was not so, and I doubt it ever will be so in the case of a human being. All this time has taught me that we are truly valuable and wonderful creatures, yet none of us is ever more than a single heartbeat away from oblivion.

Our road to greatness is on the edge of a very sharp and slippery razor!

My beloved United States of America was gone. The land was now called Amerigo, after Amerigo Vespucci, who once explored our strange lands and made wonderful maps, including the unknown land that would become America and, eventually, Amerigo in his honor.

I doubt readers will be surprised to learn that as we passed into the twenty-first century, the world became embroiled in thermonuclear war. The world as we knew it was changed forever, hardly for the better, as toxic wastes, the residue of biological agents, and radiation despoiled the land and the oceans themselves. Finally, near the close of the twenty-first century, a kind of "Stop This Madness!" mentality began to surface. Winning a war by burning down your neighbor's home at the cost of having your own domicile engulfed in flames is a no-win proposition even for the most power-hungry among us.

Amerigo was forever changed from the old America. Gone are the individual states. Gone is a cohesive national structure. The land is studded with centers of power. The strongest are those of the Federation of Amerigo, the descendant of the land I left. Amerigo has strategic centers scattered across the land, but far more numerous are the guerrilla bands of great ferocity and power, owing allegiance to none save themselves.

They do not hate Amerigo, but they seem eternally unforgiv-
ing for the madness that afflicted the world. As so many world
leaders had long prophesied, the increasingly industrialized population centers of Asia gave rise to a new world order. The Han
Empires of China joined forces with a ruthless Mongol force. In
the tradition of Genghis Khan, these bands, racing recklessly in
the wake of intense nuclear fallout, decimated central Europe
and came down through Canada to attack the United States. The
latter campaign failed, met by savage defense and attacks on the
cities of their homeland.

The long, terrible battles destroyed many cities, created new
ones, and thrust the future into a bewildering standoff of mighty
weapons and force fields. Modern Amerigo is a checkerboard of
Mongol outposts, guerrilla gangs, and Amerigo itself.

Old power structures are gone forever. The long-threatened
holy war by the Arab nations was over almost before it started.
Swarms of powerful thermonuclear weapons destroyed the great
oil fields, decimated Arab cities, and reduced their armies to
inconsequential nomadic bands. The Muslim world should have
anticipated, but never did, a new world order in which petroleum
was as unnecessary to the postwar world as candles were to light
the cities of the late twentieth century.

Even had the power centers of the Arab world not been
smashed and incinerated, their rich oil reserves would have been
ignored, superseded by the development of a fantastic new source
of power called Inertron. Oil became an antiquated footnote in
the annals of history.

Self-preservation brought about a familiar stance among
nations, who soon learned the wisdom of abstaining from the use
of weapons of mass destruction.

Gone forever were the great air fleets. A terrible undersea
war consumed international merchant fleets; new powers were
born and others faded away. Chile, to everyone's astonishment,
sided in the struggle for power not with Amerigo but with the
Mongols. Scientists from throughout the world gravitated to that
coastal land of South America. In self-defense, Amerigo allied
with Central America and the other nations of South America.
Latino nations joined together in a self-protective alliance and
became the breadbasket for all of North and South America,
leaving Europe hungry and in wreckage. Food production across

BUCK ROGERS

China, South Asia, and the Rim nations increased tenfold, giving rise to a "green revolution." Nations figuratively circled one another tentatively in nervous standoffs.

* * * * *

Much to my surprise, my experience and background in flight proved invaluable in skirmishes between Amerigo and the Mongol Empire. I flew not only in powerful Asps with energy-beam and disintegrator ray weaponry, but also in space cruisers of enormous size that could race from Earth to Mars in less than a single day. The ancient dreadnoughts of the oceans, the mighty battleships, were long forgotten, but they saw their successors in space dreadnoughts, built in limited quantities because of their immense cost in money and materials. I found myself in the thick of engagements involving these marvelous machines and was considered a valuable asset to my adopted land.

* * * * *

I write this journal—call it book or diary or whatever you will—outward bound on an interstellar flight to the distant world of Cydar, where Wilma and I have been invited. Even at many multiples of the speed of light, it will be a long journey.

But it will never be dull. Consider it to be a honeymoon across fifty thousand years of travel at six trillion miles a year.

I am 128 years old, the chronological age given me by the science of the twenty-fifth century in which life was returned to me. When these pages are finally read, it is my hope that the people of my time, my original time, the final years of the twentieth century, will be able to hold these pages in their hands and experience some of the same sense of wonder I experienced.

There is really no rhyme, no reason for why this has all happened. I am content to describe what has transpired with a phrase of my time, when I flew with wings on atmospheric lift and I could join the feathered creatures of my ancient past.

Aero, ergo, sum.
I fly. Therefore, I am.

Anthony "Buck" Rogers

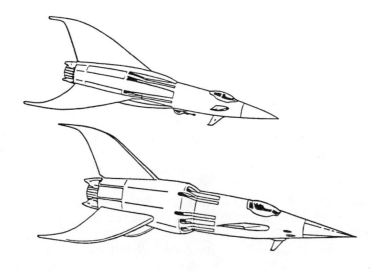

Chapter 1

"Transcon Six Three Niner, Chicago Center."

Captain Anthony Rogers glanced at the global position system display before him. Glowing letters and numbers told him with that brief glance his altitude, heading, speed, and estimated arrival time at his destination: Wittman Field, just outside the city of Oshkosh, Wisconsin. A combination of space satellite relays and the advanced computers of the huge Boeing 747 worked near-miracles with their speed and accuracy. Guesswork was a thing of the past. Sometimes it almost seemed he was watching a computerized video game instead of flying a four-hundred-ton winged giant more than eight miles above the earth.

From his right, the copilot heard a barely audible sigh. Tim Hawkings glanced at Rogers and grinned. "You still don't care for all the computers, do you?"

Rogers shrugged. "It keeps the bean counters happy. Tough to fault the front office for wanting maximum efficiency."

"I know, I know," Hawkings answered. It was a subject they'd discussed many times. Their craft was an advanced state-of-the-art jetliner. It was equipped with what they called a glass cockpit, and contained none of the old-fashioned instruments with which Anthony Rogers had learned to fly. Almost everything before him was electronic. What he saw was a whole passel of television-

screen readouts, right down to a miniature video airplane repre-
senting themselves crossing the ground. But the bean counters
who managed the costs of running Transcon Airlines knew what
they were doing. A man couldn't begin to rival the computerized
flight systems for operating with the best possible fuel efficiency.
Even before they left the ground on a flight, everything had been
figured into the electronic brains—aircraft weight, fuel weight and
burn, temperature, dew point, humidity, and traffic control calls
from Chicago Center or any other major hub airport from where
they operated.

Hawkings said aloud what they both were thinking. "The
name of the game is super-efficiency. Maximum effort for minimum cost, right?"

"Uh-huh," Rogers said, occupied with his own thoughts. Tim
was right. The airlines in the jet age were driven by cost. Passengers really didn't care what kind of airplane carried them from
one place to another. In the old days, they cared. They even spec-
ified the type of airliner they wanted for their flights. Not anymore. The single most-asked question in today's marketplace cut
right to the quick: "How much does my ticket cost?"

That was reality. You had to operate with the lowest cost possible. If you didn't, then the competition would drive you right
into the ground. And no one flew for an airline that went out of
business.

Rogers listened to Tim answering the call from Chicago Center. "Chicago, Six Three Niner with you."

There wasn't any need even to listen to the exchange. As fast
as the controller spoke, his words appeared on a glowing screen
and paper slid out from the same computer with their descent
instructions printed out for immediate or future reference if
needed. Rogers watched the screen. "SIX THREE NINER
HEAVY CLEARED OUT OF FLIGHT LEVEL FOUR THREE
TO LEVEL ONE SIX, HOLD ONE SIX, MAINTAIN HEADING
ZERO FIVE ZERO, EXPECT CLEARANCE CHICAGO
APPROACH DIRECT WITTMAN."

Neat and to the point. They were cleared to descend from
43,000 feet down to 16,000 thousand, continue their heading of
50^0, and wait for a call from the approach controller handling
Chicago traffic inbound to Steve Wittman Field at Oshkosh, Wisconsin.

Rogers's fingers moved in a blur across a computer keyboard on the console between the two pilots, punching in the movements to descend and stay smack on the numbers called out by Chicago Center. As if by magic, the power levers came back to start their descent, the computers adjusted their trim and flew the heavy Boeing downstairs as if it glided on rails. But at 21,000 feet, the smooth descent back to earth changed. The best computers ever made couldn't prevent turbulence. At only four miles high, the heat from the summer sun reflected up from the baked ground with some stiff punches in the shimmering haze and smog surrounding Chicago in every direction. Back in the huge cabin, the flight attendants would be reminding their passengers—all four hundred and ninety-seven of them!—to fasten their seat belts and move their seats to the upright position and raise their tray tables back into the safe locked compartment.

They took a sudden sharp blow that caught them by surprise, probably from another heavy jet crossing their own descent at a right angle. The big jetliners left behind tornadolike winds, long funnels of rotating air, as they descended at reduced speed and the wing flaps came down.

"Bumps and grinds," Tim said casually. "Gonna be a fun ride."

Rogers made a sudden decision. He hated sitting at the controls of a giant airplane—or a small one, for that matter—with his thumbs twiddling uselessly while some crazy bunch of black boxes and silicon chips flew his airplane. He brought his left hand up to grip the control yoke before him; his right hand went comfortably around the four power levers. Briefly he lamented the fact that they didn't even call them throttles anymore.

"I assume," Tim said with a grin creasing his face, "you are dismissing the autopilot and you are now reverting to the primitive act of hand-flying this whale?"

"Primitive? That's what you call it?"

"Natch," Tim jabbed right back. "But you do look sort of like Lindbergh. Not like Fats Molloy, though. You remember old 'Super Suet'?"

"Never mind groveling in memories," Rogers chided him gently. "Chicago is three seconds late in getting back to us. Prod them a bit." Tim Hawkings didn't need to say a word. The electronic displays flashed, and the printed words issued forth from the computer slot like a super-thin tongue with change of radio frequencies

3

and some new numbers for the radar transponder.

"We just keep right on trucking," Tim said aloud. "Approach says we have a clear path to Wittman, and we're number one to sit down."

"With all that traffic down there at the convention? There must be twenty thousand planes there for the big fly-in bash," came the reply. "Apparently the sight of the infamous Buck Rogers manhandling this very expensive Boeing onto Mother Earth is part of today's air show."

The "infamous Buck Rogers"—the name Anthony Rogers used for his flying acts with a World War One fighter plane—ignored the dig. "Put your eyeballs into high gear," he told Hawkings. "There's a lot of stuff made of wood and canvas and plastic flying around here, and I don't trust radar to pick it all up. We're sharing this sky with a few thousand amateurs, remember."

"How could I forget? Speaking of wood and canvas, you've got three in formation, dead ahead. Seaplanes, from the looks of them."

"Got 'em," Rogers said quietly.

His radio frequency was already on the numbers for Wittman Tower. It was a madhouse down there. This was the annual convention of the Experimental Aircraft Association, and pilots flew in from all over the world for the celebration, including several thousand planes that were built in garages and barns by enthusiasts with lots of enthusiasm but distressingly little experience flying among so many other aircraft.

"Wittman Tower, Transcon Six Three Niner, Seven Four Seven Heavy, long final."

A familiar voice came back. "That's a rog, Transcon. Everybody's out of your way." He recognized Harry Novogrodski on the radio. Good old Harry. He and Buck used to fly crop dusters together when they were both barely old enough to shave. "Have a tall cold one waiting for me," Rogers answered.

"You can count on it, Buck." That ended the frivolous talking. From this point on, with the field now in sight, Buck Rogers, world-famed stunt pilot and showman, was again Captain Anthony Rogers, and he was totally professional. He and Tim Hawkings were once more the same well-oiled team. Flaps, slats, power settings, gear, speed, angle, and rate of descent—it all came together in a superb blending of two pilots and their behemoth flying machine. Rogers brought her down with his silken touch, riding the turbulent air with the confidence born of long experience. As they crossed the runway threshold, Tim called out the numbers for speed and altitude, and Rogers let her float down so smoothly he seemed to be painting their tires onto the runway.

Rogers leaned back to relax while Tim taxied the huge jet-liner slowly between the rows and rows of airplanes. Tens of thousands of people watched the 747 wings glide over their heads, waving wildly at the pilots and the passengers, whose faces were glued to the cabin windows. Finally Tim parked in his allotted space, and he went through the shutdown checklist with Rogers. They sat quietly in the cockpit while service teams hooked up external power plugs to the jetliner, keeping cool air flowing through the machine. More service teams rolled high platform stairways to the door, and more than five hundred people, counting crew, began their departure.

"Ever have the feeling we're really an ocean liner with wings?" Tim Hawkings asked his pilot. "You see all those people and their luggage flowing out of this thing?"

"That's why we're here," Rogers answered, "right in the middle of the biggest, best, flashiest, most exciting aviation air show in the world. I heard they've got planes here from sixty-three countries."

Tim pointed to his right. "There's something I never thought I'd see," he said slowly, surprise still registering on his face. "Those are MiG-29s and a bunch of Sukhoi 27s—the Russian jet precision teams. They'll fly one day, then our Thunderbirds will put on a show, then the Russians again, and after that the Canadian Snowbirds . . . damnedest gathering I've ever seen. But, you know, Buck—I mean, Captain Rogers—what they really came to see are the mock dogfights."

Rogers laughed. "They're nostalgia junkies," he said. "And I agree with them. They want to see real flying, not the feet-on-the-floor stuff we do with the jets and fly-by-wire computer systems. Most of the airline boys can't even fly the old planes. 'What's a rudder for?' I hope I never hear that question again."

"Well," Tim drawled, "you know what the future holds for us. The next generation of airliners will be so automated that the cockpit will have one pilot and a dog."

"Yeah, sure," Rogers laughed. "Why the dog?"

"No, I mean it," Tim persisted. "The pilot will be there to feed the dog, and the dog is there to bite the pilot if he so much as touches the controls."

"When that day comes," Rogers told him coldly, "I'll hang up this uniform and go back to flying air shows and crop-dusting exclusively."

Tim unbuckled his harness and climbed slowly from his seat. "Starting tomorrow, Buck Rogers, daredevil ace from World War One, or whatever hat you're going to wear, you should feel right at home. You are doing the dogfight stuff, right?"

"You got it," Rogers told him. "It's like a coming-out party for me. Mike Shellane—you know him?—well, he's built the most beautiful Fokker D-7 replica you ever saw. Tomorrow I'll be the Big Bad Boche out to slaughter the innocent British and American pilots."

Tim rested a hand on his friend's shoulder. "Just promise me you'll remember that a lot of the guys flying against you do some pretty dumb things sometimes. You're the master at this, the pro. But to them it's a game, and they get too careless for my liking."

"I promise I'll be good," Rogers said with a laugh.

He had his own private agenda for the mock battles of the next day. He was going to screw his opponents right into the ground. Well, almost.

Besides, that was tomorrow. Tonight he'd be at the official welcoming party and reception for the air-show pilots and teams. He especially wanted to see his old friend, Vern, and his world-beating aerobatic performance in a Czech Zlin. Vern came as close as possible to turning the swift little monoplane inside-out, grinning all the way. He'd copped the international aerobatic championship three times running, and an air-show performance was duck soup for him. After that, the crazy ex-marine from Texas, Gower, would pull off his usual daredevil parachute jumps and scare hell out of the crowd. Most of all, he looked forward to his longtime flying buddy, the madcap Major Karl von Strasser, flying his ugly brute of a German trimotor bomber from the Second World War, the greatly modified Ju-52 they all called "Iron Annie." Karl had an absolutely foolhardy act. The bomber was incredibly strong, all angled iron and corrugated metal, its fixed-gear legs built up with high-strength steel. After he took off, ground crews would roll tall trees in big tubs onto the runway, and Karl would start down in a steep dive to build up speed. At the last moment, he'd pull out and smash into the trees. The upper branches were loaded with small explosive charges and bags of black powder, so when the Junkers smashed into the trees, a huge fireball flashed and black smoke erupted into the air. The act was a show-stopper, but only the pilots knew just how dangerous it was.

But that was tomorrow, he reminded himself again. Now someone was waiting for him at the welcoming party, someone he hadn't seen in weeks. He missed Angelina Barzoni more than he thought possible. She flew as a captain for American Airlines, but she was also a match for any air-show flyer in the world. To Buck, she was the only true love of his life. Tomorrow, after Buck "shot down" the last of his opponents in the mock battles and taxied before the crowd, the show announcer would tell the world that Buck Rogers and Angelina Barzoni were engaged to be married. Three more weeks—that was all he'd have to wait before they both could break away from their airline jobs. They'd be married aboard a Transcon 747 winging westward across the Pacific for a long honeymoon in Japan, Tahiti, and New Zealand.

Buck descended slowly down the stairway. A stunning girl in a bright scarlet-and-green jumpsuit met him halfway, threw her arms about him, and kissed him wildly as the watching crowd roared its approval.

Angelina never did anything halfway. . . .

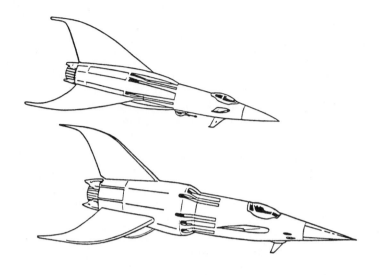

Chapter 2

One of the greatest pleasures of an air-show gathering like the annual Experimental Aircraft Association bash was that the best pilots in the world could shed the routines of their daily lives and just let it all hang out. Emerging from the blizzard of government and company regulations that at times proved stifling and always frustrating, the pilots put aside their jobs as the chauffeurs of large aerial buses with hordes of passengers. Thoughts of demanding commercial schedules and wearying routes were banished. Men and women in perfectly creased, starched uniforms shed these outer skins for snazzy flight suits and leather helmets. Staid jetliner captains shucked their company attire and dressed in coveralls and straw hats for zany flying farmer routines. Other pilots changed their names and strapped on parachutes for adventurous leaps from perfectly good airplanes, rolling and twisting and swan-diving earthward at breathless speeds, often grabbing hands and legs in colorful star and circle patterns of human bodies as the world rushed up toward them. The thrill was in the wonder of free-fall and then the final seconds when the pilot hauled on his D-ring and snapped open his chute pack, which started inflating the square chute that would bring him earthward with all the grace and control of a giant bird. If the chute failed to open or came out in a useless twirling snarl, he could experience the real thrill of the moment. He had scant seconds remaining to either untangle the flapping mess or cut himself away from the partially opened chute, fall free, and then deploy his reserve chute.

If that failed, he could always smile and wave gaily to the crowd right up to that sickening moment when his body smashed into the unyielding earth or concrete and he was instantly transformed from a functional human being into a greasy spot. One thing was certain. Up to the final moment, and especially at the last split second of fall, he held the rapt attention of the entire crowd.

Some of the flying acts, even when flown by men and women of superb skill, could never be less than extremely dangerous. Tumbling a plane through violent aerobatics, which always seemed on the edge of disaster, was actually duck soup for veteran flyers in machines stressed to survive the punishment of fourteen times the force of gravity.

It was a bit dicier for the jet aerobatic teams when they roared through their dazzling routines in spectacular tight formation, wingtips less than four feet apart. On this day a new element was added. The Thunderbirds were out to bury the Russians, and the Red Stars were only too happy to oblige with their powerful MiGs and Sukhois. The Canadians flew dainty little jet trainers, the Italians smeared the sky with large formations trailing red, green and white smoke, the U.S. Air Force showed up in ghostly bat-shaped B-2 bombers, and the Russians countered by flying a sleek Blackjack jet bomber escorting a huge Antonov An-225, their six-engined cloud smasher that weighed eight hundred tons as it barreled down the runway with the Russian Buran space shuttle hooked atop its fuselage.

These were razzle-dazzle acts the crowds had seen for many years. Slowly but surely, the call came for direct competition between pilots in mock combat. Buck Rogers and his fellow pilots recognized that appeal lay in nostalgia for the old days, when men were made of iron and their airplanes had two wings of the finest spruce, powered with clattering engines and wooden propellers, twisting in spiraling death duels.

That was one of the keys to the success of bringing back the old barnstorming acts. These planes flew low, and they were slow compared to the heavy jet planes with their sharply swept wings and booming engines. The performance of the jets was thrilling, but it got old quickly because their speed gave the crowd only a brief look as they rushed by. An airplane that topped out of its loop at twenty thousand feet was merely an unimpressive small dot in the sky, often lost to view in the glare of the sun.

But the World War One fighters, evoking the names and glory of Richthofen, Rickenbacker, Lufberry, Nungesser, Bishop, and other air aces, stayed so low to the ground that spectators could see the pilots, study their facial expressions, identify with the wind tearing at their skin and clothes. It was a ringside seat for the Great Event, and the huge audiences had made little-known pilots into famed gladiators.

And their biggest hero was Buck Rogers, grandstanding as fellow wingman to Richthofen and Boelcke, the great aces of the war of 1914–1918.

Buck Rogers made his appearance in the right-hand seat of an ancient World War One truck, without top or doors, riding on thin rubber tires, clattering and backfiring with crowd-pleasing blasts of fire and smoke from its exhaust. Wheezing down the long runway gave everyone time to push his way to the closest viewing spaces for the final battle of the day. Buck rolled close to the gleaming Fokker D-7—or at least what looked like the famous 1917 fighter plane of the kaiser's air force.

Throughout the frame and wings, lightweight metal alloys made the replica Fokker an aircraft with much greater strength than its predecessor of decades before. The rectangular engine compartment housed a modern engine of four hundred horse-power and a propeller designed by computer to squeeze every ounce of power from its Bullhead engine. Even the wings, which looked remarkably like those of the original, had been computer-modified not only to provide greater lift, but also to make the new D-7 even more maneuverable than its ancestor.

Buck would need every last one of these improvements. Soon he would be airborne and rushing into the mock but serious clash with Blacky Dillard, who had fought in the skies through several small wars in Central America and who had eight kills to his credit. Blacky would meet him head-on at the controls of a Spad 13 fighter, French-built but flown by America's top aces in the long-ago war.

It would be the speed of the French fighter against the agility and superior climbing ability of the Fokker, but in the end the outcome would be decided by the skill and cunning of the two dueling airmen.

This was a battle more than a million people would be watching from unique ringside seats. Both the Fokker and the Spad had miniature video cameras where the machine guns were usually mounted. The cameras transmitted what they "saw," duplicating what the pilots would see through their gunsights, and that image was in turn displayed on huge television screens located throughout the spectator area. Awed onlookers could look upward when the two fighters tangled in classic battle, and at a glance could seem to join each of the pilots in his plane. Adding to the realism, when either pilot pulled on his trigger, propane "guns" would fire with bursts of flame, broadcasting the simulated staccato bark of Vickers and Spandau machine guns over loudspeakers. Each pilot had a lip microphone; the audience would hear each man as if he were talking to himself in battle, right down to the grunts and rapid breathing as they pulled high gravity forces in their maneuvers.

The dogfight resembled a human pinball game. Laser sights in each fighter, continually checked by computer, would register bullet strikes against each opposing plane. If a machine-gun burst sent a spray of electronic bullets into an engine or the opposing pilot, the hits would register on the multiple television screens. The computer would also decide a kill.

One final fillip set the stage for the aerial show. Each fighter carried a container of vegetable oil. They could simulate oil leaks or smoke from flames by means of a pump, which shot the non-flammable oil into the hot exhaust to produce thick smoke.

The two men shook hands before climbing into their fighters. Blacky grinned at Buck. "Watch yourself up there, mate. You're lucky this isn't the real thing."

Buck spoke in his best ersatz German. "English swine. You are confused. *I'm* confused," Buck laughed. "I call you an English dog, but you are actually an American flying a French airplane, *nein?*"

"What did the German pilots say to each other before they took off on a mission?" Blacky asked. "I mean, the real stuff."

"*Hals und beinbruch,*" Buck answered. "It means 'break your neck and your leg.' A good-luck wish."

"See you upstairs," Blacky said and climbed into the Spad.

* * * * *

The two fighter planes taxied down the long runway directly before the crowd. Tumultuous cheering rose above the rumbling snarl of engines. Television cameras with long lenses on high stands offered tight close-ups of the pilots as they went through the final checks of their aircraft. The television screens showed Blacky in his usual unemotional preparation for flight as if it were the real thing. The crowd howled with laughter as the cameras turned to Buck in the Fokker. The propeller blast whipped his bright red scarf wildly behind him, accenting the leather flying helmet. Buck pulled his goggles down over his eyes and took a few moments to light a large cigar clenched in his teeth. He looked up into the cameras and grinned. The crowd loved it. Mr. Adventure himself, out for a great time.

A ground controller alongside the grass runway held up a yellow flag, then brought it down sharply, the signal for Blacky to take off first. Blacky knew how to razzle-dazzle an audience. He poured the coal to his engine, shoved the stick forward, stood on his brakes and immediately eased back on the stick. The Spad's tail rose until the fighter was level with the ground, the tail suspended in the air. Finally Blacky released the brakes, and the fighter shot forward and was airborne in a sudden burst of speed.

Buck watched the Spad make a steep climbing turn, leveling off at seven hundred feet. This was the altitude agreed upon for the classic one-on-one battle. Blacky would start his run northward over the grass runway while Buck flew head-on. At the last moment, each pilot would break sharply to the right, and from that moment on, it was each man for himself.

Buck started his takeoff roll to the cheers and roar of the crowd. The Fokker rose swiftly above the runway, then leveled off, scant feet above the ground, as it built up speed. Instead of making the same climbing turn, Buck rammed the Fokker forward as fast as it would go. Abruptly he horsed back on the stick, and the fighter zoomed skyward, coming up beneath the Spad, laser sights coming to bear on the surprised Blacky.

Buck smiled, knowing Blacky would be as angry as he was caught unaware by the outlaw maneuver. Buck was following a rule far more to the point than flying by the rules. The fighter pilot who catches his opponent by surprise is almost always the man who wins. In a dogfight, there is no second best, only the victor and the loser. Short of firing live ammunition, Buck was determined to win.

He squeezed his gun trigger. The television screens showed a line of red dots along the lower right wing of the Spad. Had the guns been live, he would have stitched a line of bullets through Blacky's wing. He eased in the left rudder to bring the cockpit of the Spad in his sights.

Blacky was faster than expected, and he realized immediately what Buck was doing. In a flash, the Spad turned upside down and dived earthward. The sudden burst of speed carried him barely out of the laser beam. As Buck's speed in the climb diminished, the Spad accelerated swiftly, pulling out at the last moment, using the speed from its dive to race away. Out of range now of Buck's weapon, Blacky began a wide turn, always keeping the Fokker in sight.

"Round one is yours," Blacky said grimly into his lip microphone. "Now we'll try it my way." The Spad was faster than the Fokker, and Blacky was using everything he had to come around on the tail of his opponent.

But Buck had the more maneuverable plane. He pulled the stick back hard, tramping the left rudder and slamming the throttle forward. No way could the Spad turn with him.

The next moment he realized just how good Blacky was. Instead of trying to match the Fokker's tight turning ability, Blacky went into a series of tight aileron rolls to reduce the distance between the two planes. It was a trick few fighter pilots had ever mastered, and Blacky was making the most of the moment. As he rolled, he walked his rudder slightly from side to side. With live ammunition, he'd be spraying bullets right where the Fokker had to fly; this way he had a good chance to get some laser strikes on Buck.

There was only one way out. Dangerously close to the ground, Buck threw the Fokker into a series of snap rolls, the Fokker gyrating wildly through the air as if the plane were suddenly out of control. This would bring the Spad even closer. It looked like the worst move Buck could make. Buck timed his next move perfectly. He chopped power, and the Fokker seemed to fly into mud as its speed fell off drastically. Now the Spad was close behind him but too far to one side to get in a shot. Blacky rolled away before he overran Buck.

For the next fifteen minutes of grueling flying, they parried, dived, and whirled, each trying to gain the upper hand for a clean shot. They were two fencing masters in an aerial death duel. Blacky kept trying for superior altitude so he could dive with great speed at Buck, while Buck twisted constantly to stay out of range and used his superior maneuverability to close in for a killing shot.

In a tight turn at low altitude, the Fokker slewed wildly to one side. Mistake! Immediately Blacky dived against his opponent, confident his height advantage would let him pick the perfect position to fire directly into the Fokker and end the fight.

To Blacky's surprise, Buck slammed into a near-vertical dive. Groans arose from the crowd. Buck had to pull out to prevent slamming into the ground, and when he did the battle would be ended. The Fokker seemed doomed. What was wrong with Buck? On the television screens, the crowd watched Buck's head rocking back and forth as if he were only semiconscious. Could he have blacked out from one of his wild maneuvers?

Blacky came down in what he was convinced was the final dive of the fight. In moments the Fokker would fill his sights. He held his finger on his trigger. Far ahead of him, he saw the German fighter slew to one side. Then one wheel careened on the ground, and the airplane skidded out of control.

Blacky counted off the seconds, his finger tightening on the trigger in anticipation. He watched the Fokker rock from one wheel to the other, on the razor's edge of buckling its landing gear and smashing into the ground. After what seemed an eternity, Blacky fired.

Missed! The Fokker had gone to full power. Buck clawed around on one wheel, turning into the strong wind blowing across the field. Blacky couldn't get in a shot as the Fokker flashed before his nose and then was gone.

With his speed building rapidly, Buck pulled up into a wild climb. Blacky had to pull out from his dive, and as he came level with the ground, the Fokker was directly beneath him. On every

14

television screen, bright red spots appeared as Blacky flew straight into the path of Buck's weapons. Had the lasers been machine guns, a stream of bullets would have ripped into the Spad's engine and fuel tanks, exploding the plane into a ball of fire.

The battle was ended—but not the danger. Blacky banked into a tight turn. For the moment, he couldn't see the Fokker. There was no room for Buck to break out of the climb as the distance between the two planes narrowed swiftly.

A million people watched in horror as the propeller of the Fokker sliced into the rear fuselage of the Spad. The sound of tearing metal carried sickeningly across the field. With its tail torn away, the Spad tumbled violently out of control. It careened out of the sky to smash into the ground, well away from the crowd, disintegrating into a mushrooming mass of flaming wreckage.

But Buck was also paying the price for the sudden collision. The Fokker flew through the debris of the aerial smashup, its propeller twisted into a metal snarl. Pieces of one wing tore away. Buck had practically no control left, and he was too low to bail out. In that instant, Buck saw he was going to crash directly into the crowd.

Hundreds of people would die, while others would be burned horribly as the fuel tanks exploded. With what little control he had left, he kicked the rudder hard and threw the Fokker into a flat spin, away from the screaming throng on the ground. He also gave up his one and only chance at a controlled crash from which he could survive.

In those final moments, everyone watching knew that Buck had made his final decision. The flat spin would send his plane down away from the helpless onlookers, but at a terrible price.

The Fokker spun wildly, crossed over the grass, and thundered against the concrete runway just beyond, skidding wildly as the airplane broke into pieces.

The last clear view on the television screens was of the engine bursting into flame, ripping loose from its mounts, and tumbling backward . . .

. . . directly into the cockpit, where a helpless Buck Rogers knew he was about to die.

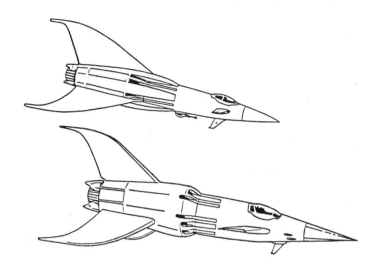

Chapter 3

Dr. Arthur Bedford gripped the shoulders of Angelina Barzoni. He held her tightly, as much to keep her from dashing past him toward Madison Hospital's Trauma Center as to keep the distraught, shaken woman from collapsing at his feet.

"I've got to see Buck!" Angie hissed through clenched teeth, forcing the words through her inner pain. "I've *got* to." Tears streaked her face, mixing with soot from the burning airplane in which her future husband had been trapped. Along with several others, doused in fire-fighting foam from the crash trucks, she had hurled herself into the flames and rummaged through the fractured metal, struggling to reach Buck to release his safety harness so that she and the other rescuers could drag him from the wreckage of the airplane before the remaining fuel geysered outward in all directions. Asbestos-suited men dragged her back from the fire, carrying her like a child as she screamed to be let free, her arms and legs kicking wildly. Through the intense glare, she'd caught a glimpse of the limp and unconscious form of Buck as fire danced ever higher along his legs. Even as she was dragged to safety, other members of the rescue crews sprayed foam on Buck and the immediate wreckage in an attempt to hold down the flames.

An armored vehicle on tracks punched into the fire and

wreckage, huge metal pincers snapping through the debris to clear the way for the rescue crew. It was the last Angie saw of her lover as the bulk of the tracked vehicle cut off her view. Above the din of crackling flames and roaring engines, she heard the fearful shout of "Down! Hit the deck! It's going to explode!"

Two asbestos-clad men fell heavily on her, throwing her down and covering her body with their own. She felt the heat of exploding fuel tanks even before she heard the deep bass boom. She fought to breathe, hanging precariously to consciousness. Strong hands moved her back against a fire truck; unseen figures clamped an oxygen mask to her face.

Hovering between consciousness and unconsciousness, she recognized the familiar *whoosh* of helicopter blades and whine of shrill jet engines. She staggered to her feet just in time to see a large white shape rise before her eyes, blurred and accelerating, a stark red cross emblazoned on the side of a medivac helicopter. Whirling rotors swirled a blast of fetid air against her. She felt consciousness slipping away, and then welcoming blackness.

* * * * *

Angie awoke slowly, her mind swimming upward through her confused thoughts, her memory struggling to cut through the murk. Her eyes fluttered. White . . . white everywhere. Could this be death? She blinked her eyes, winced with pain. No long tunnel of death. I couldn't hurt this much if I were dead, she thought. Reasoning is coming back. I'm alive. But what's all this white? She tried to move her left arm. It was locked rigidly to her side. Again she blinked and tried to . . .

"Miss Barzoni? Lie still, please. Don't try to move."

Nice face, concerned look, blonde hair, white uniform. Nurse . . . a nurse. Objects swam into focus. An intravenous bottle on a hook, dripping its contents into a vein . . . her vein. More needles. Huge white loaves of bandages. The nurse held up a large mirror at an angle so she could see herself. She saw a snowman in a hospital bed. Then it all came back to her, right up to the moment when she saw the medivac chopper lifting off the runway with Buck. She could figure out the rest of it. She had received burns of her own, perhaps other injuries. They must have brought her here.

"Where . . . where am I?" she asked the nurse. Her voice sounded muffled and hoarse through the facial bandages.

"Madison Hospital. Intensive Care Unit. You've received some serious burns, and you've inhaled a good deal of smoke and heat. You have several lacerations and cuts, but everything will be fine. Please, just relax."

Relax? Was this woman mad? "Buck . . . I want to know about Buck!" Angelina shouted as loudly as she could, ignoring the pain of moving her facial muscles and the pressure within her injured chest. "Where is he? *How* is he! I don't even know if he's alive, and you babble to me about relaxing!"

Anger brought her strength. She tore the IV tube loose from her arm and pushed away covers. She eased to the floor as the nurse, horrified, rushed to her side. With the strength born of desperation, Angelina shoved the nurse back. Half-staggering, she walked clumsily to the door and pushed her way through to the hallway. There, at the far end of the corridor, she saw the trauma center, where she knew they must have taken Buck. She staggered and weaved down the hallway until suddenly a tall doctor stood before her. She recognized him. "Arthur!" she croaked aloud. "Buck . . . how is he? I've got to talk to him!"

The doctor gripped her tightly, more to keep her from falling than to stop her uncertain progress to the trauma center doors. He motioned to an aide. "Wheelchair, now!"

Moments later he helped lower Angelina to the chair. "I'll take you inside," he promised her. "You can't get to him, Angie. He's in the hyperbaric chamber and it's sealed. But you can see him through an observation port."

"Is he . . . ?" She finished the question with her eyes.

"He's alive," Dr. Bedford told her. "I can't say much more than that. He's in the chamber under high oxygen pressure. We've got him on full life support . . . transfusions, skin coverings, that sort of thing. We've also run a current through his brain to keep him asleep so he'll be out of pain without our loading him up with drugs."

"Th—that means he can't hear me?" she asked tremulously.

"He can't hear any of us, Angie, but it keeps him out of pain. He's asleep, and we want to keep him that way as long as possible."

She nodded slowly. "How bad . . . ?" She let the question

hang.

"I won't lie to you," Bedford said quietly. "I understand you saw the crash."

She nodded slowly.

"Then you can understand why we're taking these precautions. We're giving him all the help we can. At least you can see how he's set up."

Dr. Bedford wheeled her chair into the trauma center. A huge tank dominated the center of the room. Medical technicians stood by monitors, making adjustments. Dr. Bedford stopped by an observation window and helped Angelina to her feet. Slowly she moved her body until she could peer through the port.

She felt her heart sink. Her body sagged. Bedford eased her back into the chair.

"He . . . he looks so helpless," she said finally, her voice quavering. She had expected the worst, but the sight of the man she loved drained her strength. Beneath her bandages, she tasted salt as her tears and blood mixed along her lips.

Dr. Bedford's words penetrated her bandages like the voice of doom. "There is no gentle way to say this," he told her quietly. "Mr. Rogers is completely helpless . . . at least for now."

Angelina looked up slowly. "Tell me straight out . . . what are his chances of recovery?"

"Slim to none. And if we do pull him through, I can't see how he'll ever fly again. He'd be extremely fortunate even to walk with crutches."

Angelina heard the doctor's voice as a death sentence for the man she loved. Never fly again? Buck would rather be dead.

"When will we—I—know if he'll live?"

"We'll know in twenty-four hours, Angie. Look, the truth is going to hurt. I—"

She gestured. "I know the rest, Doctor. Buck and I have both lost friends before. It's the nature of what we do."

"I know. Now, I must get you back to your room. You'll be under around-the-clock observation for at least a week. You took some pretty bad knocks yourself. I don't want you dying on me as well."

Her next words shook him to the core. "You don't understand, Doctor. If Buck dies, then inside, I'll be dead as well." She paused and closed her eyes with a pain much worse than those of her injuries. "You'll tell me if—I mean—"

"One way or the other. I promise." He wheeled her back to her room. In the bright, antiseptic light, Angie thought she had never seen anything so stark and lonely.

* * * * *

Dr. Nancy Reilly toyed with her coffee mug, staring across the conference table at Dr. Bedford. Two other surgeons sat beside her.

"You didn't tell her there's no hope he'll live?" she asked. "That in most respects Rogers is already dead?"

Dr. Rutger Claudius, to her right, shook his head slowly. "Arthur, that's wrong. For God's sake, man, he's on full life support now. His body has failed him. If we lose power for even a few seconds, he'll be a corpse."

Bedford showed no emotion. "Alive or dead," he answered, "tomorrow morning we inform Miss Barzoni that Buck Rogers died during the night."

Another doctor gestured for attention. "Why?"

Bedford turned in his seat to directly face Dr. Charles Ramirez, executive head of the Cyberdyne Medical Complex. "You know the answer as well as anybody else in this room," Bedford said coldly. "Because if we're going to save this man's life, then everyone he knows must accept that he is already dead. Otherwise, the legal and moral problems will delay things so much that it will surely kill him. Only then, for all intents and purposes, his death will take place in a courtroom."

The one doctor who had not yet spoken was not a medical man. Dr. Myron Packwood was the leading laser scientist in the country. "Listen to what Arthur says. He's right. This is a move we make now, or we can all attend Rogers's funeral services."

"But your laser program is still experimental!" Dr. Reilly protested.

"That's meaningless to a dying man," Packwood retorted. "I'm waiting to hear from Rex Caliburn. He's the government representative. If the president approves what I've recommended, then we're all protected legally and ethically. And the federal government will pay for what we're going to try. Millions of dollars." Packwood nodded to Bedford. "How long can you keep

Rogers alive—breathing and brain-alive, anyway? It doesn't matter if he's unconscious. Frankly, I prefer it that way."

"Three, maybe four months at the most. And, yes, he'll remain unconscious."

"Then as soon as Caliburn gets here with government approval, I suggest you move Mr. Rogers into total isolation. You have the unfortunate responsibility of telling his fiancée that he died."

Bedford nodded in silence.

* * * * *

Dr. Bedford, with Nurse Helen Timmons by his side, wheeled Angie Barzoni slowly and carefully into the private hospital elevator. They rode in silence to the rooftop, where Dr. Bedford moved Angie to an open area so she would have an uninterrupted view of the sky in all directions. A buzzer rang softly in a receiver behind the nurse's ear. She touched a solenoid on her wrist to activate the miniature telephone system all medical personnel carried. "Go ahead," she said softly.

"Helen, this is Anita in the communications center. Five minutes to go. They'll approach from the east."

"From the east," Timmons replied, her voice picked up by a wire-thin speaker at the side of her mouth. She turned to Angie. "The aircraft will be flying in from the east," she told Angie. She received a silent nod for answer, then a weak, barely audible "Thank you."

Dr. Bedford leaned closer to Angie. "Are you sure you want to go through with this? I mean, being up here, and—"

Angie reached deep through her misery for hidden strength. "They fly from the east," she said in a hoarse whisper, almost as if she spoke to herself rather than to the doctor.

"You see," she went on, "they always come from the east. Buck has already gone west. Did you know that?"

The nurse shook her head. "No. I'm afraid I don't."

"It's from way back in the First World War. When a man was killed in the air, the other pilots always said he'd gone west—the last flight he'll ever make." Angie paused to search the sky. "Now Buck's making his final flight. Tonight they'll all stand and drink a last toast to Buck and Blacky Dillard. I'd almost forgotten about him. He died in the crash, too-in the air, I mean. He was lucky. Bang! Lights out, you're gone. He didn't have to hang on for all those horrible days like Buck."

Nurse Timmons wanted to draw Angie out of the black mood that hovered about her. Angie was also a pilot. She knew the risks and penalties of a single mistake in the air-show routines.

"Are they releasing Mr. Dillard's ashes also?" she asked.

Angie nodded. "Yes. They had a pact. They always said that if they both went together, their ashes were to be released together from a plane. I—"

The distant sound of engines reverberated in the air. Her voice stopped, and she scanned the sky. Look to the east; they'll come from that way, she told herself silently. There they were, the old-timers, the powerful winged machines from old wars, other times.

In the center was a gleaming four-engined bomber, a Flying Fortress, the immortal B-17, shepherded by a squadron of fighter planes. Even through her tear-blurred vision, she could pick out the twin-boomed shape of the P-38, three Mustangs, two gull-winged Corsairs, a P-40, and a P-47, followed by two of Buck's friends in British Sea Fury fighters.

They swept overhead in an ear-rattling blur of thunder. Suddenly the P-38 lofted gracefully, pulling up in a steep climbing turn, leaving an open space in the tight formation. Now it was the Missing Man Formation, the final salute to a fellow airman gone west. The formation made a wide turn and circled back from the east. The planes tightened once more in a perfect formation. This time a Corsair lofted high, the final salute to Blacky Dillard.

Finally the planes disappeared into the west. She watched them dwindle until they were mere dots, heard their thunder become a thin echo, hollow and haunting. Somewhere over the mountains, a man in the B-17 would stand on the edge of an open bomb bay and release the mixed ashes of Buck and Blacky.

Angie felt a wash of blackness sweeping over her, and she yielded to an insurmountable need for release from the nonstop torment. She lapsed into unconsciousness and then a deep, deep sleep that would begin her recovery.

Oh, Buck, I loved you so! was her final thought before she lost consciousness.

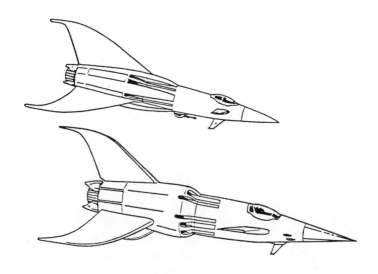

Chapter 4

Deep in his subconscious, Buck's mind played and replayed the last few harrowing moments before the crash.

The impact of the collision ripped Buck from head to toe. Instantly he knew these might be the last sensations he would ever feel, the bone-jarring deceleration as the Fokker disintegrated into wreckage. He braced himself for the fire he knew would come, but nothing could prepare a man for the sheet of blazing flames that swept around him. Then he felt the sickening fall, the loss of all control. An instant later, his reflexes took over as he punched the harness release. He still might be able to get out of this tumbling, burning death trap. He was low, much too low for his chute to have time to open, but for this kind of flying, he always wore a low-altitude system. When he yanked the metal D-ring on his chest, it would fire an explosive sabot up and away from his body, hauling the entire parachute free in less than two seconds.

Hope mocked him as he ran the possible life-saving scenario through his mind. He released the harness and the straps fell limp, but tangled metal held him like giant pincers. At that moment, the horizon whirling before his eyes as the burning wreck spun crazily downward, he caught a last glimpse of the crowd, saw Angie, her hand to her mouth. Then the concrete runway came up to smash him like a bug against a wall. Yet still it wasn't over. Enough wreckage remained to absorb some of the impact, the torn wings and fuselage yielding to the blow like shock absorbers. He refused to give up hope, to stop searching for the miracle that might throw him free from the wreckage. Suddenly he felt the fuselage break in half, the crumpled aft portion spinning away like garbage down the drain of a disposal. He might yet fight his way free!

But life plays cruel jokes, and Buck was in the midst of a prolonged comic act. What took mere seconds seemed like hours, with everything happening in slow motion. The collapsed forward structure had trapped his legs. He would die now, and his only hope was to meet his end quickly in a crushing blow or explosion when the tanks let go.

The cruelty continued as the engine ripped free of its mounts. Through the glare of flames, he saw the shadowy form of the engine tumbling backward to smash into his chest and then into his face. His last thought was one of thanks for the hammer blow that hurled him into blackness as his brain shut down.

* * * * *

"You've got to understand the kind of forces his body endured during those final seconds." Doctor Nancy Reilly glanced at her medical associates and the scientists gathered in the inner research laboratory of Cyberdyne Systems. "I will review, albeit briefly, why his life is now out of our hands. First, his burns show only the visible effects of the fire. How he survived flames that literally gushed into his open mouth and scorched all the way down his throat and into his lungs is a mystery. Had Rogers not been in superb physical condition, he would have died on the spot from the burns, trauma, and crushing of vital organs. He literally could not breathe to live. The exchange of gases in the alveolar structure shut down in minutes. Had the rescue crews not gotten pure oxygen to him, under high pressure, we'd have nothing to discuss right now. His life was saved by a rescue team that had only seconds to do their work.

"His entire cardiac system went into shock. Emergency procedures, carried out in the medivac chopper, kept him alive long enough to place him in the hyperbaric chamber. Right now pure oxygen is being absorbed through whatever skin was protected with the help of four atmospheres in the chamber. But even this is a stopgap measure. After several days under this level of pressure, the oxygen will become poisonous to his system. We are racing the clock, and we are barely keeping up," she said somberly.

"What about the skeletal system?" The brief query came from Dr. Myron Packwood, the reknowned laser scientist.

Dr. Reilly shook her head slowly. "It's easier to count the few bones, even the cartilage structures, that were *not* broken or crushed. The loss of red blood cells because of destroyed or damaged bone marrow is at least something we can handle through constant transfusions, which we've been doing from the outset. Again, we're racing time, but eventually we are going to lose.

"Finally there's the matter of internal tissue damage." She shook her head. "I've never seen anything like it." Neither had anyone else present in the secret gathering.

"The damage was not merely confined to tissue, of course," she continued, "but the organs as well. Damage is severe to kidneys, bladder, pancreas, lungs, and intestinal tract." She paused again. "Damage to the upper chest and throat is severe. Malfunctioning of the pituitary and the thyroid make for a terrible combination. We've had him on heavy hormone intake, of course, but all his other problems, especially loss of fluid through the skin burns . . . well, we simply don't have much time if we're going to go through with our plans."

Dr. Bedford studied Buck's charts. "Nancy, this tissue damage. It doesn't seem to fit the pattern merely of trauma, even severe trauma."

"No, sir. It's not uncommon in aircraft crashes. Or even high-speed vehicle impacts, except that the airman endures the cause of damage over a greater period of time. Even seconds make a huge difference."

Were Buck conscious and functioning, he might have told the doctors he knew the specific syndrome he suffered. As a test pilot, he'd sat bedside with many friends who'd survived violent crashes. The impact of collision, continuing through the violent descent, and then the battering deceleration, made a lethal combination. His body fluids had sloshed back and forth with such violence they acted as if they were heavy mercury, ripping and tearing fragile body tissues, blood vessels, nerves, sinew. He not only showed open wounds, but most of his body was also a swollen mass of discoloration, as if he'd been beaten with bamboo canes over the entire surface of his body.

He had been head-slammed and body-sloshed beyond the point at which most men would have died almost instantly. What kept Buck alive, at least until now, were artificial systems of life support, plus the fact that he was a superb physical specimen. Buck had always been a natural athlete, his body heavily muscled yet supple.

He had no control, even were he conscious, of eliminating liquid and solid wastes from his body. Both automatic systems and kind hands of nurses and medical technicians kept him from stewing in his own wastes. Within the hyperbaric chamber, where his skin permitted physical contact, those same hands massaged muscles and tendons, soothed his skin with medicinal salve. Electrical current kept his heart beating, his muscles alive, and stifled the pain that would have had him writhing even in his unconscious state.

Dr. Charles Ramirez turned from a long study of the man in the chamber. "Can we keep him alive, without further deterioration, for another month?"

Dr. Reilly took a deep breath and glanced at the other medical doctors. "A month, perhaps five weeks, but no more than that," she said finally. "Will you, Dr. Packwood, be ready by then?"

"We'll have to be ready or he dies," Packwood said brusquely. "The facts are that Buck Rogers should already be dead. With all we've reviewed, we haven't even talked about the broken ribs, the crushed pelvis, the large gashes in his intestine, the broken vertebrae, the blood vessels that must be reconnected. . . . Why am I saying all this?" He looked about, as if his pronouncements would somehow aid the shattered body in the chamber. "Let's put it on the table," he added. "We cannot hope to repair this man. The best we can hope for is to keep him alive for a limited period of time.

"Our only hope is to send him somewhere where people far more advanced than we can not only save him, but restore him to what he was. Perhaps even better."

* * * * *

They turned as the security doors at the far end of the room slid open. Rex Caliburn, with a strange gait to his walk, a subtle hint of mechanical movement, came through. They were grateful that it was Caliburn who had been with the president, who championed the extreme and costly measures they planned. Caliburn walked on legs of steel and plastic, his own legs lost years ago when a Russian missile exploded into his fighter-bomber in the Gulf War, tore it open like a giant can opener, and ripped the legs from his body. Caliburn was a living legend not only to the navy, but also to the entire medical field. He'd remained conscious long enough to pull his ejection seat handle and send the remaining half of his body up and away from his blazing, broken aircraft. Hanging in his parachute, in a nightmare of pain, he somehow managed to tie tourniquets about both legs, above the knees. Just before he landed on the desert floor, with his last wave of strength, he half-somersaulted in his parachute straps and hit the ground with his hands. Though the last part of the story had its share of doubters, legend had it that after that he'd held off a group of Iraqi soldiers with an automatic pistol until a rescue helicopter thundered to his aid, weapons ablaze.

Caliburn somehow managed to live, adapted to his artificial limbs, pulled himself together, and one day climbed back into the cockpit of a navy jet fighter and piloted it through a series of dangerous, complex maneuvers. The President of the United States had personally pinned the new golden wings to his uniform and promoted him from commander to admiral.

If anyone in this world would fight to give Buck Rogers his chance at some sort of meaningful survival, it was Rex Caliburn. He walked slowly past the group without a word, studying the still form in the hyperbaric chamber. He didn't need to ask the doctors questions. He had all their medical reports. But what he saw now didn't fit impersonal charts and words.

He wanted to reach out to touch the man, to reassure him, to tell him they were going to pull off a miracle for him. Or at least try. Caliburn had his own mental system of impressing into his conscious and subconscious mind what he saw in the form he called "the bottom line."

If ever there was a bottom line of survival, this was it. He saw a man reduced to an unconscious biological mass with tubes and lines running every which way from and into and through his body, every line connected to rows of life-supporting machines. It was as if Rogers had been clenched in the teeth of some terrible beast, chewed upon, ripped and torn, then swallowed and finally vomited out again. He was ministered to by a flock of electronic and mechanical angels that protected his life. He didn't lie in a normal bed. Even the pressure of normal gravity would have been enough to overburden what remained of his body systems. He lay suspended in a net that slowly but constantly shifted pressures on his smashed and ruptured body. My God, thought Caliburn. He's so close to the end that bedsores alone could kill him.

Caliburn turned to face the group. He took a deep breath, his face coldly unemotional, his mind totally on what needed to happen now.

"You're aware that Anthony Rogers is a dead man?"

His words startled them until they realized he was referring to what the public had been told.

Nancy Reilly spoke for the group. "We're all aware of that, sir. The planes flew over. Miss Barzoni, his fiancée—"

"I know who she is," Caliburn said impatiently.

"Then I'm sure you will be put at ease when I tell you that, as his named beneficiary, his airline has paid one million dollars to Miss Barzoni. Also, the air-show insurance will provide her with fifty thousand dollars a year for the next twenty years. She—"

"You're annoying me with all these numbers, Nancy. Cut to the bottom line."

Nancy Reilly ignored the attempted put-down. "Angelina Barzoni has signed all appropriate releases. They are filed in the proper courts. She knows Rogers is dead."

"Good," Caliburn said brusquely. "Now let's get down to the nitty-gritty. You say you believe you can keep Anthony Rogers alive for as long as it takes for medical science to advance to the point where he can be, first, revived, and second, cured of his injuries."

"Not quite, Mr. Caliburn," Arthur Bedford said icily. He didn't like this overbearing, pompous government man, and he didn't hide his feelings. "We never told you we believe we can do everything you just stated."

"Wait a moment! You told me yourself, only yesterday, that you could—"

Bedford leaned forward. "You have poor memory retention, sir. I never told you that this is what I believed. I said we are capable of keeping Rogers in a form of suspended animation—although that is not the proper terminology—in perfect stasis for one century or a hundred."

Caliburn had been through weird situations before. It was his job to cut through all the hoopla to separate the scam artists and weirdos from the real thing. "How will you do all that?" he said with open sarcasm.

Dr. Packwood laughed. "Perhaps it will be more than even you can understand, Caliburn. We're going to suspend him in time."

The statement didn't faze Caliburn. "Show me," he retorted. He patted his briefcase. "And if you convince me, I have here in my case your funding authorization for thirty million dollars to bring your proposal to reality."

The group before Caliburn—they already referred to themselves as the Rogers Team—rose to their feet as one. "Come with us, sir," Charles Ramirez said with quiet confidence.

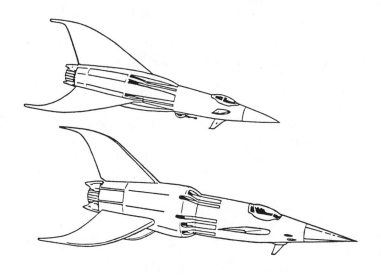

Chapter 5

The group stopped before a heavily shielded door with radiation warnings displayed prominently. Caliburn turned to study the people with him. None showed any surprise at entering what appeared to be a source of nuclear radiation danger. He remained still when Nancy Reilly pinned a radiation badge to his jacket.

"Nuclear reactor?" Caliburn asked tersely.

"Yes, sir. Modified. It's really a combination of a fission reactor and an auxiliary fusion power source. It uses helium three, so we get great power, steady and controlled, but without the danger of ionizing radiation."

Caliburn knew more than enough about radiation. He had checked dozens of sites as an inspector for the Atomic Energy Commission, but he'd never heard about any reactor at Cyberdyne. He started to query Reilly and the others, then decided they'd brief him as they went along.

The next several minutes confirmed the wisdom of his decision to wait, since he discovered that it was all a facade. They passed through massive doors that rolled heavily aside to permit their entry. Everywhere he looked, signs warned of danger areas. Flashing amber lights cautioned visitors that they were receiving low levels of radiation.

He glanced at his radiation badge. Nothing showed—not s

sign of anything leaking from a reactor, and he'd been in enough of those facilities to know there was always *some* leakage.

Warning horns sounded, and he saw men and women in radiation protection suits pass by. This is one hell of a show they're putting on, he mused. This could prove interesting. . . .

They went through two massive air-lock doors. Pneumatic pressure hissed like some prehistoric monster. Pressure changes battered his ears as the last thick door rolled into place behind them and thudded into its locks.

Caliburn had had enough of this play-acting. What had been created here had obviously cost millions of dollars, but it was all a farce. There wasn't enough radiation in this place to bother a sparrow. Caliburn stopped and touched Dr. Charles Ramirez, the chief scientist of the Cyberdyne group, on his shoulder.

"Let's put an end to the fun and games, shall we?" Caliburn said testily.

Ramirez smiled. "Then you have judged for yourself," he chuckled. "No radiation. If that was your conclusion, then you are correct."

Caliburn studied the man. "Then why all the play-acting?"

"Whenever we have visitors here," Ramirez said seriously, "from congress, or some government committee, we do our best to make them believe we're dealing with dangerous experimental systems. When they become too inquisitive, we release small amounts of radioactive gas into these chambers. It's enough to kick your rad badge into showing rising levels of radiation. Most people want out of here as fast as they can. It's our best protection against interference."

"Interference with what?" Caliburn snapped.

"The future" came the astonishing reply.

Dr. Myron Packwood joined them. The laser scientist pointed to a final thick door. "Through there," he said, "is our bridge to tomorrow. I apologize for this sideshow. Once you cross through that doorway, you will understand. I promise we will hold nothing back from you."

"Let's go," Caliburn said coldly. He wanted answers, not apologetic mumblings.

Packwood stood before a security enclave. A mechanical voice, feminine and sultry, sounded from a concealed speaker. "State your name for voiceprint clearance."

"Dr. Myron Packwood."

"Identification number, please."

"Four two two seven nine five six. Clearance level triple-Q."

"Look into the retinal scan, please."

Packwood leaned forward; a soft light flashed into his eyes.

"Thank you. Are you requesting group clearance?"

"Affirmative. One new individual. Rex Caliburn, government inspector, data on file."

"Dr. Caliburn is cleared. You may enter."

"Wait a moment," Caliburn protested. "I didn't do any of those things you did, Packwood. How could that security system know enough about me to clear me through?"

Ramirez smiled. "I'll answer for him, sir. Security is my responsibility here. Since the moment you stepped into this building, you have been fluoroscoped, X-rayed, and ultrasonically scanned. Your eyes have been examined and your retinal pattern checked with data in our computer banks. Your physical build, walk, voice tone—everything about you—has gone through security scanning. Even the electromagnetic pattern of your brain waves, along the ELF frequency—"

"ELF?"

"Extremely low frequency. Approximately twenty-six hertz. It's what your brain broadcasts. We measure it down to eleven numbers beyond the decimal point."

"Smart," Caliburn acknowledged. "But the best machines you can build can be fooled."

"That's why three guard dogs have sniffed your body odor as you came in here. They aren't machines, and they passed you through. Before you ask the question, yes, the animals were taken to your apartment so they could smell the odor peculiar to your body. To a dog, that's an unmistakable pattern."

"Enough," Caliburn said. "Open your Pandora's box and let's see what comes out."

* * * * *

Blinding light flashed past his eyes. Caliburn stood stock-still, not knowing what to expect in the next moment. As fast as it had appeared, the light was gone. A new sensation came to him, deep thudding sounds that rumbled through the steel plating beneath his feet. Packwood motioned for his attention. "It's a power surge. You'll understand in a few moments."

Caliburn nodded, suddenly angry with himself for going along so easily with these people. He had come here because of a dying man. The hopes for some sort of miracle had sustained him through all this hoopla, but he was rapidly getting tired of all the hints and muted assurances.

A final doorway split down the middle to reveal a magician's keep of dazzling lights, a medley of musical sounds. He detected a tinkling as of glass crystals ringing against each other.

There was another flash of light, but this time not into his eyes. A huge cylindrical shape stretched from his left for at least three hundred feet along the center of a vast domed facility. It reminded him of a great church he'd visited in Spain. But there was no church here; instead he saw a fantasyland of dazzling colors and hissing light beams, and he felt a sense of enormous power about them.

Caliburn recognized what he was looking at as a laser-beam generator. They'd been testing laser-beam weapons for years in the Star Wars programs, but he'd never seen anything even remotely approaching the massive generator before him. Then he looked beyond to see that this was but the first of many such generators that stood in a long row at the far end of the cylinder.

An entire wall glowed with the lights and data panels of a Mark Sixteen computer system that rendered even the great Cray computers outmoded. He saw thick cables, and more instrument panels that were completely strange to him. Light spasmed through the cylinder, and enormous solenoids clicked on and off with a sound of giant pincers opening and closing.

Caliburn addressed the group, his words slow and hushed. "Out with it. What the hell is this place?"

"We call it the Cyberdyne Dream Catcher," Ramirez said proudly. "It doesn't catch dreams in the literal sense, of course."

"Of course," Caliburn answered with undisguised sarcasm.

"But it can bring true one of the greatest and longest-lived dreams of mankind," Ramirez replied without missing a beat. "This, Mr. Caliburn, is a doorway. We said this before. It is a doorway to tomorrow. It is the means of sending selected human beings into the future."

"How far into the future?" Caliburn didn't yet believe what he was hearing, but his temptation to rake these people over the coals was tempered by the enormous complex surrounding him. Someone had put a tremendous amount of money, time, and energy into this . . . well, whatever it was. Maybe a time machine wasn't such a joke, after all.

Dr. Nancy Reilly came to his side. "Officially, we call this the Physiological Bioelectromagnetic Test Facility."

"Big name," Caliburn said, waiting for more.

"You want to know why we call it both physiological and electromagnetic?"

"It doesn't take a rocket scientist to figure that out. You've just described the human being, except for his position in life as a cybernetics system. You know, what we like to call the ability to think creatively."

"Precisely," Nancy Reilly responded, pleased that this man was a quick study. Before she could add to her explanation, a loudspeaker boomed through the area.

"CLEAR THE TEST FLOOR. CLEAR THE TEST FLOOR. TEST NUMBER ONE NINE SIX SIX FIVE WILL COMMENCE IN THREE MINUTES." After a brief pause, the words sounded again.

"Come with us, please," Packwood urged. "Into the viewing chamber. Just follow this row of green lights along the floor."

They entered a high viewing room with a thick glass wall looking down into the experimental center. For the first time since they'd come into this crazy place, Dr. Arthur Bedford spoke to Caliburn. "Looking down from this view," Bedford explained, "gives you a better idea of how everything ties together. What you see here all feeds to the power banks by the long cylinder. Including the mirrors."

"What mirrors?" Caliburn said sharply, but even as he spoke, walls slid away to reveal a bewildering array of mirrors, flat, curved, and gleaming, in a wild array of colors. Then Caliburn understood. The power banks would feed tremendous energy to laser beam transmitters. The laser beams would then be bounced through the array of mirrors, and—

"THIRTY SECONDS," intoned the electronic voice. "ALL LIGHTING DIMMED TO POINT ZERO THREE INTENSITY."

Gloom fell across the great chamber. Caliburn suddenly felt a touch of uncertainty. Laser beams as powerful as those that could come from such power banks was capable of blinding a man. "No goggles?" he asked Bedford as casually as he could.

"No need for goggles," the doctor answered smoothly. "The observation window before us will polarize the light before any harmful visible radiation reaches your eyes. Sort of automatic goggles."

Caliburn nodded; he had no choice but to accept Bedford's assurances. The final seconds flashed away. Caliburn looked about the observation room. At least another twenty people had entered, standing close to the observation window to observe the events below.

"TEN SECONDS."

Power pulsed through the floor and walls. A thin, high-frequency squeal set Caliburn's teeth on edge and made him feel as if someone were stabbing tiny glass spears into his eyes. He barely felt Nancy Reilly's hand instinctively gripping his arm. A question flashed through his mind. Why would this woman, part of the team, feel apprehension at such a moment? It didn't make—

A fusillade of events enveloped Caliburn, all virtually simultaneous. A searing emerald-green light burst into existence. One moment it wasn't there; in the next instant, faster than his eyes could blink, the light flashed through the entire complex. Still another instant later the reflected radiance yielded to a ghostly cranberry-hued glow. There were more colors, more lights, and an upward swell of energy he felt as much as heard. A thudding *boom* reverberated against the viewing window. Caliburn stepped back reflexively. He heard Nancy Reilly's voice, terse yet comforting. "Armored glass," she said, but it was enough to tell him the glass could absorb even gunfire without damage and that they were perfectly secure behind it.

Another enveloping light appeared, this time deep blue, then changing swiftly through the colors of the spectrum. Finally it exploded silently, to be replaced by a single glowing tube of blue-white radiance, not nearly as bright but somehow more important than all the others, born from the coruscating radiance that had mesmerized them all.

And even that light was but the precursor to what followed.

Light stabbed in steel-hard beams and pulsating colors from the mirrors set at varying angles about the great room. The lights seemed to appear out of nowhere; it took Caliburn several seconds to remember that all the eye-sundering laser beams were not separate light rays, but a single source being reflected from one mirror to the other at the speed of light. And anything that moves at 186,273 miles per second, even within a confined space as huge as this facility, seemed to appear all at once rather than to bounce from one mirror to another. All that had happened up to now was prelude to the final beam of incandescent fury. The beam seemed to be captured within the long cylindrical tube. It remained unmoving, solid as a mountain, glowing brilliantly from within. Now the sound itself settled to a deep infrasonic rumbling, as if a stupendous thunder many miles distant had been reduced to the grumblings of a planet's stirring.

Caliburn turned his attention to Myron Packwood. The laser scientist held aloft a powerful arm, fist clenched. His eyes shone with almost as much brilliance as the laser beams that seared the laboratory. Caliburn was a heavily muscled man, still strong from his conditioning as a special weapons officer with the Green Berets, a violent past few people in the sluggish diplomatic world knew about. In Packwood, he recognized tremendous physical conditioning, but even more an intensity that marks a man driving ahead with full mental and physical commitment. His bristling beard and dark horn-rimmed glasses had thrown Caliburn off. Of all the people here, this was the one man about whom everyone and everything else surely revolved.

Caliburn moved closer to Packwood, who turned with a smile on his face and inquiry in his eyes. "Mr. Caliburn!" he cried jovially. "What did you think of our light show?"

Caliburn wasn't there to please anyone. "Nice," he said with an air of indifference. "Super special effects. But what does it *do* besides impress people?"

Packwood's demeanor shifted from enthusiastic to serious. "Whatever we place within that cylinder," he said slowly, "with the laser system operating at full power, is suspended in time."

Caliburn didn't respond immediately. Suspended in time? That made as much sense as the ancient alchemists and magicians trying to transform lead into gold. Caliburn was no stranger to laser systems, but his work had been with target identification and destruction, not suspension. "Tell me more," he said slowly.

"The laser beam is so powerful, and moving at such speed, that it disassociates molecular, cellular, and atomic structure into particles that move at the speed of light. If I place, let's say, a statue in the cylinder and we activate the system—no, hold it. Think of a clock inside the cylinder. We activate the laser system, the clock is reduced to disassociated atoms, right on down to subatomic particles such as electrons, protons, and neutrons. They remain what they were before the laser hit them, except that they no longer have moving parts. Because now all those parts are moving at the speed of light. They have infinite mass, and you can't go faster than the speed of light. So long as the laser stream is working, the clock keeps bouncing back and forth between the mirrors—or, rather, what was the clock. Now it's simply a collection of molecules and subatomic particles. Everything is reduced to the scale of photons, particles of light. Everything in that laser beam within the cylinder becomes quanta, or particles, and—"

"Yes, I know," Caliburn broke in. "Get to the point."

"You're both impatient and disagreeable," Packwood shot back at Caliburn. "Please don't try to throw around your weight as a government man here—not with me or my group. What we've done is far beyond money. If it were money that held our primary interest, we could sell this facility to the highest bidder, which"—Packwood smiled coldly—"would go well beyond a hundred billion dollars. So, in the vernacular of the younger generation, kindly knock it off, will you?"

To Packwood's surprise, Caliburn laughed heartily and slapped the scientist on the shoulder. "Well said, sir," he boomed. "I've just learned more about you than all your fancy scientific descriptions could ever show. But let's have the rest of it. And I'll add 'please' to that request."

Packwood smiled. "You must be like a pack of wildcats in a tight situation."

"Let it go, let it go," Caliburn said gently.

"All right. In its simplest terms, light is a wave, like ripples on a smooth lake when you toss a stone into the water."

"Okay."

"But light is also quanta . . . physical matter. A particle of matter. It is one and the same, always depending upon how you study that light. It's one of the most illogical things in the universe, but it's also true. Light will be whatever you wish it to be as long as you stay within the limitations of waves or quanta."

"And in the laser beam, it isn't waves, is it?"

"No, sir, it isn't. It's strictly quanta. When we disassociate the various particles from one another, they're instantaneously accelerated to the speed of light."

"Which means," Caliburn said slowly, "that they have infinite mass. They can't go any faster than the speed of light."

"Yes," Packwood confirmed, "but even more important, they can't travel any *slower* than the speed of light. If they did, they would come apart like a clock in a time bomb . . . literally fly apart with tremendous force."

"Would I be wrong in assuming you really don't care if the clock rips apart?"

"You would."

"But if you had a living creature in that thing of yours . . . ?"

"Any disassociation of molecules, cells, or any other parts of that creature would mean instant death . . . or something even worse," Packwood finished for him. "A man could come out of that cylinder with his body turned inside out."

Caliburn had no comeback to that. He had already formulated the plan in his mind. These people were going to try to suspend Anthony Rogers in that crazy laser shock tube of theirs! Caliburn cut to the quick. "How many living creatures have you lost in that torture chamber of yours?"

Packwood didn't even blink. "Animals? About three hundred before we had our first success."

"I don't give a fig for the animals. How many people?"

"We lost five out of the first seven."

"That's a hell of a casualty rate."

Packwood shrugged. "The first three men scheduled to fly an Apollo spacecraft died in a fire on the launchpad. That was a casualty list of one hundred percent. We still went to the moon."

"Point well taken," Caliburn replied. "But I've got to ask. From where did you—"

"I'll save you the trouble, Caliburn. They were all volunteers. We also work with the federal prison system. Whoever takes the ride willingly and comes back is released, pardoned, brainwashed, and set free."

"Brainwashed?"

"Yes, sir. Our techniques work very well. Successful volunteers are in no way harmed, but they remember nothing about ever being here. It's a new narcotic, a thousand times more powerful than morphine. Whatever they are told while they are under the drug, including orders of what to forget, they will follow."

"What happens to those who come back . . . well, 'disassociated'?"

"We preserve the body parts and organs for detailed study. Come with me." Packwood led Caliburn to another room, where they went through another security check. As accustomed as he had become to combat, secret operations, plane crashes, and bloody firefights, Caliburn felt the air rush from his lungs with shock. Cold air washed over him; they kept this room at an even sixty degrees. On each wall, left and right, floor-to-ceiling shelves displayed jars containing human organs and limbs, kidneys, hearts, lungs, bladders, livers, eyeballs, sections of jaws, brains, intestines. . . . He shuddered. "Nice nightmare you have here," he said finally.

"You know as well as we do," Packwood replied gently, "we use whatever we're offered for our work. We have, ah, somewhat altered these specimens. These are the parts of failures of both animals and five human subjects. By running extensive tests, we've isolated the problems that brought on each of our failures."

"I want to see the equipment you've lined up for Anthony Rogers. Now," Caliburn appended in a no-nonsense tone.

"All right," Packwood agreed. "In the next chamber. We—"

The scientist's pager chimed softly. Packwood lifted a cellular phone to his ear. When he turned off the phone, his face looked ashen.

"Something wrong?" Caliburn asked.

"It's Rogers. He's taken a turn for the worse. Dr. Reilly just told me he'll be dead in less than twenty-four hours."

"Show me your damned magic machine," Caliburn said icily. "You'll need magic, and more, to save that man."

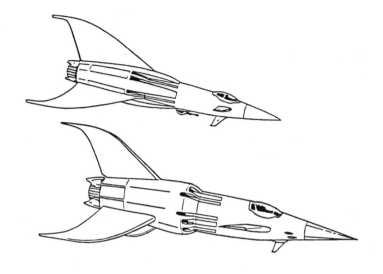

Chapter 6

They stood before another huge cylinder, glowing with a steady, unnerving light. Technicians scanned data banks, and computers glowed and flashed all about them. Medical technicians stood by the entry hatch to the cylinder. A woman approached them.

"Dr. Packwood, we're almost ready to complete the test run," she said quickly.

Packwood nodded and gestured to Caliburn. "This is Mr. Rex Caliburn. He works with us in the front office. Mr. Caliburn, meet Dr. Heiko Watanabe. She's our team leader."

Caliburn ignored the social amenities. "What test are you running, Doctor?"

The slender woman smiled. "A test of supreme confidence—my own dogs, Susie and Marki. They are Akitas, born from the same litter. Here, I will show you."

She led them to a fenced enclosure. A powerful Akita greeted her enthusiastically, ignored Packwood, and studied Caliburn with open hostility.

"He misses his litter companion . . . his sister," explained Dr. Watanabe. "Consequently he's suspicious of all strangers. To him, they might be responsible for her disappearance."

"And where is this . . . um, Susie?"

The woman pointed to the glowing cylinder. "In there. For eight months, in fact. But, of course, there is no time in that cylinder."

"So I've heard," Caliburn said sourly. "Tell me about it in as straightforward a manner as you can, please."

"Yes, sir. Stated simply, Susie was placed in the laser beam when she was eight weeks old. At that time, this dog"—she patted Marki as she spoke—"was also eight weeks old. Today Marki is ten months old. Eight months have gone by. We are about to shut down the power beam. When we open the cylinder, Susie will be inside, alive and well. If our calculations are right, then we will see a perfectly healthy puppy eight weeks old."

Caliburn had expected what he was hearing. "In short, you're telling me that for eight months time has stood still for the puppy. No growth, no change in the animal?"

Dr. Watanabe studied an instrument panel, Caliburn at her side. Then they both moved closer to the cylinder. Light shifted in a meaningless swirl. "I sure as hell don't see any dog in there," Caliburn complained.

"Of course not," the woman said patiently. "Susie has been floating—dispersed might be a better word—in an electromagnetic matrix. The electromagnetic code for Susie is in the bioscience computers. The frequency of every atom in her body—and they all vibrate at a specific frequency—is coded and retained while she is in the laser beam. When we turned on the beam, time ceased to exist, but because the atoms are moving at the speed of light, they retain the code. These mirrors," she said, gesturing, "bounce that code back and forth. In a few moments, we will shut down the laser beam transmission."

"And?" Caliburn prompted.

"Susie will rematerialize exactly as she was when we turned on the beam eight months ago."

"You're asking me to swallow one very large implausibility," Caliburn retorted. "Or impossibility."

"There's only one way to find out. We have frozen in time every element of the puppy, every electromagnetic pulse of her body and brain, every cellular structure, every blood cell, every command of hormones, every enzyme—in short, all life has simply been placed in stasis. That's why such things as food, water, muscle movement, waste disposal—none of them exist so long as this beam is active."

"And if you're wrong?" Caliburn pressed.

After a long silence, Dr. Bedford spoke. "Then we will be faced with a horrible sight—a mass of disassociated muscles, tendons, fur, teeth, eyeballs, intestines—the whole ball of biological wax. Dr. Watanabe will be crushed. The dog, Marki, will likely howl instinctively that something terrible has happened. I think you get the idea."

"If you're right, and it is one heck of an if, you will retrieve a healthy animal?"

"Yes," Watanabe and Bedford said in unison.

"I see an awful lot of emergency medical equipment in here," Caliburn noted. "That seems to suggest you're not altogether sure of what you'll find."

"We've never run a test this long," Dr. Watanabe said quietly.

"But if it *is* a success," Bedford added, his face solemn, "this laser system is the only hope of survival for Anthony Rogers. Either we send him into some unknown future when medical science will be sufficiently advanced to do for him what we cannot—keep him alive, make him well, repair his body—well, you know the rest of it."

Caliburn stood in silence. Bedford suddenly became animated. "Confound it, Caliburn, don't you understand? Rogers is dying. He could go at any moment! If we don't try this laser system, he dies. No questions about that. If we fail, then nothing has changed except that we tried to send him ahead in time where he could live. And," Bedford added slowly, "science then could not only keep him alive, but they might even endow him with certain life-protecting systems that would make him much more than he was before the crash."

"Do it. Now!" Caliburn spoke harshly, teeth gritted.

Bedford turned to Watanabe. "How long?"

"Twenty seconds."

"Go."

Watanabe's fingers flashed across a computer control board. Lights blinked off; others glowed softly. A timer chimed and digital seconds appeared on a screen, counting down.

The people in the room seemed frozen. Someone whispered, "Ten seconds . . . nine . . . eight—"

A final, hoarse, "*one . . .*"

Reality seemed to pulse in the room almost physically. The air shimmered, and the thrill of something extraordinary about to happen swept through the room. A hellish ruby-red light pulsed within the cylinder, while an invisible wind sighed about them.

Then silence.

Moving almost as if she were an automaton, Dr. Watanabe approached a code screen on the curving side of the cylinder. Her fingers danced across the numbers to depress a long curving hatch. Bedford stood by her side, lifting the hatch. Several men came forward, locked the hatch open. Everyone strained to see within the cylinder. Sounds of hoarse, frightened breathing came from everywhere. Watanabe peered through the open hatch, then her hands slipped into the opening.

There was a sound, a single, wonderful, incredible sound, high-pitched, short.

Yip!

In an instant, Marki was barking furiously, straining to rush forward as he heard the unmistakable sound of his eight-week-old littermate.

Heiko Watanabe turned, triumph shining in her eyes, tears streaking her cheeks, holding close to her a healthy, thick-furred puppy. For long moments, no one spoke, overcome with the emotion of the moment. Finally Caliburn stepped forward, holding out his arms.

"May I?" he asked softly.

Watanabe placed the puppy in his arms. Caliburn held the animal gently, feeling the fur, the damp nose. "I . . . I can hardly believe this," he said finally.

Watanabe retrieved Susie and placed the pup on the floor. Immediately the young whelp dashed across the room to the frantic older dog, greeting him with joyous cries and sharp yips of joy.

Someone tapped Caliburn on his shoulder; he turned to face the grim visage of Dr. Nancy Reilly. One look confirmed his worst fears, yet he had to voice them aloud.

"What is it, Doctor?"

"Rogers is fading fast," she said. "He may not last the hour. We've got to bring him in here now."

Caliburn nodded. He had no choice anymore. Everything was

in the lap of the gods and these people. Either they committed Rogers to some unknown, unpredictable future, or there would be a second, secret funeral service that would end this story once and for all.

"Do it now. Immediately," he urged.

Dr. Reilly spoke into her pagerphone. "Bring Mr. Rogers to Laser Prime at once. Maintain Code Blue during the transfer. Medical Team Two, get in here on the double. Be ready for time insertion at once!"

Caliburn heard confirmation to her orders from her pagerphone. "There's very little time to explain, Mr. Caliburn," she said, her words tumbling forth in a rush. "I can talk with you only until the medical teams bring Rogers in here. Just before we insert him into the cylinder, we'll have to remove all life-support systems."

"You'll kill him," Caliburn interrupted.

"No. There'll be a few minutes—we're not sure how many—when his own systems will keep him alive. We can't keep his life support operating in the beam. The moment we activate the laser transfer, all those mechanical systems will be so many free atoms and other subatomic particles. They'll be useless to him. But the instant he's sealed in the cylinder and we go to full power, he'll be suspended—"

"In time," Caliburn finished for her. "I understand. Forget about me right now. Do whatever is necessary."

A signal chimed, the far doors opened, and a medical team rushed toward the cylinder that contained the unconscious form of Anthony Rogers strapped to a gurney. They stopped by the open hatch. "Quickly, quickly," Dr. Reilly pressed them. "Prepare to disconnect. Keep him under full oxygen when you place him in the transporter. Maintain cardiac assist until the very last moment. Once he's inside, disconnect everything. He's got to be on his own. You'll have no more than a minute to make the transfer. Anything more than that is simply too long. Now, I want the air pressure built up and ready the instant you have him in the cylinder. He's got to be suspended away from the interior surface. You understand? If you have any questions, let's hear them right now. All right, everybody, *move it!*"

* * * * *

Rex Caliburn stared in dismay at the unconscious form of Anthony Rogers. Machines pulsed, lights flashed, liquids flowed through tubes into his body. The snaking Medusa head of artificial tendrils, gases, liquids, and electrical energy formed his lifeline.

The man was more dead than alive, his skin an alarming chalk-white, his face a mangled mess. Internal pressure kept his lungs from collapsing. Only one eye could be seen on the wreckage of his face, and that was blackened and swollen.

Caliburn found himself holding his breath, gasping painfully as the life tendrils were removed from Rogers. The young pilot's breathing slowed. "His blood pressure is down, still going down. Damn it, we don't have any time left!" Caliburn didn't even know who spoke the words. The medical team moved with skilled and practiced hands. In moments, they had Rogers within the cylinder. Air pressure *whoosh*ed in to suspend his form away from any contact with the circular walls of the cylinder.

"We're losing him!" a doctor shouted in alarm. "Hurry!"

Caliburn couldn't keep himself back. He moved forward into the midst of the medical teams. He looked intently at the disfigured form inside the cylinder, seemingly levitated by air pressure from all sides.

"Come on, Buck. Give me a sign. Anything, son . . ." The words hissed from him, unknowingly spoken aloud. It seemed a gesture of final futility, but he swore he saw the pilot's one remaining eye tremble and flicker open for an instant.

My God, I know every ounce of his pain, every stab of the thousand knives in that body, wracking every muscle, twisting his tendons and nerves. The sight of Buck's torn body thrust Caliburn back in time to that moment when the Russian missile warhead had exploded into his fighter-bomber, enveloping him in a ball of searing flames, ripping the legs from his body. He could hardly recall that terrible moment when he'd pulled the ejection-seat handle that blew what remained of his body out into a lashing wind, his legs going down in the blazing wreckage.

Oh, he knew. He was the only person in this group who *really* knew the agony Anthony Rogers was going through. Caliburn's face remained stonelike, but if the others had looked deep into his eyes, they would have seen the pain there.

Rex Caliburn, hard-nosed, no-nonsense agent of the government, was being torn apart on the inside. No one but he and the helpless form before him knew that Angelina Barzoni was the daughter of Rex Caliburn, and that this young man was to have become his son-in-law.

Caliburn had married Rose Barzoni, a raven-haired beauty of an aristocratic Italian family. To give up the family name was unthinkable, and she had adopted the name Rose Caliburn-Barzoni.

The name had proven too long, too clumsy, too *correct* for Angelina. Far better for her to be known in the air show as the Great Barzoni. She and Buck and Rex had kept her secret all too well.

How could he, Rex Caliburn, agree to this program, committing the still-functioning remains of this young man he had come to love to a possible life in the future through death in the present? There must be no question of the death of Buck Rogers, or Angelina would go mad thinking she might have done something, anything to save him.

Rex Caliburn trembled with the weight of his inner struggle, fighting back the tears. He wanted to embrace Buck, embrace his daughter, bring them back together somehow, but he knew there was only one decision to make. . . .

He saw no more as hands pushed him aside, closed the cylinder hatch, and secured it tightly.

"Activate!" Dr. Bedford called out. Heiko Watanabe's fingers danced on the computer console. "Full power!" she sang out. Somewhere in the distance, an enormous power surge began. Caliburn felt the floor tremble. Everything was now run by the time signals generated by an atomic cesium clock, accurate down to a billionth of a second.

The dazzling light flashed, and Caliburn felt every fiber of his body vibrating. As close to instantly as any device made by man could measure, Anthony Rogers vanished into swirling light of pulsating colors.

Trillions of cells that made up his body, molecules and subatomic particles, even the brain processes flashing with a hundred thousand signals per second, stopped, frozen in timeless limbo. Synapses, neurons, axions, everything, became pure light.

"He's gone," Dr. Bedford said shakily.

"You mean . . . " Caliburn gripped Bedford tightly by the arm. "You mean you lost him before—"

"No, no," Bedford said hastily. "He was alive when we activated the system. He's alive now, but not in a way that any human being ever experienced. And so long as our reactor keeps power flowing into this system, he'll remain just as he is now. Stardust. Maybe that's it. Stardust waiting to be recreated, reborn."

Dr. Reilly stood mute, still shaken at the spectacle of committing a human being to a great unknown.

"He's in the hands of God now," she said quietly.

Rex Caliburn wasn't so sure.

"Or the devil," he added.

He turned and left the great complex. Maybe the woman was right; maybe it was all up to God now. But Caliburn wouldn't bet on it.

One thing was certain. If anyone had ever rushed into the great unknown, this was it.

Outside again, breathing deep of the fresh, cool air—Good Lord, it was dark already!—Caliburn looked up at the stars.

Maybe that's where Rogers was headed. Maybe.

"Godspeed, Buck," Caliburn whispered aloud.

However the great experiment turned out, one thing was inevitable. When Buck Rogers regained consciousness, if he ever did, everyone now alive on this planet would be dust.

Everyone but Buck Rogers, that is.

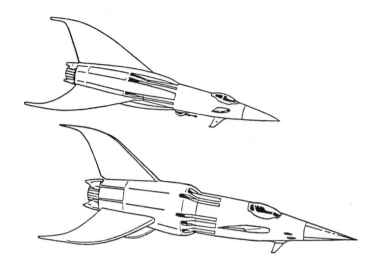

Chapter 7

Pain.

He was immersed in a river of pure white agony. Could his bones be breaking, twisting in this horror that went on and on and on?

He tried to see, but all about him was white pain. He saw an eye socket with a blazing needle being thrust into it, then realized it was his own. He felt his lungs bursting, and then a shrieking jackhammer ripped into and spun around and through his spine. A scorpion stabbed his liver, knives thrust into his kidneys, and then he was falling, an impossible plunge with whips of barbed razor wire slashing hotly at his shredded skin. . . .

Then he knew. He had been thrust into space, cast into the vacuum, and he was helpless, weightless as his breath exploded from his nostrils and mouth and ears and lungs, and he felt his blood boiling violently within him. He was floating, floating. . . .

But he must be dead!

An inner voice spoke to him, a single remaining shred of sanity: *Knock it off, Rogers. The dead don't hurt. They don't dance, and they don't prance, and they don't wear pants. . . .*

"Can you hear me, Rogers?"

A woman's voice, a cold and wonderful wind blowing through the fetid clamp of red-hot pain. How could he be hearing such a voice?

"Anthony Rogers, do you hear me? Try to answer. Blink your left eye. That's it, try! Don't talk. You can't do that yet. Just open and close your eye. That's all. Think of nothing else. Ignore the pain. Open your eye . . . do it!

He forced both eyes open. Something was wrong. He could feel movement, ripping pain, in his left eye. There was nothing from the opposite side of his face. He fought a grim upward battle against the fires burning within him. His eye opened. A white-hot needle stabbed into his eyeball. He clenched it shut tightly, wincing at the terrible effort and another wave of pain.

Strange . . . he should be in shock and feel overwhelming nausea from the pain. Don't talk, don't move. Try to feel beyond the pain. . . . Someone is out there . . . a woman . . . helping me, trying . . .

"That was great, Mr. Rogers. You may not realize it yet, but you moved your left eye. You can hear me; you understand. I know you're in terrible pain, and I understand. Now that we know your mind is working, we'll be able to move on." He could barely hear her taking a deep breath. "The pain will start to diminish very soon now. You're doing beautifully. Very soon you'll be able to see through that eye. You will be able to hear me, and you will talk to me. Sleep now. We're starting to rid you of your pain. . . ."

Her voice faded away, a diminishing tendril of sound floating about him, thinning and drifting off somewhere, somehow.

* * * * *

Dr. Jonathan Pickett, his spade beard bristling as he spoke to the technicians aligned with him before the medical levitator, nodded slowly as he voiced his judgment of the human disaster known to them only as Anthony Rogers. "Wilma got through as I had hoped. And she is correct. Despite all the physical damage and shock, he is fully functional in the cerebral sense. That means we can proceed, and I recommend we do so immediately." Pickett's heavy British accent came clearly through the hum and soft whine of electronic machines feeding power to the levitator that suspended Buck Rogers in the healing chamber. Gone was the air suspension system that had kept his torn body from contact with the laser cylinder before he was dematerialized from cells and flesh and liquids and bone into photons suspended in time.

Oxygen saturated his body, soaked into his skin, fed the human form struggling to survive and then begin the precarious process of healing. Intravenous fluids fed into his inner system, speeding high-intensity nourishment to organs and vital systems. Newly-created hormones coursed throughout his body. Vital minerals and enzymes flowed to where their life-serving energy was most needed. Buck Rogers knew none of this. He was in deep electrohypnotic sleep, his mind at rest, even his subconscious subdued to the lowest possible safe level. Nourishment, protection, and regrowth promised to keep him alive and gaining strength.

Caressed and suspended in the mag-grav coils of the levitator, he remained unaware of the medical teams already detailing the long road to survival and regeneration.

He experienced the first tendrils of conscious recovery. A superfine wire fed into his brain, terminating in the dream center, where it evoked memories, calm, serene, and most welcome to his severely strained psyche. Buck could not know, but for a long time his mind had been on the verge of shutting itself down to all external stimulation. He was surviving on instinct alone. His body continued to survive because his mind had reverted to primeval status, almost like the security of the womb.

Until Dr. Pickett directed his staff to allow those first waves and electric charges of pain to course through his body and into his mind. Pickett had assembled the best people he could find in all of Amerigo—a nation of which Buck Rogers was not even faintly aware. It didn't matter—yet.

But there was an imperative to saving and rebuilding this man. The program had been ordered by one of the most powerful men in all of Amerigo—a man respected and feared even by many of his closest associates. This man was known as Killer Kane. To his fellow officers and subordinates, he was Commodore-General Kevin Napoleon Kane, the leader of deep space operations of all Amerigo forces.

Although no one ever called him Killer to his face, Kane's appearance reinforced the image of his nickname. Stocky, his body covered with a brush of thick, curly hair, he resembled what the old history books often called the missing link between Neanderthal and Cro-Magnon Man. His brutish appearance effectively concealed his brilliance as a deep-space strategist and a master of tactical combat.

Kane had appeared before the High Council of Amerigo on Rogers's behalf. From the moment they had discovered the laser cylinder, still functioning perfectly beneath a mountain of rubble, protected by the armored shielding of the fusion reactor, Kane knew he wanted this man kept alive. On the exterior of the laser cylinder, along with operating instructions for the machinery that had kept Rogers alive for so long, he discovered a sealed container with the man's full biographical background, medical records, and special skills. Immediately Kane exercised his power as an advisor to the council, electing not to wait for the legally required vote to expend a small fortune for the program to bring Rogers "back to snuff," as Kane put it bluntly.

The council had called Commodore-General Kane on the carpet for taking matters into his own hands. Although he well knew the council had the power of life or death for anyone who violated its orders, Kane took the daring approach of demanding noninterference and full backing.

Now President Grenvil Logan looked down from his council seat at the grim visage of Kane. "We have many matters before us, Commodore-General. You know that. We will not waste time on amenities. Agreed?"

"Damn right," Kane growled. "Because if we're going to bring this man back, we have no time to lose. It's that simple."

Logan glanced at Vice-President Charlotte Hasafi, daughter of an English mother and a Saudi father, whose influence carried through much of the world. She appreciated the breach of etiquette and form visited upon them by Kevin Kane. Kane was an embodiment of his middle name, Napoleonic in nature, ego, and drive. In these brief moments, Vice-President Hasafi knew it would be she and President Logan who would pass final judgment. They would make the remainder of the council agree with their decision with no delays, no protracted debate.

In this issue, Hasafi knew, Logan was best suited to judge Kane's rash decision. Logan would know if circumstances dictated such drastic action. Logan was a politician, but like some before him, he was also a melding of ethnic and racial groups that made him distinctly individual. A combination of American-European white, African black, Jamaican, and Spanish heritage, Logan had a remarkable sensitivity to such issues. He had the brilliance and master chess-player thinking needed by a man of great power. He had years of experience in various combat zones throughout the world, and he was a born leader of men, mused Hasafi, despite the fact that he practiced ancient rites he was convinced gave him his special mental powers. Hasafi smiled to herself; there was enough superstition in this fractured world for such a practice to gain respect when it was backed up by success.

She returned the gaze of the president and nodded slightly, lowering and then raising her eyes to lock his gaze. It was a clear signal to all the council that these two had made their decision. Logan would judge and the others would support his judgment.

President Logan leaned forward, his ceremonial robe rubbing with a silky sound as he clasped his fingers and rested his hands on the table before him. "You may rest easy on your breach of procedure, Commodore."

Kane nodded; he saw no need to waste words to express his gratitude. Besides, he didn't give a fig for diplomatic procedure. Had they not been in council chambers, Logan would never have bothered with such a prissy pronouncement. Kane knew the president had to play by the rules of the game.

"Considering the highly unusual nature of this hearing, Commodore, please tell us why you chose to take matters into your own hands." Logan raised one hand to forestall an immediate reply; he wasn't finished lining up the other council members yet. "I am aware, Commodore, that you would never have acted in such a manner if you had not believed that timing was critical and that the results will justify the means. Proceed."

It was time to offer coins to Caesar, judged Kane. Give the devil his due. Logan's got to play the game. But by the looks of the rest of this crowd, I'm bloody glad I'm in full uniform. I hope these blasted medals give them eyestrain.

"This man," Killer Kane began slowly, "is more than just some freak survivor of an experiment from long ago. Most of the old records are gone. But the people who ran that laser experiment, which to us is old hat, did us a great favor. They included a complete dossier on Anthony Rogers. That's the man we're saving right now. He lived a double, or perhaps even a triple life."

"Explain, please," came a quiet interruption from Icarus, the Mediterranean councilman.

"As Anthony Rogers," Kane went on, "he had an illustrious career. He was a pilot, but that wasn't enough for him. He was an airline captain, which meant he flew machines with as many as six hundred people aboard. And he flew those machines, including much smaller aircraft, to every part of the world, which is vital to us now because he's been to places where we can't go. Before becoming an airline captain, Rogers was a military pilot. He flew anything with wings or rotors, with almost every kind of propulsion system. He was what I call a missions specialist, what in the old days they called a jack-of-all-trades for the military. The old government sent him time and time again into trouble spots throughout the world. He became a veteran of operations in jungles, deserts, mountains, ocean areas—anywhere his talents were needed. He flew old planes, but he also flew the best machines of his day and age. He flew in a manner we not only may have forgotten, but that we never really knew. Those kinds of skills, his unique experience, and above all his mind-set are exactly what I need for our air and space combat forces. Anthony Rogers—those who knew him called him Buck," he added with obvious feeling, "could be just the catalyst we need to change the attitudes of many of our pilots and combat teams."

Kane took a deep breath, pausing deliberately to let his words sink in.

"But it's more than that," Kane went on finally. "It's what we don't know about him that could prove even more valuable. He was, among other things, a world-renowned aerobatic pilot. He won international competitions for years. He was—is—a highly experienced aeronautical engineer. This man, for a hobby, mind you, designed, built, and flew his own aircraft."

Kane looked from one council member to another. He seemed to have ignited the imaginations of all seven. "Rogers is a great unknown, but he has the potential to be invaluable to us." Kane drew himself up ramrod straight.

"I want him. We need him. As soon as possible." Then he stood silently.

As he'd hoped, the other council members looked for their

decision to Logan and Hasafi. The woman gave a barely percepti-
ble nod. Logan's expression showed that he had already made
his decision. The others would follow their lead.

Logan gestured for attention, looking directly at Kane. "Do
what you must, Commodore-General."

"Done!" Kane answered.

* * * * *

Killer Kane left the council chambers immediately. Behind
him were five council members of the president's inner cabinet
who, as far as Kane was concerned, were deaf, dumb, and blind
to the realities of the present world. What was left of the United
States of America was a nation disembodied, splintered, and
divided into hopelessly squabbling factions.

It was impossible to escape from the circle of history. When
the original America was still largely a wilderness, Mongolian
hordes under Temujin—Genghis Khan himself—had smashed
through the great civilizations of both Asia and Europe and conquered fully a third of the known world. In the end, it was only
sloth and lack of new challenges that finally stopped the Mongol
tide. Eventually they returned to the great steppes of Russia and
the rich, remote stretches of Siberia, their once seemingly
unquenchable drive to conquer all but forgotten.

Only two of the council members, President Logan and Vice-
President Hasafi, knew just how grim Amerigo's present-day
prospects were. The confrontation in the council chambers had
been a charade. Prior to the council session, Kane had met
secretly with the two top leaders of Amerigo. In that private session, they had faced up to reality and had assured Kane of their
full support and cooperation. It was a pity things had to be done
in such a deceitful way, but it was important to preserve the
image of the unity of its leadership to the citizens of Amerigo.

Kane shook his head to clear his thoughts. This man from a
time so long ago, this ancient warrior, could make all the difference and return Amerigo to its former world leadership and
power.

But first they had to virtually rebuild the man. Kane had a
thousand questions to ask Buck Rogers. If he was the man Kane
thought he was, what had been lost to Amerigo could be regained

through Rogers's aggressive drive, his memories, his ability to infuse the military with new hope.

The key to making this a reality lay beyond all the experience and skills of doctors. Although Buck could not possibly be aware of it, he would survive only if something more than medicine came to his aid.

His future rested almost entirely in the skills and talents of Wilma Deering. The young woman—athletic, an experienced jet pilot, and a master gunner—was a contradiction in terms. She combined the tenderness of a woman with a no-nonsense instinct to go for the jugular when she engaged the enemy. She had earned the rank of major in the Space Corps and had fought both outside invaders and rebels in their own land. Her battleground was the sky above and the vacuum of space beyond. There were few who could match her skills in combat, but those skills would be of little help to Buck Rogers.

Kane knew it was vital that Wilma gain Buck's complete trust. He must learn to trust in her care and, even more, trust that she spoke from experience and knowledge rather than merely parroting what others told her.

Above all, she must be a woman to the mutilated man from the past. Wilma must replace the woman Rogers loved and left behind forever in the dusty pages of history. If anyone could make that happen, judged Kane, it was Wilma. The combination of being a lovely woman as well as a psychologist was more than one could hope for, but then, there were very few women like Wilma Deering. He had seen her walk slowly through a hospital ward and with no more than a gentle touch of her hand transform a desperately wounded, despondent patient into one with a renewed will to live.

Lastly, Kane knew that Wilma was something else they never mentioned openly: a sensitive. She was keenly attuned to the emotions of others as they broadcast, unknowingly, their thoughts and feelings and needs.

Such persons were to be found throughout the history of the human race under different names, including witches and magicians. Wilma was neither of those, but she was an empath, and she knew better than Buck himself what he needed to recover from his wounds and injuries, whether physical or emotional. If anyone could bring Buck Rogers back from the physical torture he had gone through, Wilma was that person.

Kane walked swiftly from the council chambers of Niagara, the huge capitol of Amerigo, also known as the Lead Orgzone— the strange political district in which the top organization and headquarters of Amerigo maintained its leadership, protected by a mag-grav shield of enormous power. Trying to pierce this shield, powered by banks of dynamos fed by thermonuclear turbines, was like throwing rocks at a thick fortress wall.

But Kane's business, for the immediate present, lay elsewhere. He needed none of the towering alloy skyscrapers, the banks of electronics, or even the suites of luxurious accommodations befitting a man of his stature. Near the center of Niagara, he went through a series of identilocks and personal security screens. An elevator dropped him six hundred feet beneath the surface of the Niagara River and the metropolitan city that lay sprawled across what had once been parts of both America and Canada.

At the deepest level of the vertical shafts, he entered another security checkpoint. This checkpoint, he knew, was armed by automated guns and laser flashrays that would fire instantly should he fail to pass every security screening. These elevators were the Achilles' heel of the Federated Orgzones since they were a key entry point into the city he had just departed.

He went down a curving tunnel and emerged into a long high-domed structure—Station Number One of the subterranean vacuum-tube train system that allowed rapid transport through the hostile territory that separated the strong points and cities of Amerigo. A single car, armored and surrounded with an eletrograv mag shield, waited for him with its door open, flanked by two armed guards. They saluted as he entered the car, eased into the front seat, attached his eight-point restraint harness, and began his prejourney checklist, including the emergencyoxy system that could keep him breathing for a week if there were a tunnel collapse or some other dire emergency.

Finally all was ready. He punched the button that slid the door closed, which in turn built up interior pressure and turned on the lights and communications systems. The long tunnel awaiting him held fiber-optic transceivers for its entire length, enabling Kane to remain in contact with his security teams.

The car shuddered slightly as the guards exited the station

and sealed the massive pressure door behind them. A chime sounded softly, and a woman's voice came through the computer system.

"The tunnel is clear of obstacles. You may initiate your journey when ready. Please confirm by retinal scan."

Kane stared into an optical sensor; it flashed so quickly he couldn't even detect the green laser that examined his eye, identifying him by his personal biological code and the implants in the soft, fleshy area on the side of his neck.

"You are clear for your journey. Godspeed." Kane grunted with distaste. Some wag in their transport shop had added that last bit at the end of the computer message. He shrugged. They still had worshipers and dreamers in a world that made a mockery of God granting speed, safe passage, or anything else.

He pressed an amber button. The car swayed briefly as it levitated in the direct center of the tube, suspended by the maglev generators in six layers. Now he looked down the beginning of a long tunnel devoid of air and friction.

He pushed back against the headrest behind him and stabbed the third button. Instantly the car shot forward, reaching its cruise speed of a hundred miles an hour in seconds. Impatient, Kane hit the overdrive command panel.

At five hundred miles an hour, he sped silently and swiftly beneath the earth. To Kane, the journey seemed interminably long. No need to waste time just sitting. He popped a Number Thirty pill beneath his tongue. Moments later he was fast asleep, untroubled by his enormous underground speed. The hypnomed pill would keep him asleep for precisely thirty minutes, a nap from which he would awaken refreshed and alert.

Seven minutes after he emerged from his sleep, the car decelerated to the subterranean station of Wyoming, Pennsylvania, a huge underground medical center deep beneath forested hills and rivers.

He rode the elevator to Sublevel Nine, then strode through the corridors and security doors until he reached a section with the glowing letters above its entrance reading, "RECOVERY."

Finally he stood before a curving viewpane of armored glass. Directly before him, Wilma Deering sat by the bedside of Buck Rogers, who was in deep hypnosleep. She held his hand in hers.

She's already started, Kane told himself. She knew even

before I did that the council would approve this program. . . .

Wilma sensed his presence. She turned her head to meet his gaze and acknowledged the slight nod he gave her. That was his only message. It was enough. Bring him back, it said. Keep him alive and on his way to recovery.

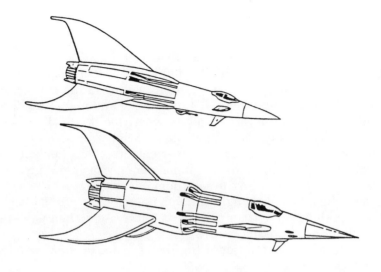

Chapter 8

"Who . . . who are you?"

Buck Rogers looked at the woman seated at his bedside. "I have the strangest feeling I've seen you before," he said slowly.

The attractive red-haired woman smiled at him. Even the sight of her was disturbing. She kept reminding him of Angelina. But that didn't make sense. Angie didn't even look like this woman. Their familiarity came from the intensity of life they resonated. Smart, quick-witted, dazzling smile. But he was sure now he had never seen this woman before.

"You have seen me," she said quietly, speaking slowly to let her words sink into his still-unbalanced powers of reasoning. "Right here, with you. Many times."

"I don't remember ever seeing you," he persisted.

"You were sedated," she explained. "The drugs allowed you to hear me, even see me when your left eye resumed functioning. But the drug blocks out certain memories. It's really quite selective. You retain only those memories your subconscious judges as pleasant, or worthwhile, and eliminates all memory of pain."

He studied the woman carefully. There was something about her he had never before encountered, a sense of sharing whatever was haunting him emotionally and the physical pain he had been enduring for so long.

Buck stopped short in his thinking. His mind was rushing off in different directions, learning little. Get a good grip on yourself, Ace, he ordered himself. Start at the beginning. . . .

She seemed to sense the questions roiling in his mind. "You asked who I am," she reminded him. Her hand rested tenderly on his forearm, one of the few places where his skin had not been burned. He felt a profound closeness to her. Was she a nurse? Whoever she was, what he was experiencing at this moment was hardly rare, he knew. It was common enough for injured men to fall for the women who nursed them back to life. At the same moment he ran that thought through his mind, he still felt there was something more than met the eye here. Again he castigated himself for not thinking clearly.

"Yes, I did," he answered finally, grateful for her bringing him back on track.

"My name is Wilma Deering. I'm a pilot."

"Oh." He studied her again. "A pilot," he repeated. "Well, isn't that a coincidence? So am I."

"I know." She smiled.

"But . . . the way you spoke, it sounded as if you've been here with me for ages. You must be a nurse."

"Not exactly, but you're close."

"I'm confused."

"Among other things, Buck Rogers—"

"Just Buck, please."

She nodded. "Among other things, I'm a medtech . . . medical technician. What you would call a paramedic."

"Uh-huh."

"And a psychologist."

"That's good. Because I feel as if I'm going a little crazy," he said, beginning to relax with her easy manner. "I mean, first of all, I don't even know how I'm alive. When that engine came back at my chest, I figured it was curtains. Then there was the fire . . ." His voice trailed away, and his face grew serious. "Wilma?"

"Yes?"

"Where the hell am I?"

She took a deep breath. This could be an unnerving time for this man. What he would learn in the next few minutes would be both a mental and physical shock, and the last thing he needed was for his system to overload. But from what she'd determined so far, she felt he could handle the impact as long as she proceeded slowly and carefully.

"You're in Pennsylvania. The MedTech Center in Wyoming—"

"Wyoming is a state," he broke in.

"Not many people know about this Wyoming. It's an advanced medical center. We named it Wyoming. Perhaps the designer of this center called it by that name because the state of Wyoming was his home."

He shrugged. The brief physical movement was like a ballet movement to her practiced eye. His instincts and reflexes were coming back quickly.

"You called it MedTech. I've never heard of that."

"You're in an advanced medical center. Everything is underground. That way we can control the air flow, contents, and temperature very precisely, with no interference from external effects such as sunlight or cold. The computers run the system."

"Okay." He closed his eye for a moment, breathing deeply. "One eye?" he said finally.

"Yes."

"But I'm lucky to be alive, right?"

"More so than you can imagine."

"Hell, I know a few pilots who have only one eye, and they can still fly anything."

Another sign. Accepting a loss, a disability that would be a crutch to many men who were pilots, to whom good vision was everything. It seemed a good time to elevate his hopes.

"This place, where you are now—"

"MedTech, you said," he broke in, pleased with his recognition and memory of where he was. He frowned. "Sorry to interrupt, but I've been out of touch," he added ruefully. He looked about them. "I've not only never seen a place like this, I've never even *heard* about it."

"I can understand that," she said cautiously. He had seized on her remark. This is incredible, she thought. Somewhere in that mind of his is a steel trap, and it's very much alive! He's quick, and his grasp of change gets better every moment. If this keeps up . . .

He was thrusting and parrying words with her, and that was the best of all signs, for now Buck was jumping ahead of the immediacy of their conversation. He's trying to trap me! she thought jubilantly. How marvelous!

"Why?" he countered.

"Why *what?*"

"Why can you understand that I'm not familiar with this place? Wilma, as far as I know, and I am very privy to advanced military and scientific programs, this place simply doesn't exist."

Her laughter was like silvery bells in a forest glade. "Very good, Mr. Rogers," she replied with feigned deliberation. "You're right, of course."

"Look," he said quickly, his hand moving without a deliberate thought to rest upon hers. "It doesn't take a rocket scientist to recognize that something here is way out of line. Your clothes, the medical gowns, the equipment around us, even the floors, the lighting, it's . . . well, it's just different, that's all. So I've got to ask you what I asked before, but sort of change the emphasis."

"You've got the floor," she answered quickly, not wanting this frank back-and-forth exchange to end too quickly. His strength was already beginning to wane.

"I do not have the floor. Wilma, I'm aware you've been devoted to taking care of me. I look like a locomotive ran over me and then made room for a couple of bulldozers to finish the job. I've seen my reflection in that glass partition. I look like the Rambling Wreck from Georgia Tech. By all rights, your smile should be a look of revulsion, but I've never seen a hint of it. So you are very, very good, and I haven't yet figured why I'm getting the twenty-four-karat-gold treatment."

"But you have some idea," she said, leading him on.

"Not really. But I sure have some questions!"

"Go ahead."

He stifled a yawn. "I'm getting sleepy. Am I under drugs?"

"Yes. They're in your system to help revitalize your strength. We have a system here, noninvasive, that monitors all your physiological parameters. That system—the bed you're lying on is an integral part of it—detects when you're overstressing yourself. You need healing, surgery. The MedSensor detects when you need rest, and it sends an EM—"

"Electromagnetic?"

"Yes. An EM signal into your brain at twenty-two hertz. That's your natural brain wave. It also begins to close down your receptivity to external stimuli. You'll fall into a deep sleep soon, but not right away. You still have some time to go."

"I'm starting to get some crazy ideas about things," he told her. "If I ask short questions, I'd appreciate short answers—but *straight* answers."

"You will receive whatever you wish, but I warn you that what you hear probably won't be to your liking. It's bound to have a shock impact, and if I feel you're going into overload, you'll be in deep sleep immediately. I'd rather you simply drifted off."

Again he shrugged. "Hey, don't hold back. Drop the hammer on me."

Once more that dazzling smile. "In your idiom, shoot."

"In *my* idiom? Why do you keep making me feel like a stranger to this land of yours? I feel like an alien."

"You're not. Let's get that clear from the start."

"Where am I?"

"You already know that."

"Yes . . . in a place that, to the very best of my knowledge, doesn't exist, not even as a top-secret government program."

"Go on."

"Did I die in that crash?"

She laughed easily. "Not quite, but you came very close. Let's simply say you were on the edge of a one-way trip. However, you did not die. You've been kept alive for a very long time." She hoped these hints would lead him to question his leap into the future.

"How long?"

"Hang on to your bed . . . tightly. Very tightly."

"Lay it on me, Carrot Top," he said with a crooked smile.

"Do you remember the story of Rip Van Winkle?"

"Sure. A man falls asleep. Something—I don't remember what—keeps him zonked for years and years. He wakes up with a long white beard in a future time. Why?"

"Do you think something like that might really happen?"

He studied her carefully. "Wilma, you're setting me up for something."

She nodded.

"Are you trying to tell me," he said slowly, very deliberately, "that I'm somewhere in the future? From my own time, I mean?"

"Yes."

"Why?"

"It was the only way to keep you alive. The medicine of your time couldn't save you. We can. In fact, we have. You're living proof."

He closed his eye, leaning back in the bed. He fought off a sudden wave of drowsiness. "Whoa! Hold on, lady. You mean I've been kept on ice for—" He looked directly at her. "How long?"

"First things first. It's obvious you were thinking about an experimental process of your day called cryogenics. It involved freezing a body in supercold liquid and, as you say, keeping it on ice until some future time when medical science could cure what was incurable while the patient was still alive."

"Is that what—"

She gestured for him to wait. "No, we didn't put you on ice. Nor did scientists of your time use such a procedure. It simply didn't work. The problems—crystallization of the blood, brittle tissues, hardening of vital nerve networks—were endless. You can't stop time and the aging process that way."

He stared at her, knowing she was leading him to where he must believe the unbelievable. "Let me get the crux of all of this first. You know, the short synopsis." Again he fought off the wave of sleep descending on him.

"How—what—happened? You're telling me I was kept alive artificially?"

"Yes."

"But *how?*"

"There was an experimental program in your day—secret, but heavily financed. It was a matter of dematerializing biological material."

"That's me. Thanks," he said wryly.

"In the most basic of terms, if a biological creature—you— could be reduced to the most essential, basic structure of his mind and body—"

"That's a big if," he broke in. "You'd have to get all the way down to subatomics."

Elation gripped her. "Exactly."

"They—scientists—did that to me?"

"Yes."

He was hearing her words now in a thickening fog. "How?"

"Laser dematerialization."

"You're telling me they reduced me to primordial soup?"

"Much more than that. The best way to say it is that you were transformed into a state of quantum energy. You—or rather, the atoms and subatomic particles of your body—were reduced to light quanta."

"Photons?"

"Yes. This enabled them to accelerate what was you to the speed of light. Are you familiar with time dilation?"

"Yeah." He felt he was mumbling, groping in his memory for what he knew of mass and the speed of light. "Einstein. The old boy's theories—realities, I mean—that if you travel at the speed of light, time stops."

"Excellent."

"But—but you can't go faster than light. Infinite mass. Crazy as hell, but they proved it would . . ."

"That's enough for now. You'll sleep deeply."

He was spiraling downward, struggling to ask the one question burning in his mind. "What—what year is this?"

"Twenty-four twenty-nine."

He gaped. The enormity of the numbers overwhelmed him. "Four hundred and thirty-three years," she added as his eye closed. The last words he heard were, "Welcome, Buck Rogers, to the twenty-fifth century."

"Good God." He was never sure if he really spoke those words as consciousness left him.

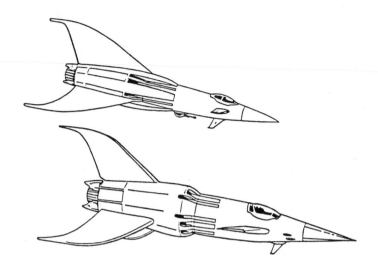

Chapter 9

"So I'm going to be a descendant of the original bionic man . . ." Buck laughed, a sound that startled him.

"You were going to say something else," Wilma prompted.

"Oh, yeah. I don't suppose you ever heard of that television show about two people who got torn up in accidents and were rebuilt through bionic science."

"Buck, it's been more than four hundred years."

"I know. Forget it. I was going to add that I feel like a character in some movie. And the heroine in this story is the prettiest I've ever seen."

"Compliments," she said with a smile, "will get you everywhere. But to answer those questions, you may be surprised to know that bionics was not the answer. Oh, it helped, but it's just stopgap medicine. It's an excuse, really, for doing a job that medical science of your day couldn't yet manage. The real answer is genetic control and helping the body to do what nature created it to do."

"Which is . . . ?"

"Heal itself."

Buck gestured to take in his entire body. "You can heal someone who's ill or injured," he said defensively, "but this—what's left of me—well, I'll put it this way. I'll take all the artificial parts that work, thank you."

"We'll do better than that. Look," she said earnestly, holding his hand in both of hers, "we'll make you as good as, if not better than, the original. But we'll do it with biology, not bionics."

"That sounds as if you're going to grow me back in a nutrient tank."

She leaned back, sharing his smile. "In a sense you're right. The world is nothing like you remember, and—"

"You've never explained that. Only hints and inferences. I get the idea I'm in for a shock, or I may not like what I find."

"Possibly. But you have an adaptive mind," she responded quickly. "As I told you before, everything in due time and in its proper order. The first priority, above all else, is a whole, well, and fully functioning Buck Rogers."

She halted, obviously searching for the words that would best explain their program. "Let me put it this way. We know how to rebuild you as a bionic man. With several centuries of technology behind us, the science of replacement parts of the human body is old hat. But it has several major flaws, and they're as much psychological as they are physical. In fact—"

"Let me guess," he broke in suddenly, his manner intense. "It's like the mechanical man from the Wizard of Oz."

"I'm really not acquainted with your fantasy world, Buck."

"Oh, it's fantasy, all right. It was a movie, about a Kansas farm girl who gets picked up by a tornado, along with her dog, and is somehow whirled off into a fantasy land and—" He chuckled. "Never mind. The point is that there was a mechanical man in the movie, a sort of lovable, clanking parody of a man. But he was miserable because, while his body and brain worked, he didn't have a heart. No ticker inside his chest. His life's dream was to get himself a heart so he'd be a real, whole man."

"Is that what you believe might happen with you?"

He laughed. "That question is loaded with traps, so I think I'll step around it and just say that I don't know. I've never been bionic or mechanical or anything but myself."

"That is precisely what we want," Wilma said immediately. "But you'll be even better than the original. When you get into the surgical and restructuring program, the idea is to make you not only what you were, but an improvement."

"Hell of a speech, Wilma."

She flushed. "I didn't mean for it to sound like one."

"Take it again, one step at a time." His expression showed his seriousness. "Please?" he added.

"You are familiar with biogenetics?"

"Somewhat."

"All right. A good proportion of your skin was burned. You already know that."

"I know. You can prevent the escape of water from a body with temporary measures until the skin has time to scar. You end up with skin that's like wrinkled tarpaper, but it's better than nothing." He sighed.

"That won't happen with you."

His one eye widened with surprise. "Why not?"

"Your genetic code was determined with a small patch of unburned skin. The computers provided the code down to the smallest detail. Since you arrived here, we've been busy growing your own skin. Soon we'll be able to replace every burned part of your body with that skin. Since there's no danger of rejection, the old and the new will join together and follow your genetic pattern."

He remained silent, then placed a finger over the mutilated space where his other eye had been. "And what about this? A miniature television camera? Fiberoptic hookups to the optic nerves? That's bionics, no matter how you cut it."

"We're *growing* you a new eye—an exact replacement of your own. For all intents and purposes, it will be your eye." She hurried on with her answers to his questions, both voiced and unspoken. "We'll do the same with broken or crushed bones, nerves, tendons, sinews, muscles, arteries, veins, capillaries, even your lungs. That includes that ear you lost. It's being grown right now, including the inner organs of hearing. It's called rebirth through genetic medicine, Buck."

"Look," he broke in, "I had a friend who was busted up in the crash of his jet fighter. His leg was broken in several places. There was bone loss. Even in our times, the doctors could fix him. We had something called bioglass. It had just about all the characteristics of real bone. They connect the busted ends with bioglass. His leg bone latched on to it and began to grow over the bioglass. No rejection. What's wrong with that?"

"The bioglass doesn't have bone marrow, so it doesn't produce red blood cells. The body must function by robbing from other sources. In its simplest terms, there's a deficiency of needed life materials, even though the man might walk or run again. Nature took many millions of years to create what we are. Artificial substitutions, like cardiac pacemakers, worked for a while, but they were never as good as the original. After the first experimental surgeries, heart implants became as good as the original, because the new heart *was* the patient's own heart."

Wilma took a deep breath. "It isn't just medicine, Buck. It's the very philosophy of life. If you had brain damage, we couldn't really help you. Your brain has a hundred billion neurons. That includes the glial structure that supports the brain. But if the cerebellum is damaged, we ease a patient's difficulties, but we can't replace that part of his brain that is the mind. We *can* do just about everything else."

Buck let out a tremulous sigh. "So I go into deep sleep, you do the Humpty Dumpty routine on me, and—"

"Humpty Dumpty?"

"A children's fable. About a humanlike egg that falls off a wall and gets all cracked up, and nothing can put it together again. But it sounds as if you've solved that problem. I go to sleep, and while I'm in dreamland, I get a whole new bod, so to speak."

She smiled, but there was something different about the look on her face.

"Sorry, my friend. You don't get off that easily. Except for a few special procedures, you remain awake during the entire process."

He was startled with her words. "Hey, I can grit my teeth with the best of them," he said quickly. "You know, Joe Hero and all that. But there's a limit, Wilma! You'll have me screaming like a madman."

"We'll block the pain, but not with drugs."

"What then? Are you going to use a sledgehammer to put me out?" he asked in mock seriousness.

"There are already probes implanted in your brain to stimulate a rush of endorphins that flood your body. We kick them off with electrical vibrations. They function better than any morphine or other painkiller. You remain aware of everything that's going on, but you're not tortured with pain. We've got to keep you alert and responsive so we're sure we're on the right track with everything we do. We test as we go along, fix anything that isn't right."

"I sense I'll be something like a guinea pig."

"Are you feeling sorry for yourself?" she demanded.

"Anything but," he replied. "Befuddled, confused, bewildered, overwhelmed—you know, the thin line between acceptance and insanity, I guess."

"You'll do fine. Do you know there are more than sixty probes already implanted inside your body?"

"When? I don't recall anything like that."

"Of course not. The probes were put in place when you were in stimulated hypnosleep."

"Where are they? How come I can't feel them?"

"Each probe is so small it's almost invisible. Most of them are made of pure gold. Some are an alloy of iridium oxide and plantium. They're extraordinarily precise in transceiving physiological signals. In fact, they're capable of gathering data from even a single nerve cell. All together, they provide us with a precise real-time look at your nerve stimulation. We can tell how you're doing at a glance, because everything is telemetered to a computer that gives us ongoing readouts of how your body is functioning. That includes hearing, vision, kinesthetic sensing—"

"The whole ball of wax, I guess," he broke in.

"Crudely put, but true nevertheless. In short, we not only receive the data that tells us how your systems are functioning—or not functioning—but we can also transmit messages to your body to bring things on-line. The moment you're functioning normally, the probes become quiescent. They go on hold, so to speak, until they're needed."

"And if something isn't working up to snuff?"

"Each probe is paired with a microelectrode to determine needs for hormones, enzymes, electrolytes. or other needs. After a while, your body learns when to react to a need or problem, and your system takes over for itself."

Buck grinned. "I feel like a laboratory rat."

"So you are," she said easily.

"When does all this start?"

"It began three days ago."

"Three days! How come I . . ."

He fell into the deep hypnosleep programmed to begin at precisely that moment.

* * * * *

Black Barney stood before the viewing window that looked down on the entire AkshunGames contest field. From this high, the figures below seemed ridiculously small. An upward glance showed every detail on a huge, curving television screen.

Barney snorted with disdain for the crowds that filled the Niagara Orgzone energy-shielded dome. The worst place to watch the competitions was right here in these bleachers and box seats. People were so distant from the real action that they needed soniplugs held in place against their skull to hear the sound, including men and women gasping for breath in their exertions. By wearing the plugs, you could even hear the scrape of floatsneaks against gravel in the relay races. And if you wanted to feel as if you were "down there among them," all you needed to do was to turn on the hologram viewer, and right before your eyes the competitors appeared in amazingly detailed three-dimensional holograms. Grimaces, bleeding, thudding body blows, teeth spit forth like white candy—whatever you wanted, it was right there.

But still they came to fill the bleachers and the front-row boxes. Although Barney now felt disdain toward such devotion, he, too, had once been one of the most avid fans of the sports games and competitions. The Gamesmasters really knew how to draw them in. Watching the games through electronics gave one a terrific view, but it lacked something the crowd needed.

"Watching even a 3-D," Barney had once explained to a group of friends, "is like kissing your sister. Something's missing."

He knew what it was. It was the same thing that drew thousands of people in the distant past to live circuses, jammed with exciting acts and stunts and dozens, sometimes hundreds, of animals to thrill the crowd. The circus in Buck Rogers's time had been a great crowd pleaser, with the smell of sawdust, the roars and bellows and stink of lions and elephants and horses and— Barney let this train of thought die. There hadn't been a circus band for hundreds of years. Everything came out of the computer now, and it was too good to keep you hanging on the edge. Lack of perfection was its own music sometimes. Barney laughed silently at himself. He was acting like a traditionalist, immersing himself in a world only one man among them all really knew.

BUCK ROGERS

He watched that man at this moment as Buck Rogers went through his training regimen, with Wilma Deering riding him constantly, urging him to ever-better performance. She compelled him to run faster, jump higher, and throw farther—track and field, swimming, climbing, wrestling, all of it.

And despite her efforts, Buck was going to lose just about every competitive act in the book. That was part of the program. Barney watched as other men, one by one, exceeded the best of Buck's performances in everything from pole vaulting to hurling the javelin. Finally he saw Buck stride away in disgust. He stopped before a training bench and dumped a pail of water over his head to wash away the sweat and cool down his body. Wilma followed him, laughing, and threw her arms about his neck, hugging him tightly. Barney nodded. The pairing of these two as a team was working better than they could have hoped for. Barney aimed a spinband helical antenna onto the field. He could hear every sound within a fifty-foot circle of the two people he watched.

* * * * *

"You've done it, Buck. Congratulations," Wilma told the exhausted man. Buck sat on the bench, soaked, drinking fortified dran, a mixture of juices, herbs, and electrolytes that would soon have his body ready for further testing. "This wraps it all up," Wilma continued.

Buck stared back, shaking his head. "Wraps it up? I just won the loser's cup, lady! I got my butt whipped by everybody out there, men and women!"

"Of course you did," Wilma replied, smiling patiently. "There was never any doubt about that."

"Then why the big charade?"

"It wasn't a charade," she said. "This wasn't a competition, even though we led you to believe that. Until now, that is. We had to learn your full physical parameters. Competition, or what you thought was competition, is the best way to bring that out. When you ran the track, you were up against men and women biologically altered to run faster than anyone else alive. The same with the swimming, the weight-lifting, all of it. Every competitor you faced was a champion in his or her own right. But if you averaged out the performance of all the people today, you'd end up as one of the better-performing athletes out there."

He took a long pull of his energy drink. "And you're satisfied?"

"Better than that. The physical preparations are over. You're as sharp, as fast, as strong, as you ever were in your entire life. And you can apply those attributes to whatever you do." She paused. "You're ready now for what may well be a lot tougher for you to handle than anything you did today."

"I'm all ears, lady."

"Tonight you learn what happened to your world after you were suspended in time. It's not a nice story. Psychologically, it could be devastating."

He started to ask her why, then clenched his teeth. He had a hunch she might be right.

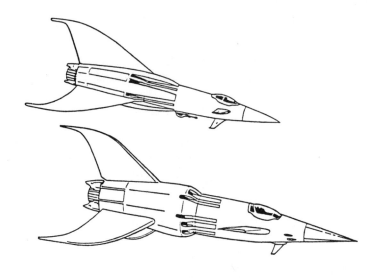

Chapter 10

Buck sat within a learning cubicle in Niagara, running through three-dimensional holograms of a bewildering variety of fighting skycraft. Wilma presented flight scenes of the craziest machines Buck had ever seen. Very little made sense to him. Here he was in the twenty-fifth century, and he had been presented with an amalgam of aerial machines that ran from primitive canvas-covered ancient biplanes to clattering helicopters, from huge aerial battlewagons to sleek supersonic jet fighters.

His indoctrination came to an abrupt halt with the sudden appearance of Air Marshal Marcus Bergstrasser, a tall, lanky man with scarred features and the weathered look of a professional battler. He yanked open the cubicle door, ignoring the indoctrination program.

"Wilma, shut off that damned toy of yours," he commanded.

With a quiet, "Yes, sir," she did as ordered. The cubicle went silent, and the moving map and illuminated strongholds vanished. Soft lights came on. Bergstrasser closed the door behind him.

"We can talk here with full security," he announced to Wilma and Buck.

Buck smiled. "Full security here? Right in the command center of your whole outfit?"

Bergstrasser leaned across the command panel and stabbed several computer keys. "All right. We're isolated now." He turned to Wilma. "Get me the data on the Half-Breeds. I want their main installation, peripheral guard battle stations, the works. Bring up the display showing their numbers, equipment, and current status."

"Half-Breeds?" Buck echoed aloud.

"Yes," Bergstrasser snapped, watching Wilma's fingers flying across the computer data boards. A glowing map of what had been the contiguous forty-eight states of America appeared on the screen. In the area just northwest of what had once been the metropolis of St. Louis, a group of glowing amber-colored lights appeared, surrounding a single large red glow.

"We don't have time for a full history lesson, Rogers," Bergstrasser said. "I can't really give you any orders until you're a sworn member of the Niagara Orgzone—our nation, or what's left of it. If you agree, I'll swear you in right now as a major in the Flight Combat Task Force. That's my outfit. We deal with atmospheric combat on tactical levels. We get down-and-dirty with the opposition. Damned little of the high-tech combat stuff. We don't defend cities or battle space cruisers or any of that nonsense. That's up to people like Black Barney, Killer Kane . . . people like that."

"I don't get your drift. Who are these Half-Breeds?"

"You'll understand in a few minutes," Bergstrasser promised. "I don't know how much Wilma has told you about the continental area, but the country you knew is gone. Except for our major strongholds and those of the invaders—the Mongols, the Chileans, the Golden Dragons, and some others—the country is a vast territory with guerilla outposts here and there." More lights flashed on the board; Bergstrasser pointed to different glowing sites.

"Here's where we are—the Niagara Orgzone, which simply means that's our organizational zone. We're the single most powerful outfit in the whole country, but we're a long way from controlling the rest of the land. Not that we haven't tried, but just holding our own is what we've settled for. If," he said with a tired pause, "we could bring together the feudal outposts and the roving guerilla forces, we could triple our strength and expand our influence across most of the country. It's a big if, but you may be the key to breaking the deadlock we're in."

Buck stared at the glowing dots and colors across the three-dimensional map of the country. All of a sudden he forced himself away from the map. "Wait a moment," he protested. "You're going way too fast for me to make sense out of what you're saying. Guerrilla bands? Mongols? In the United States? And Chileans? That's just a small, backward country at the butt end of the Andes Mountains! You also said something about Golden Dragons. You know what you sound like, Marshal . . . ?" Buck hesitated, groping for his name

"Air Marshal Marcus Bergstrasser," came the reply. "Let's dispense with the rank and titles if you don't mind. Marcus will do just fine. And obviously Wilma hasn't had the opportunity to give you even a condensed version of what's happened to this country—or the rest of the world—in the last several hundred years."

"You just won the prize for the understatement of the year," Buck murmured.

"I'd hoped to bypass, at least for the moment, an elementary history lesson," Bergstrasser said, grimacing.

"No way," Buck said adamantly. "Whatever you've got up your sleeve, Air Marshal—Marcus—you're leaving me on the thin end of a long pole by not filling me in on what's gone on. Right now I seem to be in the middle of some cockamamie world with all new players, from what I've heard so far. And the old outlines of countries are the same, but inside the boundaries, I'm living on what seems like an alien planet. Just about anywhere I turn I'll be walking into something I don't understand. Take the time, Marcus. Anybody who gets into a fight with only limited knowledge of what he's facing has already lost half the battle. I want better odds than that."

Marcus Bergstrasser sighed audibly. Finally he nodded, realizing the time schedule he had in mind was unworkable. "Wilma, take over," he directed. Bergstrasser grabbed a chair, shoved it back against a wall, and lit a long, thin cigar.

"Well, I'm glad to see not all the amenities have been lost," noted Buck. "It takes a civilized man to appreciate a good cigar. Although I'm puzzled. Where in this crazy country do you have the space or the time to cultivate tobacco farms?"

Bergstrasser rolled the cigar in his fingers and flicked ashes into a wall receptacle. They vanished in a thin curl of smoke. "We don't," he answered. "We don't have the time, the open country, or enough hydroponic farms for tobacco. This cigar is cultivated from seaweed, mixed with the fibers of the hemp plant, and infused with synthetic nicotine. It tastes like the best of the ancient Cuban cigars, but there aren't any harmful effects. Would you like one?"

"Later," Buck said. "Let me get the background now from Wilma."

She nodded. "All right. We'll do this with a combination of historical and current names and organizations. For a while, there will be so many you won't be able to retain them all, even though they all play a vital part in whatever the air marshal has planned for you."

"It sounds like you're going to run a film past me at full speed and all I'll see is a blur," Buck said with obvious impatience.

"Point well taken," Wilma admitted. "But tonight, when you're asleep, you'll be in hypnomemory training. Everything you see and hear now will be fed into your memory cells while you're sleeping. When you awake, everything you've learned will be as familiar as if you've lived in our present all your life."

"Neat trick," Buck murmured.

"Let's go back to your time," Wilma went on, ignoring Buck's comment. "How would you judge the state of the world in—1996, right?" Buck nodded.

"The danger of major war had diminished, I believe," she said.

"That's only partially true. The Second World War was more than fifty years behind us, but there were plenty of other wars— Korea, Vietnam, Algeria, a dozen or more wars in Africa. South and Central America were a hotbed of small wars. India, Pakistan, Afghanistan, Turkey, Iraq, Iran, Tibet, Argentina—well, we averaged between thirty and forty wars every year."

"Please keep that in mind," Bergstrasser asked. "It's important. And what about America? Your own country?"

"We were smack-dab in the middle of many of the small wars," Buck admitted. "Fifty thousand dead was pretty much the norm." He frowned. "You can add a few million missing and wounded to that."

"And you regarded this as *peace?*" Wilma asked with obvious sarcasm.

"Compared to what might have happened, I suppose we did," Buck answered. "It isn't that simple. It wasn't black and white, but a mass of gray. We ended the Second World War—"

"How many dead?" Bergstrasser asked, his tone making it clear he already knew the answer.

Buck shrugged. "It depends upon who did the counting. By conservative estimates, about seventy million. More realistically, more than a hundred million. A lot more would have died if we hadn't ended the Pacific War with the atomic bombs we dropped on Hiroshima and Nagasaki."

"And that," Wilma said coldly, "led to *another* kind of war. Dozens of smaller, confined wars with mass killing, but not the end of civilization as so many had feared when the United States and the Soviet Union had so many hydrogen bombs. What if *that* war had broken out?"

"Thank God it didn't," Buck replied. "America and Russia were at each other's throats for years, but we never again dropped an atomic or hydrogen bomb on anybody."

"How many warheads were available? Nuclear and thermonuclear?" Bergstrasser pressed.

Buck frowned. He didn't like the direction this exchange was taking. "All are estimates at best. The actual numbers were secret. The best guess was between sixty and eighty thousand. The point is, what we called the Cold War—the standoff between America and Russia—ended without a fight. The Soviet Union collapsed from within—decadent, miserably poor, a dictatorship. Living under Communism was pure hell. Finally the whole rotten mess fell apart. Russia broke up into many smaller countries—"

"And the smaller wars continued," Wilma pressed.

Buck nodded. There was no way to ignore that reality.

"Plus a new danger presented itself," said the air marshal. "As the next several decades went by, more and more countries, to say nothing of power groups and terrorist groups, began to accumulate their own nuclear weapons. I don't want to describe anything that isn't accurate, Buck. Is what we've said, and what you have told us, true?"

"It is. But what's the purpose of all this? All we're doing is rehashing ancient history," Buck shot back angrily.

"Not quite," Bergstrasser said soberly.

"What do you mean by that?" Buck demanded.

"You had your accident in 1996. Just about the time that you were placed in the laser dematerializer," Wilma interjected, "came the beginning of the end. In Russia, Moscow lost control of its territories—republics, I believe they were called. The new so-called free republics turned on Russia. When a republic declared itself free, Moscow reacted predictably with full military power. By the end of the twentieth century, only a few years after you were out of the picture, Europe was tearing itself apart. Many of the breakaway countries joined together to fight the Russians. The fighting in the old Communist lands began to spread. Someone launched a salvo of nuclear warheads against France and Spain. They retaliated. Within a week or so, all Europe banded together. France demanded that England come to its aid. The English refused, saying it wasn't their war. Turkey and the Czech countries, along with Germany and Poland, made their move to control oil sources by launching a massive war against the Mideast countries of Iraq, Iran, Saudi Arabia, Yemen, and Kuwait."

Wilma leaned back in her seat. "From that moment on, there was no stopping the spread of fighting. Missiles, planes, anything that could carry a nuclear weapon got into the spreading war. England took a barrage of hydrogen bombs, but that was nothing compared to the biological agents that were thrown against the islands. The United States felt compelled to go to their aid, but the big question was whom were they going to fight?

"So the United States reverted to what your people called the Big Stick policy. They figured that if the leading cities of the warring countries were obliterated, those lands would be so devastated, the people so overcome, that the fighting had to stop."

"It was a big mistake," added Bergstrasser. "A very big mistake. America should have taken a hard look at the other side of the world. By the end of the century, the Chinese had built an enormous military machine. All the signs had been there, but your country, the old America, was just too smug to recognize the real danger. For many years America and her European allies had looked down on the Chinese as a backward country. China allied itself with Mongolia and the Siberian outposts. The Russian military bases in the Far East had been isolated from their homeland. They had no hope of reinforcements, and now they faced a truly powerful enemy right on the Asian mainland. China, Mongolia, Japan, Siberia, Vietnam, Sumatra, Singapore, New Guinea, all had felt isolated, and now they banded together. They came to the conclusion that it was time to put the white people in their place.

"They used everything they had—more than two billion fighting men, and no one knows how many tens of thousands of planes, tanks, heavy weapons. And a submarine fleet no one even dreamed they had. The Pacific became an enormous battleground of submersibles, but America and England, as well as those French and Russian subs that could escape from Europe, were vastly outnumbered. I'm sure you recall the kamikaze attacks the Japanese used against America in the Pacific War. That was an act of desperation. But now the Asian forces had superiority in both numbers and weapons, and millions of combat men willing to die just as long as they took enemy ships, submarines, and planes along with them.

"The world was tearing itself apart. Vast areas were radioactive wastelands. Terrible epidemics swept across entire continents. Asian armies moved across the Aleutians and swept over Canada with virtually no resistance. They gathered their forces to a billion strong and poised for the death blow against the United States. In the meantime, to the south, the Central and South American lands saw the handwriting on the wall. There was no United States able to protect them. Either they threw in their lot with the Asiatics, or they'd be ground to dust. The Chinese and Mongolians wouldn't even have to invade. Biological agents would devastate them all. So the South Americans announced, first, they would remain neutral, but that facade didn't last long. It was either join the fight to erase the long superiority of the white man—and the same thing was happening in black Africa—or they'd be crushed. In fact, the uprising in what was South Africa was a bloodbath that equalled anything ever written about in the Old Testament. The countryside and the rivers and lakes all ran red with the blood of people hacked, cut, speared, or blown to bits. But there was a new player that emerged from the savagery. That was Chile and its immediate neighbors."

"I don't understand about Chile," Buck reiterated. "Strung out the way they are—"

Wilma stabbed the computer console buttons and Chile appeared magically. "The geography of Chile was perfect for submarine operations. Considering their long coastline, that was number one on their list. You couldn't get at Chile from the east because of the mountains. Argentina saw the handwriting on the wall and joined Chile. There had always been a powerful Japanese presence in Brazil. They set off biological plagues in the main cities, which in turn devastated normal commerce. Factories closed down, electrical power almost disappeared, rivers closed, airports were shut down by terrorist squads, food distribution died, communications faded away—"

"I get the picture," Buck said moodily. "And I can make a guess at one more thing. Because of the Andes Mountains, Chile stood apart from the mainstream of air currents. They stayed largely free of radioactive fallout and biological epidemics. All of a sudden, with nearby countries supporting them, with the Chinese and Mongols pouring supplies into their country, they became a dangerous power."

Wilma sighed again, worn out from her dissertation. "Air Marshal, please wind this up," she asked Bergstrasser.

The tall man stubbed out his cigar, lit another, and waved it in the air like a baton. "It was short and sweet, Buck, even though it took a few hundred years. First, southeast Asia was now the main concentration of power in the world. Along their northern flanks, they had the Himalayas as a natural barrier. To the west, jungles and swamps and local national infrastructures had been devastated. All people wanted was something to eat. Nationalism disappeared. If the Chinese would only feed them, they'd devote themselves to the Chinese cause—and they did. Australia was left to die a slow death. Why bother with a country that was ninety percent desert, cut off from any meaningful aid or supplies, and could barely feed itself? Finally the Chinese got tired of Australia still proclaiming itself a bastion of democracy. Eighty Japanese supertankers, modified to hold troops, landed nearly a million fighting men and machines at several points along the coastlines, and Australia was chewed to pieces.

"That left New Zealand. The Chinese and Mongolians were smarter in the sociological sense than anyone had ever given them credit for. They didn't touch New Zealand. They let it be known that, so long as New Zealand gave up its military armaments, the new Asiatic warlords would let it be. The country was rich, beautiful, and was completely out of the way. In the European, Latin, and other countries, New Zealand became the Great Escape. The rich, the powerful, and the greedy flocked to New Zealand, unhindered by the Asians. Because they could live there in luxury, a sort of modern Rome developed, protected by its enemies. It also gave the Asiatics a single dominant place for contact with what had been the Western World."

A long silence followed the verbal disintegration of the world Buck had known. Despite the cruel impact of the words he heard, Buck wasn't caught entirely by surprise. He had grown up and lived in a world of massive lethal armaments, of endless successions of wars small and large. He had been aware that just one tiny shove could send it toppling over the brink into a madness that would affect the entire world. But this new war wasn't for profit or greed, but to prove that the Asiatics, with the oldest civilizations on the planet, were the true leaders of the world. Now they would prove it once and for all.

"What happened in Africa?" Buck asked finally.

Bergstrasser snorted with disdain. "For a while, Africa was all cheering and huzzahs. The white man was finally getting his comeuppance. Then two very grim realities of life set in. First, virtually all trade with the rest of the world came to an end. Food, medicine, industrial parts—just about everything— couldn't get in, and exports couldn't get out. The entire social and economic structure disintegrated. They were on the edge of anarchy, but apparently they figured it was worth the travail, because as soon as the rest of the world settled down, it would need African products and commerce."

Buck broke in. "I can figure the rest of that scenario. They had never really understood the Asian mindset—the Chinese, and the Mongols especially."

"You are correct," Bergstrasser confirmed. "The new warlords considered the blacks inferior. Nonindustrial, bereft of scientific structure—in brief, their only value was in inexpensive labor. It wasn't quite slavery, but the Chinese hauled them off by the millions to help clean up the destroyed cities, and they paid them barely enough in food and housing to keep them alive. They became the postwar serfs, treated with utter disdain. I don't know how many millions died. Since then, the survivors have hardened—those who still live in Africa, that is. They've formed into tribes and bands again, they stay out of sight, and this time they swear they'll die fighting before they accept what the Chinese call 'Asiatic generosity.'"

"Sounds pretty much like the Second World War," Buck added. "When Japan set out in the thirties on its program of conquest, it said it was creating a greater coprosperity sphere for all Orientals and Asians. That was their fancy name for conquest. They butchered, tortured, and enslaved millions of people." Buck paused. "But we're getting sidetracked. Let's get back to the power base that emerged and what we face today—the Half-Breeds, for example."

Bergstrasser turned to Wilma. "You take this one."

She nodded. "It's not a pretty story, but it generally follows what you've already heard. The year when you had your accident, the world had a choice of a bright new future or reverting back to a period very much like when Hitler and other fascist leaders were coming into power. Space travel was coming into its own. It was a time, you'll remember, of American and Russian cooperation in space—the big shuttles, the Russian stations, the interplanetary robots. All over the world, different countries were sending up satellites. Programs were under way for international cooperation in returning to the moon and building permanent stations there. Sixteen countries were sending ever-larger ships to Mars. Manned expeditions were coming off the drawing boards. The computer revolution had become an explosion. Everyone in the world could be in immediate contact with everyone else. The science of genetics was leapfrogging into the future. Scientific and technological advances were extraordinary.

"But the world couldn't get its feet out of the mud. Your people had their eyes on the stars, but wars all around the world kept bogging them down. The United Nations was a joke. It was probably the most amazing period of world history ever. Space travel existed side by side with outhouses, even in America. Genetic advances in food production were near miracles, yet millions of people starved to death every year."

Buck took it all in silently. Finally he asked his first direct question about what had happened to the United States. Despite all he'd heard, he felt something was still missing.

"Look," he said slowly to Wilma, "this all seems like bits and pieces to me. Let me ask you some fast questions, and keep your answers short and sweet. I'll fit the pieces to the puzzle in my head. If I'm missing something, you can fill me in later." He waited as Wilma glanced at Bergstrasser. He nodded.

"Today—and I mean right now—who's running the world? I can't tell from what you've told me whether it's the Chinese or the Mongols or both."

"For the most part, it's the Mongols. But it's not all that neat and tidy. After they swept most of the world, they began to fight the Chinese. Winner would get to be top dog. While they were in the middle of seeing who was king of the hill, the United States took a desperate measure."

"Seems like anything would be desperate under the circumstances," Buck said acidly.

"It was. Our country was a long way from being defeated. We still had a powerful submarine force throughout the world—forty-thousand-ton boats, superfast, thermonuclear drive. They didn't need refueling, produced their own water, even manufactured basic foodstuffs. Anyway, we had over a hundred of them dispersed around the globe, at least sixty beneath the Arctic icecap. I've already said the Mongols came down through Canada. When they hit the United States, things really got wild."

"Who won?" Buck was holding true to his promise of fast questions. The look on his face made it clear he wanted equally fast answers.

"For a while, the Mongols."

"And then?"

"Do you remember the Minutemen from the original American Revolution? Well, Americans turned up everywhere, heavily armed. They let the cities go and took to the countryside, fighting the Mongols like Indians. It slowed down the Mongol advance considerably."

Buck knew a bit more about combat than field action. "Where was our headquarters?"

"Washington was gone. Hydrogen bomb. So were Detroit, New York, Los Angeles, and most major American cities."

Buck recalled the underground command centers that had

been built when America and Russia were on the brink of war. "So that leaves—?" He let the question hang.

"You're in part of it. Niagara. The government was split into organizational zones . . . orgzones. There was a whole city beneath Niagara Falls and the rivers. Other places such as Cheyenne Mountain—"

"The old headquarters for the North American Defense Command, built under a mile of solid rock," Buck noted.

"Right. Old salt mines. Even deep underwater domes. Massive structures of steel or armorglass. Most of them are at least two miles beneath the earth's surface."

"How do they communicate with one another?"

"Data compression, satellite hookups, hydrosignals. Even if they're picked up, the routing is random."

"And the language?"

Wilma laughed. "Ancient languages predating even Sanskrit. And they're changed all the time."

"How tight is the national organization?"

Bergstrasser leaned forward in his chair. "It stinks. We're fragmented. There are Mongol outposts throughout the country. A few are allied with us, but most of the others are still loyal to Toutka and Chamka."

"Whoa! That sounds like a song-and-dance routine."

"Sorry. They're the two big problem children of the Mongol Empire. They're not really leaders, but rather ministers of power. They stay behind the throne of the Celestial Mogul."

"This is getting to sound like a Chinese menu. Please, spell it out for me," Buck said impatiently.

"The Celestial Mogul is the number one man of the Mongol Empire," Wilma explained. "He's known variously as Aseptic Majesty, the Celestial Mogul of Mongolia, Potentate of Asia, Dean of the Ever-Living Nobility, Overlord of the Mongolian Emperors of Amerigo and Europe. To the Mongols, he's a venerated world ruler. He holds court from a monastery in Tibet."

"Would you believe he's two hundred and thirty years old?" Bergstrasser added.

"Sure. If he's in a tank of glucose with his brain hooked up to a bioscience computer. But if he's that old, well, he can't be running the big show."

"He isn't," Wilma confirmed. "Toutka and Chamka are his

left and right arms. They run the Mongol Empire, but they keep the old boy alive because his age is revered by the Mongol subjects. It keeps a lot of people in line."

"And no one's tried to knock him off?"

"Not us," protested Wilma. "If we did, we'd have a holy war on our hands. Our policy is to let him be. His ministers are the ones we deal with. And they've calmed down ever since the Israeli Vengeance War."

"Israel?" Buck knew his voice sounded hollow. "I can't imagine they're much more than a splinter in the woodpile."

"Even a small splinter, in the right place, can be a terrible thing," said Bergstrasser. "And the Israelis made some pretty big splinters. The Arab and Indo-European oil fields had all been pretty well ripped up. Wherever there was oil, those areas became prime targets for occupation. The Arabs, who had developed submarine fleets of their own, lobbed hydrogen bombs on the Venezuelan oil fields. We blew up the Alaskan fields to keep them from falling into enemy hands when the Mongols came pouring over the top of the world.

"But the Arabs have a habit of ignoring reality. To them, the global war represented a sign from heaven. Allah was calling for his people to destroy their oldest enemies. And there were the Jews, all packed neatly inside a small area, just ripe to be squashed. While the rest of the world was beating each other up, the Arabs judged the time ripe for the jihad, the final holy war against the descendants of the ancient Israelites. Whatever armies they had left attacked Israel. They threw everything at them—poison gases, biological agents, and millions of soldiers whipped to killing frenzy. Israel never stood a chance, but they were ready for such a moment, and they had always vowed that if they went down, they would exact a terrible price. They told their enemies that if they attacked, not one Arab or Indo-European city would be left standing."

"I'm familiar with the Sabra," Buck said slowly. "The fighters of Israel . . ."

"The Israelis had underground airstrips ready for such a moment. They also had vertical takeoff fighters and bombers in those bases and on ships. Over two hundred attack planes were in the air almost at once, each carrying two thermonuclear bombs of twenty megatons. Behind them, waiting for launch, were the big Negev Mark Four missiles, each with a single warhead, one gigaton per missile."

"A billion tons . . . my God," Buck whispered.

"They launched one hundred and seventy missiles. Almost all hit their targets," Wilma said. "They incinerated most of the Arab and Moslem world—where it counted, anyway. What they didn't destroy outright was wiped out by massive radioactive fallout.

"Most of the world decided the United States must be behind this kind of nuclear savagery. It didn't matter that Israel itself had been slaughtered. People don't reason clearly when everything about them is being torn to pieces."

"So whoever had missiles and bombers left," added Bergstrasser, his expression suddenly grim, "took dead aim at us. That should have been the end of this country. But our scientists had developed enormous power transformers capable of firing a tremendous jet of heat at incoming warheads and bombers. The result was that we were able to stop most of the attacks."

"But we were already badly hurt," Wilma said sadly. "Pockets of this country had been devastated, turned into slag. For the most part, the big cities were jungles of wreckage. You can picture the rest of it. Yet," she said, forcing a smile to her face, "there was a benefit to all this."

Buck shook his head. "How could that be? There must have been something like a nuclear winter with all that ash and smoke thrown into the atmosphere. Biological weapons must have taken hundreds of millions of lives. Farming couldn't have been much of an industry anymore. And distribution must have been nearly nil. What could be positive in such a scenario?"

"The future," Wilma said with sudden forcefulness. "You see, everybody was just about out of long-range missiles. There were no more factories and industry to replenish them. All this was history. Gone. The cupboard was empty. One of the few things that was left were the aircraft, most of which were small machines, fighters and tactical planes. They couldn't be gathered into really large units. No one was making advanced jet engines. Most electronics systems were worn out, and the ones that worked were guarded jealously and kept for special purposes."

Buck leaned back in his chair, looking from Wilma to Bergstrasser. "It sounds as if most of the world simply sank back into history. All you had left to fight with was junk your people could piece together."

"Yes and no. A really determined effort could build ground armor for fighting. But everyone felt worn out, and a new mood seemed to affect most people. If an attack was made by air, the defenders reverted to the old kamikaze ethic. They'd ram the enemy. Some of them bailed out in time, but most didn't. That kind of determined fighting became a detriment to further mass attacks. Air duels between a few opponents became the norm. Kind of like the old medieval days of chivalry and knights in armor."

"It beats mass suicide," Buck observed.

"But it led to a static world. There was more than enough hatred to go around. People wanted to get even. The big armies began to break up into isolated fighting units, and those, in turn, became new towns and cities."

Buck laughed. "Castles and feudal barons."

"There was still one trump card to play," noted Wilma.

"Not that difficult to figure," Buck broke in. "Shipping. Plenty of ships still left—big, small, it wouldn't matter much. Odds are that most people returned to the barter system of trade."

"For the most part, yes," confirmed Bergstrasser.

"But this place"—Buck gestured to take in the gleaming metropolis that was Niagara—"doesn't seem to fit the scenario you've been describing. This all looks pretty high-tech—electronics, computers, underground vacuum railways, and all that."

"There are perhaps eight such cities in the entire country," Wilma explained. "The only way to start major power centers like this one was to bring in the best people remaining from all over the country—from anywhere in the world, for that matter. What we have in Niagara, Chicago, and a few other places are like castles in a ruined land."

"I bet that gets a lot of people upset," Buck said quickly. "The haves and the have-nots. Which means those who don't have are ticked off and would like to redistribute the goodies you're stashing here."

Bergstrasser nodded. "A bit crude, but true."

"Globally, we have world disorder. South America began to boom. So much material had been poured into Chile that when the mass fighting was over, they found themselves a real power-house among the countries that remained. And what they have is protected in mountain redoubts and great undersea caverns."

"What happened here, in the good old U. S. of A.?" Buck persisted.

"Your 'good old U. S. of A.' was history," Bergstrasser snapped. "We were just as responsible as anyone else for what happened. Much of the world died because of our weapons."

"Don't drag me into your philosophy of how and why. All I care about are the results," Buck said.

"It's a mixture of world disorder and uneasy truce," Wilma said. "Entire countries were hanging on to survival by their fingernails. Russia was a vast wasteland. The Mideast still glows at night from residual radioactivity. The lower Pacific regions—Indonesia, Malaya, Borneo, Java, New Guinea, all those places—cut themselves off from the rest of the world. No planes can land there; no ships can dock. They live in total isolation. Maybe they're right. They're making it. We've already explained what happened to New Zealand. The general attitude of the countries who came off better than most is, we've got ours and the rest of you can go to hell."

"Stay with what happened here," Buck persisted. "Like how come the name America is in the trashcan and we're now Amerigo?"

"Because someone in the council," Bergstrasser said with sudden heat, "finally got some smarts. "We allied ourselves with Central and South America. No more trade barriers. No more American ownership of the countries. No more looking down on the Latinos as second-class citizens. No more destroying native jungles. We became a single nation from the Canadian border right on down to the tip of South America. And changing the name to honor the past, Italians and Spanish and the locals, was a stroke of genius. Overnight we were no longer the damn Yankees intruding on their lives. We rebuilt the highways. The Panama Canal was redredged. Shipping was a coastal matter, and critical goods began to flow back and forth between north and south. Frankly, I believe that move saved our hides."

"I can't believe that what you're telling me was enough to drag ourselves up from the bottom of the pit," Buck told him bluntly.

"How true," Wilma said sadly. "You're right. It wasn't, and it still isn't. We still haven't put our own house in order."

"Would I be right in assuming Amerigo is largely a land of splintered power groups?" Buck asked.

"You've hit the nail on the head," Bergstrasser said quickly. "Amerigo, and the world as well, is a dichotomy of stark contrasts. We live our daily lives—as a nation, anyway—in conflict, disorder, and distrust—anything but working together as a nation. Most of the country is still back in the past somewhere, yet scientific advances have also been made. We've been to the planets. There are actually space fleets out there. If we could work together, we could speed up the rebuilding of this country and much of the world tremendously."

Buck didn't hide his distaste for what he'd just heard. What they were saying reminded him of how millions of people felt in the 1960s. The United States and the Soviet Union spent hundreds of billions of dollars sending men into space in unbelievably expensive rockets. They went into orbit and they walked on the moon, and when it was all over, if you asked the man on the street, "How did the Apollo program make your life better?" he'd laugh in your face.

"Save the science for later," Buck said, pushing aside the issue. "We're just starting to get back to square one. Let's get back to the Half-Breeds. Seems to me that's what this powwow was supposed to be about."

Wilma glanced at Bergstrasser, then looked directly at Buck. "How do you feel about risking your life in a duel?"

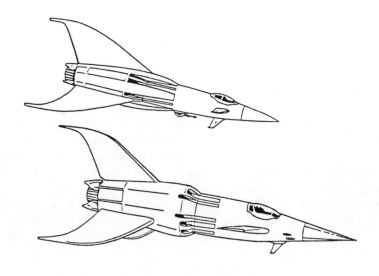

Chapter 11

You're an idiot, Rogers, you know that? Buck chastised himself. How in the name of blue blazes could you have let yourself in for this? Here you are in the twenty-fifth century, and you're on your way to fight some local hot dog who wants nothing more than to fill you full of hot lead. You don't know this cat—what's his name? Oh, yeah—Rocky Hoffman. Sounds like a pug from some rundown boxing gym. But names don't mean anything, and you know it. The whole country is going to be watching on the television circuits to see who goes down in flames. . . .

Wilma really slipped it to you. She and that slick Marcus Bergstrasser. They pump you full of historical folderol until you don't know which way is up, and then she slips you the Mickey.

Why should I risk my life in a death duel? for crying out loud. Tomorrow morning, over the North Carolina hill country. A duel at dawn, like some whacko fight of honor from the First World War. And here I am in this resurrected museum piece of a fighter—a bloody Messerschmitt, for crying out loud—while this Hoffman character has a hot late-model Mustang to take me on.

Buck shook off the foul mood that had hung with him through the night. He'd had little sleep. He found it impossible to doze while he ran through aerial maneuvers through his head, trying to remember all the little things that could make all the difference when you're in a death dance. Wilma Deering and that smug air marshal were gambling that Buck was as good at the controls of an airplane as his history indicated—ace aerobatic jock, veteran combat fighter pilot, airliner captain, and all the rest of it.

Unlike Buck, Rocky Hoffman hadn't had the chance to fly hundreds of vintage planes. He lacked that kind of experience, so he might not have knowledge of the moves only those fighter pilots who lived through dozens of combats knew about. But Wilma hadn't left anything out. Hoffman came from the crazy bunch called the Half-Breeds, whose stronghold was a powerful military area in Missouri. He'd been flying since he was a kid. The Half-Breeds had only a few jet fighters, but they had a cache of planes dragged out of museums and stored in underground hangars, and they fussed over them day and night to keep them in top-notch condition. The Niagara Orgzone had done the same. They had samples of the old weapons so that they could be duplicated if it should ever prove necessary. But a German Messerschmitt! Buck would dearly have loved a Bearcat or a Mustang, or even one of those souped-up Sea Fury fighters they flew in wild races in the old—

The old days? Those times were hundreds of years ago, but Buck had flown in such races, had fought it out on the deck around the pylons in Reno and Scottsdale with the best of the fighter gang. Mustangs, Bearcats, the Tsunami modification, even the big Lightnings with boosted Griffon engines. As hot as those races were, they weren't the stuff of which great fighter pilots are made.

The Half-Breeds, one of the most powerful guerrilla bands in the country, affected most of the other tightly-knit armed groups spread throughout Amerigo. So long as they remained free of control from any national organization, there would never be any hope that Niagara could pull the country together.

So that's how the big contest was set up. Buck cruised at 33,000 feet, the powerful Daimler-Benz engine throttled back to economy cruise, purring with the smooth power the Me-109G had been famous for. The cockpit was cramped, a porcupine pit with knobs and controls in all the wrong places. Even the cockpit canopy was something disdained by the Mustang and Thunderbolt pilots who viewed the world through a beautiful domed plexiglass canopy with superb visibility. You looked out of the Messerschmitt through flat-paneled armored glass. The visibility was lousy, and the airplane one of the most uncomfortable he'd ever flown.

He couldn't help the smile that came unbidden to his face. A long time ago—forever, it seemed—he had spent time with Adolf Galland, who had commanded the entire fighter force of the Third Reich. Galland worked with the Americans to rebuild the German air force after the war, and he spent much time in Arizona and Nevada at the fighter training schools. There Buck had not only met the German ace who had more than a hundred kills to his credit but also had the great advantage of listening to how Galland had survived eight years of war, starting in 1937 in Spain.

"There is only one creed for the successful fighter pilot," Galland said over a drink late one night. "You fly to fight, and you fight to kill. You catch the enemy by surprise if you can, and then you ram the throttle forward and you dive at top speed, eyes bulging and your blood lusting to kill, and you do whatever it takes to defeat your opponent. That way," Galland said with a smile, "you will return to your home field to fly and fight another day."

They had talked about the merits of the fighter planes. Buck had always wanted to know why the top German aces, including Hartmann, who racked up an incredible 352 kills, refused the more modern Focke-Wulf FW-190 fighters, choosing to stay in the older, cramped, uncomfortable Messerschmitt. "Ah, the Focke-Wulf is a beautiful airplane. Its lines are superb, and it flies like a dream. The Messerschmitt? It is designed to do one thing—kill the enemy. And I do not care what anyone says. It is better fighter plane—assuming the pilots are of equal caliber—than anything else in the world, including the Mustang and the Spitfire. The secret is to know what your airplane can do for you. You must become one, the man and the machine, and that is the winning combination. . . ."

Buck had never forgotten those words. When Wilma asked Buck about dueling, so abrupt and startling, Bergstrasser looking on, poker-faced and not saying a word, Buck realized there was so much more to that query than a one-on-one contest with some crazy pilot from the powerful Half-Breeds.

"Risk my life?" he repeated her words. "It depends. Look, lady, nobody is ever more than one heartbeat away from ending his life. I imagine you'll spell out the why of all this, but I've got to say something first. I'm here, talking and breathing and in great shape, only because you people gave me back my life. This is also my country even if you've named it after this Vespucci cat. So I owe you, and I always pay my debts. The answer is yes. So now tell me what this is all about."

Before either Wilma or Bergstrasser could reply, the door to the hologram cubicle opened. Buck turned to look at Commodore-General Killer Kane. He wore a combat flight suit with space fleet insignia. Entering the room, he was followed by President Grenvil Logan. Kane stepped to one side as Logan slowly seated himself.

"I've heard the question, and I'm gratified for your reply," Logan said quietly to Buck. "There is great risk in what we're asking you to do. Why we're asking you to accept that risk, and what it means to this country, is something I wanted you to hear from me directly."

He turned to Wilma. "Major Deering, bring up the free armed forces on the holoprojector, please."

Wilma keyed in the computer, and a glowing map of Amerigo appeared. One by one areas glowed in different colors. Buck recognized what he'd seen before—the area occupied by what the others had identified as the Half-Breeds.

President Logan pointed to the projection. "The Outlaws," he said. Another area glowed brightly. "Wyoming, please." Another spasm of color flashed across the screen.

"Altoonas." Light appeared in an area to the west of the territory of the Wyoming Gang.

"Nagras."

That one surprised Buck. Killer Kane saw his questioning look. "They're only a hundred and twenty miles from here. Wildest bunch you ever saw. They call themselves the Nagra Gang. They come from all over—blacks, whites, latinos, islanders, desert people, mixed into every kind of mongrel human you can imagine, and they're proud of it. Got a bunch of Indians as well. We keep them supplied with food, medicine and other necessities. We do *not* mix with them. They won't have it. They act as scouts for this city, prowling the countryside, and we keep them going. It's a great deal for both of us."

"Pineys," President Logan intoned. More lights glowed in what had been New Jersey.

"Sacramentos . . . Now, there's a gang of crazies, but they're made up of combat veterans, men and women both. Their kids learn how to shoot and kill almost as soon as they can walk. They're the best survivalists in the business. They live off the land, and they rebuild some amazing weapons as well as improvising their own. The Mongols—and the Han, mainly Chinese—have wanted to wipe them out ever since they sent up an old missile and blew hell out of a Han TransPacific liner. Killed everybody. They stripped the dead bodies, cut up the wreckage for spare parts, and fed what was left of the crew and passengers to their wolves."

"Wolves?" Buck immediately felt like a foolish echo.

"Trained wolves, bears, other animals," Kane broke in. "They've got some kind of psychic connection with those beasts. We don't know just what it is, but nothing on the ground can get near them without all hell breaking loose. Even their falcons carry miniaturized electronics signals to use when they spot anything."

"Sandsnipers." President Logan went on. "They work the beaches along the northeast coasts. A horde of small subs. They live in trees as well as other natural facilities. Like the Sacramentos, they have an affinity with sea mammals. Orcas, dolphins, seals, and other sea creatures are trained and fight to protect the humans."

"Susquannas." Bergstrasser added to his voice to the others. "An offshoot of the larger Wyoming group, which is big enough to be considered an orgzone of their own. They're at odds with the main Wyoming bunch, so they've named themselves the Delaware Gang."

"And here," Wilma said as more lights came on, "is the Wyoming Gang. We've mentioned them before, but they're another concentration that's grown big enough to be an orgzone. They're actually organized into a widespread group of camps, much as the old Roman army. I was part of this gang."

She paused, and when she resumed, Buck hung on her every word. "The leader called himself Brutus Magnum. He claims he's a reincarnated centurion. I was a lot younger then, and I was his woman. I didn't like the idea of being tied down to someone who had the fighting skills of a Roman but no more brains and sense than a common drunk, which he also was every chance he had. I bring this up for only one reason. He lost me in a poker game to some of his cronies. I was supposed to be their mistress."

The small room was silent. "I killed Magnum with a poisoned dart from a crossbow. Then I offered to take on the rest of them as well. I got away with it because the other women of the camp stood by me. They said the killing was justified because of the loose way Magnum played with my life. But I left the gang after that. Commodore Kane heard what had happened, and he felt any woman with that kind of guts belonged in his outfit. He sent in a chopper team at night. They detonated blinder flares, and in the confusion, they snatched me out of there. End of story."

Kane picked up the thread. "What we've been trying to get across to you, Buck, is that there're another thirty or forty gangs out there, spread all across the country. Split up the way they are, they control only their own immediate territories. They don't work together at all. If they did—well, you would see the beginning of a unified force in Amerigo, something we haven't had for a very long time."

President Logan gestured for attention. "Wilma, dim the lights, please." The holographic presentation darkened. "Now bring in the Han Airlords."

Fifteen bright lights speared through the gloom. Every one was topped with the forked-lightning insignia of the Mongol fighting command. Buck couldn't believe it. Mongol enclaves throughout this country?

Logan seemed to read his thoughts. "I know. It's hard to believe that even after decades of war, this country still isn't free. Nor does it work well as a single organization."

"But how . . . or even why do you permit these enemy garrisons to remain here?" Buck spoke the words slowly to fight back his astonishment.

"Frankly, we're exhausted," the president replied. "All of us. We've been engaged in nearly constant battle for almost a hundred years. The population of this planet was once nine billion people. Seven billion of those are dead, and another half-billion are merely surviving. Many of them, badly irradiated and infested with toxic wastes and biological agents, live on the brink of death. Buck, we are just plain worn out. We and the enemy as well." He saw the changing mood on Buck's face and gestured to forestall an interruption.

"The only reason we still exist, even as a fragmented nation, is that both sides decided that we simply had to end this insanity of mass destruction. If the war had kept up, we would have been throwing rocks at one another. We no longer had fleets of missiles. Our bomb production plants were destroyed. We destroyed their ability for mass delivery of their most effective weapons."

"Stalemate?" Buck spoke up again.

"In a way. Perhaps you'll understand this better if you take a hard look at your own history. In the First World War, the Japanese were allies of America. In the next war, we were bitter enemies, and we did everything we could to kill Japanese anywhere we found them. We were allies with the Russians in the Second World War, but as soon as it ended, we stood on the brink of nuclear hell with them for nearly forty years. This country came into being because we fought a life-and-death battle with the English, and when that fighting was over, we could hardly have been closer allies. Look at Korea! Fighting a war by special rules that limited the area of action and even the types of weapons. Berlin, Vietnam, Iraq, Iran . . . the list is almost endless, and you lived through most of it."

President Logan turned to Kane. "Take it from here, Kevin. Run through the high points of the drill, please."

Kane picked up the narrative without a pause. "You already know, Buck, that the Chinese and the Mongols mounted a massive offense against North America. They had already taken over most of the Asian lands, and we were next in their master plan. At the same time, while Europe was fractured by its own fighting, the Mongols swept through most of that continent. Perhaps that was what saved us, because those battles and the subsequent occupation of Europe tied down enormous enemy manpower and weaponry. Then we had another stroke of fortune. The Mongols that swept out of their remote regions were a different breed than the men who had followed Temujin—Genghis Khan—centuries before. Genghis Khan's hordes were barbarians in almost every aspect of life, not simply against their enemies, but even within their own ranks. They lived under brutal conditions, severe weather, limited food production, and with nothing that approached the mechanized industries of the West. What they did have was a ruthless approach to their opponents. They were superb horsemen, experts with bows and arrows and lances, and deadly with swords. Nothing could stand up against them in those early days of Mongol conquest.

"If we had fought such men when the Mongols came ripping down through Canada, the war wouldn't have lasted a month. The best horsemen and great armies in the open are helpless against the effects of hydrogen bombs. We could have killed them off like bugs. No one lives through a few million degrees of heat, to say nothing of thousand-mile-an-hour winds and ionizing radiation. In fact, we took out a good half of their armies that way.

"But this is a different breed of Mongol. They're ruthless, but they're also cunning. They're terrific horsemen and foot soldiers, but they were right up there with us in operating modern weapons. What we didn't know, when we were slaughtering their invasion force, was that the Mongols held their Chinese allies in contempt. Almost all of the troops we destroyed were Chinese, not Mongols, who were never very great in number. They sent in the Chinese as cannon fodder.

"They attacked many of our cities with hydrogen bombs, just as we wiped out their cities. But they pulled off one of the neatest stunts of the war. They managed to occupy several dozen of our cities without venting their barbarism. What they did, in effect, was to entrench themselves in those cities, so to get them out, we'd have to destroy our own populations as well."

Buck nodded. "Standoff again."

"Exactly. Keep in mind they were not embroiled in occupation on different continents. Communications were going to hell in a handbasket, so the different power groups within the Mongol organization began jockeying over who would be top dog. Over the years, the dust began to settle.

"Their tight-knit organizations in China began to unravel at the seams. As soon as they occupied China, history repeated itself. The Chinese cooperated with them. They obeyed them and offered no resistance. The Chinese have done that for thousands of years, and what worked before worked again. As of right now, and for the last hundred years, the Mongols have managed to isolate themselves across the Asian lands. They no longer have the capacity to explode out of Asia. They're totally corrupt. New leaders are killed off regularly. They operate under what closely resembles an ancient feudal system, and the Mongols who occupied so much of our country do everything in their power to make sure it stays that way."

Buck kept his questions to short phrases. "How do they manage that?"

"The Mongols in Amerigo call themselves the Han Airlords. They are intelligent, capable, tough as nails, and above all, very realistic. Once they had exhausted ourselves in their hundred-years war against us, a sort of uneasy truce set in. Nothing was set on paper; it was just plain common sense for all concerned. Lobbing hydrogen bombs around had become insane. No one used nuclear weapons anymore. Again, stalemate. They lacked the forces in Amerigo to overcome us, and we were in the same boat. We were so spread out and splintered we couldn't mount any major offensives against them."

"Where are we now?" Buck pressed.

"Amerigo—the former America—is broken, like a clay tablet that's been dropped on the floor. The pieces can be put back together again, but not until we shift the balance of power between ourselves and the Han Airlords. They're the real masters of the worldwide Mongolian Empire. They ignore Europe because it's devastated. They couldn't care less about Africa. The Mideast looks like one enormous sandy garbage dump. South America supplies us with foodstuffs and does the same for the Han, who rule their empire from the fifteen major cities they occupy."

"You let the food get to them?"

"Of course! We'd be in real trouble without that food. We don't have the agricultural foundation anymore, and we don't turn out synthesized food on a mass basis—not yet, anyway. We need food from South America. So we get ours, and we let the Mongols get theirs, and nobody interferes with those shipments. We would both rather be able to eat than starve."

Buck shrugged. It made sense, in a way.

"The Mongol organization has several different major factions. The Han Airlords rule what they can here in Amerigo. They haven't made any mass attacks for many years, being content to enjoy the spoils of war. That's all in our favor. They're entrenched behind their defenses, and without opposition or competition from us, they have slowly been poisoning themselves. They're not as sharp as they used to be, except for a few select groups who want to rule their own areas."

"What's their main base?"

"The entire Los Angeles basin, with direct underground connections north into San Francisco and south into San Diego."

"Someone mentioned a bunch called the Golden Dragons."

"The Mongol Secret Society. Something on the order of what existed in your Germany. The Gestapo and SS. What the Japanese called the Kempi Tai, or Thought Police. The United States had its CIA, the Russians their KGB, the Hungarians their AVA, the British their MI-Five, and so on. The Golden Dragons are spread throughout the Mongol Empire, but ruled from the United States, with the Asceptic City, or Celestial City, as the main center. There's one in China, but the main headquarters is in what used to be Chicago. That's where the Celestial Mogul holds court and runs the works. Wilma, bring it up on the holo, please."

Buck and the others studied an enormous domed structure thirty miles in diameter at its base, a translucent dome encompassing a magical scene of beautiful buildings.

"Is that shimmer I see real or just an effect of the holo projector?" Buck asked.

"It's real. They've developed genetic science to the point where they all live an average of a hundred and forty years or more. The place is absolutely antiseptic, sealed off within the dome. The shimmer, as you call it, is a force field against bacteria, viral invasion. It's about as germ-free as anyone could make it."

"Which also makes it terribly vulnerable," Buck mused aloud.

"Very good," President Logan spoke up. "Obviously, if we were able to punch a hole through that crystal palace, their population wouldn't last a week."

"It seems to me you could take out their brain center with a single stroke," Buck said, pushing the point. "My next question is why you haven't done that."

"Because we can't follow through with enough manpower or firepower to go through another damned war!" Kane barked. "What we have now is a delicate, crazy balance. If we took out that blasted dome center without being able to follow up, those Chilean naval and submarine forces would blockade all food shipments to us. We're not ready for that yet. We're working as hard and as fast as we can to make ourselves self-sufficient, but it takes time. First we've got to get our act together, get the various gangs of Amerigo to start working with each other."

Silence followed Kane's last remarks. It lasted long enough for the pieces to come together for Buck—for this is where he entered the picture.

"So now the Half-Breeds think you're just a bunch of patsies." Buck grinned. "Which is just what you think of the Mongols in their germ-free city with its plastic cap."

"Ouch!" Kane blurted out. "That hurts, but I'm afraid it's accurate. If you succeed in taking out this Hoffman fellow, that could be the spark to get our people thinking of themselves as a nation again instead of a bunch of renegades who don't give a damn about anyone except themselves. But even they realize that their long-term future is hollow. It's the same old story—we pull together or we go down together."

"If I do shoot down Hoffman, what happens next?" Buck asked very deliberately.

Logan rose to his feet. "The Half-Breeds have said if they lose that battle, if we emerge victorious, they will throw in their lot with us. They'll swear allegiance to the Federated Republic of Amerigo. And if they do that, we know that several other gangs will be right behind them."

"What if Hoffman takes me?" Buck asked.

Wilma spoke up, her voice strained. She grasped Buck's arm. "Don't even *think* about that!" she exclaimed. "Don't you understand? It's almost as if some supreme power is giving us a second chance. Here you are, out of nowhere, and now you're the fulcrum for all of us! If you lose, we all lose."

He stared at Wilma, hardly believing what he saw. Tears ran down her cheeks as she wept silently. He had the strangest feeling those tears were for him.

Kane joined Wilma. He rested a hand on Buck's shoulder. "We've told you only parts of the whole picture. It's too much to take in all at once. You need some time to absorb what's really at stake here. You see, we're also running out of energy. Our nuclear reactors are junk. Even the thermonuclear plants are desperately short on fuel. You can't operate a deepspace fleet on oil or coal."

"What?"

Kane raised his eyebrows. "I said you can't operate a deep-space fleet—"

"Hold it right there!" Buck interrupted excitedly. "We have a fleet in space?"

Kane had a crooked grin on his face. "The start of one, any-way. We need to rebuild our lunar industrial bases. The helium three is our key to just about everything in our future—"

"Hold it again," Buck said, then his voice rose. "Just hold it!" He shook his head. "I'm going to fight a battle to the death in an airplane more than four hundred years old, and you're talking about space fleets? This is crazy!"

"Maybe so," Kane shot back, "but it's real."

"Look, it's getting late. If I'm taking off in the morning to fly to Asheville, I want to do another check on my plane from nose to tail to make sure they did the modifications exactly as I ordered. We can pick up this insane conversation later." He paused. "If there *is* a later, that is. One more thing. Wilma, you can help me with this. I want to pack my parachute personally. From what I've heard, you people use flying belts or something like that?"

"Yes," she confirmed. "But they're too big for the cockpit of your fighter."

"As long as the parachute fits."

An uncomfortable silence followed her words. Buck glanced from one face to another. He didn't like what he saw. Finally Wilma broke the impasse.

"There—there aren't any parachutes, Buck. We thought there were, but when we tried to repack one, it fell apart."

"No parachutes," Buck said in a hollow voice.

Killer Kane slapped Buck heartily on the shoulder. "Well, there's only one thing to do then, Buck. You'll just have to whip that crazy loon's butt."

Marcus Bergstrasser moved forward. "I know how these peo-ple fly, Buck. This Hoffman is good, but I'm convinced you'll beat him."

So why do I feel like a fly about to drop into the spider's web? Buck wondered.

* * * * *

Buck eased the Messerschmitt into a gentle climbing turn so he could look behind him. The lowering sun glinted with golden light off the wings and rotors of turbine choppers. One big jet transport and at least six other machines, filled with people, accompanied the ancient German fighter. Buck eased back to level off the plane and checked his flight chart. Asheville lay dead ahead, a long strip atop steep-sloped hills. He eased back on the throttle to start his descent.

The closer he came to his destination, the more he realized just how far the word must have spread about the upcoming duel. Alongside the runway, he saw dozens of vehicles and a bewildering variety of flying craft.

There must be more than a thousand people down there, he realized.

A thousand people like those who attended air races, auto races, boxing matches, skydiving contests, all of them waiting to see someone make that final mistake that would cause flames to erupt or a parachute release to fail.

Buck took a deep breath. Tomorrow morning, at ten o'clock sharp, the contest would begin.

An inner voice seemed to call to him.

And that's when it's time for you to whip that guy to a fare-thee-well, Mr. Rogers.

"Yea, sure," he said aloud and suddenly laughed at himself long and loud.

He put the Messerschmitt down like a feather dropping gently to earth.

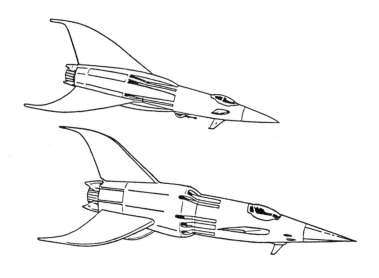

Chapter 12

Wilma sauntered across the airport ramp, high heels showing off shapely legs, a short, pleated athletic skirt swirling in a wispy flow. Her breasts were outlined by a form-fitting top with just enough cleavage to keep hundreds of eyes following her every movement as she headed for the Mustang fighter on the ramp. She watched Rocky Hoffman as he stood on the wing, looking down into the cockpit to make a last-minute check. She nodded to herself. All their reports were perfect. The way Hoffman looked at her, his expression changing from mild interest to a bold leer, told her the nature of the man she was already thinking of as a creep. She played her part perfectly: the female entranced with the ace pilot. Hoffman almost seemed to peel away her clothes with his eyes. She stood close to him, giving the appearance of two people planning future get-togethers.

Okay, Buck, time for your entrance, she thought. She smiled to herself. Buck had figured out his adversary right down to his toenails. A lady-killer, a big hero within the ranks of the Half-Breeds . . . crude, masculine, and completely endeared to himself.

She saw Buck coming across the flight apron, his strides bespeaking anger at the sight of Wilma with Rocky Hoffman. Finally he stood before them and stabbed a finger at Hoffman. "What the hell are you doing with my girl?" he demanded.

Before Hoffman could reply, Buck turned angrily to Wilma. "I warned you about this guy. Stay away from him!" He grabbed Wilma by her wrist, pulling her toward him, almost dragging her along as he strode away from the Mustang.

"Hey, flyboy!" Hoffman shouted, laughing. "What's the matter? Can't you stand a little competition? Maybe your lady wants a real man instead of some retread!"

Buck stared straight ahead, barely able to conceal a grin. "Don't turn around," he told Wilma. "He fell for it hook, line, and sinker. The big he-man. Now he'll waste half his time thinking of how he's going to steal you from me."

She chuckled. "He did everything but drool."

"You'd make any man drool," he told her with admiration. "But thanks. Really," he emphasized. "It's working."

"Fill me in, Buck. I have a general idea of what you were doing, but you're the fighter plane expert here, not me."

"It's pretty simple," Buck said, laughing. "Hoffman just met me, and already he's convinced he's beating my time with you. Big hero type. Nothing has changed in four centuries when it comes to guys like him. He's all puffed up, and he'll be thinking of making time with you instead of clearing his mind of everything except this dogfight. What you just did increases the percentages for me."

For several moments, she remained silent. Then she slipped her arm through his. "Would it bother you," she asked quietly, "if he really was making time with me?"

Buck stopped, facing her directly. "Wilma, I—" He cut himself short. "I want my head clear of everything except the duel. Do you understand?"

She squeezed his arm, then slipped free. "I understand. Go get him, Ace," she said and walked away.

He went to the waiting German fighter. Representatives from the Niagara Orgzone on one side, the Half-Breeds on the other, watched his approach. He faced the small group of Half-Breeds gathered near the two planes. "Let's get right to it. Any change in the rules?"

A burly man in leather glared at him. "No change. You two take off and climb to three thousand feet. Hoffman comes back across the field from the east, and you come at him, same altitude, from the west. You both break to the right. You're the hotshot,

Rogers. You don't need special instructions."

"I'm going to kill your boy," Buck said quietly.

The man's jaw dropped, and then he regained his senses. "Go right ahead and try, mister. Hoffman eats iron nails for breakfast and spits out tacks."

"What's your name?" Buck demanded.

"Who? Me?" Sudden laughter. "Lombardosa . . . what about it?"

Buck smiled. He was rubbing nerves every chance he had, and this clown might just jar Hoffman a bit more than the Half-Breeds liked. "Listen, Lombardosa, it looks like what hair you have left is brown. We can always change it to red."

"Yeah? How you gonna do that?"

"Change places with Hoffman. You get your big fat butt into that plane and I'll meet you upstairs. When I scramble what few brains you've got all over the inside of your cockpit, everything will be one big red mess. Want to try me?"

Lombardosa jutted his chin forward. "I wouldn't want to take Hoffman's pleasure away from him," he said with a sneer.

"Big talk," Buck said coldly. "Anytime you want to back it up, just let me know." Immediately Buck turned to the watching groups, then looked directly at Killer Kane. "Once we're in the air, there aren't any rules, right?"

Kane looked at the Half-Breed group, and to a man they nodded. A woman in a leather outfit stepped to the front. "Just so there's no doubt, flyboy, it's kill or be killed. If you bail out, Hoffman will gun you down in your chute."

"I'm not going to bail out. I haven't got any chute, and I won't need one. But thanks for clarifying the rules. It's kill Hoffman, whether he's in the air, on the way up, floating in midair, or on the ground. It should be interesting to see that blowhard try to outrun cannon shells." Buck smiled sweetly. "I might just slice him into chopped liver with the prop."

He walked back to his own group, nodded to them, then started for the ramp where the two fighters stood. Black Barney went with him. "That woman wasn't kidding, Buck. It's a fight to the death, all right, whatever the circumstances. If he bails out or crash-lands and tries to walk away from the wreckage, you've got to kill him. The way the Breeds look at things, if you let your mortal enemy escape when you've got him down, you're a weakling and a fool."

Buck shook hands with Barney. "Take notes, Admiral. This should prove interesting to you."

He climbed into the cockpit, checking every control and switch. Then he fired up the powerful engine and ran through another gauge check. Barney stood on the wing, fighting the powerful airstream from the propeller. He leaned down, placing his mouth close to Buck's ear. "*Hals und beinbruch!*" he shouted.

Buck looked up at the man in surprise. "Where did you learn that?"

"I did my homework. I finally discovered what it means. German pilots always said it to each other before battle. 'Break your neck and a leg!' " He banged a fist on Buck's shoulder, climbed down, and pointed to the sky. A green flare arced high above them, the signal to taxi out to the runway for takeoff.

The wind was from the south. Perfect, Buck thought. They would each take off from opposite ends of the airstrip, each staying to the far right so they would pass one another as they lifted from the ground. Lined up, ready to go, both men watched for the bright red flare that would be their signal to take off and then do their best to kill one another.

* * * * *

The Buck Rogers at the controls of the lightweight Me-109G Gustav was no longer the quiet, amiable pilot he had been on the ground. Buck had adapted his persona from flier to fighter-pilot killer. In the air, a dogfight had room for only two kinds of people—the man who killed and the man who died. Dogfights were never won by rules but by the men who thought things through the best and flew all-out. Buck was determined that everyone watching would witness a lesson in execution.

As the rules called for, they took off in opposite directions. They were to climb to three thousand feet, make a wide turn, and come back head-on at one another directly over the field. Then both pilots would break to the right and begin their aerial dance of death.

That's the way the rules went down, but Buck had been in fighter combat before, and he'd listened to every word of that old master, Galland.

Buck began his fight the moment his wheels came off the runway, howling with increasing speed for takeoff and a swift climb. That's what Hoffman expected. He didn't expect what happened.

As he moved the throttle forward, Buck hauled the stick as far back as it would go, his propeller blowing a mass of air back against the raised elevators. This rammed his tail down against the ground as power built up. The Mustang was already rolling when Buck popped the stick forward, went to full power, and jammed his rudder pedal down as hard as he could to keep slipstream and engine torque from spinning him around. The Gustav shot forward, accelerating swiftly. Buck glanced at his left wing, saw the Handley-Page slot moving back and forth, increasing lift to well above that reached in the same amount of time by the Mustang's laminar-flow wing. Then the slot slammed smoothly into its place against the wing, and Buck knew he had the speed he wanted.

The Mustang raced along the runway to pass him. Immediately Buck banged the stick to the left to lower his left wing and kicked in his right rudder. The Messerschmitt slewed wildly, seemingly out of control, careening directly toward the oncoming Mustang.

Hoffman stared in disbelief at the other fighter. He was sure Buck's plane was out of control and hurtling toward him, making a collision almost inevitable. Cursing, Hoffman knew he had to get out of the way of that clumsy idiot in the Messerschmitt. With barely enough speed to leave the ground, he horsed the Mustang off the deck, banking sharply to the right to escape the Messerschmitt.

Buck smiled. Hoffman was trying desperately to get enough flying speed for full control response, but he hadn't had time yet. The Mustang trembled on the edge of a stall. One mistake now would put Hoffman into the trees and end his flight in a huge ball of fire. Hoffman lowered the Mustang's nose, holding the wings level for maximum lift, not daring to bank, sucking up the landing gear. Like the thoroughbred she was, the fighter accelerated smoothly from its long moment of peril. Hoffman smiled with relief. Now he'd show that fool Rogers!

It's the small things that count; the preparations make all the difference, Hoffman thought confidently.

The Half-Breed's plane was much heavier than the Gustav he intended to destroy. No doubt Hoffman had access to the records that ballyhooed the Mustang as the greatest fighter of the Second World War. It never occurred to him that those records were compiled by the people who had won the war and thus could say anything they wanted. It was true that the Mustang was a superb fighting machine, but it takes more than that to wax your enemy.

Hoffman flew "by the book." He had no other source of information, so he followed the manual and had the fuel tanks of his fighter filled to the brim. That meant additional weight. Weight translates into less speed, slower climbs, and less maneuverability. Plane for plane, the Mustang and the Gustav were remarkably similar.

Buck had planned the combat with all the expertise of a chess master. He loaded enough fuel for no more than thirty minutes at full power. Anything beyond that would result in too much performance penalty, so he flew with less weight. That gave him performance advantages, especially in the tight maneuvers for which the Messerschmitt was justifiably famed. Buck also had his ground crew, who had babied this machine in its museum for years, remove the underwing gondolas housing the heavy cannons and shells. Those were intended for battle against American bombers, when massed firepower was a key factor. A pilot skilled in marksmanship could do far more damage against another fighter with only one nose cannon and two machine guns, provided he could put that firepower where it counted, in the opposing plane. Hoffman had taken off with six fifty-caliber machine guns, all with full ammunition loads. More weight, less performance.

But the Mustang was obeying his commands. Now he was building up speed so he could maneuver into position to battle Rogers on even terms.

Buck never gave him that chance. The only way Hoffman could gain a workable position in the air was a wide, climbing turn, so he could break away from the Messerschmitt, gain critical altitude, and keep his eyes peeled for his enemy.

What he never had the chance to see was the Messerschmitt building up great speed while the Mustang still floundered in its near-disastrous takeoff. Buck climbed straight sunward, overboosting his engine to develop every ounce of power he could get. The Messerschmitt hauled upward with bulletlike velocity, its engine screaming. Buck brought the stick full back, flowing into a beautiful high loop, arcing over on his back and then accelerating downward. He came out of the sun like an avenging angel, aiming for the airspace through which he knew Hoffman must fly.

The Mustang pilot scanned the sky, squinting as his gaze brought the bright morning sun into view with its blinding glare. Could that be a bird flitting across his vision? Then sunlight glinted off metal, and Hoffman knew he was caught in a trap of acceleration and climb, a metal insect about to be pinned against an invisible wall.

Buck fired. The nose cannon and machine guns arced away in curving tracer patterns. Explosions tore the engine cowling from the Mustang, smashing fuel and oil lines. Bright flames gushed back, penetrating through the firewall between the engine and the cockpit to lick out at the screaming Hoffman.

The Mustang canopy slid back. The desperate burning pilot threw off his harness and hurled himself away from the blazing fighter. Shuddering with pain, Hoffman knew he could still save his life—not with ancient technology but with a product of twenty-fifth century science, a jumping harness of Inertron with small but powerful reaction jets. As he fell from the wreckage of his fighter, he twisted the control on his chest. A small battery of enormous power energized the Inertron, feeding the superalloy into a pencil-thick wire connected to the miniature combustion chambers. As quickly as the belt was activated, tiny spears of flame reduced Hoffman's effective weight to barely five pounds, slowing his fall to a gentle downward drift. He had ten minutes of Inertron energy in his belt, more than enough to lower him safely to the ground. Just above the runway, autostabilizers took effect to keep his body upright, and his boots touched the surface.

He'd made it! He heard cheers from the watching crowd of Half-Breeds, but they were drowned out for the moment by the explosion of his fighter plane. Hoffman stood erect, burned and injured, but still defiant. He watched the Messerschmitt make a low turn over the nearby woods, nose down, the propeller a gleaming disc in the sunlight. Hoffman shook his fist at the approaching plane. Rogers hadn't won, after all! You had to kill your opponent for victory to be claimed.

He was still standing with upraised fist when the propeller of the German fighter hurtled straight at his head and shoulders, a terrible whirling scythe that would in a matter of seconds slice him to ribbons. Hoffman prepared to die as the winged death hurtled toward him at more than four hundred miles an hour.

At the last possible moment, Buck hauled in the left rudder and snapped the stick to the right, crossing the controls. The left wing passed mere inches above Hoffman's head, the edge of the whirling propeller terrifyingly close. And then the plane was gone, curling upward into a giant victory roll. Hoffman collapsed limply to the ground. A hush fell over the watching crowd, afraid of what they would see.

Then Hoffman managed to rise to his knees, wobbly, struggling to stand erect. He stared in disbelief at the receding Messerschmitt, just as the crowd stared in disbelief at what surely seemed to them a dead man come to life.

* * * * *

Air Marshal Marcus Bergstrasser poked an elbow into the ribs of Killer Kane. "My God, did you see that? I think the whole group of Half-Breeds has just gone into deep shock."

Kane lit a thick cigar, clenching it happily in his teeth. "That was some beautiful flying, but the ending— Now, that was finesse. He could have gunned down Hoffman anytime he wanted to, in the air or on the ground."

They turned when they heard strangling sounds at the side of the runway. Wilma Deering wiped her mouth with the back of her sleeve.

"That was the finest 'execution' of its kind I've ever seen," laughed Bergstrasser. "Major Deering," he added with unexpected stiffness, "I do recall that you, I, the Commodore here, and in fact every one of us warned Rogers that if Hoffman lived through this episode, then Rogers would be judged a failure. Shooting down his opponent wasn't the point—"

"But, damn, it sure was beautiful!" exclaimed Kane. "I've never seen any flying like that! Our young man is an *artiste*." He looked at Wilma, "No one is closer to Rogers than you are. Do I or do I not recall you warning him to be certain to kill Hoffman—exhorting him, in fact?"

"Yes, sir, I did," Wilma said meekly.

"You're letting yourself get upset over details, Deering. Calm down, Major."

Bergstrasser looked at Wilma with an expression of deep satisfaction on his face. "Do you realize just what we can accomplish with what happened here today? It will be all over the internet by now. They'll be carrying pictures, video, background on the pilots. Before the next twenty-four hours pass, every outfit in the country will know the Half-Breeds have joined with us. There'll be another six or eight more gangs by the end of the week."

"And we'll blow up Rogers's skills to where he'll seem like a giant before we're through," added Killer Kane.

Wilma looked at both her superior officers with distaste. "Why do you feel you must push what happened? You'll get a lot more mileage out of this affair if you don't say anything. Everyone will expect us to crow about what happened. If we simply let the story get around by itself, it'll grow on its own."

Kane nudged Bergstrasser. "She's right. Let it be. The tale will spread on its own."

"I need Rogers for our tactical air operations," Bergstrasser said cautiously to Kane. "But I'm worried about getting him. After today, he'll be a legend. The Half-Breeds have touted Hoffman as invincible. He's taken down at least twenty of our Manta fighters. He was hell on wheels with those disrupter beams."

Kane shrugged. "What you're saying is already history. Hoffman and his legend of invincibility is gone. I don't know where you intend to mount any significant air action, Marcus. After today, who are you going to fight? We've just proven—or rather, Buck Rogers has—that we can bring the guerrilla outfits in line without mass fights or killing. Your need is for defense against mass attack. Anybody who sends out a fleet after today is simply offering a great target. You can do better than that, Marcus. Rogers is far more valuable as a champion, white horse and armor and all that."

Marcus scowled. As quickly as she dared, Wilma stepped between the two military leaders. "Air Marshal," she said to Bergstrasser, "how do you think Rogers will do in a Manta or a CF fighter? The Manta has disrupters, ray beams, even lasers.

But it's a clumsy craft at best. It can't maneuver like those old planes we just saw fly. Buck would probably hate it. From what I've learned of him so far, I believe he could modify the Manta into a really potent weapon."

"Stop prattling, you two," Kane growled. "You can't see beyond your noses. I want Rogers for space ops. Can you imagine what kind of magic tricks he'll be able to pull off in deep space? Our fly-by-wire systems are a joke. Most of our rocket fighters are more like lead sleds. You both know that. It's like throwing rocks out in space."

"I suppose you want him on the Armstrong complex on the moon," Bergstrasser growled.

"To hell with the moon. That's engineer territory—mere plumbing problems as far as I'm concerned," Kane snapped. "We need him on Mars—for starters, anyway."

Wilma held up both hands. "Sirs?"

"What the hell is it, girl?" Kane demanded.

"Permission to speak frankly, Commodore. Off the record."

Kane made a sour face. Bergstrasser laughed at him. "Take your own advice, Kevin. Do what you told the major. Calm down. Besides," he added with a grimace, "we're both too late."

"What does that mean?" Kane glowered.

"Look for yourself," Bergstrasser advised, pointing to a group clustered across the runway beside the Messerschmitt. They all recognized Admiral Benjamin Black Barney in close conversation with Buck Rogers. Several junior officers from Barney's command stood by silently, paying close attention to the words of the two men. Kane and Bergstrasser could have directed a miniature laser receptor to pick up their conversation even at this distance, but that was something they never did to one another.

"Wilma," Kane said quietly, "you know more than you're telling us. Lay it on us, woman."

"Sir, it's classified," Wilma said stiffly.

Kane grinned at her. "Very good, Major. Now I'm addressing you as your superior officer. Tell us what you know, Major. That's an order."

"You won't like it, sir."

"Do you want to be a lieutenant, Major Deering?" Kane asked, only partly in jest. "Spit it out!"

"Admiral Barney met with the council this morning, sir. He

has their agreement for a special mission he's about to launch, and Rogers is part of his team. By the way, sir, Rogers is now a full colonel, courtesy of the dramatic defeat of one Rocky Hoffman."

"And just what is this mission?" demanded Bergstrasser.

"The admiral believes they've located the lost empire of Atlantis." Wilma waited for her words to sink in.

Both men dropped their jaws and said simultaneously, "*What?*"

"Atlantis, sir. What they call the Lost Continent."

"I know what they call Atlantis!" Kane said acidly. "There are other names for it I can think of. Poppycock and balderdash are some of the more common ones."

"The others aren't spoken aloud in mixed company," Bergstrasser joined in. "Crazy, insane, foolhardy, or just plain nuts. Those will do for starters. Major, there have been stories about Atlantis for a couple of thousand years! Every time they find a squared-off rock or what seems like a stone road buried in the sea, the rush to Atlantis is on again. What's set it off this time?"

"The Chileans, sir."

The two men held their silence as they studied Wilma. She was doing her best to maintain a poker face.

"What else do you know, Major?" Kane said finally.

"They're serious about this, sir. Intelligence has been on the matter for several weeks. We've monitored everything we could pick up about Chilean activity. We've done everything we could think of short of reading their mail, and I'm not absolutely certain we haven't tried that. But the Chileans seem to be dead serious about this. They're mounting a major expedition to the site."

"Where, damn it?"

"That's the problem, sir. One of their DeepDivers was on a research mission off Puerto Rico—the main trench. It goes down twenty-seven thousand feet. Their sub sent a coded message that they found evidence of the remains of an enormous city and strange installations they couldn't figure out but that seemed capable of generating tremendous power."

"Nuclear?" Bergstrasser asked.

"No, sir. Whatever the Atlanteans had—provided there really

was or is an Atlantis—is nothing like we've ever seen or imagined. Admiral Barney made his case to the council that we can't afford not to get down there ourselves."

"But . . . we're talking about pressure of tons to the square inch. Our subs can't touch that kind of pressure. And if the Chileans can, then they've got equipment that I'm not familiar with."

"Yes, sir," Wilma said politely.

"Wilma, damn it, you've got canary feathers all over your face. You still know more than you're telling us. I suppose if I gave you another order to tell us the rest, you'd disobey me?"

"Yes, sir," she said quietly. "And may I say, sir, those are the orders I received directly from Admiral Barney himself."

"One last question, then, and I'm talking now to Wilma Deering, not Major Deering. You got that?"

"Yes, sir."

"How come you know so much about this project? It's got to be top secret."

"Yes, sir, it is."

"So?"

"I'm going on the mission, Commodore. I'm assigned to Colonel Rogers, sir."

Kane studied her for several moments. "Are you sweet on that fellow, Wilma?"

"With the commodore's permission, sir, I prefer not to answer that question."

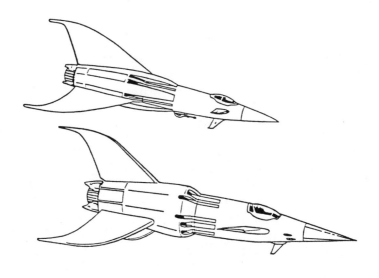

Chapter 13

Benjamin Black Barney rested his boots on his desktop, leaning back in a heavily padded chair with wide armrests. Buck Rogers stood before the admiral's desk, taking his time studying the rows of buttons and controls mounted in each armrest. He had already learned enough of the science and technology of this divisive world to recognize that Barney was a man of his times, extracting from the past everything that might be useful and at the same time employing every scientific device that had emerged from the heavily protected research laboratories of the Niagara Orgzone and its scattered cities throughout North America.

Barney was both a man of his times and a throwback to the best fighting men of Buck's own era in the Twentieth Century. Buck appreciated the "throwback" aspect of the admiral. Barney came from that very special class of leaders of fighting men who never demanded of his subordinates any action he would not undertake himself. He was proficient with every weapon in his navy's arsenal, which was as lethal and diverse as any Buck had ever imagined.

Barney gestured to a comfortable chair near his desk. "Make yourself comfortable, Colonel," he said easily. "If you're going with us on this underwater rabbit hunt, we'd best get to know one another. That way you'll understand my orders instinctively and won't need precious time to think them through. You'll do what's needed and do it fast."

Barney laughed, a deep, booming sound that echoed off the curving walls of his spacious office. "Funny the way a man falls into his own traps, isn't it?" he said finally, chuckling. "Here I am preaching to you about fast actions, swift reflexes, and going all-out in a fracas, and you've just cut that Hoffman character into chopped liver. I've watched the videos of that dogfight you had. I like what I saw. You're good, damned good. But you know what was even more important to me?"

Buck didn't answer immediately. He was considering every aspect of this extraordinary man, his skin as black as shining ebony, eyes equally dark and fierce, his skull shaved and polished to a gleam. And there was more. Buck had seen the way he moved, with all the grace of a panther, almost effortless in his movements.

"You know, Admiral, in my day, we'd have no trouble fixing a label on you . . . no disrespect intended."

Barney smiled. "You didn't answer my question, Rogers."

"I was getting to it. I was trying to judge what you'd see in me based on what you are."

A broad smile met his words. "Well, that's certainly different—a man from the distant past putting a label on poor old Black Barney."

"Poor old—" Buck laughed out loud. "Is that the label you want from me, Admiral?"

Barney leaned forward, elbows on his desk. He pressed a button near his left hand. A bottle rose steadily from the desk. Buck failed to recognize its contents, but he got the impression it was both powerful and unusual. Behind the bottle were two empty glasses. Barney took his time pouring, then slid one glass toward Buck.

"Drink up," he said quietly. "I bet you've never tasted anything like it."

Buck held his glass to the light. No help there. Through the thick, heavy glass, he saw an amber-colored liquid. "Mind if I ask what this is, Admiral?"

"Hell, no. Ask away. What you're about to drink is a whiskey that didn't exist in your time. Combination of deep-sea plant extract, synthetic chemicals, sour mash for bite, and some energizing catalysts that'll make your heart dance and your mind prance."

"Poetic," Buck said noncommittally.

Another booming laugh. "You'll never drink anything I won't drink myself. We call this stuff orcade. Got the strength of a killer whale, fills you full of fizz and fight, tastes great going down, kicks off a real buzz, and the effects are gone in three minutes. No drunken stupor, no rotten hangovers." Barney scowled. "If my men want to tie one on, that's up to them when we're not committed to a mission. So they drink orcade instead of the regular rotgut. It has one more advantage, Rogers. For several minutes, you're soaring as if you've had an amphetamine boost. It sharpens the mind and your claws. And you, my ancient friend, have claws. Hoffman found that out. Drink up, blast you!" Barney lifted his glass in a silent toast and tossed the liquid down his throat in a single swallow. He grinned owlishly at Buck.

There was only one thing to do. Buck held up the glass, brought it to his lips, and drained the contents. He couldn't quite identify the taste. It was like cognac, but with a sweetness he'd never tasted before. Then he forgot about the taste. Suddenly his vision sharpened and colors took on a dramatic intensity. Admiral Barney seemed to be seated beneath a clear and revealing light. Buck felt incredibly light, as though he still had all his body mass and strength, but only retained a fraction of his weight. He breathed "Wow" quietly, trying to concentrate on the immediate effects of the orcade. "Strange name for something this good. Sounds like what we used to drink during sports or heavy workout sessions. They called it Gatorade."

"Have any real gator juice in it?"

Buck laughed. "Hardly. They called it that because it was developed for the football team of the University of Florida, the Gators, who were right in the middle of alligator country."

"This is named after our friendly killer whale," Barney noted.

"The gladiator orca," Buck added.

"Right on, Ace." Barney filled two more glasses. He sang out, "Drink hearty, my friend, and then it's back to business," and once more drained his glass in a single long swallow.

Buck was still in the clouds when Black Barney got back to the matter at hand. "Let me give you some additional background, Ace," he rumbled. "We've got a lot of black dudes in our outfit—"

"Admiral Barney," Buck broke in, "I don't care if they're black, green, white, pale pink, brown, or striped purple. I don't even know why you brought that up."

"Because not all your history is lost in the limbo of the past," Barney said immediately. "I seem to recall mention of some, uh, racial inequalities. . . ."

"So you want to know where I stand?" Buck asked.

"I knew before you walked in here, and you've let me know in other ways," Barney said with obvious satisfaction. "Just so you know I'm not in the least offended by your pale, pink-white, pasty color." He grinned dazzlingly.

"Okay, that's out of the way," Buck replied. "What now?"

"How much have they told you about the Atlanteans? I know they were supposed to slip you some data about them during your indoctrination."

"Not much," Buck suggested. "Atlantis has always been the heart of some sort of imaginary great treasure hunt. Books describe this ancient, brilliant culture, far advanced in science, medicine, mathematics, engineering, technology—existing for thousands of years before the first farmers ever planted their crops alongside the Tigris River. The Atlanteans supposedly pre-dated not only the Sumerians, Persians, Babylonians, Hebrews, and Romans, but they were going great guns when cro-magnon man was busy trying to wipe the deck clean of his neanderthal predecessors. Find Atlantis, the story went, and you could not only rule the world but also own the future."

"And the people of your time did some heavy searching, I suppose?"

"Oh, sure. Who wouldn't go for the pot of gold at the end of the rainbow?" Buck answered. "It would be like finding Aladdin's lamp."

"What's that?"

"Another marvel of our day. A lamp, the same kind used to burn oil and incense, but this one supposedly had magic proper-ties. If you found it and you knew what it was, you were supposed to rub the sides and mumble some magical incantation. Smoke would spew from the top of the lamp and a genie would appear."

"Slow down, confound it. A genie?"

"A sorcerer of unlimited magic powers. Not of the earth we occupied. He existed in some indescribable la-la land, and he could be summoned through the lamp. He would grant the holder of the lamp any three wishes he wanted, no matter how impossible they seemed." Buck laughed.

"So . . . a children's fairy tale," Barney said.

"Some adults believed in it."

"Were all the people in the Twentieth Century that nuts?"

"Admiral, you're walking on thin ice. Do you believe in God?"

"I don't know."

"How about your men? Or your women? Any religious people among them? Any church services, any chaplains?"

"Well . . ."

"Any of them ever tell you they've seen or talked to God?"

"What *is* God, Rogers?"

"Don't ask me a question the wise men of this planet have been trying to answer for tens of thousands of years, Admiral! I don't know. Call it a belief. That's as good an answer as any. But when it comes to faith, it is describable, it is measurable, and it can be relied upon."

Admiral Barney started to pour himself another drink, hesitated, then changed his mind. "Example, please."

"I'm a pilot. Tens of thousands of other men and women have been pilots. We all share the same absolute belief, a belief as strong and sustained as belief in any supreme deity, or angel, or demon. Maybe stronger."

"Don't stop now."

"To be a pilot, I have to have absolute faith in the reality of flight, although I can never see, feel, hear, watch, or otherwise judge with my eyes what lifts me from the ground. The power of lift from an airfoil is invisible. It doesn't even seem possible. In fact, the more you study it, the less possible it seems. Yet I and my fellow pilots have absolute faith in its reality."

Barney drummed thick fingers on his desk. "You'd make a helluva preacher."

Buck laughed aloud. "I've done my share of praying, but usually it was because my butt was about to catch on fire."

"Okay, you're part of my team now." Barney waved his hand to cut off questions for the moment. "It's been cleared all the way up through Kane and Bergstrasser right to the council. Even

President Logan gave his stamp of approval."

"I don't get it, Admiral. I'm a pilot. You know, up there in the clouds with the birds and the angels? If you're on the hunt for Atlantis, you're going the other way—like down." Buck stabbed a finger at the floor. "Down there . . . well, I'm out of my league."

"Sure you are. I know that," Barney said.

"Then I don't get it."

"Do you want to go with us on this expedition to nowhere, Rogers? You have a choice, you know."

"Frankly, I didn't know. Somehow I was made a major, and after I waxed Rocky Hoffman, someone said, hey, man, now you're a colonel, so that means I take orders like anyone else."

"This mission is risky . . . groping through dark waters into the unknown, threading needles miles beneath the ocean—great entertainment like that. Nobody on my team is under orders to go. You can say no, we'll have another drink, and I'll send you back to Niagara, and that will be the end of it." Barney chuckled. "Of course, you're likely to go stir-crazy there after a while. No more dogfights for you, my friend. President Logan has decided that if you get knocked off in a soiree upstairs, no matter what the reason, everything they've gained by having the Half-Breeds coming into our camp goes out the nearest window."

Buck stared at the floor, not answering. Black Barney seemed to be able to read his thoughts. "Take your time, fella. You're not really under my orders yet."

"I'm sure you want me to be straight with you," Buck said cautiously.

"Anything less and I'd have you tossed right out the front door," Barney told him, looking down through half-closed eyes.

"You're cute, Admiral, you know that?"

"I think we're on the same frequency, Buck. The last thing I want is for you to return to Niagara and be tossed to the wolves—"

"I think I would prefer sea wolves," Buck countered.

Barney boomed with laughter. "You're even better than I gave you credit for. You figure out yet where you are?"

"Not precisely, at least not in terms of location. Nothing to do with triangulation or latitude or longitude, which would be meaningless in any case. But in another sense? Sure I know. We're several hundred feet beneath the sea. Or within the sea, I should say."

Barney leaned across his desk and stabbed a button. The

lights dimmed to only a trace. Slowly and steadily the walls began to lose their solidity. What seemed to be metal and stone changed before his eyes to glass.

"You're looking through a piece of zoron-glassite," Barney said with noticeable pride. "Actually, the glassite was developed in the mid-twentieth century."

"I was a kid then," Buck remarked, "but I've heard of glassite. Our scientists first used it in their deep bathyscaph experimental deep-diving gear. Flotation tanks of gasoline were on top of the vehicle. Pressure equalization kept the extreme depths from collapsing the tanks, and underneath the tanks—or usually, one tank—was the spherical vessel for the human crew."

"Very good," Barney said with open admiration. "You remember the vessel?"

"Look Admiral Barney, I'm no seer. This was common knowledge in my time for any advanced science programs. And in addition to aerodynamic engineering, I spent two years at Annapolis doing deep-diving sub research. I—"

"That comes as a welcome surprise. There isn't anything in your dossier on that," Barney noted. "I'll let you read the whole package later. But how did that tie in with the *Trieste?* That is the vessel to which you're referring, I presume."

"Sure. I also did a stint flying B-1B bombers out of Guam and Saipan for a while. We flew long range by refueling in midair with KC-10s. But we also had extra time on the ground, so we went scuba diving. There were a couple of old-timers there who had supported the deep dives."

"Details, please."

Buck shrugged. "It was in early 1960. One navy man, Walsh, and Jacques Piccard. They went all the way down in the Marianas Trench—right to the bottom of the Challenger Deep, in fact—and—"

"How deep?"

"Thirty-five thousand, eight hundred and three feet. They touched bottom."

"Pressure?"

"Seven point one-five-two tons per square inch."

"What was their biggest surprise?"

"That science was all wet—no pun intended—about water being incompressible. I remember that point clearly, because later, when I went into astronautics studies and got into extrapolation of alien liquid planets, that fact could be critical. It turned out that seven miles down, water could compress as much as five percent. And compression equates to temperature increase. Sure as rain, the temperature went up by one degree Centigrade."

"How would you describe a bathyscaph?"

"Clumsy, awkward, dangerous—like a thin-skinned balloon."

"Good. That's what it was and what it is now."

"What has all this got to do with one, me, and two, Atlantis?"

"It depends," said Black Barney, frowning.

"You're leaving me pretty much in the dark, sir."

"You've got plenty of company. Together we may just be able to bring some light into the picture."

"Sir, are you serious about this search for Atlantis?"

"As serious as I know how to be."

"Then you must know a hell of a lot more than anybody before you."

"Could be," Barney replied noncommittally. Buck had no choice but to ride it out.

"Ace, if you believed Atlantis was real, at least at some time in our past, where do you think is the most likely place it would have been located? That's a lot of ocean out there."

"Yes, sir."

"Don't patronize me, Rogers. If you just want to listen to my comments without being aware of what the hell I'm saying, then I've got to understand that. Got it? It stinks, but I've got to buy whatever is your position."

"One hundred forty million square miles, accuracy within one percent, of liquid surface area."

Barney's eyes narrowed at this sudden recital of the total square miles of ocean surface on the planet. "Good start. Keep going, but I want everything you say to point to Atlantis. For the moment, we'll accept the theory that it once existed, even if there's no trace left of it. Which," he added with a thin smile, "may not be the case. So what about this hundred and forty million square miles?"

"It's the liquid surface area of the planet, sir," Buck said, knowing full well Black Barney knew it as well as he did.

"And?"

"There are three hundred and thirty million cubic miles of

water covering the planet. Four-fifths of the oceans' volume is below nine thousand feet, and the average depth is thirteen thousand feet."

"What does this tell you?"

Buck smiled. "Give me enough bulldozers and enough people to run them so I could level the land mass of this planet, and I mean leveled down to what is now mean sea level, and—"

"And what would we have?"

"A world covered by water to a depth of about two miles."

"A water world."

"Of course."

"Give me some more of these wild numbers, Rogers."

"Well, sir, salt is one of the best ways of getting the point across."

"Do tell."

"Yes, sir. In the oceans and seas of the world, there are about fifty quadrillion tons of salt."

"Spread that salt out over the land surface area of the world and we get . . . ?"

"If we spread that much salt over the entire land mass, we'd have an ocean of salt over every inch of land from the surface to a height of five hundred feet."

"I'm glad to see you studied your textbooks, Rogers."

"I wonder why you're tweaking me, Admiral?"

"Call me Blacky. Ask me what the hell I'm after."

"Okay. What are you after?"

"Atlantis."

"Wrong answer, Blacky. I'm as dumb as they come in that game."

"No way. Obviously you have well-grounded knowledge of this little planet of ours. Concentrate on this being a water world, as we both agree—the only water world in the entire solar system. There are liquid oceans on some of the outer planets and their moons, such as Titan, but that's not water. Methane, ammonia . . . inhospitable crud like that."

"Are we that sure of what it's like on those worlds, Blacky?"

"Hell, yes." His next words rattled Buck to his core. "I've grav-floated across the oceans of Titan. That crazy moon has seas, rainfall—poisonous to us, of course—and some appreciable land mass as well. Big islands, small islands. Colder than the backside of a frozen penguin."

Buck stared. "You've really been there?"

"Would I kid a new member of the Black Gang?" scoffed Barney. "By the way, that's the name of the outfit you just joined."

"The Black Gang."

"Specialists in deep undersea exploration."

"Frankly, Blacky, I'd much rather be outbound than inbound. Like the moon, for example."

"Lousy view. Dusty, airless, no trees, no hamburger joints. Makes even the Gobi Desert look like an oasis. I should know. Busted up one of our cargo loaders on the far side. Radios dead, couldn't even contact the main base through comsats orbiting the moon. Dark, nasty. Recent meteorite shower obliterated most landmarks. We couldn't ride, we couldn't fly, we couldn't grav-float. The inertron supplies messed up when our old-fashioned reactor irradiated the inertron into slag. We had to walk one hundred and sixty-two miles in pressure suits in a race against dwindling air and water supplies. The only thing that kept us going were the rolls of solar cellsheets we had. We dragged them behind us like bridal gowns. That kept us alive. When searchers scanned the surface, they found us by sheer luck; the cellsheets reflected light and set off the photocell alarms in the roboscouts hunting for us." Barney shook his head. "Hell, man, go somewhere else if you're going outbound—someplace like Mars."

"I want to go there, too," Buck said with sudden heat. "When I was wiped out in that crash back in my time, we had sent probes out through the solar system. Six manned teams had walked on the moon—"

"That was Apollo?"

"Yes. But we never went back with men after that. Not while I was there, anyway. We landed probes on Mars and Venus and—"

"I know the details," Barney interrupted. "Schoolboy stuff compared to today. Antiquated, even quaint."

"My point was, Admiral, I've requested space duty with Commodore Kane in his Deepspace outfit. It's being dangled in front of my nose as 'sometime in the near future.' "

"And you'd rather be in that outfit than this one?"

"Yes, sir. I've nothing against this operation, Blacky, aside from the fact that this really isn't my bag, and—"

"And you believe this mission is a wild-goose chase," Barney finished for him."

"Yes, sir."

"You remember the Hubble telescope from your time, Rogers?"

"Yes."

"Then you remember that it confirmed the existence of planets orbiting stars within a fifty-light-year radius of our system?"

"So our astronomers claimed. But as good as the Hubble telescope was, it couldn't get us anything close to detail of such worlds. Too far away for the optics, even across the full spectrum."

"When did you mash yourself into hamburger, Buck?"

"Nineteen ninety-six."

"Too bad you weren't around for another forty or fifty years. By that time, the Hubble 'scope was a museum piece. In fact, it still is. Kids look at it all the time in holo studies in school. To them, it's like the Wright Brothers plane was to the jetliners you flew."

Buck waited in silence. Barney would get to his point in his own good time.

"Imagine a jump of scientific advancements of fifty, even a hundred years, Buck. About thirty years after you bought the farm, astronomers made a quantum jump in the light-gathering powers of new telescopes. Liquid helium systems, maser collectors, mirrors that made the Hubble mirrors look like rough-cut glass. The details don't matter, but what they got was a detailed look far out from our planet. We found other worlds with the spectral lines emanating from our own planet. You see the connection?"

Buck eyed Blacky cautiously. "When you say the spectral lines, are you including the emanations from industrial systems?"

"Yep." Barney looked a tad smug; it was obvious he was cherishing this conversation.

He's leading up to something, mused Buck, and I'm just getting the first real hints. . . .

"High atmospheric?" Buck asked.

"Contrails from high-flying machines of some kind. Chemical traces of rockets. A whole wide band of chemical elements from nuclear drives. Fluctuations in the gravity fields that don't relate to planetary or other celestial phenomena."

"In other words, manipulated energies."

"Along the lines of what we do with our antigrav systems," Barney added, "but the lines are sufficiently different to lead us to believe that our systems are horse-and-buggy hardware compared to what we've detected."

"Blacky, you're about to explode with what you're leading up to," Buck said.

"Are you jerking my chain, Buck?"

"No way. That grin keeps escaping your mouth. You can't even hold it in. What's the real surprise?"

"Clear signs of antimatter drive. The energy release is so violent it threw some warbling effects into the gravitational fields. We saw pulses of gravity waves we've never detected anywhere else out in space. And they're repeated."

"Explosions?"

"Hell, no!" Barney exclaimed. "They seem to indicate regular runs between not only planets, but also nearby star systems. And the best of all is that in an area of galactic collision, two spirals grinding together at least twenty to fifty thousand light years from Earth, we traced what seemed a long, thin black hole. By long I mean several light years. By thin I'm talking the width of a human hair for comparative purposes."

"But that's impossible!" Buck's burst out.

"Not if what we have observed is FTL," Black Barney said very slowly and deliberately.

"You mean faster-than-light drive?" Buck asked in awe.

Barney leaned back and poured another two glasses. Buck needed it this time. He drained his glass in one long swallow.

"Fifty thousand light years from Earth," Buck repeated, his voice sounding hollow.

"Or more. What I have found most interesting is that the most likely source—considering the time interval between when light from that system started out on its trip to us and when it arrived—is that it's a galactic area of binary stars."

"Hold it, Blacky. That's hardly earth-shaking. Even in my time we knew that two out of every three stars we could see with our instruments were binaries—really two stars in close proximity, each orbiting about a central gravity point."

"Neatly said, lad. You just made the jump to what this is

really all about."

"Which is?" Buck asked quickly.

"Not quite yet," Barney said, his voice making it clear that Buck had yet to pick up on unspoken keys in their discussion. "You've left out a few important points. First, nearby stars don't mean a bloody thing. It's what *type* of star that matters. An F or G—"

"Yellow, G-type, like our sun," Buck interrupted quickly. The look on Barney's face told him he'd spoken the right words at the right moment.

"What else?" Barney asked with mock innocence.

"Distance from the parent star. Size, mass, density, rotational speed, water content, axial angle, moon or moons—for beginners. All the ingredients necessary for a planet to support conditions for life and allow it to evolve."

"Right on the button," Barney exclaimed, pleased. "Now let's go back in time a bit. The earth-type planet—three of them, actually—revolved about a yellow G-type sun, just like ours. But it had a binary companion. It was small and blue-white, which meant it was a young star, burning intensely—burning so intensely, in fact, it was going to rip itself apart. It was already shedding some of its outer gas layers."

"Caused by what?" Buck asked.

"A rogue star traveling through their system. It yanked the blue-white out of gravitational balance, causing it to swing inward toward the yellow. It didn't take long for the interactive energy of two powerful gravity engines—the mass of the stars themselves—to start raising havoc on those planets, all three of which seemed to be occupied by advanced cultures of some kind."

Then it hit Buck. He was so stunned by the conclusions that for several seconds he sat in silence. Barney didn't intrude on his thoughts, waiting to hear what Buck had to say. Finally Buck stirred, climbed to his feet, and began walking slowly about the room.

For the first time, he noticed the walls had become fully transparent. Just beyond the glass extended a huge enclosure through which several giant sharks swam slowly. He stared long and hard at the powerful animals.

"I suspect," he said slowly, "you've gone through all this just to prepare me for the finale."

"You're faster than I gave you credit for, Buck. Those sharks perk your interest?"

"Yes. They're not sharks."

"Oh?"

"Not like anything else on this planet. They're breathing through nasal inlets instead of gills. In fact, they don't have any gills. This is crazy. What I'm seeing is impossible—a cartilage-based creature in the water, extracting oxygen, but not with gills, that looks like a shark, swims like a shark—"

"And kills at a distance by electrical charge, like some immensely powerful electric eel," Barney finished for him. "These sharks, in fact, lack the DNA with which every terrestrial creature is linked, from midge to whale. Nature could never create this animal from our ancestral heritage of amino acids. And there's one more thing."

Buck knew his voice sounded hollow. "You're no end of surprises, Admiral."

"Our Earth sharks, especially the makos and the great whites, have an inbred, fanatical hatred for these creatures. The great white isn't supposed to be capable of emotions like hatred, but if it even senses these things, from miles away, it moves with all possible speed to attack, and it won't stop fighting until these things are torn to shreds."

"Who usually wins?"

"The Earth sharks. These things are just as tough, but when they're sighted, it's as if an alarm bell clangs through the ocean. The makos and great whites come in droves. It's a slaughter. So most of these fellas have gone into hiding or remain away from the main action."

"That means they're no longer loose in the open ocean."

"I thought you'd never get there," Barney said, showing a hint of admiration.

"So they congregate in one or two main areas? That's a question, not an opinion."

"Either way, you're right."

"Is all this fitting together the way I'm starting to think it's fitting?" Buck asked.

"Try it. Short and sweet, Ace, like sound bites."

"There were intelligent, advanced life-forms on this planet we're discussing. A passing rogue star knocked out the gravitational balance, and the local binary solar system was doomed. There was radiation buildup, planet-wrecking tidal gravitation—the whole nine yards."

"Keep going."

"Their solar system was dead, or it soon would be, even the outermost planets. So their only hope of survival was to find another world within their reach that could sustain their form of life. They'd need a yellow F- or G-type stable star like ours."

Buck locked eyes with Admiral Barney. "And ours turned out to be the best bet," Buck went on. "If they had instruments capable of spectral analysis better than ours, they could determine the nature of this planet, and when they discovered it was a water world, it was like a miracle to them."

"What would you have done if you were in their place?" Barney asked.

"There would be only one thing to do—throw every resource you have into getting to this world," Buck said at once.

"Across a distance of fifty thousand or more light years?"

"The odds are they had either close-to-light-speed travel or they had *faster*-than-light travel. They found some way around the Einsteinian block that nothing can travel faster than light because of infinite mass."

"And if we had FTL—faster-than-light—capability—?"

"The whole galaxy and beyond would be in our hands."

"Take it one step farther, Buck. What if this alien race, and we'll assume there was such a race, came from a planet that was even more of a water world than ours? And when they traveled across space and came here, they found the land surface of Earth was filled with hostile creatures, all manner of viral and bacteriological dangers, terrible weather—"

"You can stop right there, Blacky. They'd go underwater."

The two men stared at one another, and then they breathed the same word simultaneously. "*Atlantis.*"

"Again, assuming everything so far is correct, they built huge underground facilities, and in some remote area of this planet, surrounded by a great deal of water surface, they raised their above-ground city, or city-state, or whatever. And rather than spreading out across a hostile surface, they concentrated their energy into this one place they considered their new home." Barney threw up his hands. "And we come up again with Atlantis."

Barney leaned forward again to stare intently at Buck. "Forget wondering if there ever was an Atlantis. I know, I know—people have been searching for the fabled land of Atlantis forever. It was supposed to be in the Mediterranean, or off the coast of Japan, or in the Atlantic, or it was part of Polynesia. Anywhere and everywhere."

"So something else has happened—recently, I mean."

"That's why you're here, m'lad." Barney smiled broadly.

"I need more," Buck told him.

"We need you for a special mission to Chile. Specifically, to the coastal area of Chile."

"But I don't—"

Barney cut Buck off in midsentence. "You used to fly jetliners from Miami to Santiago, Chile, right?" He waited as Buck nodded. "You did it for years. You know the routes, the mountains, the valleys, lakes, coastal areas. And to top it off, didn't you fly for a National Geographic television special in that same area? Don't answer. Nobody alive in our country today knows that area better than you."

"But why is that so important?" Buck protested.

"Because Atlantis wasn't in the Mediterranean, and it wasn't in the South Atlantic or anywhere else that everyone has been looking," Barney said with growing excitement. "Didn't you ever wonder how the Chileans were able to leapfrog centuries of technological progress and suddenly burst forth from what was essentially a third-world nation into a nation that was capable of building energy weapons, all sorts of electronics, and especially submersible craft that put everyone else to shame?"

"Of course I've wondered," Buck admitted. "But from the fragments of information I've received, it looked like they got their help from the Mongols and all those international mercenaries who sold them the best hardware we or the Europeans could produce."

"That's just the tip of the iceberg," Blacky said. "Several hundred years ago, during the period when we were all tossing hydrogen bombs at one another, the bombs that were used for deep penetration before they detonated caused more than a few crust-destroying earthquakes. They tumbled mountainsides, ripped open chasms, caused tremendous tidal waves, stuff like that. We learned only within the past several years that one of

131

those quakes carried along a fault line where the Andes Mountain extend well out into the Pacific Ocean."

"Don't tell me—along the coast of Chile," Buck broke in.

"Right as rain, Ace. A few years after that particular earthquake and its subsequent subterranean disturbances the
Chileans seemed to flower overnight. Today we know they didn't
do it on their own. And they didn't do it with help from us, or the
Mongols, the Chinese, the Europeans, or anyone else we know."

"You're telling me," Buck said slowly, "that the Chileans
found Atlantis?"

"Exactly. They found Atlantis, or what was left of it after tens
of thousands of years. We come to believe that an alien race came
to this world as a life-saving, desperate measure. They chose a
site in the Pacific close to the coastline. While they still had their
energy devices, they tunneled deep beneath the ocean floor into
the Andes in Chile. This was their conduit from their underwater living habitat to the land. To protect themselves against
whatever prowled, flew, or crawled in the Chilean jungles and
mountains, they decided they needed a surface city, or center, or
whatever you want to call it, so they could better understand and
deal with the surface life-forms of this strange new world.

"That city, which we have designed Hidden City, is in an area
marked on the charts as Crater Lake. It's the crater of a huge
extinct volcano. The entire water surface of the lake is a sham.
Oh, it's water all right, right on down to some floating vegetation
and native canoes and the like. But the water is only a few feet
deep. Beneath the surface, there's a layer of some alien glasslike
alloy. When the Atlanteans needed to come up for surface exploration or research, they could drain off the water or use tunnel
exits with thick air locks. When the twentieth century began, the
Atlanteans discovered that men had learned to fly and would
inevitably soon be exploring much of the planet that had previously been beyond their reach.

"About this same time, as best as we could determine, they
also came down with a terrestrial virus that decimated their
numbers. Technologically, they were far beyond anything else on
this planet. But their numbers were few, and their strength had
been drained away by disease. So they accepted the Chilean
natives. They used their advanced systems to teach and train
them. The Chileans became their willing servants. They became

expert technicians, and on this basis, Chile began to build an undersea force like the world had never known—huge, advanced submarines, powered by some crazy stuff we can identify only as liquid air. It's not nuclear fission or fusion, like our subs. It gives them tremendous speed and weapons that can knock the stuffing out of any opposition.

"Apparently the Mongols somehow got wind of what was happening. When they did, they went after Chile with two huge airfleets. Their ships were clumsy things when you think about it, but they figured they could set off some big underwater blasts with nuclear bombs, and the shock waves would put the Chilean defenses out of commission long enough for them to send down several thousand fighting men into the mountains. Well, the Mongols that landed on that artificial lake surface were sitting ducks. They came down with flying belts. That went well enough, but once they were down on that slick surface, the belts were low on power and couldn't get them back up again. The Chileans, using Atlantean weapons, simply sent massive electrical charges through the lake surface. In one stroke, they killed off most of the Mongol invasion forces."

"What about the bombers?"

"Whatever powers the Atlanteans possessed gave them the ability to control weather," Barney explained, "at least enough to create enormous thunderstorms that generated incredible electrical charges. Prodigious lightning bolts were drawn to the Mongol bombers by the static discharge of their movements through the air. The bombers were totally wiped out. The credit for all this, by the way, didn't go to any Atlantean. They're always shadowy figures hovering in the background. The Chilean military people took the credit. Admiral Ricardo Benez Castillo runs the show."

"What kind of air power do they have?"

Barney gestured dismissively. "Hell, it's nothing more than a motley collection of old junk. Some choppers, a few old jet fighters and bombers. It doesn't amount to a hill of beans. They don't really need air power in the same sense we do. Submarines are their big gun. They're faster than anything we have. And, of course, they might have other things we don't about. I'd like to know more."

"One thing puzzles me," Buck said after much thought.

"Where and how do you get your information about this? From what you've described, the Chileans are pretty well covered in almost everything they do. And you also seem to know what happened to the Mongol forces. I don't imagine the Chileans told you about that."

"Have you heard much about the Golden Dragons?"

"I've heard about so many crazy outfits I can't remember. I guess I heard mention of them, but not much else," Buck answered.

"In a nutshell, then, the Golden Dragons started out as a Mongol secret society. To keep their new empires and conquests under tight control, the Mongols knew they needed up-to-date information on resistance movements or weaknesses in their own organizations. So they created this outfit—much like the old CIA or the Russian KGB—to keep tabs on everybody and everything. It was a hotbed of spies, trying to keep track of who was doing what to whom, and what the latest advancements in science, weapons, and technology were. They have two leaders, both of mixed Mongol and Chinese extraction. The man who runs the eastern half of the globe is Om-Ka-Zoril, and his partner, who keeps an eye on the west, is Morke-Ka. They're slick, dangerous, and ruthless. They started out as a Mongol arm, but as the years went by, the leaders got power-hungry. Instead of keeping to their sworn duty of wrecking our orgzones and keeping everybody on their knees, including the Mongol leaders in occupied Amerigo, they became an entirely new power faction in the world."

"What's their connection with the Chileans?"

"Smart," Barney said acidly. "The Golden Dragons befriended the Chileans by supplying them with materials and technology they couldn't easily procure from around the world. In turn, the Chileans gave the Golden Dragons free access into and out of the Hidden City in Crater Lake."

"But how did you get into their system?" Buck asked.

"Like I said, the leaders are hungry for power. It's simple. We gave them a couple of offers they simply couldn't refuse. First we gave them all kinds of money in the form of technology. Then we traded electronics for information. When they thought they had us by the throat, we let them know that the first time they tried anything against us, we'd let the Mongol Emperor in Asia know what was going on. There's nothing a Mongol hates more than a traitor."

For several minutes, Buck didn't speak, choosing to watch the strange alien sharks cruising beyond the thick glassite walls. He let out a long sigh. "All this has been fascinating, Admiral," he said finally. "I understand your interest in my experience with the Chilean coastline and in the mountains. You're right. I went through much of that country by jet chopper for that television crowd doing documentaries. I even got to know some of the locals pretty well."

"And you speak their language," Barney added.

Buck nodded. "Spanish is my second language. That should be no surprise, Blacky, not with all the flying I did down there. But you've left me with one nagging question."

"Let's have it."

"From the way you described how the Chileans wiped out the Mongol airfleet, I don't see how you could possibly want me to fly down there now as part of an aerial task force or whatever. It doesn't make any sense."

"You're right," Barney replied. "That's why you're going down there with me."

Barney laughed. "By submarine."

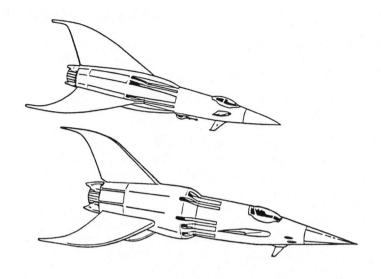

Chapter 14

Buck's muscles seemed paralyzed despite the deeply padded chair in which he was sitting. In the lower forward bow of *Io*, his attention stayed riveted to the extraordinary sights before him. Compressed glassite curved almost completely around the viewing chamber, so that Buck seemed to be floating in some sort of dreamlike underwater fantasy, with fantastic sights drifting by on each side as the huge submarine made its way steadily southward. He felt virtually no sensation of movement, certainly no vibration or spasms of the enormous engines that sped seventy thousand tons of submersible craft through the deep ocean without apparent effort.

Far behind the bow section, three compact nuclear reactors, each only a fifth the size of the reactors that drove the great missile-launching subs of Buck's time, generated a smooth flow of invisible power. No great screws pounded the deep ocean waters; no shrouded propellers emitted an unmistakable shrill whirring sound. *Io* forged ahead propelled by a swift flow of the very liquid through which it moved with amazing speed. Down to eight thousand feet, the huge submarine, heavier than most battleships of the Second World War and larger than anything else that had taken to the seas in the twenty-fifth century, moved with silken grace through the inky depths. Open channels along the rounded flanks of *Io* sucked in water and pumped it back at great speed in a strange form of jetlike propulsion. MHD—magnetic-hydro-dynamics—formed the heart of *Io*, named for the violently volcanic moon of the great planet Jupiter, in honor of that scathing little world lashed by the gravitational tides of its mother planet.

MHD had forged far ahead of the first systems tested hundreds of years past, but then the power source languished in obscurity during the hundred years of nuclear savagery that befell the world. Then it was put back into development again, perfected in round-the-clock research teams under the absolute, even despotic, prodding of Admiral Benjamin Black Barney.

Buck was still reeling from the wonders of the machine and how it came to be. Yet his attention suffered repeated interruption from glowing creatures, strange fish of often enormous size with some sort of built-in bioluminescence so that streaks of light along their sides served as running lights in what would have been absolute darkness. Except, of course, for the lights of *Io* itself.

But the fantastic underwater machine and the strange creatures of the deep weren't the only sources of Buck's wonderment. Buck had never known a woman like Ardala Valmar, the captain of *Io*. She sat in a padded contour lounge chair off to his right, a long thin cigar held aloft in her left hand, gesturing at the changing panorama of the subterranean valleys through which *Io* passed. Buck found it impossible not to take a few moments to study Ardala's profile. She was in every way a magnificent woman, yet within her easy grace of movement, there was undeniable power, a coiled spring of energy she might unleash at any moment. No man or woman became the captain of an astounding vessel such as *Io* without having competed with the best naval officers in Amerigo. Competed, and bested the lot.

"I'll make sure you meet the captain of *Io* when there's not a crowd around her," Barney had promised. "Otherwise, you may never be able to get in a few words of your own. Besides, she's asked for a private introduction."

"I'm flattered, but I also feel as if I'm somewhere out in left field," Buck answered. "Why would Captain Valmar be the least interested in meeting me? I'm no submarine man, as I've told you, and—"

"Come on down here with me, Buck," Barney had said with impatience. "We don't mince words, you and I. Never forget that."

"Admiral, you have a way with words. Are you sure you're not a reincarnated drill sergeant?"

"I take it that's a compliment?"

"Damn right it is." Buck paused and grinned.

"Shall we get down to business?" Barney asked, obviously sensitive this morning as they prepared to leave the deep channel far out beyond the radioactive junkpile of what had once been Philadelphia. "I've got a million things to do right now, Colonel Rogers, and I want to get this over with in a hurry."

"Got it," Buck said simply.

Barney went to a holocontrol in his cabin aboard the sub. His thick fingers flew like cables across the control board. A holographic image of a woman's face appeared. Buck drew in a long breath. He'd never seen a face like this before on man or woman. Every feature seemed to be chiseled from marble; her skin was the white of ivory. Her brows swept rakishly upward at sharp angles and then curved to the sides of her forehead. And her eyes! They seemed limitless in depth, as black as black could be, reflecting light in strange pinpoints like a diamond. Her lips were perfectly, delicately tinted with mixed red and purple lipstick. High cheekbones told of her Russian-Asiatic background, and the set of her face bespoke rich intelligence. In short, she was breathtaking.

Barney clapped Buck on his shoulder. "This is a holo. Wait until you meet her. She's devastating."

"I can imagine."

"Nope, you really can't. The toughest part of Ardala Valmar is her mind. She's as fast as a computer, as wicked as a card sharp, as brilliant as any scientist, and with it all goes strength of command and a wild sense of humor."

"And she's the captain of *Io?*"

"You'd better believe it, my friend. The best naval officer in the entire country. You've probably noticed how quiet this tub is. The MHD is the main propulsion source, but what few people know is that Ardala modified the system. The equipment sets up a tremendous contained magnetic field in the forward area. An opposite repulsive electromagnetic force is applied from the stern. It pushes against the entire vessel, just like an old-fashioned rocker. But Ardala designed the tubular sluices along the hull. They magnetize the seawater, draw it into the sluices, and compress it—not much, but enough to eject it at tremendous speed behind the sub, adding to its propulsive force. It isn't easily detected because the water remains cold instead of pouring out heat like the nuke boats."

"How fast can this thing go?"

Barney smiled. "Based on tonnage, mass, cross-section, and everything else that goes into the equations of determining speed at various depths, we should have a top speed of about forty or fifty knots."

"Our nuclear killer subs could do that in my time," Buck noted.

"Sure they could. But they didn't weigh seventy thousand tons, and they didn't carry six negs that could be deployed any time we want to whip along at nearly two hundred knots. And notice I said what her top speed *should* be, not what it is. Just under one hundred knots, fella. In an emergency, half again as fast."

Buck whistled. "That's getting up there with a lot of planes at long-range cruise speeds."

"Well, put this in your thinking cap. With the way Captain Valmar modified the MHD system, *Io* can operate at maximum power for three years without fuel replenishment because the main drive fuel is the ocean itself."

"I'd like to meet our captain," Buck told Barney. The admiral switched off the hologram. "Oh, you will. She's scanned your dossier and everything else about you. She's studied our holos of you talking, walking, and flying. According to her, you were born four or five hundred years too soon."

"What's that supposed to mean?"

Barney laughed. "That you were made for the twenty-fifth century. Your cross-training, your skills in so many fields, the fact that you're a maniac in an airplane—a maniac who knows how to *win*—all these are the things she considers. I told you her mind was like a computer. She mixes and matches everything."

Buck remained quiet for a while. Finally Barney closed off their compartment and energized the maximum security screening. "Might as well get the rest of it out in the open now," he said.

"That sounds ominous."

"It could be. You're in a closed environment within *Io*. Wilma Deering is your almost constant companion. Her orders are to bring you up to snuff about our present time. But let's face reality, Buck. Wilma is a dynamite looker. When she was younger and had time for that sort of thing, she walked away as the winner in every beauty contest she entered. Add to that her experience and skills and qualifications and you've got pure nitro in each hand." Barney shrugged. "But don't sweat it. Wilma's sweet on you."

"Now, wait a minute—"

"Just hold on, Ace. That's a fact of life. Wilma is what we call a sensitive when it comes to ferreting out other people's emotions, but she can't hide her own worth a damn. The problem isn't Wilma—and don't tell me you're not heavy on her as well—the problem is Ardala. In the past, she and Wilma have been in a running contest as to who's the fastest, the best fighter, the best woman—you name it and they're on each other about it."

"And I'm caught in the middle?"

"Yep."

"But I haven't even met Captain Valmar!"

"I know that. Wilma knows that. But when she wants to be, our captain can be quite a—what is that blasted word?"

"Vamp?"

"That'll do. I'm telling you all this so you'll be ready and won't be caught off guard."

"I'm still not sure I get it, Barney."

"You know Wilma picks up on emotions and feelings. She can read other people as easily as you and I scan a holo. And from the way she's looked at Ardala, she's convinced our captain has designs on you. You're a magnet, Buck. Full of life and vinegar. So watch yourself. Both those women can be deadly."

Barney grinned foolishly and added, "You lucky dog, you."

So why don't I think all this is great? Buck wondered.

* * * * *

He didn't meet Ardala Valmar until their voyage was well under way. Buck didn't expect the captain to be anywhere but at the helm of the giant submarine. Threading through the coastal waters was a nasty job. The sea bottom was an enormous junk-yard of sunken ships, rusting hulls jutting up from the bottom like great knives waiting to scour the bottom of any ship passing nearby.

Buck piped the bridge. A lieutenant commander answered. "Permission to come to the bridge for observation. Colonel Rogers on the pipe. Security clearance activated."

He heard, "Stand by, please." Moments later a small electronic chip surgically implanted in his neck glowed dimly; Buck knew the security system was activating the chip, running its data through the security banks.

"Colonel Rogers, kindly come to the bridge. This is Lieutenant Commander Sally Cortez. I'll meet you on your arrival. The green deck flashers will lead you directly here. Cortez out."

Glowing green lights appeared almost magically as Buck moved toward the command center of *Io*. At another security checkpoint, Cortez met him personally. She was a brown-skinned, trim woman with flashing eyes and obvious high intelligence. "You can see we're on a tight watch right now," Cortez explained. She handed Buck a flyweight earpiece. "Wear this. You'll be able to listen to everything that's going on as we move out to sea."

"Thank you, Commander. I'll try not to be in anyone's way."

She flashed him a warm smile. "Anything special before I return to my station?"

"Yes, if you have a moment." She nodded and he continued. "We're heading for the lower Pacific coastal regions off Chile," he said, noticing a slightest widening of her eyes. Clearly she was surprised to discover he knew what most of the crew still did not know: their ultimate destination.

"I'm wondering if we'll go through the Panama Canal or if we'll make an end run around the bottom of South America, through the Drake Passage and around Cape Horn."

His question caught her by surprise. After several seconds, she smiled. "I forget, Colonel Rogers. Excuse me."

"I don't understand, Commander."

"There isn't any Panama Canal anymore. That entire area was melted down in the Mongol strikes. They used a kind of bomb that sustained an unusually high temperature for several hours after it detonated. It burned everything. It also melted the locks. The entire area is landlocked again and still highly radioactive. So you're half right, Colonel. It's around Cape Horn. We'll stay clear of the Falkland Islands and other such places because they have listening posts all through the area. We'll swing wide, go well out into the Pacific, and then do our end run up the coastline along the western edge of Chile. That would seem to be the last place they'd anticipate something as big as *Io*." She glanced at the bridge crew. "Excuse me, Colonel. I'm on duty," she said and departed quickly.

* * * * *

An hour later, Buck was seated in a padded lounge chair in the forward observation deck of *Io*, awaiting the arrival of Captain Ardala Valmar. He had been introduced to her in a brief, rather stiff meeting on the bridge. Running the giant submarine through the obstacles off the port of Philadelphia left little time for social niceties. He'd shaken hands with her, taking note of the worksuit she wore, stained with hydraulic fluid. Obviously she wasn't afraid to get her hands dirty working with her crew in any area where her expertise might be needed. The more he heard about Ardala, the more he realized how highly the crew regarded her. To them, she was captain, saint, medical doctor, engineer, scientist, and a gifted undersea combat veteran.

That certainly wasn't the woman Buck watched now as she came into the observation deck. Buck found himself glued to her every motion as she stood close to the glassite, looking out. Finally she nodded to herself as if meeting some personal requirement. She turned and stood before Wilma's lounge chair, then quietly, as though shrouding her power in warm greeting, she spoke in husky, feminine tones to Wilma.

"I haven't had time to take you personally through *Io*, but I will at the first opportunity. Allow me to welcome you aboard, Major Deering." Silhouetted against the ocean background through the glassite, she was startling in her presence. The Ardala he had seen briefly with the work gangs of the submarine was gone. In her place was a superbly conditioned woman whose best features were accentuated by nothing more than a skin-tight gold lamé jumpsuit plus a small touch here and there of jewelry, including the communicator, which looked more cosmetic than utilitarian, against the bone behind her ear. Long jet-black hair, previously concealed beneath a work cap, now flowed freely to her waist in stark contrast to her jumpsuit.

She never gave Wilma an opportunity to reply to her warm greeting. Instead, she eased closer to Buck with silky motion and came to a stop before his chair. She looked down at him and smiled. "Have you enjoyed your cruise so far, Colonel Rogers?" Buck saw a flash of white, perfect teeth.

"You're a far better sight to the eyes than Captain Nemo," Buck said with mock seriousness.

A shadow seemed to flow across her face. "I'm not sure I understand. . . ."

"Forgive me," Buck said quickly. "A literary reference from antiquity. Captain Nemo was the master of the submarine *Nautilus*, a creation of one of the master science fiction writers of my time—actually somewhat before my time, to be perfectly accurate."

She smiled again. "I am rarely caught by surprise. I remember now. This country's first submarine was christened *Nautilus*, was it not?"

Buck nodded. "In honor of the writer, Jules Verne."

"Our age has an unfortunate dearth of fairy tales, Colonel," she said quietly.

Buck gestured to take in the enormous vessel about them. "This boat is a fairy tale to me, Captain Valmar. It's truly astounding. I understand you were the main engineer, the architect of *Io*."

"Certain people are quite free in their praise," she demurred. "There were many of us who helped create this marvelous boat."

Buck laughed. "I'm pleased to see that our undersea language has prevailed. No true submariner would be caught dead describing his submersible as a ship. They were always boats."

"From the Germanic?" she asked, knowing the answer even as she asked the question.

She's testing me, Buck realized. "Of course," he answered. "From the *Untersea Boot*—the infamous U-boat of both our world wars."

"The deadliest peril of the high seas," Ardala said, now on certain ground from her knowledge of submarine history.

"Not quite," Buck replied. He could have remained silent, letting her slip of history slide by, but long ago he had recognized the necessity of meeting strength with strength.

"Would you explain that, please? And we may dispense with formal titles except when they are necessary? My name is Ardala. I know yours is Anthony, but your friends have always called you Buck. And I hope we will be friends."

"We will," Buck said with confidence. He glanced at Wilma, who sat silently, seething at the smoothness with which Ardala had cut her completely out of their conversation.

"Most people believe the German undersea fleet sank more shipping than anything or anyone else," Buck said. "But for the record, the deadliest submarines of the Second World War were American. Eighty percent of all the merchant and combat ships lost by the Japanese, from 1941 to the middle of 1945, were sunk by our subs. They finally choked off Japan, isolating her from imports, and hampering the flow of reinforcements from the home islands to Japanese forces spread out across the Pacific."

"I will remember that." She flicked a thumbnail; flame appeared magically to relight her cigar. Microminiaturization was a handy thing, Buck thought. A lighter completely covered by her nail.

Buck turned as several other people entered the lounge. The prime crew—Gold—ran the great submarine at this point, and it was a rule of the crews who prowled the depths in boats that when you had the chance to relax, you never passed it up. Buck nodded to Black Barney. He was surprised by the appearance of identical twins. Barney made the introductions. Ricardo Sanchez and Ricki Chavez were two of the most sinister men Buck had ever seen, with pointed beards, neatly trimmed sideburns and brows, the eyes of hawks, and sharp noses. Obviously they were of Spanish extraction. Barney had briefed him on these two but had never said a word about their being twins. Their different surnames were no doubt to avoid familial association unless they were known personally. "Those two operate through the underworld of South America," Barney had explained. Cocaine kingpins for global trade in the stuff."

Buck had been amazed. "Running cocaine today? In a world where everything that flies is suspicious? Without free trade or unencumbered shipping? And you *know* they're running coke and you still allow it? Good God, Blacky, that stuff almost destroyed this country hundreds of years ago!"

Barney nodded. "Right on every count." He paused. "Except one, that is. First, we know how rough coke is. In fact, the stuff that's grown today is much rougher than anything you knew— genetic modifications, that sort of thing. And before it gets shipped, it's blended with some very esoteric chemicals. The addict is hooked as if a spear had been thrown right through his heart."

"Then how can you allow this stuff to be sold?" Sudden anger surged through Buck.

Barney laughed. "You don't get it, do you? You think we're crazy to allow that stuff anywhere in Amerigo. Buck, dealing, shipping, selling, or distributing cocaine in Amerigo carries a death sentence if you're caught. No long trials, no appeals. Immediate appearance in court, and you get trial by three judges, no jury. Ninety-nine times out of a hundred its execution by firing squad that same day."

Other possibilities came to mind. Buck looked carefully at Barney. "You mean . . . ?"

"Don't stop. Figure it out yourself."

"The Mongols. You've got a supply line right into the Mongols!"

"In both Amerigo *and* their home territory, my friend. And I'll tell you something else. They're hooked. By the millions. The stuff we add to the powder, after about six months, begins to eat away at their brains. It doesn't kill them, but they begin to think like carrots and cabbage. If we can keep it up long enough and they don't cotton to what's going on, there'll be a Mongol empire of vegetables. It beats slinging hydrogen bombs at each other."

* * * * *

Looking forward through the glassite bow introduced Buck to a world that had always been about him—the hydroworld of Earth—but about which distressingly little was known. His journey southward in *Io* was a revelation in many ways.

Now, as he stared into the stygian darkness, he suddenly saw bands of light and color far ahead of *Io*.

His startled exclamation brought Ardala to rest her hand on his arm to assure him that no danger threatened the great submarine. "The lights are from autoprobes," she explained. "There are three robot probes twenty miles ahead of us, another three at ten miles, three more at five, and another three at one mile. The video from the probes, which are controlled by computer, allows us to see well ahead of our position. Each probe is equipped with detectors for changing temperatures, salinity, radiations, sound pulses, and anything else that goes on in the ocean. If it doesn't fit within the parameters programmed into the computer, alarms notify us immediately, we go to condition red, and we assume battle stations. *Io* could take out an entire fleet."

"Perhaps you'll explain something to me," Buck prompted.

Ardala nodded. Others on the observation deck heard Buck; they all turned to hear his question and the captain's answer.

"We're going down pretty deep," Buck said slowly. "How deep I don't know yet, but it must be on the order of twenty thousand feet. That's enough pressure to crush the best boat we ever built in my time as flat as a pancake. How can *Io* take that kind of pressure on her hull and still maintain performance?"

Ardala smiled. "You are aware this boat is named after the volcanic moon of Jupiter, *Io*."

"Yes. And well named, too. *Io* has the same kind of power."

"Well said, Colonel. The secret is in the hull design. Simply stated, we're overbuilt by a factor of nearly thirty. You see, *Io* was never intended to be a submersible operating in the hydroworld of Earth."

"That means . . ." Buck let his words fade away as Ardala smiled.

"You're quick at putting pieces together. I can tell by your reaction you must understand."

"Let me try," Buck said. "You have main antigrav power generators. They're large, inefficient, and they consume enormous amounts of power. You'd need that to lift *Io*, or whatever she was called before you changed her mission, well above Earth. It would be essentially a beam-generated antigrav."

"Correct."

"And then a main drive would cut in. If I figure this right, a nuclear booster would have been added on as a power stage to accelerate to orbital speed. That also means more g-forces than a man can handle. But as soon as you have orbital velocity, the booster cuts off and you're in free-fall. Than you bring up the crew in personnel carriers."

"Exactly. And did you determine the original mission of *Io*?"

"You were going to take this boat into the atmosphere of Jupiter and Saturn."

"Excellent!"

"The pressures in those atmospheres, to say nothing of the contents, would be enough to rip apart any space vessel. So you built it like a submarine to drive through the atmosphere of two worlds where the atmosphere is even denser than the oceans of Earth."

"That's why we have a triple hull," Ardala explained. "Jupiter is especially deadly. Its atmosphere is terribly corrosive, made up of hydrogen, helium, ammonia ice, methane, ethane, acetylene, phosphine, germanium tetrahydride—with temperatures ranging from hundreds of degrees below zero to fourteen hundred degrees above zero. To say nothing of lightning bolts a half-mile or more in width. The point is, *Io* is built to handle all that. But finding Atlantis is our priority now."

"So you think there is an Atlantis off the coast of Chile."

"I'm not paid to speculate on matters I couldn't possibly know about. I—" She became silent as a gong sounded. By her silence, Buck knew she was receiving a message from the bridge.

She rose to her feet. "We're going down to the bottom. The roboprobes have detected several hunter boats well ahead of us, and they're not ours. We could take them out easily enough—we've got the firepower—but that would only give our presence away, and I'd rather keep whoever is out there guessing. My guess is they're Chilean boats on a wide sweep, but they're not expecting any company like us. However, we'll dive well beneath them. I'm afraid I must return to the bridge. You and Wilma enjoy the ride." Without another word, she was gone.

Wilma looked at Buck. "There's a harness in your seat. Strap yourself in."

He followed her instructions. Moments later the bow dropped, and *Io* began to dive at a steep angle for the bottom.

Twenty minutes later they were far out from the coastline, running deep near an ocean floor that changed from cavernous furrows and rock formations to what looked like a sandy plain. There wasn't a sign of life, not even an occasional fish. All signs of vegetation had disappeared. At a hundred knots, *Io* ran just above the bottom plains, the bleak floor of the ocean broken occasionally by the hulks of sunken ships—shattered merchantmen, warships, even the tangled wreckage of bombers from several wars past.

"We're south of the Hudson Canyon now," Wilma related. "It's deep and dangerous. Once you're in it, the canyon walls shift without warning from wide to narrow. At this speed, even *Io* could be damaged by impact with the canyon walls. We'll slack off speed and go to silent running."

The bottom began to change again. The bleak ocean floor gave way to tumbled hills. They were entering the Hatteras Canyon, a wide slash in the descending slopes of the continental shelf. Their speed increased again. "You might as well take a break now," Wilma offered. "You've got time for a meal and a shower and some sleep if you feel tired. Everything should remain pretty bland until we get a good way off the Florida coastline. Then it gets interesting. We'll be traveling through the Blake Escarpment. It's a craggy, rough area of tumbled cliffs. There's been so much breakup of the slopes that maps from a few months ago are useless. We have at least twelve to fourteen hours before we get there."

"How about getting something to eat together?" he asked.

"With or without our precious captain?"

"Your claws are showing."

Wilma shrugged. "I don't play games with a man I like and respect."

"Yes, ma'am," Buck said.

He ate a meal of steak and fries and several cups of strong black coffee. Immediately afterward, he returned to his cabin and fell into a deep sleep.

Some time later, the alarm sounding battle stations brought him fully awake and alert.

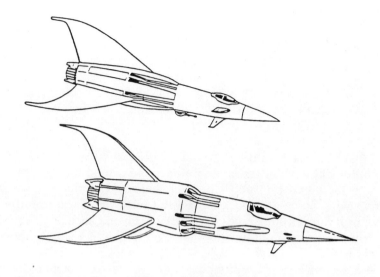

Chapter 15

Buck came to his feet immediately, hitting the overhead light switch and grabbing for his clothes. He was in his jumpsuit in seconds and pulling on his boots when a fist hammered at his cabin door. "It's open! C'mon in!" he yelled.

Wilma stood in the doorway, the red flash of battle stations reflecting like a blinking traffic light across her face. Buck pressed the self-sticking tapes to tighten his boots and looked up from the edge of his bunk.

"What the hell is going on?" he asked.

"Ambush," came the immediate reply. "We're well into the Blake Escarpment. It's a perfect setup for the kind of trap we just ran into."

"Never mind the geography lesson," he snapped. "Ambushed by whom? And how? What's out there against us? And what the devil am I supposed to do besides play stupid tourist?"

"I've heard from the bridge. Captain wants us both in the Response Bay. Don't ask me why. We'll find out soon enough. Just finish dressing and let's get out of here. Pull down that hatch to your right. There's an emergency breathing mask and communicator in there. Put them on." He followed her example as she donned the emergency breathing system and pressed a switch. He did the same. "Can you hear me?" he heard.

"Loud and clear."

"Good. If you get any calls from the bridge or anywhere else. they'll automatically cut into our frequency."

"Got it. Let's go." They started out at a steady trot along the lower passageways of the great submarine. Crewmen in different colored emergency gear hurried past them, everyone tightly disciplined and moving steadily, controlled.

"We've got a minute or two," he called to Wilma through the communicator. "Has there been an attack against us?"

"I don't know. I don't think so, or they'd be flooding these areas with flame-dousing gas. It won't hurt you if you breathe it in, but it knocks out flames in a hurry. I haven't seen any yet, but if you see a cream-colored vapor cloud, don't sweat it. That's what it is."

They emerged from the passageway and stood aside as several combat teams went by at a dead run, then climbed the ladder leading upward to the Response Bay. "All the teams that take action against an attacker get their orders and equipment here," Wilma said quickly. "As soon as we're inside, Security will activate your security chip and log you into the computer. Then we wait for whatever orders they have for us." They entered the Response Bay.

Commander Sally Cortez turned from a situation console. She gestured them to her. "I'll fill you in. We're on full red alert and battle stations." She tapped keys on her computer board. The large transparent map above the computer flashed into colored lines. "This is the Blake Escarpment. We're, um—" she hit another key—"right here." A blinking light represented *Io*.

Buck looked at the three-dimensional holodisplay of the ocean bottom. It looked worse than the cratered moon. Cliffs jutted upward from the ocean floor, jagged and split in many areas.

"This whole surface is like an obstacle course," Cortez said. "Many of the cliffs have caved in, and there's uncharted debris everywhere. We're getting a sonar readout in realtime of what's around us. See here, to the east? You'll notice the cliffs curve toward the Caribbean Basin."

"It looks like cliffs of clay that have been exposed to heavy rainfall," Buck noted. "Like storm runoff."

"Much the same effect. There's a powerful current running off the mainland, and it sweeps into these cliffs, breaking them up." She pointed to the map. "See this narrow strip of deep, curving sea floor? And just beyond this flattened area, there's a steady rise of low mountains, higher than the abyssal hills. The hills are a natural barrier to any boat coming from this direction. Anything moving our way to bushwhack us would have to rise pretty close to the surface. But if they've been lying in wait for us, along this narrow channel, and they haven't been moving, there's no way we could detect them."

"Who are they?" Wilma asked.

"Our best guess is the Chileans. Possibly some of the bigger Mongol boats. They don't have many left, and they're inefficient, but they carry heavy armament. To put it mildly, we're outnumbered, and they've got the high and the low ground. For us to go over the abyssal hills is to leave ourselves wide open to attack. If we go down, we get into that curving channel, and they can hit us before we have a chance to find them."

"Can we outrun them?" Buck asked.

"Captain Valmar judges that's exactly what they expect us to do. They'll have us in a three-way crossfire." Cortez frowned. "What I don't understand is how they knew exactly where we were. It's as if they've been expecting us."

"The Mongol boats tell the answer," Buck said quickly. "Want to bet a buck to a doughnut that Golden Dragon outfit is playing both ends against the middle? They're getting paid by us and they're getting paid by the Mongols and the Chileans, and they're selling information to both sides. There's an old expression for this. We've been suckered."

Captain Valmar joined them. "Sally, expand the area on the situation map."

Immediately the area in view enlarged. "If we go east, we're wide open to detection. There's the Vema Gap. It widens into the Nares Abyssal Plain, and there's no cover for us."

"What about south?" Buck asked.

"If we get far enough south, we can drive straight into the area of the Puerto Rican Trench. It goes down more than five miles. They wouldn't be able to follow us there. But first," Valmar stressed, "we've got to get through this ambush."

"Commander, can you get a scene of the area south of Swan Island?" Buck asked.

Again the scenes shifted on the situation holodisplay. "That's it," Buck said quickly. "Hold it right there. Captain, I once made some deep dives there while I was cross-training with the Navy. That area is a drowned coral atoll. It's an undersea plateau that starts six thousand feet down and then rises to barely a hundred feet beneath the surface."

"We'd be a sitting duck there," Valmar broke in. "There's hardly any room for maneuvering."

"Knowing we were coming this way couldn't give your enemy enough information to pinpoint where we are," Buck answered. "You've been tracked the whole time since we put to sea."

Valmar looked hard at Buck. "How do you know that?" she demanded.

"Can you find out if there's been any unusual aircraft activity along the coastal area? Philadelphia southward to where we are right now?"

"Yes, but why?"

"I'll explain later, but please get me that information now. It may explain a lot."

Valmar signaled to an officer and relayed the message from Buck. "We'll know in two or three minutes."

Cortez gestured to the holodisplay. "It won't be any too soon, Colonel. See those three red dots moving toward us? They're Chilean boats. Once they move, our sensors can identify them."

"Data," Valmar snapped.

"Fast runners," Cortez replied. "Six thousand tons each. Nuclear drive. They're pouring out radiation for us to pick up and identify. Each boat carries twelve high-speed torpedoes with UDXR warheads, six hundred pounds each."

"That's a break for us," Valmar replied.

Buck's eyes widened. "Torpedoes with high-yield explosives are a break?"

"The moment they fire those torps, we'll send out a sweep of microtorps of our own. They'll pick up the sounds of anything coming our way. The Chilean boats have liquid-air engines, but not their torps. They're old-fashioned, clumsy things. They use a rocket booster to initiate high speed and then they use propellers. Make a racket you can pick up for a hundred miles."

"Captain, incoming torpedos," Cortez interrupted, her voice incredibly calm.

"Fire first interceptor sweep. Nine Mark Six killers. Launch!" Valmar snapped.

Everything worked as anticipated. Streaks of white light marked the micros rushing toward the incoming torpedoes. "Seventy seconds to intercept," intoned Commander Cortez.

"That's a whole minute, Rogers. I have your data. There's been a single aircraft, very high altitude, flying slowly up and down the coast, every now and then adopting a wide circular flight pattern."

Buck slammed a fist into his other hand. "Just what I expected. We're being tracked from above."

"How?" Valmar shot back.

"It's MAD."

"Rogers, are you crazy? Mad about what?"

"You misunderstand, Captain. It's obvious that some of the systems we had in my time have been lost or forgotten. I—"

He stopped in midsentence as the streaks of white met the incoming red lights. Brilliant flashes speared the display. Combat Center relayed data to all hands through their receivers in the oxygen helmets everyone wore.

"Eight incoming torps intercepted and destroyed." Dull thunder rolled through the sea, a deep low rumble against the great mass of *Io*. "One torp still incoming. Tracking is ineffective with defensive micros. Damage Control, activate hull defense systems immediately. All hands, brace for impact."

Wilma grasped the edge of a computer bank. Buck did the same. He was startled to see Captain Valmar standing in a crouch, ready to absorb any shock through her stance.

"You'll find this interesting," she said to Buck. He couldn't understand her calm. She must have nerves of pure steel. . . .

An explosion boomed through the hull. *Io* rocked gently, sliding to one side from what was obviously a direct hit from a torpedo. Buck scanned the combat center. He could hardly believe the calm and discipline of everyone in sight.

"Damage report," Valmar said calmly.

"One direct impact. Defense system activated on schedule. No damage to system. Hull breach closed."

"Very good. Keep me informed of any change," Valmar replied.

She turned back to face Buck. "We have a sensor system

built all along our hull, encircling the boat. The sensors detect the pressure wave of anything coming toward us at any speed. The computers immediately determine the point of impact. Our outer hull instantly expands a pod at that point with heavy nitrogen. The blast is absorbed by the pod, which vents the pressure away from the hull. You can liken the hit to a mosquito bite."

"Amazing," Buck said, obviously impressed.

"Let's get down to something less amazing. You were saying something about mad?"

"MAD," Buck repeated. "It means magnetic anomaly scanning. Even back in the early sixties—nineteen sixties, that is—we had planes that could cruise five miles high with MAD detectors in booms trailing from the tail."

"And they could detect submersibles from that height?"

"Absolutely. They were so good they could just about tell you the name of the Russian sub captain. Not even *Io* can screen out its signal, unless you're very deep. If electronics have advanced like I think they have, then whoever has a modern version of our MAD systems can pick you up several miles down. In the magnetic spectrum, you're like a bright light."

Valmar leaned back against a console. "The Chileans don't have large aircraft capable of such flight," she said.

"It must be Mongolian control," Cortez added.

"You may be able to take care of those boats out there waiting for us," Buck told the assembled combat team of *Io*, "but as long as you're being tracked from above, you can't hide down here. That's how these boats were able to set up their ambush. They could even work out a timetable for when you'd arrive."

"Markham!" Valmar called. An officer appeared immediately.

"Look at the holo. See those boats out there laying for us? Do they look close enough to the cliffs?"

The officer, wearing the red jumpsuit of the ordnance team, grinned. "Yes, sir! I've already studied that situation, Captain. If we put a couple of big torps into those cliffs, we'd set off a hell of a landslide. Those boats will have to move, and fast, just to keep from being buried under a few million tons of rock. Most of their sensors will turn to mush from the debris the explosion churns up. Mud, dust, heat . . . the whole nine yards."

"Well done, Markham. Our sensor torps, of course, will be just as blind. How many negs are ready to launch?"

Buck turned to Cortez. "Negs?"

"Negative buoyancy boats. Long, slim, maximum nuclear drive with minimum cross-section. Since they're negative buoyancy, they've got to keep moving or they go down."

"Just like an aircraft," Buck noted.

"Precisely, Colonel. They're as tough as a steel girder. Two-man crews and a slew of stingers. Pencil-thin torpedoes with needle-nose warheads. If the negs get anywhere near those Chilean boats, they'll be dead meat. They're very maneuverable and fast."

"But taking out those subs isn't enough," Valmar broke in. "Markham, prepare the Mark Nine torps to blow away those hills and scarps. The minute everything comes sliding down, send out six negs. I want those Chilean boats hit from all sides."

She turned to Buck. "But unless we get rid of that thing overhead, we'll be a sitting duck as well."

"Captain, remember that sea mountain I mentioned a little while ago? That drowned coral atoll?"

"Go on. Quickly, Colonel. We don't have time to spare."

"Captain, it's a magnetic madhouse around there. I don't know what causes it, but every time we sailed over it or flew over that area, our detection equipment went haywire. The magnetic compasses just spun about like crazy. If you rest *Io* alongside that plateau, or even on top of it, they won't be able to pick you up. The area will screw up their gear."

Valmar turned back to Markham. "Two EM decoys ready to go. Follow procedures I've given you for the big torps and the negs. The moment that's done, send the decoy out headed due east. About two thousand feet down, speed nine zero knots."

She turned back to Buck. "The decoy is a roboscout. It sends out an electronic signal that exactly matches the size and shape of *Io*. If what you say is true, then that plane—"

"Will go after the decoy," Buck finished. "Just like the decoys in the old days. We used them in the air and under the sea."

"And once they've taken the bait, you're going upstairs to shoot down that Mongol plane."

"*What?*"

"Commander Cortez," Valmar ordered, "escort these two to the aft launching bay." She gestured toward Wilma and Buck. "Give the colonel five minutes in the simulator to study the controls. What he doesn't know or remember can be filled in by Deering. All right, everybody, *let's move!*"

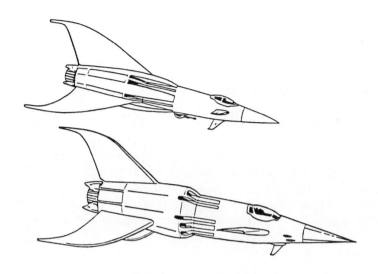

Chapter 16

Buck sat forward in the tandem seat of the Skua. The trainer was an exact duplicate of the combat machine.

The Skua had the feel and touch of a stub-winged killer, its small wings swept back rakishly. Wilma ordered him to slide into his body harness. "You've got to be able to get out of this thing faster than you can climb in," she said sternly. "I've flown ships in orbit that have the same general controls, but there's nothing out there that can compare to the this for performance in atmosphere."

Buck felt the controls. "Green knob, left hand, jet engine throttle?"

"Right. The blue controls the latch-and-free mechanism for compressed-air launch, and *that*, mister, is one hell of a kick in the slats. At least fourteen g's to boost into the air, and then— that red grip? That's the rocket boost for maximum climb, with a reserve tank that combines the ramjet with a rocket engine for emergency power in the air. Now put your hand back to the green knob. Twist it left and right. When you twist left, this thing falls like a rock. When you twist right, you're almost a hovercraft. We're not big enough for antigrav, and for our purpose, it's a luxury we don't need."

Buck wrapped his right hand about an old-style fighter plane grip to his right. His forearm rested in a padded groove. He felt a sense of familiarity with that system. It was the right-hand stick control instead of the larger stick mounted in midfloor of the cockpit. Even the F-16s he'd flown awhile had the side-mount stick, as did several of the bigger jetliners of his day.

He glanced up at Wilma. "Firing controls?"

"Two buttons in the front of the right-hand controller. The top button is for homing stingers. They have a combination of seeking devices—infrared, electrical, radar, and magnetic. They all work at the same time, so one of them is bound to do the job. You have fourteen stingers. Each trigger squeeze sets off one missile at a time. You want a bunch of stingers out there, just beat a tattoo on the stick."

"Lower button?"

Wilma took a deep breath. "Laser," she said slowly. "We don't know how it works in atmosphere, because it scatters the beam and attenuates the power charge."

"Then what the hell is it doing in the ship?" Buck demanded.

"It's designed to work in space," Wilma said. "I can cut the heart out of a . . . a battleship of your time out there, because the laser is really a disintegrator ray. There's no attenuation in vacuum. We get full power. It also sets up a vibration where it strikes. It turns molecular and cellular structure into mush, and the laser beam keeps right on going to gut the interior of your target."

"But we don't know if it works from *this* flybaby," Buck insisted.

"We'll find out soon enough," came the rejoinder.

Buck turned back to the flight instruments and controls. "Fly-by-wire, right?" Wilma nodded. "You put pressure on those controls, the computer senses your requirements and makes corrections two hundred times a second. The Skua is basically unstable. Without this system, it would tumble like a toy thrown by a child and—"

"Rogers! Admiral Barney here. Come in." Barney's voice came to them simultaneously.

"School's out, Colonel. Get the devil out of that oversized toy and into the real article. Deering, you reading me?"

"Yes, sir!"

"Then get with it, woman! I want launch in three minutes or

less. You have anything left to tell Rogers, you do it while you're on your way upstairs. Go!"

"We're on our way, Admiral," Buck answered for them both.

They slipped away from the simulator and crossed into the adjoining bay where the launch readiness crew awaited them. Buck moved into the front seat; everything was exactly the same as the simulator. Except that this thing is a winged bomb, he told himself. This ride is going to be for keeps.

"Get rid of that oxy helmet," Wilma ordered from the back seat. "Put on the globe helmet. The tech crews will fasten everything and hook us up for radio communications."

The crew was there immediately. A bubble pressure helmet went over Buck's head. There were no wire connections; everything was high-frequency FM within the ship, including their spoken words picked up by their mikes and short-beamed to radio communications with *Io*.

"You clear, sir?" a tech asked.

"Clear in front," Buck replied.

"Clear in back," he heard Wilma's call.

"Closing and sealing the canopy," They heard the tech's voice through their helmet headsets. A rounded clear glassite dome lowered from a back hinge. It seated tightly against the fuselage, and Buck felt the change in pressure as the Skua was sealed within its own systems.

"All right, people," Wilma sang out. "Clear the launch bay. Open the doors and flumes."

Buck felt the thudding sounds of thick protective hatches slamming into their lock-and-hold positions. "Launch leader, give me a ten countdown for jet start."

"We're ready, Major. Starting now. Ten . . . nine . . . eight . . ."

"Throttle advance for the jet engine to thirty percent," Wilma called. Buck eased the green knob forward with his left hand. He kept his right hand on the sidestick controller. He never wanted to remove his hand for any reason when they prepared for launch or during flight.

At the call of "One" and "Jet start," Buck felt and heard the booming roar of the powerful ramjet behind and beneath him. The engine howled like a banshee, causing the Skua to quiver in her restraints. He was impressed. They were only at thirty percent power, and he felt as if he had more juice at his disposal than all four engines of the jetliners he had flown back in the twentieth century.

"Buck, through launch, I'll handle the power sequence and you fly this mother. Got it?"

"Got it."

"You can climb out at any angle you want."

"One last question." He knew the final seconds were rushing away. "What's the climb rate?"

"One hundred and thirty thousand feet a minute. Save the questions for later! Final check. G-suit inflated?"

"Go."

"Harness?"

"Set."

"Get your head back hard against the seat rest behind you."

"Okay, set."

"Launch crew," Wilma called through her mike. "Five-second count and launch."

"Roger that, Major." More hatches moved. Buck felt a sudden pressure buildup; even in the enclosed space of the Skua cockpit, he felt the trembling of compressed air ready to blow.

" . . . three, two, one. *Launch!*"

There wasn't even time for Buck to feel the explosive surge of compressed-air energy around him in the angled launch tube. At the same instant he heard the word "Launch!" he realized the upper hatch cover leading to the exterior of *Io* was still closed, and they were being hurled straight into the thick metal plate.

* * * * *

A tremendous surge of compressed air shot violently upward from *Io*, much like a great slug of ice-hard water. At the same moment, the firing officer depressed the launch button and a circular metal hatch swung to one side, leaving behind a frangible fiberglass covering between the ocean and Skua.

Everything worked as designed. Buck saw the world before him turn violently white. Simultaneously the charge of compressed air blew the Skua upward through the angled tube. Buck barely had an instant to see the fiberglass housing erupt into a thousand pieces. Everything happened with blinding speed, like a motion-picture film being run a hundred times faster than normal.

Acceleration mashed him back against his seat, glued his head and helmet to the padded headrest. The g-suit bladders squeezed his legs, thighs, and stomach like a giant vise, but at least he was prepared for the physical blow.

Then water took over the world as the Skua hurtled upward, still encased in its great slug of compressed air. Before he could even worry about whether they might be damaged or trapped within the ocean, green yielded to brilliant sunlight. For a moment, weight fell away. The Skua poised in midair, slowing almost to a hover, well away from Io and safely above the ocean surface.

Before the killer fighter could begin to fall back toward the water, a green light flashed on the control panel in front of Wilma, and a computer voice, in a frantic tone, boomed, *"Fire!"* Wilma had been ready for it, but even if she had been incapacitated by the wild lunge away from Io, automatic controls would have taken over the climbout.

She tried to call to Buck to hang on, but the words never had time to change from thought to voice. She squeezed the rocket motor grip. Sound smashed back from the Skua, booming through the fighter, and in that same instant a huge pillar of fire blasted into existence, white-hot, shrieking, a dinosaur cry of uncontrolled energy.

Flame shot back into the ocean, exploding into a huge geyser of foaming steam erupting skyward. It never touched the Skua. Two hundred and sixty thousand pounds of blazing rocket thrust blew the Skua skyward as if shot from a monster gun. The killer ran for the high heavens.

Buck sat transfixed, amazed, overwhelmed by the rapid sequence of events. Suddenly Wilma's voice, straining against the high g-forces, came grating through his headset. "Fly this thing, damn you!" she shouted. "Zero three zero heading, *now!*"

Buck pulled himself together and concentrated. He moved the sidestick controller to the right, then barely touched the right rudder pedal. He wondered how the aerodynamic controls could overcome the surging rocket thrust, realizing almost with the same thought that the stick control and rudder pedals must be linked through the electronic control system to the rocket motor, which was gimbaled to allow any combination of up-and-down or side-to-side movements in response to his control pressure.

He realized just how right he was when an invisible force from his right mashed his body against the side of the cockpit. The Skua turned in response to his controls and was veering east from a northerly heading to Wilma's call for 030 degrees, the change in direction bringing on the sideways g-loads.

Buck had climbed skyward in some hot fighter planes, but this was like a continuous, nonstop blast from some giant cannon. Clouds appeared as if by magic; the ship flashed through them as if they were faint traces of vapor.

"Ten seconds," Wilma sang out. Digital numbers appeared, glowing, directly before Buck's eyes on the cockpit windscreen. The HUD glow told him everything. Without taking his vision from where was flying, he was able to get all the data he needed from the heads-up display. Wilma's call meant their rocket boost would be gone in ten seconds. By now they were rushing through the sky with such speed the ramjet had more than enough air smashed into its burn chambers to continue ignition.

He directed his attention to the engine gauges as the seconds of remaining rocket thrust flashed away. The air gauge read 115 percent, more than enough for the ramjet to continue at full power. What a bird! he exulted. And everything works just as advertised. . . .

Abruptly he was thrown forward against his harness. They were climbing at supersonic speed, and in that virtual silence, the rocket thunder remained far behind them. As quickly as the rocket burned away its last fuel, even before it could tail off in sputtering flames, the automatic controls set off the pyrotechnic charges to separate the spent rocket casing from the Skua. Now they flew on ramjet thrust alone, and the Skua responded much more easily and quickly to his control inputs.

"I have the target locked into the sweep search," announced Wilma. "Still at zero three zero degrees, but it's accelerating and climbing, turning to a more easterly heading."

"Range? Altitude?" Buck said quickly.

"One niner miles slant range; we're closing steadily. The enemy aircraft—"

"Just call it a bogey," Buck said, reverting back to the old combat aircraft calls.

Wilma hesitated only a second. She was sharp, fast, supporting him beautifully.

"Bogey at seven-two thousand."

"And no contrails," Buck noted.

"Buck, I'm picking up unusual gamma radiation," Wilma said quietly. "Much more than we should expect up here."

"Stand by one," he replied, switching to open frequency. *Io* would be trailing an antenna that would pick up his radio calls.

"Barney, you on the line?"

Admiral Benjamin Black Barney answered immediately. "Five by five, Buck. Go ahead."

"We're closing in on the bogey—"

"We've got you both on the scope."

"Okay. Did you read Wilma on the gamma radiation?"

"Affirmative. I don't like it. That's their main power source. We've checked back at Niagara Orgzone. That thing has been in the air for the last three days and nights."

"Which means they've got power coming out of their ears," Buck said grimly. "The crew has to be far forward in a compartment that protects them against their own radiation, as well as blast effects. I don't think we can keep our laser firing long enough to bother them. From what I know of these designs—and we worked on them, too—it's probably armored in all its vulnerable points."

"Buck . . ." Barney paused, and the momentary break brought a scowl to Buck's face. "Our computer shows they produce more than free radiation from their reactor. They can direct a beam of gamma radiation directly at the Skua. It won't hurt the structure, but it will go right on through your canopy. You'll be okay for about ten or twenty minutes, but then it's . . . well, you know."

"Sure I do," Buck said. "It's called a death sentence. Wilma?"

"Go."

"We can still use the disintegrator. It won't take the plane out, but in a bird like that, with their electronics, they'll seal off the crew compartment inside their blast and vibration shields. Which means they'll be viewing everything through video-holo scan. They'll be inside a winged tank, and with our laser working, there's no eyeballing us directly."

"Range nine miles, closing steadily. Bogey is now at eight-three thousand, heading zero eight two. Okay, Buck. What you just said. We use the laser disintegrator to keep their heads down inside their cockpit. We can fire the stingers at them at the same time."

"Wilma, it isn't good, baby. That ship is a flying tank. Either we get a direct hit on the reactor or penetrate the crew cockpit; otherwise we can't stop them. The only other way is to send some stingers right up the tailpipes of those jet engines. That way we can bust up their plumbing and—"

"Skua, Barney here. We show four missiles directed at you. Radar-homing, computers on board the missiles. You better do some fancy flying, fella, right now!"

Buck watched the incoming missiles in his heads-up display—four bright lights racing toward them. "Wilma! Do you have decoys in this fancy toy?"

"Yes."

"Set for radar disruption and absorption. Fire two at the missiles coming in from the right. Fire *now!*"

Two decoy missiles, slender and accelerated by pencil-thin dazzling green fire, flashed away from the Skua, rushing to intercept the larger missiles curving toward their fighter.

"Buck . . . those two on the left—" Wilma let the sentence hang.

Buck knew he had to time this perfectly. If one of those missiles hit them directly, the party was all over. But he still had a few tricks up his sleeve.

"Wilma . . . the decoys with the radar signal beacons? The moment you see the stingers explode those missiles on our right, fire them directly ahead."

He hadn't spoken a moment too soon. Two enormous roses of boiling flame followed his words. He barely had time to shout, "Fire decoys!" Wilma was ahead of him. At the first glare of the explosions, she had launched two simulator missiles, each radiating a powerful signal to attract any radar-homing device.

"Buck . . . those missiles coming in . . . " Wilma's voice showed strain. He didn't have time to explain.

"Time to impact from the two on the left," he said calmly.

"Seventeen seconds," she snapped out.

"A lifetime, baby, a lifetime," he said with an unexpected lilt to his voice. "Count me down at eight seconds."

"Eleven seconds to impact."

"*Now!*" he shouted. He forgot about Wilma, about the enemy

aircraft, about everything save those two missiles boring in and what he could do now to thwart them.

His hands and feet moved in a blur. The Skua seemed to go wild. He tramped left rudder, and the fighter whipped into a dervish of aileron rolls to the left, whirling crazily. The two missiles coming in lost hard acquisition and veered toward the radar decoys Wilma had fired directly ahead of them.

Now Buck slammed the right rudder, brought the stick to the right, and then again to the left. The Skua slewed wildly, tumbling. Buck felt blood running down his lips—a g-force nosebleed. He'd had plenty of them, but the sight his wild maneuver produced was worth it.

Two enormous explosions filled the sky with great clouds of flaming smoke. Immediately Buck rolled the Skua back to the right and then shot straight ahead. Just short of the mushrooming smoke clouds, he horsed back on the stick. G-forces squeezed him painfully, and Buck felt gray along his peripheral vision. They must have pulled fifteen to twenty times gravity. He shot upward, half-rolling to the left, climbing inverted so he could keep both the two remaining missiles and the Mongol plane in sight.

"What's the speed of those missiles?" he asked quickly of Wilma.

"Straight and level at Mach two."

That would work . . .

"Are they following us?"

"Yes! I've set your screen up so you can see our position relative to the missiles and—"

"How fast can this buggy go?"

Mach three, but we burn fuel like mad that way."

"We don't need much. Hang on to your hat, Wilma! And keep tracking the missiles."

"Will do. I'll let you know if they close in on us."

His next words almost paralyzed Wilma. "That's just what I want them to do," he said, laughing. "Okay, baby, down we go!"

He whipped the Skua into a rolling turn, coming out of inverted flight into a punishing, curving dive in pursuit of the Mongol plane. With gravity working with the Skua, their speed jumped quickly to three times the speed of sound and kept increasing. The great winged shape of the enemy aircraft expanded swiftly.

"Buck! Two more missiles coming at us. They're in a fan spread!"

"Just what I want."

"*Are you crazy?*"

"Nope. Just like the admiral said, more like a maniac. Turn on our transponder. Full sweep."

"But . . . they'll home in on us. We'll be a sitting duck for—"

"Save the speeches for later. *Do it!*"

She switched on their ultra high frequency broadcast signal. To any radar tracking system within a hundred miles, the Skua was now a perfect illuminated target. The missiles veered toward them.

Buck's timing was exquisite. When it appeared they must surely be hit, he threw the Skua into wild barrel rolls, enormous around-and-around maneuvers describing a great corkscrew in the sky. Tracking the powerful signal from the Skua's transponder, the electronic brains in the missile warheads did exactly what they were designed to do—they followed the Skua.

Or at least they attempted to. One of the four missiles tumbled wildly from its gyrations, flipping out of control to crash into another missile, causing another fiery explosion in the sky.

"Two down!" Buck shouted.

"Can you get the others?" Wilma asked, just realizing that Buck might yet extricate them from what seemed to be certain death.

"Hell, no. I want them chasing us. Pump up that g-suit as tight as it will get, Wilma!"

The Skua hurtled downward at nearly four times the speed of sound. Buck's maneuvers had brought him high above the huge nuclear-powered aircraft. It grew swiftly in the heads-up display.

"Buck, they're flooding us with that gamma ray emission!" Wilma called out.

"We won't be here long enough to worry," he answered. He aimed directly ahead and slightly to the right of the other aircraft. In rapid-fire succession, four stingers flashed away, rushing ahead of and to the right of the Mongol plane.

"Instinct is a wonderful thing," Buck sang out. "Watch those slant-eyes twitch, because I just pulled their string. They'll turn as hard as they can to the left now because they think my aim stinks with those stingers going to their right."

Exactly as he had expected, the huge swept-wing machine bent into a steep turn to the left. Buck dove wildly toward the airplane, curving just off its left wing. "Now!" he shouted. "Hang on, baby!"

The Skua dove perilously close to the Mongol ship's left wing. As they passed the wingtip, Buck pulled the tightest zoom climb he could with the controls. Even the Skua's powerful structure groaned in protest. Just as grayness rushed into Buck's peripheral vision, the beginning of a blackout, he had a glimpse of the Mongol plane close to their right as the Skua shot skyward.

The two remaining Mongol missiles had followed him in his madcap dive. From his last vestige of peripheral vision as gray was followed by black, he saw the missiles following the Skua.

* * * * *

"Barney! Valmar here. What in the world is happening up there? Our tracking is muddled. We're getting a powerful transponder signal, and then the scope tracker says the sky is filled with all sorts of . . . well, pieces of metal. Are you in touch with Rogers or Deering?"

Barney shook his head. He didn't know what was happening far above their heads. Everyone in tracking and monitoring had heard that maniacal laughter from Buck as he maneuvered like a man possessed. The Skua's seats were equipped with noninvasive medical monitoring, so they had a telemetered readout of the physical condition of the two pilots. Wilma's pulse was going right through the roof, and her blood pressure was going up and down like a yo-yo. The amazing reports from Buck showed his pulse up, but only slightly, and his blood pressure rose and fell in concert both with his changing g-loads and his shouting.

"Captain," Barney said as calmly as he could, "Buck took out the first two missiles and—"

"What about those two closing in on him from the front?"

"Captain, I don't know. It's crazy, but Buck maneuvered to have those missiles fired at him head-on, and that reduces his maneuvering room and time and—"

"Hold it, Barney! Our scanners are picking up another explosion—really big blast this time. The radiation counters are going off scale. . . . Damn! We've got a target coming almost straight down, spinning and burning. . . . That's the radiation source! It's the Mongol plane. But we haven't any track on the Skua!"

Barney felt his blood chill. His first thought was that Buck had placed the safety of the great submarine above all else. The Mongol plane bristled with powerful armament. Maybe that gamma radiation could be concentrated in an intense beam so that even a few seconds direct exposure would start shutting down Buck's and Wilma's vital life processes. Maybe, maybe, maybe . . . It was driving him crazy—

Wait a moment . . . he's got a separate code in his transponder. . . .

"Ardala! Switch to transponder squawk 1776. Hurry! See what you get."

Within seconds, she was reporting back. "I don't understand this, Barney," Ardala said. "We're getting a clean signal on that frequency. It's climbing rapidly, and it's past ninety thousand feet, slowing down. What's going on?"

Barney broke out in peals of laughter. He tried to talk, but realization of what Buck must have done and relief at hearing the signal almost choked him. He spluttered and coughed as he tried to speak clearly but failed.

"Damn it, Barney, stay where you are. I'm coming right there," Valmar ordered.

Barney collapsed in a chair, wiping perspiration from his face. He switched his own tracking scopes. Sure enough, on the 1776 squawk signal showing on his scope, there it was . . . a bright dot. It was the Skua, now at 93,000 feet and no longer climbing. As Barney watched, he saw the dot moving slowly but accelerating as it began losing altitude.

Then Barney knew what must have happened up there. "I'll be damned," he said quietly to himself.

Valmar burst into his tracking room. Barney held up both hands. "They're alive. The Skua is still in one piece, but I think they're out of fuel, coming down with a dead stick. Buck got the Mongol. If you're tracking with your radar, you'll see it spinning like a top as it comes down."

"No power in the Skua. He can't ditch that thing in the water; it's too fast, and besides, it can't float. I'll do anything to get those people back." She gestured to his tracking scope. "Is there anything else up there? A second Mongol plane?"

"Just the Skua. Everything else is clear."

"All right, Barney. We're going to break all the rules. I know what my orders are, but my crew will never be worth a hoot if they don't trust me to do anything to recover my people when things fall apart. Now, here's what we're going to do. You keep tracking the Skua; we'll do the same. I want to know when it's low enough for them to use their belts.

"And hang on, Barney. We're coming out of the water like a whale breaching."

Barney grinned, knowing what was coming. He held up a thumb. "Let's get 'em, Ardala!"

* * * * *

Ardala Valmar moved quickly back to combat command. She spoke in rapid, quiet, assured tones, what her crew recognized as no-nonsense, no-question time. "Cortez, I want timed-release explosive charges for every Chilean boat you can detect out there. Circling maneuver, figure eights, then random pattern. They're to release a charge every forty-five seconds to keep those boats worried and waiting for something heavier. Commence firing *now!*

"Markham! Double those heavy torpedoes into the cliffs. Bring down the whole lot. Keep firing one extra demolition torp every two minutes. I want the water boiling with mud and muck in every direction. Schwartz! Hedgehog pattern every sixty seconds, random detonation in the vicinity of the enemy boats." She turned and stabbed a finger at another firing officer. "Draper, send out the drummers. Random pattern, maximum noise, laser signals and smoke in the water. Every third launch is with high-intensity flares, low over the bottom. The closer you get to any targets, the better.

"All hands, listen up," she addressed her firing crew. "If we get any hits on those boats and the crew takes to the escape systems, release the biosensor sharks. Set their homers to go after anything moving in the water. I don't care if it's fish or people,

169

they all get chewed up. Set their receivers so that we can disable the attack mode and bring them back for recovery. Launch in sixty seconds, a bracket of ten."

Markham looked at Cortez with raised brows. "I don't know what's going on," he said quietly, "but with those robosharks out there going after anything that moves, there's going to be an awful lot of blood in this ocean."

Sally Cortez grinned, her hand poised on her firing console. "You'd better believe it, fella!" Her hand went down, and a bracket of explosive homers rushed away from *Io*.

"Admiral Barney! Valmar here."

"I'm on, Captain."

"Did you copy my orders?"

"Right on, Valmar. Brilliant."

"Keep me informed on the Skua."

"Will do. They're down to forty thousand feet now, still descending."

He turned back to his communicator. "Colonel Rogers, come in, come in. Deering, if you receive me, please reply. I repeat, please reply."

He heard only static. Buck Rogers had timed everything with split-second accuracy. Wilma still found it difficult to believe he had deliberately drawn the enemy missiles toward the Skua and then, in the most amazing exhibition of flying she had ever seen, had outwitted the electronic homing systems of the missiles. Those violent rolls and corkscrewing maneuvers were aerobatics with which she was completely unfamiliar. Atmospheric flight, she now realized, demanded levels of skill and knowledge that she had never realized.

And how he drew the missiles in behind them was nothing short of amazing.

She almost screamed at Buck for them to dive away from the Mongol bomber. They could never stay in close enough to use the laser disintegrator. That demanded a precise, steady flying maneuver of at least ten seconds for the laser to agitate the molecular structure of the big aircraft, after which the laser would punch through to send searing heat into the fuselage.

But ten seconds with a powerfully defended bomber was more than a lifetime. Holding a steady, straight-line course for that length of time was a death sentence! It also made them a sitting duck for the gamma ray beam. Nothing was more frustrating than the next blast of bad news—that their own stinger missiles could be rendered useless by defensive systems, and that even the explosive charges might never have a chance to break through the heavy armor plating of the Mongol plane. It had so much power from its nuclear power system that it weighed at least three times as much as normal, and all the extra mass was in the form of battleship-like armor.

But the defensive missiles fired by the Mongols were much more powerful than their own stingers. Buck had maneuvered wildly, had performed the most incredible reversal in position and direction. His bruising dive toward the big plane had to be timed with exquisite precision; his own missiles brought the enemy pilots to veer to the left. This meant the aircraft had to bank sharply, left wing down, and it was at this instant that Buck dived scant feet by the wingtip, passed the bomber, and then pulled the most violent upward maneuver he had ever flown in his life. Behind and below them, the bomber banked again to the right—a perfect homing target for its own two missiles.

Now the electronic homing devices performed precisely as they were designed—before them was a target, and they smashed into the wing of the Mongol plane and exploded.

Even as Buck and Wilma rocketed skyward from the force of their violent pullup and lapsed into blackness from the g-forces that drained blood from their eyes and brains, the huge wing folded in two, collapsing sideways back over the fuselage and cockpit. The Mongol plane whipped instantly into a violent spin, whirling around its right wing like a seed pod falling from a tree. Within that hapless machine, the nuclear reactor cracked open, and the thick fuel lines and coolant and pressure chambers came apart at the seams. Lines and tubes whipped about like striking cobras. Intense radiation flooded the interior of the aircraft. The crew was trapped, unable to use their escape devices to eject the capsule into which they were crowded. But even had they done so, they were doomed by the fierce radiation ripping through their bodies. Had they ejected successfully, they would all have been dead within the hour.

They were not given that hour. The bomber, shedding pieces, was in a death spin that would continue all the way to the ocean below. . . .

* * * * *

Slowly Buck and Wilma recovered consciousness, groggy from the rush of blood and oxygen back into their brains. Within seconds, the darkness was gone, but still they saw through a filmy haze. Finally Wilma was able to make out her instruments.

"B-Buck," she called in a voice that quavered from shock and physical punishment, "do you hear me? Please . . . please answer me. . . ."

Buck sucked oxygen deeply, his head clearing rapidly. He heard Wilma's voice, but at the moment he was paying full attention to the data readings on the heads-up display before him. The Skua was in a steep spiral, its engine dead, but still accelerating due to its weight. Buck concentrated on two instruments, the altimeter and the rate of descent. They were going down at four thousand feet a minute and passing the twenty thousand foot level. He answered Wilma's call in the best way possible, by pulling the Skua out of its death spiral, righting the wings, and bringing up the nose. Moments later he was in a controlled, powerless descent.

"Wilma, are you with me?"

"Y-Yes . . . I think so. My head feels like its been beaten with a hammer."

"Worry about that later. This thing glides like a brick. There's no way we can make a water landing and just waltz away in a dog paddle."

"We won't have to, Buck." He heard strength returning to her voice. "The seat cushion . . . and the backrest, Buck. They have pull tabs on them. Try to reach them."

His hands groped until he felt the backrest tabs. Moments later he located the seat tabs.

"There's only a little time left, Buck. Do exactly as I say."

"Go ahead. That ocean is coming up pretty fast."

"In that pack is a sheet of Inertron. You saw how it worked with Hoffman after he left his fighter plane. It reduces your weight to about five pounds. We'll drift down slowly, but we've got to be out of the ship no lower than three thousand feet so we can decelerate. The Inertron is set to a maximum fall of about ten miles an hour, but that's only when you're a short distance above the surface. Fasten those tabs, Buck. Do it now. They won't activate until we're out of the Skua."

"That's fine and dandy, but this thing doesn't have any ejection seats, and we're moving at a pretty good clip."

"There's an Inertron package in each wing. It's good for about twenty seconds. When I activate the system, it has the same reverse gravity effect as our personal packs. It will slow us down to about forty miles an hour and stop the rate of descent. But we have only those twenty seconds to clear the ship."

"You'd better do it *right now*. We're running out of everything fast."

"All right. In three seconds, I'll hit the switch. Ready?"

"Ready!"

The Skua slowed in midair as if it were floating beneath a huge parachute, but without the shock of an opening canopy. Thirteen seconds after Wilma activated the antigrav unit, they were down to about thirty or forty miles an hour, a mild breeze compared to their former speed. Their descent rate could hardly be detected.

"Release the canopy! Now!" Wilma shouted.

He hit the switch. Clamps flew back, and small pyrotechnic charges blew, hurling the canopy above and well behind them. "Now, Buck! Get out!"

He stood on the wing, one leg still in the cockpit, one hand bracing himself against the wind rushing by.

The seconds flashed away. Wilma was screaming at him now. "Jump! For God's sake, Buck, get off the ship! Your pack won't activate until we're clear!"

Still he hesitated, looking down at the ocean several thousand feet below. Buck had jumped from aircraft before. He'd gone through survival training, had earned his extra set of wings as a member of rescue teams, and he'd gone skydiving just for the fun of it. Seventy-four jumps in all.

But I had two parachutes then . . . one big one to let me down nice and easy, and a reserve canopy just in case something went wrong. All I've got now is this skinny Boy Scout pack . . . and I'm supposed to jump?

"*Jump!*" Wilma shrieked, her voice deafening in his headset. He looked behind him just as Wilma leaped from the wing. She's not in the right body position . . . no balance. She'll tumble . . .

Oh, hell, here goes nothing. . . .

He dived off the wing, immediately arching his back, his arms outstretched, knees bent, assuming the proper balancing position for a stabilized sky dive. Wind noises increased as his falling speed swiftly increased to 140 miles an hour. He dreaded looking for Wilma. She had to be falling out of control by now.

He hurtled past Wilma, who looked up at the astonished face of Buck as he whizzed by. She was drifting gently downward, almost as if seated on an invisible chair. Again her voice came painfully through his headset.

"You idiot!" she laughed. Even as her peal of laughter banged against his ears, he felt the deceleration as the Inertron antigrav system activated. The howling wind was gone. It was like floating down beneath a huge parachute— only there wasn't any chute.

"This is incredible!" he whooped. The air felt like a giant marshmallow beneath him. He was a leaf riding gently earth- ward, sliding along a downward-sloped invisible mountain of cot- ton. He saw Wilma above him, waving. He waved back, his faith restored—or just discovered—in an energy system he couldn't see, feel, or even understand.

The ocean was less than five hundred feet below him now. He felt the first deceleration, his descent slowing steadily until he slipped toward the water at less than ten miles an hour.

Then he became aware of deep booming sounds. Water rose from the ocean less than a thousand feet away as huge blasts of foam erupted. It looked just like the depth charges they'd dropped against submarines. The sound grew in intensity as he dropped lower. The ocean boiled furiously from unseen forces.

Then there was another sound, as if the ocean were being ripped like a huge sheet of canvas. "They're here!" Wilma called out.

Buck turned to look. To his left, the ocean swelled. A huge mound of water, perfectly rounded, kept rising from the sur- face, the lower part of the mound dark green, becoming nearly white with boiling foam near the crest. An immense dark shape burst from the dome, a huge rounded bow thrusting from the water like some gigantic, impossible whale leaping into the air. The entire, immense structure of *Io* appeared, magically, impossibly, wonderfully, water streaming from its rounded flanks like a giant waterfall pouring over a high mountaintop. Then the great submarine rested level, its hatches sprang open, and swift, flexible motor launches raced toward where Buck and Wilma would alight.

Black Barney stood tall in the boat rushing to Buck.

"Welcome aboard!" the admiral shouted.

Buck's feet barely touched salt water, and that was all as eager hands grasped his body and guided him into the launch. Barney hugged him fiercely.

"You're just in time for lunch," he boomed.

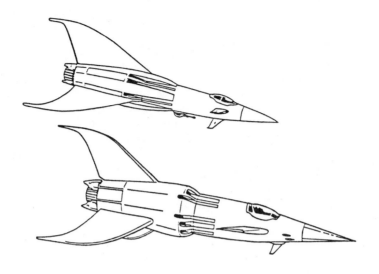

Chapter 17

Captain Ardala Valmar came through the *Io* sick bay with concern creasing the lines of her face. Considered by her crew to be implacable, pragmatic, and given to cold, analytical observation of her crew and their performance no matter how demanding the moment, they could hardly conceal their surprise as they saw her grateful greeting to the two pilots who had flown a near miracle in support of the great submarine.

The captain slipped a small flask beneath the covers of Buck's hospital bed. She leaned forward, her face close to his ear. "According to the dark one," she said, referring without name to Black Barney, "you are quite fond of this potion. When this is gone, just hand it to Nurse Beth, and it will be replaced with a full container."

"Thanks," Buck said to her. "I don't know whether to call you ma'am or sir."

"Ardala is fine. And you are Buck rather than Colonel Rogers." She smiled, a radiant sight. "We'll save the diplomatic and military formalities for when it is necessary for the crew to hear. Otherwise, after what you and Wilma have done—and I admit to being overwhelmed by her performance—that—"

Buck's face went serious. "Ardala, listen to me. I don't want to leave this unspoken or to pass it off lightly. Without Wilma, we would never have destroyed that Mongol bomber."

"Can you see her across the corridor? In her room?"

"Yes. Isn't that Markham with her?"

"It is. He has been debriefing her. Every detail of your mission is being data-compressed and sent off to Niagara. She has been raving about *your* performance. You were really quite remarkable up there today, Buck."

He shook his head. Immediately he brought his hands up to each side of his face. The room whirled about him. Ardala placed her hands over his. "Gently, gently, my friend. Those gyrations have left your inner ear less than happy. That, and the dosage of gamma radiation you received. It was more than any of us expected. It will affect your balance for several more days."

He glanced down at the intravenous needles protruding from his arm. "Is that why you people have been using me as a human pincushion?"

"You *and* Wilma." Ardala glanced at the blonde woman talking with animation to Markham, relating again and again the details of their wild flight and combat. Everything was being recorded; the mission profile on all the radar scopes and scanners was being integrated and fed to Niagara.

"Have you met Li Yandai?" Ardala asked.

Buck glanced up. "That sounds like something from a Chinese menu. Who is he?"

"Don't be misled by his Chinese name—or his face when you meet him. Li is American-born, but was raised as a young priest in a Chinese enclave in the Dakota Badlands. He is utterly faithful to Amerigo and is married to the former Carlotta Domingo. Mixed Spanish and Italian, I believe. Li is a poet, a scientist, a strategist of pure brilliance, and he is also the chief of whatever air forces and planes we have left. He watched your encounter with that Hoffman fellow from the Half-Breeds. They have since joined with us and have brought at least another dozen of the wild ones with them."

"Does he fly?" Buck asked.

"Like an angel. He lacks your particular skills and he prefers flying, whenever possible, in a glider. I think that's what it is called . It has no power, and its wings are extremely long and thin, like—"

"It's a sailplane."

177

"That's it. Thank you. Li will remain aloft for days in that birdlike contraption of his. He even sleeps when he is aloft. He is masterfully self-trained so that, if necessary, any upset of his bird—as he is fond of calling his sailplane—brings him instantly awake. He has not yet met you directly, but he hopes to do so when this mission is completed. In the meantime, he is gathering all the records of your contest with the Mongol machine, as well as everything from Wilma, and then he is going to the Mongol Enclave, where he'll meet with Soo Kassar, ruler of the American Mongol forces residing in our country."

"He's going to sit down and break bread with a Mongol ruler in Amerigo?"

Ardala nodded. "The two of them are old friends. Each remains faithful to his own people, but they are sensible enough to realize that open warfare is insanity. The world has too long been on the edge of poisoning itself. So he will meet with Kassar and give him all the records of your battle with the bomber. You see, the Mongols have boasted that not even ten of our fighters like the Skua could destroy a single machine, as you did today. Li believes this will reduce the number of flights over our parts of Amerigo. It's just one more step in breaking down the barriers."

"Where is this Soo Kassar?"

"In what was once Chicago. He lives every day with underlings doing their best to capture, unseat, or kill him. There is no peace within those people. They feel they are regarded as outcasts by the Celestial Mongols in China and Tibet and are looked down upon almost as subhuman."

Buck shook his head and laughed. "What goes around comes around, Ardala. Everything you just said could be taken right from the words and actions of my world in my time. You have lots of super gadgets and gimmicks, and many of your people are great, but you're still burdened with the same problems and prejudices that burdened us."

Ardala held her silence for a few moments. "You understand that Li Yandai would rather die than knowingly betray Amerigo?"

"If you say so. But how can he trust this Soo Kassar?"

Ardala laughed. "I turn to history, to your own time, for that answer. Shall I say he knows on which side his bread is buttered?"

"So we keep him in power."

"He is a known factor. He is honest and faithful with the Mongol government. But he is not stupid or burdened with their native hostilities, and he feels that one day we will either join together or we will fight furiously to the finish."

Buck studied her face. "Ardala, I wouldn't count on wrapping this up with a tea party. One day you'll either reclaim all of our country, without the Mongols maintaining an armed camp here, or there will be full-scale war. Let me give you another bit of history. Those who ignore the lessons of history are condemned to repeat its mistakes."

"I will remember that. And now do you feel up to some serious conversation?"

"I could do with a thick steak first."

"Done. Nurse Beth will signal me when you are ready. You will be moved, along with Wilma, to the observation dome. Our conversation will continue there."

Whoever was chief of the mess knew how to do things right. Buck was never that certain what was in his thick porterhouse; he knew that most of the "meat" served aboard *Io* was first run through food converters as a soupy mess from the sea, to which nutrients and vitamins were added, and then into the "steak factory," where it was processed to look and taste exactly like steak, right down to the bone on which he chewed afterward. Kitchen-fried potatoes and several mugs of steaming coffee left him sprawled back in his bed.

Black Barney was his next visitor. He closed the door and increased the air-conditioning flow through the room. Buck watched him in silence until Barney pulled a chair up to the side of the bed and, still in silence, handed him a long, thin cigar. Finally he spoke. "Enjoy, son. Just take a sharp breath. That thing is self-lighting."

Buck sucked in air. Immediately the end of the cigar glowed and sent up thin curls of smoke. "Amazing. I guess this must be made from seaweed, too, but it sure tastes like Jamaican tobacco."

"It is Jamaican." Barney smiled. "We trade in many things, but they have the world market cornered in great tobacco."

Buck took two long drags, letting the smoke drift gently from his nostrils. "Okay, Barney, all this kid-glove treatment makes me feel like a new man." He grinned. "Now that you've fattened the goose for the kill, what do you have up your sleeve?"

White teeth flashed in the dark face. "We'll go into it in detail when we get you and Wilma up forward. Did Ardala talk to you about the gamma radiation effects?"

"Sure did. Said I'd have some woozies but only for a few days. My guess is it messed up the inner ear a bit and—"

"More the medication than the gamma, but she's right. Three days from now you'll be as good as new."

"Barney, damn it, you're bursting at the seams! Whatever it is, spit it out!"

Barney chuckled. "You know we're going around the Cape and up to the main Chilean base on the west coast of South America."

"Yeah. To pay a call on our Atlantean visitors from way out yonder—the Pleiades, or whatever they call home."

"It doesn't matter. Fifty thousand years or more from a destroyed solar system is a long way off. The big question is whether they're really here."

"Got some news?"

"In a way. You've met Ricardo Sanchez and Ricki Chavez?"

Buck frowned, trying to remember, then nodded. "Sure have. The Bobbsey Twins, right? Twin brothers, but they use different names. Slicker than owl snot on a brass doorknob, from what I hear."

"What else do you remember besides their slick ways, Buck?"

"They're the meat-and-potato combo of South America; they've got smarts, contacts, money, power; they speak a bunch of languages; and they deal in drugs, slaves, and other nasties from their home base somewhere up in the Venezuelan Andes. They do odd jobs for Amerigo, and in my book, they're the worst kind of slimeballs, who ought to be ground under our boots."

"Neatly spoken, and I agree." Barney added, "I'd be glad to do it myself except for the fact that they're more important to us alive than dead."

Buck shrugged. "It's not for me to decide. But if you hang around in a pigsty long enough, it's tough to get rid of the stink."

"I take it that's a criticism."

"Barney, we once promised not to snow one another. Of course it's a criticism! They're roaches!"

"Useful roaches, however," Barney reminded him again. "They have a number of high mucky-muck Chileans who depend upon them for their supply of the finest grades of coke and heroin."

"Somewhere in all this there must be a point."

"You're an impatient man, Buck."

Buck laughed. "I've been looking for answers for nearly five hundred years. Cut to the quick, okay?"

"Their cocaine and heroin buyers, very high up, as I say, can be maneuvered to say anything when you string them out. Hold back on their supply and they're ready to eat their children to get the stuff. This time, at our request, Sanchez and Chavez—"

"The Blues Brothers of the underworld."

"Explain that to me some other time. My point is they left a few of their highest buyers way out on a limb. They were screaming for the stuff. The brothers, as you say, dropped the hammer on them. Either they came up with some good answers about the Chileans and Atlantis, or they could die from the screaming meemies."

Buck bolted upright in his bed. "And?"

"I told you. In a little while, in the forward observation lounge."

"Then get me out of here! Now!"

"I thought you'd never ask. I'll send for your clothes."

*   *   *   *   *

They gathered in the forward observation lounge and waited for latecomers. Finally Ardala Valmar called and said she and several others would be delayed for some time from the highly secret meeting. The crew didn't ask questions. Their captain had placed the forward lounge area completely off limits, with guards and heavy blast doors sealing them off from the rest of the submarine.

Buck, Wilma, and Barney had some time to once again be mesmerized by the rapid movement of *Io*. Sonar and maser probes painted a startling holographic display of the ocean bottom well ahead of the submarine. It gave them an even more amazing sense of unreality when a tiny submarine floated in hydrospace on the holoprojection. It was like watching themselves, as though they were witnesses from high above.

With the furious engagement with the Chilean submarines

181

and the Mongol bomber far behind them, the passage around the bottom of South America went without interference. *Io*'s sensors kept up constant probing of the depths, and Valmar kept three UAVs on constant patrol.

The small unmanned aerial reconnaissance robochoppers were powered by overlapping twin rotors—no tail boom, no aft controlling rotor. They burned little fuel and kept constant contact with combat teams in *Io*, sending back a flow of video and other visual observations. The most activity they encountered was a huge pod of whales moving in stately procession to their feeding grounds off Antarctica.

Io had other eyes as well. Two-man-crew negative buoyancy submarines ran thirty and seventy miles ahead and flanked the course of the submarine.

Now that they were starting to enter the waters of the Pacific, the ocean floor presented a startling view of what might be found on some distant, alien planet far from Earth's solar system. "It looks like some of the roughest mountain terrain I've ever seen from the air," Buck noted to Wilma. "It's hard to believe that most of what we're seeing was once above mean sea level, that the ocean surface was below these ranges." He swept his hand in a wide gesture to take in the sea bottom, "This is the result of continents shifting, crustal plates bouncing off one another. . . ." He shook his head. "It's astonishing and incredibly beautiful." Buck was deep into the wonders of the sea that had fascinated him as a youngster, much as he had been mesmerized by the promise of flight.

"You did some deep-ocean exploration, didn't you?" Wilma asked. "I overheard Admiral Barney talking about a deep valley or trench of some kind."

"The Marianas Trench in the far Pacific. At the bottom is the Challenger Deep. We sent down some research vessels. They touched bottom at nearly thirty-six thousand feet. But don't give me credit for that, Wilma. I was just in the research group that supported the deep dives."

"You have a rueful look on your face."

Buck laughed. "I never said I didn't *want* to go down there. But you know what? Those same people who did the deep dives would give their eyeteeth for a trip like we're taking right now. We're in a submarine as large, as heavy, and as strong as a battleship, and we can view everything in incredible comfort. In my day, Wilma, what we're doing right now was strictly a distant dream."

"Consider it a dream come true," she said warmly. Off to her right, in stygian darkness, flickering lights caught her attention. She grasped his arm. "Buck . . . look over there." She pointed. "We're so far down there's no natural light from above, but that looks like signals of some sort."

"They are," he replied. "It's from an octopus, and how big they get is anybody's guess. But they're highly intelligent, and they have bioluminescent capability. Along their arms they grow what we'd call lights. They flash them on and off in different colors. We finally determined the sequences were signals."

"Intelligence?"

"Advanced. It's sort of a visual Morse code, but infinitely more detailed. They're 'talking' to one another, and the more we study them, the more we learn about both their intelligence and their ability to communicate. When we descended, at a thousand feet we reached the point where we left sunlight behind. It's utterly black down here, as far as light from above is concerned, anyway. But another five hundred feet down, especially if the observer stays down long enough, he encounters a world he never even suspected was there. Turn out the lights, Barney. Can we have the neg boats kill their lights also—just for a short while? They've got sweep sonar and other stuff to navigate with."

"Can do," the admiral replied. He passed on the request to the bridge and Captain Valmar agreed. The observation deck went utterly black. They waited quietly for their eyes to adjust to the slightest light beyond the submarine.

Then it began. They passed a large area of octopus flashes of color, then complete darkness again. Suddenly Wilma cried out in astonishment. Ahead, there were explosive bursts of light in the distance, as bright as skyrockets, dazzling in white and yellow.

"What . . . what was that?" she asked, awed.

From the darkness to her right, she heard Barney's voice. "I wish we knew, Major. Ninety percent of what goes on down here is a mystery to us. We've only been exploring the sea for about ten thousand years, but we're still groping."

"Would you believe," Buck added, "that at least half of all life-forms down here have bioluminescent ability? There, off to our left. It looks like fog, sort of filmy, like pale milk."

"I see it," Wilma said.

"Keep your eyes on it. It's a giant squid, and they're amazing."

"How deep are we?"

"Three thousand feet. Look!"

A cloud of burning particles spread out like a starburst, twinkling and sparkling, red and yellow and orange intermixed with rays of dazzling white.

"What—what is that?"

"It's the squid, trying to fend off an attacker. It's probably deepwater sharks, or a sperm whale on the hunt for its favorite lunch. They'll fight like two giants battling. Sure enough—see?"

Against the background of scattering light, the silhouette of a huge sperm whale came into view, its jaw agape, ripping at the squid. The froth was visible from the luminescence of the struggle. Other animals had gathered to watch the battle and to feed at the scraps that would be left over, a dinnertime call announced with flares and spotlights.

Directly before *Io*'s deck, riding the pressure wave of water flowing back as if it were breaking surf, swam a procession of hundreds of strange fish. They remained invisible in the darkness, except that along each body was a line of bright dots, like the portholes of miniature submarines.

"Those are the favorite food for big barracuda down here," Barney explained. "The lights keep them all in touch with one another, but it's also a great danger because it attracts killers. That's why they're hanging on to us as long as they can. To the predators down here, we're the biggest fish in the sea, and little fellows like these are too small for us to bother gobbling up. . . ."

A soft chime sounded. Barney took the message on the frequency code of the chip embedded in his skull. "Roger," he said, turning on a dim red glow in the deck. "I'll tell them."

"Captain Valmar asks us to be patient. Another hour or two. Would you like to return to your quarters to rest up?"

"And leave *this?*" Wilma exclaimed. "Not on your life, Admiral! I vote to stay. Buck?"

"I'm with you. Barney, if we could get some strong coffee up here, that would be great."

"No sweat. Oh, we're being joined by someone I've wanted you to meet for a while. Dr. Takashi Inoyue. He heads the overall strike teams of our undersea fleets. He's my second-in-command, and he'll be critical to us when we reach the Chilean strongholds. Let me give you a thumbnail sketch of him."

The coffee came first, and with it three small vials of the special drink Barney espoused as "good for the heart and soul." By the time they'd finished the vials and were sipping coffee, Barney had begun his brief on Inoyue. "First, he's small. Don't let that mislead you. He's built like spring steel, and he's a superb athlete. He has to be to carry out the research he's done in the oceans. For several years, he headed our underwater demolition teams—much like the SEALS of your day, Buck. In fact," Barney said after a long pause, "we were the lead team."

Wilma studied the dark face in the red gloom. Admiral Barney was many things to her, but she'd never thought of him as a skilled special warfare killer. You never really know the people you think you know best, she sighed to herself.

"The most amazing thing Takashi did," Barney went on, "was to modify his own body. He worked with our best medical scientists and genetic engineers. He had his whole blood system, his oxygenation, altered to approximate that of animals like seals and whales. They can't breathe underwater, but their blood system is tremendously enriched with oxygen, so that they can store up enough oxygen in their bloodstream to remain underwater for an hour or more. That's why some of those creatures can dive to four thousand feet or better. On top of that, he spent years studying the recordings and behaviors of the small-toothed whales when they were communicating. He got so he could mimic the sounds of dolphins and orcas, as well as pilot whales and similar creatures. He'll swim out to sea and go underwater, and after he's sounded off, there's a whole swarm of those animals circling about him like they're old friends. He's incredible.

"But there's another side to him. Takashi is mixed Japanese and Mongolian. He was so successful in raids and attacks against the Mongolian sub fleet that they assigned an entire special team to kill him. When he thwarted their attempts, sinking their subs and ships left and right, they resorted to going after his Achilles' heel. A Mongolian team captured his wife and flew back to their home country in a mountain redoubt. They said if he tried to rescue her, they'd kill her immediately, but if he switched sides, joined his blood heritage, so to speak, and joined the Mongols, he'd be welcomed with open arms, made a high-ranking officer, and he'd be reunited with his wife."

"Tough offer to turn down," Buck said.

"Especially if he really loved his wife," Wilma added.

"Accepting their offer would have violated everything he stood for," Barney went on. "So they began a long and slow torture of Chieko, his wife. First she was gang-raped, and then her skin was peeled off in strips while she was still alive and feeling everything. The torture went on for weeks, with Chieko dying piece by piece. Finally she went mad. It was her only escape. They cut her up while she was still alive. Arms, legs, ears, nose—"

"She was *alive* through all this?" Wilma gasped.

"She was. Mongol doctors kept her alive so she could see what happened to her limbs. They fed them to the pigs. Finally she willed herself to die. And she did."

Silence followed his description. "I told you all this because Takashi will kill Mongols every chance he has. You see, they videoholographed everything and then sent him the laser disc. He was uncontrollable after that. He was determined to kill a Mongol for every single minute she was in their hands and being tortured. So far he's notched more than two thousand lives on the belt he wears beneath his clothes. There's room for plenty more. One more thing. From that time on, Takashi has never once smiled or laughed. Don't expect warmth from him—just absolute loyalty to those who join him in fighting the Mongols."

Wilma felt a cold shiver run through her body. "I'm infinitely glad he's on our side."

"Barney, how does Takashi fit in with our heading for Atlantis?"

"In every way. If the Atlanteans are there, they spend almost all their time underwater. They appear to be allied with the Chileans, and the Chileans are allied with the Mongols, even though they once fought each other like wild men. That's just the way it is. Which mans there may be Mongols there, and certainly there will be Chileans who are partial to the Mongols, so to Takashi it's a perfect setup. Besides, he can get around underwater like a fish. The rest of it—" Barney shrugged— "well, let's wait and see."

They lapsed back into silence. No one said a word when Takashi Inoyue joined them. He slipped into the observation deck and took a seat in silence.

* * * * *

Around the southern edge of the South American continent, running at high speed, flanked and led by the neg subs, *Io* forged ahead steadily. The ocean bottom now showed signs of its violent past of continents battering at one another. Plateaus rose from the rugged bottom, their upper edges flattened and broad. To Buck, he might have been looking down from the air at Grand Mesa in Colorado, or the famed mesas rising in Venezuela, where from one such high plateau boomed the world's highest waterfall, Angel Falls, with a drop of more than three thousand feet.

But this was different in other ways. The bottom had the appearance of having been sliced by a huge cleaver tearing along sideways to create the hydromesas. It looked like some sort of strange liquid Monument Valley from the Amerigo southwest.

They continued to sweep over the ocean bottom, curving around the tip of the continent. The underwater terrain about them was shredded and fractured, as grotesque in its appearance as the blackened lava swirls of the Craters of the Moon in Idaho. The ocean bed was split and wrinkled, tossed with undersea mountains and cliffs, a cacophony of formations splitting into new cracks and fissures.

They received a signal from one of the lead neg crews. "Home Base, we've got some unexpected activity up here. We're seventy-four miles out in front, and there seems to be some sort of sub-surface volcanic eruption ahead of us. Neg One, over."

They all listened on the broad-wave frequency, their implants picking up the broadcast exchange between *Io*'s command center and the neg subs far ahead. Markham's voice was unmistakable.

"Roger that, Neg One. Have you got parameters yet?"

"Command, we're not sure of that. It appears that the ocean floor has a broad fissure running generally east and west, but it goes on for miles. It's like a volcanic vent, and there's thick black smoke pouring up from it. Visibility ahead of us is practically nonexistent, even with sweep-ranging light torps. All they show is boiling smoke. Over."

187

"Roger, Neg One. Any open fires or volcanic lava flow at the base?"

"Negative, Command. And I don't like it. We've got a fair sweep only with sonar. We have maximum possible penetration with the masers. The blue-green pattern cuts through somewhat, but I'm confused about the sonar. It's getting reflections like aluminum chaff dropped from planes to screw up radar, only right now whatever stuff is out there is playing havoc with our sonar."

"Neg Two, this is Command. Do you concur?"

"Affirmative, Command. And there's something else. This whole situation stinks. It's the heat patterns from the vents. They're consistent—*too* consistent. There should be variations in our thermal readings. There should be places where the sea floor is more broken up than others, but what we're seeing is almost a straight line."

Buck noticed Takashi Inoyue leaning forward, intent on every word, his body poised like a coiled snake.

"Neg Two, Command. Can you break that down some more?"

"Command, it's too clean. Everything is too orderly. No expected natural variations. We don't like it, and we've armed all weapons."

"Neg One, Command. You agree?"

"Yes, sir. We've done the same. There's something else. The sea life around here is acting real skittery—as if they're fleeing from something."

Captain Valmar came on the frequency. "Do I get the impression that you feel what you're encountering isn't natural? Immediate response requested."

"Yes, sir. That's what we think."

Valmar's voice overrode all other radio activity. "Red Alert, all hands. Secure the boat. Battle stations, battle stations!"

Barney and Inoyue fairly leaped from their chairs and set off at a dead run for Command Center. Wilma started to leave, but Buck grabbed her wrist. "We'd only be in the way back there. Besides, between the observation hull and the holographic scenes, we can see as well as anybody."

"I feel naked sitting here," Wilma complained. "There's only that window between us and, well, whatever is out there."

"It's safe. If things do start coming apart, we'll put on the emergency suits. They're in those wall lockers to your left."

"But—"

"Quiet!" Buck hissed. He was listening to an exchange between Takashi Inoyue and Captain Valmar.

"I've had this experience before, Captain," he heard Takashi say. "It's not the Chileans. Give me a holomap projection, please. From fifty degrees latitude down to fifty-five degrees, coastal area of Chile." In seconds, the holoprojection flashed on the combat situation wall. Takashi pointed to the Archipelago De Los Chonos.

"That whole coastal area is a natural minefield. Without proper charts, you'd get lost in minutes. It's a labyrinth of the worst kind. And here"—he pointed to Isla Magdalena"—is a huge underground facility—subterranean rivers, enormous caverns, all blocked off by the mountains. It's a natural fortress."

"Are you saying it's not manned by the Chileans?" Valmar said quickly.

"Pirates."

"*What?*"

"Pirates," Takashi repeated. "Argentinian for the most part, some renegade Mongols, a mixture of Brazilians, other countries. Criminals who escaped in the confusion of battles. Anything that comes through this area by surface vessel is in danger of encountering so-called 'natural disasters.' The pirates—and they're all capable seamen and submariners—have a fleet of old-fashioned boats, all heavily modified. When something comes in range, they set off those volcanic smoke eruptions. Oil fires under pressure create a line of smoke that looks dangerous to cross. Let me have a robochopper view from above."

The scene switched. The robochopper video cameras showed the ocean surface ablaze with burning oil. "There's the trap," Takashi went on. "Ships, even cargo boats, coming in from the south run right into this barrier. The ships slow down. Same with the cargo boats. The pirates don't fire torpedoes or other weapons. All of their boats have short range, but they use a modification of the Chilean liquid-air drive. They have plenty of defenses—mostly smoke, fire, and confusion. Their boats have enormous barbed steel prows, and they ram whatever ships or boats come their way. Ram them, lock in tight, and take them to the inlets and islets that make up their defensive maze."

Barney's voice came in. "Only they never expected anything

like *Io*, I'll wager."

"I agree," Takashi said. "This boat has enough firepower, especially with the negs out there, to wipe out at least half their force."

"And slow us down some more," Barney broke in. "It seems we're losing sight of what this mission is all about."

"The admiral is right," Captain Valmar broke in. "But we just can't ignore them. They're likely to try to follow us, and I don't want a full-scale battle on our hands. The sounds will carry for thousands of miles—" She stopped and studied the wall projection of the Chilean coastline. "It's nine hundred miles north to Valparaiso, just east of Santiago. That's the main Chilean base. If they pick up a battle royal here, they'll be expecting us, and that could make a real mess for us. We've got to arrive there unannounced."

Buck's voice broke into the joint frequency. "Captain, Rogers here. Permission to come to the bridge. I have an idea about how to handle this without a fight."

"Make it quick, Colonel."

Buck and Wilma ran steadily to the bridge and combat center. Buck took a deep breath. Valmar wasted no time. "Let's have it, Colonel."

"Mister Inoyue, you said they use steel rams to capture ships?"

The Asian fixed cold eyes on Rogers. "Correct. Your point, please?"

"*Io* has a triple outer hull. That means we can isolate the interior from the outer two hulls. Is that right, Captain Valmar?"

"Yes."

"Can you set up a powerful electrical charge to the outer hulls?"

Valmar looked at Markham. "Yes, we can do that."

"Then why not use the negs out there to herd those enemy boats directly toward *Io*? Let them know how big we are—a prize bigger and richer than anything they've ever seen before. If they hold true to form, they'll ram us. Only this time they'll come in a major force. We're too big and heavy for one or two of their ships to handle, so it will be a concerted attack."

"Aha!" They turned to Inoyue. "The colonel is right! If we direct our electrical field to our outer hulls and they ram—"

"We'll be sending a tremendous jolt directly into their boats," Barney finished.

"And no explosions," Buck added.

Valmar turned again to Markham. "How long will this require?"

"Twenty minutes, sir. That will give us time to isolate all our machinery and the crew, just in case we get a backlash of the electrical current."

"Mr. Markham, make it so. Admiral Inoyue, kindly stay with Mr. Markham. Barney, you fill in anything we've forgotten." She looked at Buck and Wilma. "Permission to remain on the bridge."

She opened her communicator to the entire crew, explained the situation quickly, and ordered preparations made immediately. One of *Io*'s reactors would direct its entire energy output to turning the great submarine into a floating electric chair.

* * * * * *

"We've got to time this right. The negs can run around these pirate boats like they're standing still. They'll pursue the negs. I want *Io* ready to move into that smoke cloud. We'll need automatic buoyancy control from the thermal upwellings within the smoke. Start moving in now. Do everything you can to give those bandits a good target. I want them mean and hungry for the kill. Commence a steady pace into the smoke."

The operation went like clockwork. There's nothing easier than drawing in a hostile force whose main purpose is in pillaging and killing innocents. They're convinced they have a helpless prize on their hands, and Captain Valmar did everything to encourage that feeling.

The negs ran through the enemy submarines like the latter were wallowing in mud. Then just as quickly they slowed down, seemingly confused, and ran for safety—straight toward the boiling wall of smoke from the oil fires far below.

Io rolled from side to side as the submarine penetrated the oily upwellings. Under Captain Valmar's orders, *Io* emerged from the thick smoke, then appeared to make an emergency turn to plunge back into the roiling darkness.

The pirate subs came after *Io* like hungry sharks. Here was the perfect, plump target for the taking. Three boats came in

191

abreast, their ramming spikes extended, and slammed into the hull at high speed. The spikes penetrated the outer layer, then pushed forward to the second hull and closed the circuit for the electrical charge being generated by *Io*.

Blue-white lightning flared brilliantly in the dark sea, crackling violently as it pulsated about and through the enemy subs. Electricity surged through each of the pirate boats, electrocuting the crews. In seconds, it was over. Bodies stiffened, jerking wildly; they had no time to signal the other incoming pirate boats. *Io* put on a sudden burst of speed at full power; water drag ripped out the ramming spikes, leaving three lifeless pirate subs to begin their long final plunge to the bottom.

Again a sweep of enemy boats came in, and again Valmar controlled *Io* so as to present a helpless target. To all intents and purposes, she was a defenseless cargo carrier.

Three more pirate subs died in surging currents of lethal electricity and were subsequently shaken off to slide downward in their last voyage.

After twenty minutes, only four of the pirate boats remained. Their crews held off from attacking. No one answered their frantic calls for explanations. They couldn't access the frequency of *Io*'s transmissions with the negative buoyancy submarines cruising like great barracudas.

"Neg One and Two, this is *Io*."

"Two, go ahead."

"One. We're on, *Io*."

"Time to turn the tables. Can you track those enemy boats? There are still four of them out there."

"Roger, Command. They're in close enough for us to pick up their propulsion systems on strike sonar."

"Negs One, Two, this is Captain Valmar. You will attack the enemy boats, but not with weapons. No torps. Repeat, no torps or explosive charges. We've had a close look at these things, and they're old Chinese Long March models. They can't take much punishment. You will ram at three zero knots in the stern area. That should put their steering mechanisms out of commission and bust up those liquid-air-cycle drives as well. Exercise caution. Do not exceed three zero knots. Do you copy?"

"Yes, *sir!* It'll be our pleasure, sir. They're sitting ducks. We're going in now. . . ."

* * * * *

They gathered in the officers' mess with hot coffee all around.

"I have a feeling of deep satisfaction," Inoyue said quietly. "Those men were nothing but scum, preying on helpless people."

Barney was his usual ebullient self. "Not anymore they're not." He filled a bowl with steaming beef stew. "That sort of rhumba makes a man powerful hungry. Buck? Wilma?"

"I'm not really hungry, sir. Thanks, but I'll pass," Wilma replied. She was still thinking about the hundreds of men, and perhaps women, in the destroyed submarines. No matter how many battles she had seen or fought in, she couldn't shake her revulsion of bloodshed.

"What about you, Buck?"

"Pass the stew and the bread," he answered. "I'm hungry, and there's just enough time for a drink and a nap before we arrive off Valparaiso."

Captain Ardala held up her coffee mug. "On to Atlantis, gentlemen!"

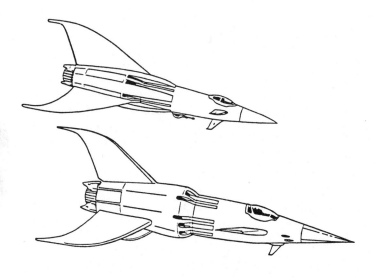

Chapter 18

Io eased northward along the western coastline of Chile at slow speed, taking advantage of every concealing swell of ocean bottom, island, and strong currents to reduce to a minimum any chance of early detection by the Chileans.

"You know what this reminds me of?" Black Barney remarked dourly to the group assembled on the bridge of *Io*. "Fabled crystal palaces and flying dragons that can kill an elephant with one swipe of their claws, then roast it for dinner with a blast of fiery breath. Can you imagine what that would have been like? Good old King Arthur and his sodden knights, traipsing around the countryside with a hundred pounds of armor, taking advantage of any unfortunate maiden they encountered. History has a way of showering nonsense with respectability, covering the foul deeds of miscreants with fables of honor and loyalty to some lofty cause. In the ancient times, I can think of nothing more stupid, more foul, more selfish, or more bloodthirsty than the so-called nobles of medieval Europe and their crusades against the so-called heathen of Islam. Bad enough that good King Richard led so many of his men to slaughter at the hands of the so-called primitives of the Mediterranean lands, but the darkest pages of all were written with the Children's Crusade!"

"Who turned you loose?" Ricardo Sanchez asked, then looked

sideways at his twin, Ricki Chavez. They were both enjoying listening to Barney, who held high degrees in history.

"Don't push me," Barney snarled. "Remember you're on board this boat by our good graces. But let's not pretend we're bosom buddies or that I have any inkling of affection for either of you. You're merely allies of convenience, and I doubt if I'll ever get the stink of you off of me."

Ardala Valmar moved in between them. "He asked a perfectly reasonable question, Admiral. These two haven't done a thing to earn such a barrage from you. What's turned you on like this?"

Black Barney leaned back against a console, his eyes still blazing with anger. "I'll tell you what brought it on, Captain," he said, still speaking in harsh tones but without his former blustery volume. "It's where we're going and the fact we're taking this garbage along with us. If there is an Atlantis, then we are about to encounter a people from a very distant past who, from everything I've heard about them, are basically a gentle folk. They possess no great military forces, no grand armies or navies. None of that. They're a people who came to this planet simply to escape the death of their own. I'd have liked to meet them in something other than a death machine."

"You mean this boat?" Valmar asked coldly.

"Yes! This boat," Barney answered. "I'm sorry, Captain, but it's just been festering inside me."

"We didn't dictate this mission, Admiral Barney," Valmar replied in her same steely tone. "Perhaps it might mitigate the situation if you remember that it is the Chileans who are the purveyors of weapons here."

"You don't know that," Barney growled.

"And you don't know otherwise," came Valmar's immediate rejoinder.

"Perhaps," Sanchez said with a smile, closely examining his fingernails, "the admiral might be less rigid if he examined his own history."

His twin joined in. "Don't get him started," Chavez said hastily. "Before you know it, he'll be moaning about the great slave trade. People like him lean that way at every opportunity."

"Baiting me won't do you one damn bit of good," Barney spat. "The fact is there isn't a single race on this planet that hasn't practiced slavery. White, black, brown, tan, red—we're all guilty."

He shrugged. "Just once I'd like to encounter another group with an open hand rather than a gun."

"That might be a good way to get your hand chopped off," Buck interjected. "Remember, Admiral, we all bleed the same color."

"Ah, a white man with a sense of color," remarked Sanchez. "My compliments, Colonel Rogers."

Inoyue raised a hand. "If I may say something?"

His quiet tone caught them by surprise. "Everything each of you says has merit. And you are all saying the same thing, only in different words. I honor my ancestors for their love of life, respect for the aged, and sacrifice for their country. I think of laughing children and beautiful flowers and poetry. But the same blood that flows through each of you has stained these memories. If we did not practice war and slavery on ourselves at different times, it is only because we did so against other people."

Ardala Valmar knew when it was time to put an end to a conversation. She recognized the signs of cabin fever and pent-up energy. The fight between Buck and Wilma and the Mongol bomber, and the unexpected slaughter of the pirates, had taken a high toll. This was the emotional aftermath. It came as no surprise to her. She had seen it happen aboard a submarine many times before, and now she needed to turn the acrimonious exchange to the issue at hand. Their goal was much too close to waste time in a war of words and useless accusations. "Enough!" she snapped. "I have a mission to perform. So do all of you. It has import that may exceed anything we can imagine, and I want you to save your energies for the task at hand."

Uncomfortable silence filled the bridge. Buck kept a close eye on Barney. He was a rogue of the old school, and to Buck, it was obvious he would have liked nothing better than to wrap his powerful hands about the necks of the drug-dealing twins from Venezuela. His great fists clenched and unclenched as he forced himself to calm down. He took a long shuddering breath.

"I apologize, Captain," he said abruptly. "Even admirals can go off half-cocked at times. And I extend my apologies to anyone I may have offended. It was not my intention."

Sanchez and Chavez acknowledged the apology with slight bows of their heads. They recognized the perfect right Ardala Valmar had to become angry and enforce her rules aboard her ship. Everyone backed off. The emotional tension eased as the minutes went by.

Yet Black Barney's words had struck a sensitive nerve. Barney really didn't care a fig who liked or disliked what he said or his attitude. He had fought all his life for the things in which he believed, and taking a back seat to nonsense wasn't in his makeup. Buck caught an icy stare directed by Takashi Inoyue at his lifelong friend and companion in combat. Whatever his reasons, Takashi is angry with Barney for sounding off. . . . Oh, well, I don't know what their rules are, but— Buck forced it from his mind. He was swept up in the growing excitement of the possibility of Atlantis being virtually at their fingertips.

* * * * *

Ardala Valmar's dislike of unrest among her crew on duty dampened the flames of argument. She strode about the boat for hours, her body language making it absolutely clear she would brook no more bickering, no matter what a person's rank or position. Quickly the crew settled down to the matters at hand.

Amidst the uneasy truce, the voice of Sally Cortez suddenly cut through the tension. "Captain, bridge reports our destination approximately forty miles due north."

"Any signs of underwater facilities?" Valmar said quickly.

"We're picking up something, sir, but we can't make out what it is. Coastal fortifications are consistent with our earlier aerial reconnaissance. But the water temperature is increasing steadily."

"Any major movement toward us?" Valmar asked.

"Nothing unusual, sir. All sensors and scopes indicate normal activity, but increasing in depth and scope."

"The Chileans are devious people," Ricki Chavez said. "We have dealt with them for many years. We have an operative within their community. She has the means to send a burst transmission from an isolated position in the mountains to one of our comsats, which in turn retransmits it back down to us. That includes the incoming code for this submarine."

Valmar looked sharply at Chavez. "Why haven't I heard of this before now?"

Chavez shrugged. "If there was anything important to report, you would not have missed it, Captain. It would be received by your own communications center. You would know it even before I did."

Valmar nodded. His words made sense, but she didn't like anything that might affect this mission being kept from her. "From now on, Mr. Chavez, you will inform me of any and all activities relative to this boat. Is that clear?"

"My apologies, Captain. I will do as you order. But I repeat that while I am aboard *Io*, I could not communicate beyond this vessel without your cooperation."

"Cortez," Valmar called out on the boat frequency. "Any changes?"

"No, sir. We are now thirty-one miles from destination."

Valmar made an instant decision. "Reduce speed to slow forward, ten knots. I don't want us barging in like some underwater battlewagon. That could easily be mistaken for an offensive move on our part."

"Captain, we are moving into Chilean waters. We've been at odds with these people for years. You can't assume a peaceful reception," Barney reminded her.

"I remind you, Admiral, the Chileans have also been at odds with the Mongols for an equal period of time." Valmar frowned. "I don't know why, but I have the strangest feeling we're being invited into their complex."

"That's what the spider said to the fly," Inoyue said quietly.

"Thank you for that slice of wisdom," Valmar retorted sarcastically. "But we are not spiders and flies. There's something strange going on here. It's almost as if I'm receiving a message of some kind that we're being invited."

"After what we did to those Chilean boats?" Barney was incredulous.

"When we had that encounter, Admiral, they didn't know who or what we were. Plain common sense would be to intercept us. And now that they know they've got a lot to handle, they'll be very careful about rubbing us the wrong way." She hesitated. "And I repeat what I said before. I do not want us to come barging in like we're on a mission of destruction."

"Captain?" Valmar turned to Buck. "You said you had a strange feeling that we're being invited into the Chilean complex. Have you ever felt anything like that before?"

"Never. It's a strange feeling, and it goes completely against the grain." On a sudden impulse, she stabbed a finger at Chavez. "You said you had an operative within the Chilean community."

"That is so," Chavez said, nodding.

"Tell me about her. Limit it to the salient points, if you please."

"Certainly. First, she is known to your high council, by name and mission."

Valmar glanced at Barney. "Admiral, you know about this?"

Barney shook his head. "Not a whisper."

"All right, Chavez, let's have it."

"Her name is Dawn Noriega. Mixed Spanish and Chinese ancestry. I regard her as a genius. She speaks many languages fluently and seems to have a sixth sense about her—knowing in advance what direction people will take. She is quite uncanny that way. She is loyal to Amerigo, but not because we are more appealing than other peoples."

"How do you mean that?" Valmar pressed.

Chavez smiled. "Noriega always seems to know which side of any conflict is the stronger and thus will prevail in the long run. She trusts us more than she does the Mongols. Perhaps they are more difficult to understand. Certainly many of them remain barbarians, while others, as you know yourself, are slothful. Your drug program works very well. The Mongols are at their best when they are fighting. Without war, they crumble. All this is known to Dawn Noriega. That is why she works with your country. The decision to keep her work as secret as possible was not made by her or my brother or me, but by Vice-President Hasafi herself."

"Why?" Valmar demanded.

"May I answer?" Inoyue spoke up. "We—that is, Japan—have suspected this for some time."

"On what basis?" Barney snapped.

"A secret that is not repeated remains a secret."

"It's the old security game," Buck offered. "Makes sense, too. It operates by the need to know. If you don't know something, you can't let it slip to anyone else."

"Damn it, Takashi," Barney said heatedly, "I asked you how you knew about an operative inside the Chilean camp. I don't want parables or homilies."

"We simply traced backward," Inoyue answered. "It is not so difficult, yes? We were aware of the supply of drugs to the Mongols. There must be a highway of information as well as supply. It took us more than a year, after we first began to suspect the situation, to accept that your country has what you call an 'inside plant.'"

"Or maybe," said Ricardo Sanchez, "you also have a plant on the inside, and that's how you found out."

"I am not aware of any such plant," Inoyue said smoothly.

"Captain Valmar." Buck's quiet tone caught their attention. They turned to him.

"Look at Wilma," Buck said softly.

They had pushed Wilma Deering from their thoughts during their exchange, but what they saw now commanded their attention. Wilma was crouched alongside a computer console, rocking back and forth gently on her feet. She held both hands to her head as if she were in pain.

Buck went immediately to her side. He held her gently. "Wilma? What is it?"

She looked at Buck with pain-filled eyes, her expression one of complete bewilderment. "There's—there's this pain inside my head," she said, forcing out the words.

"A headache? They can stop that in minutes," Buck told her, realizing even as he spoke she knew far more about the medical facilities aboard *Io* than he did.

"No. Not a headache. At first I thought I was hearing voices. It was . . . confusing. Then it became clearer . . . like a sense of warmth. Warm light, a gentle feeling."

"Anything specific other than that?"

She reached out with one hand to grip Buck's arm. "No. It's . . . like an emotion, but not anger or fear. It's like . . . when two people feel good about one another." Her eyes held steady with his. "Do you understand?"

Buck had a strong desire to hold her in his arms. He caught himself suddenly. In the middle of this crowd, that didn't make sense.

"Buck, do you have any ideas?" Valmar asked.

Buck helped Wilma to her feet and led her to a padded chair. She sat gratefully.

"Captain," Buck answered. "Wilma is an empath."

Valmar said nothing for several moments, then asked, "How strong is she?"

"Very."

Without turning away from Wilma, Valmar addressed Ricki Chavez. "Every time I ask you about this Noriega woman, you never finish your answer. Do it now, Mister, and be quick about it."

Chavez responded with a slight bow. "We believe she is perhaps forty or fifty years old, but she looks more like a woman in her twenties. She is most beautiful. She operates places of pleasure throughout the world—you understand what I mean?"

"A brothel is a brothel by any other name," Valmar snapped. "Get on with it."

"Those places are her safe havens. Her, ah, employees are also quite beautiful, and they are superb in their ability to give pleasure to their clients. Men would kill to spend one night with Dawn Noriega. But she holds men in contempt. Many men are endeared to her, so she is always kept protected."

"Chavez, all of it, damn you. Now!" Valmar said in an icy tone. "You leave anything out, Mister, and I'll have you thrown in irons."

Chavez paled. He was convinced that Captain Valmar knew much more than she had let on. "She is a triple operative," he added.

"What the hell does that mean?" Barney broke in. "Sounds like she's working for everybody."

"Precisely," Valmar snapped. "Go on, Chavez."

"The admiral is quite correct. She has never broken her word with your Vice President Hasafi, who is aware of all her contacts. "The Han—both the Chinese and the Mongol lords—believe she works for them as an agent deep within the workings of the Amerigo Council. She reports to the Han—mixing fact with fiction, of course. She also is accepted completely by the Chileans. I do not know what hold she has on these people, but as I say, she plays all sides. She derives her real pleasure from living on the razor's edge—that, and amassing power and great wealth of her own. My own opinion is that she is loyal only to herself."

"Thirty miles," came the voice of Sally Cortez from the helm.

"All stop," ordered Valmar. They could feel *Io* slow to a standstill.

"I know what she is." The voice was Wilma's, and once again they all turned to her. "It is not the Chileans she covets."

"Then what is it?" asked Valmar.

"I understand now," Wilma went on. "The pain is gone. I have been receiving messages." She looked from one person to another.

"Dawn Noriega," Wilma said slowly, "has joined with the Atlanteans."

They stared at her.

"You mean to say there *is* an Atlantis? Are you are certain?" Inoyue asked, his eyes wide.

"There is," Wilma said with confidence. "They have been trying to let us know we are in no danger from them, nor from the Chileans. You see, the Atlanteans control the Chileans. It was not always so, but it has been for more than a hundred years."

"How can you possibly know any of this?" Barney thundered.

Wilma smiled. "Dawn Noriega is a telepath."

Silence met her last statement.

Valmar broke the tension. "Barney, you know by heart every major engagement our navy has had for the last few hundred years. Right?"

Barney shrugged. "Of course. It's mindphase-imbedded in my memory. No problem with the implant for data recall."

"Have we ever fought an engagement with the Chileans at the base we are approaching? Or within a few hundred miles of this area?" Valmar pressed.

Barney stood silently for several moments, then shook his head. "No, never."

"Don't you find that unusual?"

"Unusual?" Barney snorted. "Hell, it's amazing. If we had really wanted to take out the Chileans, all we had to do was wipe out this base. The Chilean navy was ten times stronger before than it is now. They whipped the Mongols in one battle after another, but in the process they lost most of their own forces. And since then—" he paused to consider his own thoughts— "they've been a pain in the butt to us as well. We've had some scrapes, like we did on the way here. But, no, Captain, we've never attacked this base or fought any battles near here."

"How do you explain that?"

Barney stared. "I never thought about it."

"Wilma, can you explain what you just heard?" Valmar asked.

"Until several minutes ago, no. I didn't understand even an iota of all this. But since Dawn—and those with her—have been sending me the sensations I've related to you, believe I am beginning to understand. Aggression toward this particular base is blocked. The protection takes enormous effort, extreme energy. And it requires a *gestalt*—the efforts of many talented or special people concentrating on a single aim."

"You're telling us," Valmar said slowly, "that bringing together a group of these people, who may be telepaths—"

"They are," Wilma said quietly, totally confident.

"Assuming that this is so," Valmar went on, "then, by mental power alone, they have been able to thwart any plans to strike at this base."

"Yes." Wilma stood quietly, her hands clasped before her. She seemed apart from her own group, uncaring of their questions.

"Hold it," Barney said. "There's still another possibility. Buck, even in your time, nonlethal weapons were the big thing for the military. Powerful electromagnetic beams on the same brain frequency—twenty hertz—could confuse thousands of enemy soldiers. The soldiers lost their balance, couldn't concentrate, and were unable to fight while they were being beamed. We had the same equipment for a while, but we didn't fight many pitched land battles, so it was simply ignored. The point is, this planet itself generates a radio wave frequency that's the same as the brain—twenty hertz—so a signal sent out from generators is enhanced by the planet's own energy, and it carries for a long distance. We could be experiencing the same effect here, especially since we don't know what kind of generating equipment they may have."

"You should know better, Admiral," Wilma told him.

"What do you mean?"

"Wilma's right," Buck stepped in. Your EM frequencies won't work underwater—not for any distance, anyway. I'm talking a mile or two as maximum range."

"Captain?" Barney turned to Valmar. He didn't need to voice his question. If anyone knew energy levels in the sea, it was Ardala Valmar.

"He's right," she said. "It can't be an EM band."

"We're getting nowhere," Takashi Inoyue broke in. "We bicker

among each other, and this woman"—he pointed to Wilma—
"purports to tell us why. Doesn't it occur to you that this is the
chance to pursue the Chileans in their home base? That this is
the opportunity to wipe out their seat of power, once and for all?
You are thinking like children, not military people!"

"Wilma." Buck had to repeat her name twice before he could
break through the confusion she was feeling. She turned slowly
to face Buck.

"Why aren't the rest of us sensing or feeling what you're
receiving?" Buck asked.

"Damn good question," Barney said. "There's been way too
much talking instead of acting."

"Deering is an empath," Valmar broke in. "That much we
know. She is a sensitive, able to home in on the emotions and
feelings of others. The council has employed her talent many
years in just this way."

Inoyue moved toward Wilma and stood facing her. "Are you
also telepathic?"

Wilma smiled. "No. I cannot, read minds. My talent—I do not
even have a name for it—is empathy. If someone is feeling pain, I
also sense that pain. I share it. If they are troubled, I, too, am
troubled. If there is fear, I will sense the fear. If they are joyous, I
receive impressions of well-being and happiness. But I cannot
read the thoughts of any other person," she repeated.

"But this Noriega woman, Dawn—are you certain she is telepathic?" he pressed.

"I am not certain of anything," Wilma replied. "I have felt
these thoughts, I have received . . . word pictures—no, not words.
Impressions. I sense a feeling of arms held wide open in welcome
emanating from this complex. Is it Atlantis? I do not know. I feel
that it is. That is the best I can do."

"Captain Valmar?" Buck said suddenly. She turned to face
him.

"Sir, something very much out of the ordinary is happening
here. Wilma is acting as sort of an antenna, and somehow she
receives signals along a wavelength we can't even identify. But
the rest of us also are feeling something . . . something decidedly
mental. But if I may say so, Captain Valmar, indecision has
killed just as many people as aggression has."

His words seemed to galvanize Valmar. She shook her head

sharply from side to side as if casting out any mental intrusions. Her hands closed into fists. Buck studied her carefully. She's digging her nails right through the skin of her palms, he noticed.

Valmar's voice rang out like a clang of steel upon steel. "All hands!" she snapped, her command carrying to every member of her crew. "Condition Red. I repeat, Condition Red. All defensive shields and systems up and ready."

She looked at Barney, who rewarded her with a cold smile and a nod.

"Battle stations! All weapons at the ready. All warheads activated. One-third ahead. Probes out, unarmed."

"Captain, may I recommend—"

"Forget the diplomacy, Rogers. Say it."

"Leave all our lights on. Everything. The probes, this boat . . . light everything up like a Christmas tree. People don't hide in the light."

"Your point is well taken," Valmar replied. She gave the order for every light to be turned on to maximum brightness.

"Deering!" Valmar turned to Wilma. "Listen to me carefully, Major. And get that wimpy look off your face! You're an officer and a member of this crew on a mission. Do you read me?"

Wilma seemed jolted by the harsh tones.

"Yes, sir," she replied, strength returning to her voice.

"Markham! Follow my orders. Confirm."

"Markham here. Yes, sir, go ahead."

"Activate emergency plan Marblehead immediately. Confirm activation."

They stood silently. What the hell is Marblehead? wondered Buck. One look at Black Barney told him the admiral knew. The admiral didn't like what he heard, but he was obviously in agreement.

Markham's voice came back within a minute.

"Captain, Markham here. Confirm plan Marblehead activated and primed. You have the firing sequence. Please confirm."

"Confirmed, Mister Markham. Remain on standby."

"Yes, sir."

"Major Deering." Valmar's voice was ice. "Listen to me carefully. I—" She held up a hand. "No, wait. Markham, send off the signal to the council, direct attention of President Logan. 'Status Marblehead, and we are continuing our program and will make every attempt to sustain peaceful contact. Chance of finding Atlantis is—' " Valmar looked at Wilma—" 'nine zero percent. Confirmation or refutation the moment we are certain.' Get that sent off immediately."

"Yes, sir."

"Now, Major Deering, I don't know if this Noriega person is really telepathic, so I don't know if she can read your mind, or simply send messages like those you've been describing.

"The closer we get to the base," Wilma said quietly, "the stronger the signal. But even now the messages are sometimes confusing."

Valmar's impatience showed. She rested an elbow on a control console. "What language is she using? How is she speaking to you?"

"I don't sense a language. Scenes, faces, seascape . . . strange faces, white, faces of pure white, with large green eyes . . ."

"Noriega speaks many languages," Valmar broke in. "Her primary language is Spanish. You also are fluent in many languages, including Spanish. Is this correct?"

"Yes."

"Have you concentrated on Spanish?"

"Eight languages, Captain. But I have no recognition of this one."

Valmar was becoming impatient. "What is the language of the Atlanteans?"

"They . . ." Wilma's brow furrowed in concentration. "Captain, I get no indication of a language—spoken, I mean. They read the thoughts of one another, paint mental pictures, including schematics, technical details. As fast as these are thought by one person, any other member of their race can read the same thoughts."

"Listen to me carefully, Wilma. You've just described an immense power. Can they plant ideas in our minds without our being aware that those thoughts may not have originated within ourselves?"

Wilma hesitated, holding both hands to her head. She winced as if in pain, then nodded slowly. "Yes, they can," she said in a half-whisper.

"Have they been doing this to us?" Valmar asked sharply.

"No, sir."

"How in blazes can you know that?" Barney shouted.

"I don't *know*. I just *feel*. . . ."

A wan, sad smile came over Wilma's face. They looked at her, startled, as tears formed and slid down her cheeks.

"Child, what's wrong?" Valmar asked, gently this time.

"They will tell you soon. But there is no danger to us unless . . ."

"Unless what?" Valmar demanded.

"Unless we bring it upon ourselves. I don't know what that means."

"It could bloody well mean a hundred things," Barney broke in again. "Captain, we're going around in circles! May I recommend we go right in?"

"We are, Admiral."

Markham's voice came into their receivers. "Captain Valmar, we have first visuals from the probes."

"What do we have?"

"Sir, there's an enormous depression in the sea floor ahead of us, at least three thousand feet deep, maybe ten or fifteen miles in diameter. A great circle. And there's some structures in there. We can't get details. The probes go in only so far, and then they're up against some kind of an invisible wall. They're stopped dead."

"Stand by, Markham." Valmar turned back to Wilma and nodded to Buck.

"Major, will they allow you and Colonel Rogers to penetrate that shield or whatever it is? You'll go unarmed, wide open, as naked as jaybirds to avoid any possible misinterpretation of your actions as hostile."

Wilma closed her eyes, concentrating. Suddenly she opened them wide and nodded. "Yes, they will."

"Cortez, stand by with a two-man probe . . . glassite bow, full circumference, hydrostats for propulsion. No weapons of any kind are to be aboard. That includes sidearms. I want that probe absolutely clean."

"Yes, sir. Right away."

"Rogers, apparently the people up ahead, Atlanteans or whatever they are, haven't been painting any pictures in your head. Is that correct?"

"I haven't felt or sensed a thing, Captain."

"Good. You'll handle contact with us. Your probe has an aft violet maser that can send radio signals for at least fifty miles, which should be considerably more than you'll need. Stay on open line with us. Report as you go along."

"Yes, sir."

"Rogers, I have to say this. You are not required to undertake this assignment. You're here as a volunteer, and—"

"Captain, I wouldn't miss this for the world," Buck said with a grin.

"Commander Cortez! Report here immediately, escort Deering and Rogers to the probe, and launch at once."

* * * * *

They eased ahead of *Io* with well-oiled precision. Buck and Wilma were strapped in to the side-by-side control seats, an instrument and data panel shining softly before them. Buck needed little more than a quick survey of the controls to figure out how to handle the probe. Everything was simple and reliable. Propulsion came from tekron batteries that would propel the little sub for at least five hundred hours, much more than they required. Buck checked the maser communications system. It was transceiving perfectly.

"Wilma, turn on every light this thing has on it."

"Right." She snapped down control switches. A maser strobe flashed brightly atop the sub, at the stern, and beneath it. The forward strobe was left off so as not to interfere with their visual acuity.

"Does this thing have a sonar pulser?"

"Yes. Do you want it on?" Wilma asked.

"If we had flags and skyrockets, I'd be using them as well," Buck told her. "I want no doubts left that we're making a perfect target of ourselves. No use in getting these people upset."

"They're aware of what we've done."

"How far are we from that circular depression Markham reported?"

"Eight miles. Our speed is a steady thirty knots. We're less than fifteen minutes away."

Before them, stretching away until visual sight was lost, moved an immense array of undersea life. Huge plants rose up like sunflowers, swaying in the ocean currents. Buck had never seen so many fish, most of them recognizable. Others were strange, unlike anything he'd ever seen.

Far ahead the ocean began to change. A dim glow appeared, growing steadily brighter as they forged ahead. "That's their city," Wilma announced. "The lights are to welcome us. They've lit up their city to maximum brightness, just as we've done with *Io* and the probes." The huge submarine was some ten miles behind them now.

"They're sending out an escort," Wilma said. "I have a picture of something bright, with people inside. It will lead us into the city."

Within minutes, her mental image materialized before them. It was another submarine, but obviously it was never meant for conflict. A material that looked like glassite covered the entire outer structure of the vessel. Interior lights showed the propulsion system, bridge, and long viewing sections on each side of the submarine. The sub swung around to one side, always visible to Buck and Wilma, then took up a position directly ahead of them.

"They want us to follow them," she said.

Buck reported this new development to *Io*, then concentrated on following their escort. Before them, the lights grew ever brighter and larger. Their escort began a steady descent, with Buck following.

"Looks like we're going into that circular area Markham described," he said.

"It's their city."

"City?" he echoed.

"They'll turn on their other lights, which will illuminate everything."

"Another message?"

"It's like a film now, a video or hologram. Everything is three-dimensional."

"We have a few moments before we get inside, Wilma. Those orders that Valmar gave Markham . . . do you know what Marblehead is?"

"No. I never heard of it before."

"Well, it sure fired up Admiral Barney. He knows."

Wilma shrugged.

"And Takashi Inoyue knows, too. Something about what he heard yanked his chain pretty good."

"Barney and Inoyue have been together a long time. Perhaps

they both share the same information."

"Yeah. Maybe. And pigs have wings."

"I don't understand."

"Never mind. It's not important now, and—"

Several swimmers came into view, wearing globe-shaped helmets and pressure suits. They crossed beneath and at an angle to their sub."

"It's a Chilean work party."

"A what?"

"Workers. They do the maintenance here at—" her voice dropped to a whisper—"here at Atlantis."

More lights appeared, flooding the ocean. "They've illuminated the whole area," Buck radioed back to *Io*. "I've never seen anything like it. They're not floodlights or anything like that. The whole ocean is light. It's like daylight above the surface. The light comes from everywhere, as though the water itself is glowing."

Wilma laughed. "It is glowing—the ocean, I mean. The water itself is producing the light."

Atlantis came slowly, steadily, breathtakingly into view. Buck was speechless. There was something so totally alien about it that he was captivated. He'd never seen anything like it—an entire city, thousands of feet beneath the ocean, all of transparent material, gleaming, dazzling with color.

As they continued their descent, he saw something else. If this was the fabled Atlantis, it was not of earthly origin, nor was this undersea metropolis in good condition. Rubble formed talus slopes along the base of the spires and lay in odd clumps about the ocean floor.

The overwhelming impression was one of decay.

"How do we make contact with . . . with the Atlanteans?"

"They are coming to us now."

Dim forms, ghostlike and moving slowly, rose from the depths.

"They're swimming in open water," he reported to *Io*. "Bipedal, like us. But they're . . . white. I mean white like the color of snow or ice. No pink. Just white. They have large eyes, but no pupils. . . ."

He nudged Wilma. "How can they stand the pressure?"

"Like all sea life. Internal pressure is equal to outside. The same way we withstand the pressure of air at the surface."

Buck understood. Take a man out to the fringes of space, where the pressure was but a fraction of sea level, and without pressurization he'd explode like a watermelon dropped from a mile high onto concrete.

"Think of them as albinos," Buck radioed. "They swim with little effort. Their bodies seem extremely supple and fluid, like sharks cruising. I'll bet my bottom dollar they aren't terrestrial. In many places, their city is crumbling. There's some serious problems here. I'm so close now I'm getting impressions like Wilma was receiving before aboard *Io*."

"Describe the feelings," Valmar asked.

"It's . . . not comfortable. I can feel their pain . . . and these people are tired. Very tired. There's a sense of futility, of an ending to everything."

"That could be deliberate," Valmar said, "to get you off your guard."

"Whatever the reason, I don't believe we need to be on guard. It's as if they're glad we're here. They want to share their history with us before . . ." He let out a cry of pain. Wilma had cradled her head in both hands. She was weeping.

"Rogers! What is it?"

"I can't believe this. They're in my mind. And they're . . . they're waiting to . . ."

His voice faded away. He felt a crushing, terrible sadness.

"Rogers! Report!"

"They're waiting to die. There are hundreds of them around us now, swimming alongside us, inviting us down."

"*Io*, this is Deering. We're being taken to a pressure dome. Once we're inside, they'll evacuate the water and establish normal air pressure and oxygen for us. I—"

Her voice was cut off as the little submarine rocked sharply. A sound like deep thunder rolled through the sea, alarming the albino figures about them.

"We've just felt the shock wave from a seaquake," Buck called in immediately. "From what I can determine, they've been having a lot of these lately. That would explain the debris and decay in the city itself. *Io*, there's nothing here that even smacks remotely of military installations. Maybe Wilma can get some more from them."

She turned to Buck. "They'll explain once we're inside the pressure chamber. They've told me . . . somehow . . . that they are in danger. So are we. And *Io*, too. There's something else. I'm having difficulty understanding what they mean . . . it's something about *Io*. . . ."

Spell it out, Deering!"

"They'll explain," she said, "after we're in the chamber so we can talk . . . no, not talk. Communicate directly with our minds. We're almost to the building with the pressure chamber. As soon as we can, we'll call back and report. But they . . . they say the mountains will fall soon. I'm not sure what that means. Deering, out."

Wilma shut off their radio. "I'm sorry, Buck. They say there's no time to lose. We must meet with them now."

Buck saw a ring of lights surrounding an oval entrance to a long chamber. He eased the sub inside, stopped their forward motion, and they settled to a flooring. Behind them, they heard a huge door closing, and the shriek of air pressure resounded through he sub's hull. All about them the water drained away. Then they were approached by several of the strange people. "They're asking us to come out now," Wilma told Buck.

* * * * *

They sat around a large oval table. The surface was slick stone, polished and cool to the hand. Before them were six of the albino people. The sense of sadness was almost overwhelming. Everyone looked up sharply as a roll of thunder passed through the pressure chamber. Several sharp impacts followed.

"Quick, Buck. Take their hands in yours."

He felt strangely calm and safe with these people. He reached out his hands and grasped their slender, white fingers. Six fingers, he noted.

They're looking straight ahead rather than at us, he noted, as if they're not seeing. . . . My God, they're blind. All of them!

"Wilma, I—"

"Yes, I know," she broke into his words. "They've been blind for centuries. They do not have speech. They did, long ago, but it became unnecessary. They see through the eyes of others. Through the Chileans. The animals . . . dolphins, seals, whales.

212

They enter other creatures' minds and see through their eyes. Buck . . . empty your mind. Please. Just let your thoughts go . . . you'll understand. . . ."

He closed his eyes and relaxed totally. Pictures came clearly to him. A beautiful world floating in space. Blue and white and green, like Earth . . . but not Earth. Splendid cities, with people in harmony with their world. Swiftly the scenes changed. He felt a rushing upward from the planet, like hurtling through space. He was staring at a star, angry, as hurling streamers of violent fire shot outward. The star seemed to tremble as if wracked by terrible internal forces.

The planet again. The same star seen from the surface of the world. People suffering. Heat. Oceans steaming and boiling away. Volcanic eruptions spewing molten lava across hills and fields. Quakes . . . buildings toppling.

Another scene. An enormous spaceport of the future. A huge craft, with people hurrying to get inside. The violent eruptions increased. He was inside the gigantic spaceship, looking down through an observation port. The world beneath him seemed to fall away as the great ship lifted silently through turbulent clouds and lightning-ripped skies.

Then he saw stars through the port. The stars became blurred streaks of light, turning yellow, orange, then red as the spaceship reached some enormous speed. The stars winked out. Blackness.

Time . . . countless years. Most of the people were in some sort of suspended animation. . . . Then the stars came out again. Far ahead, he saw a single yellow sun. Deceleration. A planet orbiting the sun coming closer and closer. All forward motion stopped.

In his mind, Buck looked down upon Earth perhaps fifty thousand years before as the huge vessel lowered gently to a mountainous countryside. There were verdant valleys and fields, with an ocean beyond. The Andes in Chile . . . the spaceship on the ground, people ecstatic with their new world.

But not for long. The radiations from the star were strange, unforeseen. People stumbling, holding their hands to their eyes.

It rushed through his mind like a silent, turbulent wind. They were going blind from the sun. Frantic, they raised their ship again, drifting off the coastline, and descended into the ocean. Machines brought from the ship gouged out the deep circular depression. Buildings going up. They learned to modify their blood and oxygen systems so that, like seals and other sea mammals, they were able to enrich the oxygen in their blood until they could remain underwater for an hour or more at a time.

They could not live on the surface. They needed the protection of the ocean to shield them from the radiation of their new sun. But they needed food grown on land as well as raw materials during the many years that passed.

During this period of acclimating to a new life, they developed latent telepathic abilities. Since they were blinded, nature provided through direct mind contact what it had taken from them. They learned to reach the minds of the higher animals, to "see" through the eyes of other creatures.

A new creature entered upon the scene, and men began to flourish across the land. As the aliens drifted across the countryside in antigravity machines, resplendent in the sky, then plunged back into the sea, the legends began.

There was a hidden civilization beneath the sea. Rumors of a powerful nation, of a magnificent city that had slipped beneath the waves, spread throughout the world. The land came to be known as Atlantis. Navies and armies began to search for the fabled city, the unseen land. The people from space came to be regarded as gods. The natives of Chile were pressed more and more into service as the Atlanteans found returning to the surface ever more dangerous.

Surface radiation had taken its toll. The skin of the Atlanteans became as white as chalk. Their brief forays onto the surface, sometimes witnessed by Earth people, gave rise to stories of aliens landing from space—but no one knew when or how long they had been here.

But the Atlanteans were slowly but steadily dying out. Their birthrate fell steadily. Fewer and fewer children were born, until finally the aliens had become sterile, weak. Natural disasters took their toll. Deep undersea storms, earthquakes, and volcanic eruptions pounded the city.

* * * * *

The sense of sadness became like a physical weight on Buck and Wilma. In their minds, they saw the extinction of the Atlanteans. Shock waves rumbled through the sea. A powerful earthquake was in the making. The Andes would crumble, tear apart. Volcanic vents would burst open, and the mountains would slide into the sea . . .

. . . onto the fabled nation of Atlantis, sealing its doom. They were tired and were ready to accept their death.

If their guests were to live, they must leave immediately and head with all possible speed for the open sea, far from where the mountains would crack like brittle clay and where torrents of blazing rock would pour from the coastline. The sea floor itself would break open to spread molten magma across the ocean floor.

There was a final series of scenes, of Buck and Wilma entering their submarine, sealing themselves inside. The pressure chamber filled with water, the entryway opened, and they returned at once to their great undersea craft, which in turn must make all possible speed due west. Not even *Io* could withstand the violence that was about to come.

* * * * *

"*Io*, Rogers here."

"We read you, Rogers. What's happened with you two, anyway?"

"No time for explanations, *Io*. Listen to me. The Andes are about to undergo a tremendous earthquake. They're going to tumble into the ocean from the Chilean coastline. It can happen any time now. We're coming back as fast as we can. When we're aboard, you've got to go to head due west at full speed."

"That's an awfully big pill to swallow all at once, Rogers."

"It's real, damn it!"

"Give us something to go on, Rogers," Captain Valmar came back. "We can't just change plans like—"

"Maybe this will convince you, then," Buck broke in. "We have a message for you. They told us you would understand immediately."

"Spit it out, Colonel."

"They told us, in pictures, of an enormous explosion, a fireball within the sea at least thirty or forty miles wide. They said for you to disarm Marblehead, whatever that means."

"*They* told you that?"

"Affirmative."

Aboard *Io*, Captain Valmar looked with shock and disbelief at Admiral Barney. "Blacky . . . there's no way, no way at all, they could know about Marblehead! Rogers and Deering don't have even a suspicion of what we were prepared to do!"

She returned to communicate with the probe. "Rogers, do you know what that was they showed you—that fireball?"

Buck glanced at Wilma. She gestured for him to continue. "I can guess, Captain. If something went wrong when we got to Atlantis, if they were an armed enemy ready to do battle with us or destroy or capture *Io*, you would detonate a very high-yield hydrogen bomb you have aboard. My guess is a hundred megatons or more."

"Buck, Barney here. What about that woman, Dawn Noriega? Was she there? Is she telepathic?"

"She was there, Barney. And she's for real. Call her telepathic or psychic or whatever you want, but there's no question that she's for real."

"Buck, you're certain of that?"

"I sure am, Barney. She stayed with the Atlanteans to be taught by them. That's why she's so good at sending mind pictures."

"But . . . if everything you say is true, she'd die with the Atlanteans!"

"No, she won't. She's in the probe with us. And she's scared."

* * * * *

They brought the small probe back aboard *Io*. The moment the boat was sealed again, Captain Valmar stood at the helm.

"Commander Cortez, maximum speed, full ahead, course two seven zero degrees. Let's get the hell out of here."

Six hours later, the mountains came down.

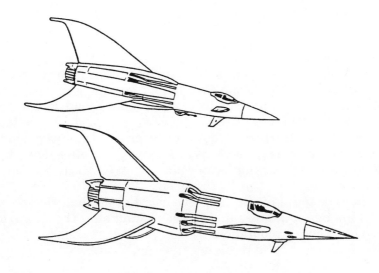

Chapter 19

"Buck, will you please stand still? If I'm ever to make you presentable to the High Council, you've got to stop squirming like a child trying to get out of a visit to the dentist." Wilma smiled as she needled Buck, who stood uncomfortably before a glowing three-panel mirror.

"Damn it, Wilma, I thought I left all this folderol behind me," he grumbled. "In fact, I left it behind me more than four centuries ago. You'd think that in all this time civilized people would have gotten rid of all these fancy costumes in favor of some comfortable clothing." He glared at his reflection. "I look like a bloody popinjay."

"Whatever that is," Wilma said, ignoring his tirade. "You're being made a high officer, someone who will report directly to the council. I don't even know what your rank will be."

"As if it matters," he groused. "No airplane ever knew the rank of the pilot behind the controls."

"Oh, be quiet. This isn't a cockpit you're going into. You're being honored—promoted—and from what I hear, Commodore Kevin Kane is going to personally request that you be assigned to his command."

Buck half-turned, his interest suddenly piqued. He pictured in his mind the brutish-appearing, stocky man built like a keg of nails. Kane would have been right at home in a wrestling ring, but there was no doubting his reputation as a master tactician and strategist.

"Isn't he the head honcho for space operations?" Buck asked.

"If 'honcho' means the commander of space-ops, yes," she replied. "He's been in the military ever since he enlisted in the space force when he was sixteen. They would have thrown him out when they learned his age, but he passed his entry exams with a perfect score. There was no stopping him after that. He's also known to favor the Latin countries in Central and South America."

Buck snapped his fingers. "I've heard about that. He named both his headquarters and his command ship the *Admiral Vespucci*. Quite a reputation."

"He's as crazy and reckless as he is brilliant."

"You served under him?"

Wilma nodded. "Uh-huh. Stand still! I've almost got this. . . ." She stood back to examine his reflection in the mirror. "You'll do."

"Did you serve under Kane?" Buck pressed.

"Under and with him. I got to be close friends with Nanette."

"Who's that?"

"His wife. She's a full commander, the best code and communications expert in the business. She's broken every code the Mongols have ever used. She's also learned the language of the Tiger Men."

Buck gave a blank look. "Who and what are the Tiger Men?"

"They were the dominant race on Mars."

He stared at Wilma. "Girl, I'm miles behind you. A dominant race on *Mars?* And I believe you said they *were*—you know, like past tense—the dominant race on that planet. What are they? Aliens? I thought the only aliens were from Atlantis, and they're a page in history now."

"I couldn't begin to tell you in two minutes."

"Then take two hours," Buck cajoled. "Take two days if you have to!"

"There's no time now. It will take us ten minutes to reach the council chambers if we start right now, and we're due there in eleven minutes. Buck, please don't kept the council waiting for us!"

"I want to know about Mars."

"You will . . . from the council itself."

"Oh . . ."

They went quickly to the terminal droptube, where they plummeted several hundred feet before they eased to a stop. Then their bullet-shaped car rotated and slid into the antigrav force field of the inner-city tubeway. Wilma looked directly into a computer eyescope for retinal identification and clearance. "Cent—" she began, then stopped. "Buck, sit down, will you?"

An electronic voice sounded softly. "Please repeat your instructions, Wilma Deering."

"Central, please. Nonstop."

"Central nonstop confirmed. Commencing in five seconds," the voice answered.

"Wilma, why do you say 'please' to a computer? You're not talking to a person."

Before she answered, the overhead and side lights of the vacuum tube became a blur as they shot into motion.

"Perhaps not. But this particular computer and I have been talking back and forth for years. She—I guess it's a she; sure doesn't sound grouchy, like you—recognizes small things about me. A pattern, you can call it. After a while, the manner of speech, innuendos, tone, volume—and courtesy—is in the security memory banks, and Diedre—"

"Who's Diedre?"

"The computer, silly. Who else did you think I was talking to?"

"You call the computer by name? Sort of personal, isn't it?"

"Of course. If I called her Sally, she'd know something was wrong, and security would block any further movement. Besides," Wilma laughed, "you do the same thing."

"I do?" he said dubiously.

"I've heard you! When you're flying, you talk to your airplane. You say things like 'Come on, baby' or 'Atta girl,' and you pat the instrument panel and call her 'Sweetheart.'"

Buck kept a poker face. "Well, that's because the airplane hears me, and she understands. You get better performance that way. I'm not talking to some dumb computer." He stopped and looked about him, eyes wide.

"Nothing personal, Diedre," he added to the walls of their car.

"No offense taken, Colonel Rogers," came the reply, and Wilma and Buck broke out laughing.

They eased into their station at Central, and the door slid

open with a sibilant hiss. As they left the car, Buck paused and patted the backrest of his seat. "Nice job, girl," he said and went into the station with a grin on his face.

* * * * *

Buck hated pomp and circumstance. He'd always detested it when he received medals for combat missions, when he was feted "in the old days" as an outstanding aviator, or when he set new flight records. It was easier flying through a thunderstorm than standing stiffly before hundreds of people, lights glaring in his eyes while he searched his mind for something to say that wouldn't be insipid. The old discomfort came back full force as he and Wilma entered the waiting room before entering the council chamber. He felt like stiff cardboard in his dress uniform, which actually fit remarkably well. Wilma had explained that the material was thermal-sensitive and would adapt to his body weight and shape. Black jacket, fitted gleaming gold scarf, dark gray shirt, silver lapels, a nine-pointed iridescent star over his left breast. He liked the feel and heft of the thick studded belt, but he'd bet a dollar to a doughnut it wasn't real leather—more likely it was lizard or sharkskin. Best of all were his boots, engineer style, high on the ankle. When he first slipped into the boots they felt clumsy and uncomfortable. Several minutes later he felt he was wearing slippers of amazing comfort.

"They're designed the same way as your flight suit," Wilma explained. "Thermal and sensitive to the shape of your foot. They actually adapt to fit your foot—uh, feet." She giggled. For the moment, he didn't react to her gentle humor. It wasn't that long ago when his legs were mangled flesh and bone. Amazing the things that brought back to his mind the medical miracles these people had performed on him. Wilma mistook the quiet smile on his face as response to her words, but Buck was smiling in silent gratitude. Suddenly the uniform didn't feel so stiff and formal. Ease up, fella. They're paying you honors. . . .

* * * * *

Buck stood, with Wilma by his side, before the council members. He had already studied holograms from every different angle possible of their faces. He didn't want to go through any last-moment memory searching to respond to whomever might be addressing him or asking questions.

Behind the curving black stone counter—cut, he had been told by Wilma, from the nucleus of a comet and brought back here to Niagara—sat the Supreme Council. From left to right, the council consisted of Benjamin Black Barney himself, in a uniform smothered with medals and ribbons, a strange, glowing rank insignia on his shoulders, and a form-fitting skull headpiece of gleaming metal. Buck almost laughed out loud; he had a sudden memory of a motion picture based on Camelot in which the magician, Merlin, had worn a headpiece identical to that worn by Admiral Barney.

To Barney's left was the imposing figure he recognized immediately as President Grenvil Logan, leader of the seven-state federation that made up Amerigo, elected to the presidential seat by the leader of each of those states. Buck recalled that Logan often identified himself wryly as the quintessential human mongrel, a product of seven different and distinct races. He also, Buck recalled from his studies, still practiced in private certain ancient sorceries and rites. They were the scandal of the government, but no one knew for certain whether Logan believed in his alchemy or simply tweaked his opposition in his own particular way.

He recognized Charlotte Hasafi immediately, the dark-haired, hawk-nosed woman reputed to have extraordinary skills in political matters—and an I.Q. that went clear off the charts. She smiled at him quietly, sensing his discomfort with the moment.

A side door to the chamber opened. Filing into the room and taking seats on the dais were several officials and officers assembled specifically for this encounter.

First came Commodore Kevin Kane, Commander of Military Deepspace Corps, who had already befriended Buck and supported him openly to his own following among Amerigo's armed forces. His fiercely devoted supporters throughout Central and South America considered the naming of Kane's command spaceship *Admiral Vespucci* a clear signal that Kane accepted those hundreds of millions of people as brothers-in-arms. Buck had already learned that Kane's wife, Nanette, was the leader of Amerigo's encrypting and communications center. Buck did not question why Nanette Kane was absent. None of my business, anyway, he thought briefly.

He was caught completely by surprise to see Dawn Noriega occupy the seat next to Kane. Noriega wore a severely austere jumpsuit and boots, her hair pulled back tightly and bestudded by glowing jewels, which matched her earrings and the rings she wore on her fingers. "She wears crystals of some amazing power," Wilma had explained when they had first rescued Dawn from Atlantis in the final hours before its destruction. "I don't know what they do, but her body is a very compact and powerful energy source that seems to increase her telepathic powers."

There were others. Wilma had provided holographic background on those she was told might attend this special session. If Dawn Noriega was as powerful telepathically as she had seemed on the *Io* mission and she was trying to create a group of people with real but undeveloped talents in this field, the future could be very interesting indeed.

Buck glanced from Dawn to Wilma by his side. As impressive as Dawn was, Wilma was even more so. Her appearance was stunning, and Buck was button-bursting proud that he and Wilma were about to be recognized as a team of great fighting talent. Wilma had created her own attire for the occasion, a body-smooth, floor-length dress that reflected light in a random pattern. She was a shimmering rainbow of gentle colors, which helped accentuate her own stunning figure.

Two more men took their seats. Buck recognized Vladimir Kharkov, a swarthy man of mixed Russian and Mongolian extraction with a fierce handlebar moustache and scars that covered much of his body. Kharkov had led the ground forces in repeated forays against Mongol and Han outposts in the far country of Asia, Alaska, and Canada, almost invisible behind energy shields and the frozen wastelands. He had gained no small fame within the Amerigo government for his deadly strikes against enemy garrisons and fortifications, especially through his favorite tactic of rapid tunneling beneath the snow fields by means of a nuclear-powered auger, from which his force would suddenly spring to attack and destroy the enemy.

Kharkov took no prisoners, and since his battles were far from the cities of either side and no nuclear weapons were involved, he was considered a guerrilla leader and left to his own devices. His records had captured Buck's attention before he first laid eyes on the man. When the Mongols first exploded across Europe, behind a rolling barrage of tactical nukes and massive armored columns, they regarded the Russians and Europeans as unworthy of mercy. Prisoners were handed over as gifts to the Han to serve as slaves. Vladimir Kharkov was the sole survivor of his small city in which every other man, and all the women and children, had been butchered. The city was held up to the rest of Europe as an example of what would happen if there were continued resistance to the massive Mongol forces. Vladimir survived by cutting open the belly of a recently killed horse and removing its innards, after which he crawled inside the carcass and hid for five terrifying days and nights. He had never cleared from his nostrils the stink of the decaying animal or the smell of death of his own family and friends. He worked his way to an Amerigo strike team in the Mediterranean, swore absolute fealty to the Federation, and through bloodthirsty and successful missions of his own, worked his way up through the ranks to the rank of Field General.

The last of the group entered the chamber with heavy boots thudding against the floor. Buck and the others turned to see a tall man with a shock of salt-and-pepper hair, sunken eyes in a gaunt face, and the look of a man who had known the extremes of life and death for most of his life. He wore an artificial buckskin shirt and trousers beneath a rumpled hat. He strode with open arms to Wilma, grabbed her in a bear hug that lifted her off her feet, and kissed her soundly on the lips. He put her back on her feet, surveyed her before him, and boomed, "When I bring 'em into the world, you can bet they'll be smashing great lookers!"

Without pausing a moment, he turned to Buck, clapped him on one shoulder with one hand, and shook his hand with the other. "So you're the wonder from the past. You don't look much like a neanderthal to me, Rogers!" He let out a loud guffaw and winked at Buck. "Not to worry, friend. I am Hieronymus Huer. Doctor Huer, that is. I birthed this young woman"—he threw out one arm—"as well as the Logan brats and a few hundred others. You can call me Doc." He spun about, waved to the group, and took his seat.

It was as if a whirlwind had passed through the room.

223

BUCK ROGERS

* * * * *

President Grenvil Logan was a merciful man. He knew that men like Buck Rogers and Black Barney and Killer Kane hated the formal trappings of state and its ceremonies. He was mercifully brief.

"Anthony Rogers, I would have enjoyed hearing the complete story of your recent adventures and superb performance for Amerigo. You, however, know full well what you accomplished, so I will not belabor the issue by sounding like a politician running for office. Besides"—he gestured to take in most of the people on the dais—"I have been informed in detail of much that has transpired. I am aware also that medals and similar honors are not, in your own idiom, your 'cup of tea.' So we will put all that to rest."

Logan paused, and his demeanor assumed a more serious look. "Please allow me to get right to the point. We wish you to continue serving the Federation. Is this also your desire?"

"It is, Mr. President," Buck said with quiet conviction.

Logan nodded. "Commodore Kane has expressed himself to me most clearly. He would be grateful if you would accept his invitation to become part of his DeepSpace Operations Command."

Buck started to speak, then reminded himself to shut up until he was asked to do so. Logan didn't keep him waiting.

"Are you of this same inclination, Anthony Rogers?"

DeepSpace! This is like a dream. . . .

"Yes, sir!" His voice echoed through the chamber. Logan smiled.

"Then, henceforth, that is your assignment. And from this moment forward, you are now Brigadier Anthony Rogers. My congratulations, sir."

"Thank you, Mr. President. But—" He faltered, groping for the right words.

Logan seemed amused. "Yes, Brigadier?"

"Sir, Major Deering and I have become a very special team. It would be . . . well, if accepting this promotion means breaking up our team, I'll have to pass—with all due respect, sir."

"So you believe in loyalty, Brigadier Rogers?"

"Yes, sir."

"Then you shall have your wish. Colonel Wilma Deering will be officially assigned as your combat partner."

The word blurted from Wilma before she could stop herself. "Colonel . . ." she managed, her eyes wide.

"If that is acceptable to you." Logan was almost laughing.

"Oh, it is, sir, it is!"

Logan stood. "Then this ceremony is ended as of right now. Let the records be secured in the computer with distribution to all commands." He picked up a gavel. "This is somewhat antique, I admit, but no one has come up with anything better." The gavel slammed against the stone with a loud bang.

"Case closed!" announced the president. "We shall retire now to the dining room where, I dearly hope, you will all divest yourself of rank and ceremony and, in a moment all too rare in our lives, thoroughly enjoy yourselves with superb food and wine."

* * * * *

Logan sure knows what he's doing. Back in that chamber, these people would never be as loose and gutsy as they are here. I don't know what we ate, but it was great, and the wine— Of course. It's that same drink I had before. Gets you whacked out for a few minutes, and then you're back with both feet on the ground. It's time to get together with Kane and Doc Huer. The good doctor knew what Buck wanted most to hear.

"Ah, the Tiger Men. I sense you're fairly bursting at the seams to drub me with all your questions, Rogers."

"You're Doc. I'm Buck, okay?"

"Agreed." They clasped hands firmly.

"Look, Doc, I know we've been on Mars. Even before I left the dark ages of my time, we'd landed probes on that planet. You know that we and the Russians landed on Venus and surveyed all the planets, as well as most of the moon. We didn't quite get closeups of Pluto, but that was next. We had plenty of manned flights, and we went to the moon and— Please pardon me, sir. I'm not telling you anything you don't know."

"But you are, m'boy, you are. You see, when you talk about it, there's fire and pride and a feeling that everything is very personal to you. So I get the taste of it this way."

"That's precisely what I was going to say to you about this

race on Mars," Buck answered immediately. "We both know I'll be going through all the holo records on whatever manned expeditions we've made to Mars—"

"Stop. Not expeditions. It's a regular run, just like those big-bellied aluminum cans in which you dragged people all over the world. Amazing how you did all that without Inertron and beamed energy and antigrav. And your computers were just about on a par with the abacus."

"I admit we were clever little savages," Buck said with mock seriousness. "C'mon, Doc, tell me about the people on Mars. You interacted with them from what I hear. That means you communicated with those folk, got to know them somewhat."

Huer made a sour face. "That's true, despite the fact that the Mongols are really the big cheese up there."

"I didn't know that."

"Between the Han and the Mongols, with a couple of billion people at their beck and call, they could afford to throw away lives. When we stopped lobbing hydrogen bombs at each other back here on Earth, we started throwing rocks at each other on Mars. The rocks were made up of all kinds of weapons—disintegrator beams, antigrav force fields, huge atmospheric electrical spasms, waves of electromagnetic energy. Fortunately, we didn't do in the whole planet. The problem is that when we started fighting the Han and the Mongols on Mars, they outnumbered us ten to one. Nevertheless, we clobbered them. We were killing off seven of them for every man or woman we lost. Can you do quick math in your head?"

"I see what you mean," Buck said, nodding. "When your last one is wiped out we're down to zero, they've still got three."

"Crude," Huer said, gesturing with a goblet, "but accurate."

Killer Kane slipped into a chair to join them. "Doc's a bit gung-ho with his numbers and that silly-ass math. As bad as it was up there, it wasn't all bad. Besides, there are time frames. It was terrible in the early days, but right now we're pretty much on an even footing with each other. What happens now and in the near future will determine not only what happens on Mars, but also who's running the show through the asteroid belt and beyond."

"I hear what you're saying, Commodore, but you're jumping from pillar to post," Buck complained. "It's tough to keep everything in perspective. Can we stick with one issue at a time until I'm up to speed on the whole scene?"

"Doc, damn it, be cool, will you?" Kane prodded the older man.

"Stop interrupting, you space scalawag. Where are those cigars you promised me?" Doc demanded.

Kane grinned and reached into his jacket. "Temple Halls," he noted. "The bloody best. There's two dozen of them in here," he said, handing them to Huer.

Buck looked at the cigars. "Barney used those. Veggies, he said. Self-lighting. Are these the same?"

Doc Huer busied himself snipping off the end of one cigar and flicking flame from a fountain pen. "I can see you don't know much about cigars," Huer said. "This is real tobacco, grown on one of our private farms. Very expensive, but who lives forever? Even the aroma, taste, wrapper, smoke . . . it's real."

"How about the Tiger Men, Doc?" Buck reminded him.

"All right, all right! Pushy, aren't you?" Huer replied with a twinkle in his eye. Then he leaned back in his chair, blew out a plume of smoke, and got down to business.

"First things first, Buck. Not until I was able to review what happened when you sailed on *Io*, trying to find Atlantis, did I realize that many of the beliefs we held about the Tiger Men of Mars and the Golden People— Damn it, don't gape like that. You're likely to have a frog jump down your throat."

"Two distinct, separate races?" Buck pushed.

"We used to think that. But if you include that albino race of undersea Atlanteans, that makes three. My personal opinion is that the albino effect was an evolutionary change, brought on by thousands of years without any direct sunlight. It can happen that way. Pigmentation mutation, that sort of thing.

"My feeling is that when this group arrived in our solar system some fifty thousand years ago, they didn't just go to Earth. One group did because they wanted to settle on a water planet. Like most cultures, however, they had different groups with some severe divisions among those groups. So one bunch opted for Earth, and a second crowd went to Mars. Then *that* group split up. I'll get to their differences in just a minute, but first I wanted to establish the time frame from the very beginning. Fifty thousand years fits in."

"Perhaps more than you realize," Buck replied. Immediately he had the rapt attention of both Doc Huer and Black Barney, who barely looked at Wilma as she joined them. "Look, for fifty or sixty thousand years, people on this planet have been seeing strange things in the sky. This isn't a local advertisement for UFOs or flying saucers or whatever. It's a page right out of history. There are caves with granite walls in China. Radiocarbon dating puts their age, and the carvings in the granite, at about fifty-seven thousand years ago. The pictures carved into the granite are unquestionably of spacecraft of some kind—discs and rocket shapes."

"The discs," Barney offered, "could be skimmers, both atmospheric and sea surface. Figure it out. If they had plenty of power, which we know they did, and some sort of antigrav, the flying disc makes sense as a runabout. A spaceship to cross the universe it definitely is not. But for something that's suitable local transportation in a world then without roads, it's perfect."

"Like the helicopters of your time," Huer offered.

"Precisely. You had some big suckers, too. With all those turbine engines screaming and the rotors churning like mad—well, to natives isolated from the rest of the world, you'd be considered gods who had come from outer space."

"Okay, then," Buck said, anxious to go on about the next phase. "Time rolls by. With greater population on the planet, more and more people are reporting these things. Even the Romans had discs on their gold coins. Most UFO stories were just so much nonsense, but not all of them. Then they died out. Oh, people still saw strange things, but the real ships in the sky, why, they began to fade away like a strange dream. It's funny—or not so funny—how this coincided with the Atlanteans finally making their decision to remain underwater. And there's one more bridge tying all this together."

Barney smiled. "Let me guess."

"Guess, hell, Admiral. You're not the only one who knows about USOs."

Huer seemed puzzled. "USOs?"

"Reports started coming in from all over the world of great, glowing discs diving into the ocean, or bursting upward from the sea and tearing out into space. There were numerous reports of huge glowing wheels racing through the ocean, passing beneath ships or sometimes skimming the surface. Don't you see? That's what happened here on Earth. And it probably ties in with your two races on Mars."

Doc Huer leaned back and held up his goblet in a silent salute. "Buck, lad, I'm all ears."

"What was Mars like in the past? The probes, the orbiters and landers, left no doubt that water once ran freely on Mars. Deep channels, warm temperatures, the whole enchilada for people from space looking for a new home. The gravity was light, and they were fifty million miles farther out from the sun, so solar radiation was diminished—"

"Oops! Bad supposition there," Barney broke in. "Thinner atmosphere and greater distance didn't help. Because of the thin air, the surface radiation was just as bad."

"But it was warmer? And with water?" Buck persisted.

"With fauna, fertile soil, changing seasons, excellent planetary rotation for the weather engine. They simply didn't expect the place to fall apart on them," Barney finished.

"That's where your albino race has been adding the missing pieces. Even the computers say we now have a ninety-seven percent chance of knowing accurately what happened."

"Go on," Wilma urged, her own interest prompting her to join in the discussion.

"The people who came here," Huer explained carefully, "separated into two divergent groups. One remained on the surface and gambled that they could protect themselves with their science and technology. They built massive structures that blocked radiation. They even built enormous domes under which they raised their crops and kept their farm animals. We've already found remnants of such a civilization in archeological digs, although we haven't had much opportunity for any real scientific input about them. But what we did find put us on the right track."

"Then what happened to them?" Wilma asked.

"Mars lost its atmosphere, or almost all of it, so the surface people had to either stay inside their pressurized domes or wear pressure suits if they went outside. They developed pressurized surface vehicles. Then, with all their water freezing and water vapor sublimating into ice crystals, the planet rapidly lost its warmth. Dust storms raged across Mars, just as sandstorms do on Earth. The finale was a sudden outburst of volcanic activity. Most likely some big asteroids rammed great holes through the surface right down to magma. All hell broke loose. Volcanoes ten miles high rose from the land. The buildings in which these people lived were wrecked. So were their crops and the other things they needed to survive. These were the Golden People. But they didn't die out; they wouldn't give in quite that easily.

"The solution was to try to work out a deal with that other group, the ones we now call the Tiger Men."

"The Tiger Men made it through all this?" Buck asked.

"I've spent time with those people," Huer acknowledged. "They'd built massive underground structures that rolled with the punches of quakes. Force fields around their subterranean buildings held off the lava when it splashed across the surface and down the channels. They survived in surprisingly good shape. But by now their numbers were dangerously low, so a deal was struck. The Tiger Men take in the Golden People if the Golds would agree to sustain hydroponics and other agricultural work. Funny thing about that. The Golds seemed to be more advanced than the Tiger clan."

"That they were," Barney added. "Nevertheless, as part of the agreement, they assumed the position of servants to the Tiger Men. They were completely protected that way, so there was no real enmity between them. It was something like old Rome, when the head slave often had more power than anyone except his master, usually a big landowner or a senator."

"How did they get those names—Golden People and Tiger Men?" Buck asked Doc Huer. "If you spent time with these people—"

"Normal evolutionary process for the Golds. They were sharp with biogenetics. Both groups were. The Golds engineered new outer skin, an incredible dermatological adaptation fed by genetic adaptation. Their outer skin became hard, almost like a flexible shell that protected them from the cold and unfiltered radiation. They got their name from their skin color, if you want to call it skin. It's more like an armored shell."

"And the Tiger Men?" The question came from Wilma.

Huer smiled. "A branch on the genetic highway. They knew that, in the long run, living underground could be extremely dangerous biologically, so they prepared for it. They adapted feline genes to their systems. They grew long, thick hair, like fur; it's really the same thing, but denser and covering almost the entire body. They picked up some unexpected bonuses in the tens of thousands of years that went by. They developed—literally—tiger stripes in their fur. They're fully human—or as similar to humans as you can get when you're from outer space—except they see much better than we do in the dark. Their inbred animal senses have given them many positives. I got to know them when I was part of a military scouting expedition. We got into a fire-fight with the Tiger Men; we were faster and had better weapons. When it was over, a sandrover of the Tigers was on its side, and the crew was pretty well banged up. A couple of them were near death. I took care of them, fixed their wounds. They couldn't believe it. My group was standing guard with blaster rays and I was saving the lives of their people."

Doc put down his cigar. "It doesn't matter where you are, in one world or another, if you're a doctor. You tend to those who need you. From that day on, after the word spread, I was something of a shaman to those people. They swore they would never knowingly harm me. And they never have."

"Doc, there's a question I've got to ask," Buck put in.

"Shoot."

"If these people, here on Earth and on Mars, crossed space, did they ever expect anyone else to follow them?"

"Damned good question, son. The fact is, they did. They all got together to build some form of monolith that could be seen from many millions of miles away and could be detected even light-years away. The first thing they put up was an automatic, constant radio signal on the hydrogen band. It had all the math necessary to figure out the spatial navigation needed to find our sun, and they were able to transmit the specific spectroscopic signatures of the sun. Anybody with at least their level of science would know where to home in. They built a couple of towers, each fed by its own thermonuclear reactor and computer. Then—and I guess this was to leave a visible mark—they constructed an enormous structure on the surface. It made the Egyptian pyramids look like clay tablets in comparison."

Buck's eyes widened. He could hardly believe what he was hearing. "Cydonia!" he breathed very softly, almost humbly.

"That's it," Barney confirmed. "Way up there in the northern latitudes. Your old space agency got pictures of it from the early Viking orbiters. But all they got was the face and a helmet. That alone is a mile and a half long by a mile wide. The original monument was the entire body in a pressure suit, maybe fifteen miles long, with the arms outstretched to make it just about as wide. Quakes and landslides crumpled everything but the face. You ever see those pictures?"

Buck nodded. "There was a lot of argument about the face. Scientists said it was all tricks of lighting and shadow."

"Still dumber than the south end of a mule headed north," Doc remarked. "Some things never change."

"Other people said it was a human face, and they got into fights with still more people who said the face was like that of a humanoid ape."

"A perfect description of Benjamin Black Barney," Doc laughed. "But they were all wrong. The face was that of a feline-type human, a perfect picture of a Tiger Man in his pressure suit. You'll see it yourself when you get to Mars."

"Don't you mean when *we* get to Mars?" Wilma asked coyly.

"Watch out for that weak sister act, Rogers," Kane told him. "Our new colonel has been there before. She heads a division of rocket fighters that have done battle with the Mongols off Earth."

Buck turned to Wilma. "You never told me that."

She shrugged. "I told you I was a pilot. You didn't ask any more, so I didn't say anything else."

"Let's get this discussion back to an even keel, people." The serious tone of Killer Kane's voice held their attention.

"We've got a war going on across Mars," Kane said. "Some of the Martians—we may as well call them that—are allied with the Mongols. They got to that planet in force before we did, and they brought with them vast amounts of what the Tiger Men needed—food, distillation plants for fresh water, oxygen generators. . . . It's a long list. In return, the Tigers joined forces with the Mongols and presented them with new antigrav systems and, above all, a gravity-wave system that converts space-time energy into a propulsion system unlike anything we'd ever seen before. It generates a thrust on a continuous basis that's like an atomic bomb going off steadily, just like a damned nuclear piston engine. It's so big and powerful, it's not even used in their ships."

"How powerful, Admiral?" Buck broke in.

"Powerful enough to shove small moons around without any trouble. Powerful enough for you?"

Buck nodded. "I think I'm out of my league here."

"You won't be for long," Kane told him. "Tomorrow morning you go into intensive indoctrination and training. Astroscience. Spatial navigation, maneuvering with thrust systems only in zero-g, energy beam weapons that really work well in vacuum. You'll go through the direct-feed mind systems that will lock all these things into your memory. When that's done, you have two weeks of in-space flight training and mock fighting. Colonel Deering, by the way, will be your main opponent. Watch yourself, Rogers. She's very good, and we'll judge you on the basis of your performance, not your team relationship with our brand-new colonel."

"Yes, sir," Buck said. Anything else would have sounded stupid.

"You're not the only one, of course," Doc Huer added. "Dawn Noriega will be subject to the same intensive training and flight experience."

Buck and Wilma showed their surprise. "Think!" Kane almost spat the word. "She's a telepath. We don't know if her talents will work against the Mongols when we mess with those people in space. She has to learn to think in their visualizations, not her own. If she can throw those people off balance in a tight fight, it could swing a battle in our favor. Can she read the minds of the Tiger Men? That could give us one terrific jump on them. The only way we'll find out is to get out her out there on Mars and see what happens. By the way, Colonel Deering, Dawn will come under your command. It may be that your particular abilities as an empath might just produce a new wrinkle that will work to our advantage."

"Dawn Noriega and Wilma Deering in the same outfit . . ." Buck didn't realize he had spoken aloud and drew immediate critical looks from Barney and Huer.

"There's more to that than you've just said, Rogers. Let's have it," Barney ordered.

"I was thinking of an old expression, sir," Buck replied carefully.

"And what that might be?"

"Oil and water, sir. They don't mix very well."

"Then you make sure it's not a problem, Brigadier. Do you read me?"

"Loud and clear, sir."

"Good."

"Question, Admiral?" Buck continued.

"Ask," Barney said.

"Have we—I mean, Amerigo—started terraforming Mars yet?"

"You mean reshaping that old world into a paradise for us?" Doc Huer interjected.

"That's the general idea, Doc."

"Keep one thing in mind, Buck."

"What's that?"

"Mars isn't our planet to play with. The real prize in all this is, first, gaining clear ascendancy over the Mongols. Second, and above all else, the planet Venus. That might well be the next home for mankind."

"*Venus?*" Buck asked, obviously in disbelief. "That planet is like Hades—pure, unmitigated hell."

"Buck, that's just what Earth was like a very long time ago. Keep your hopes up."

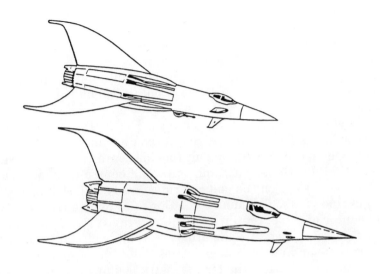

Chapter 20

I hate this damn thing, Buck cursed to himself, his lips pressed tightly together as the Asp fighter made a mockery of his attempt to control the supersensitive beast. The Asp was half engine and fuel, powered with a mononuclear thrust engine and a battery of small reaction-control rocket ports for precise maneuvering. Jutting from the aft end of the barrel-shaped space fighter was an extension of the power plant, a marvelous thrust chamber with the strength of a steel girder and the flexibility of a water snake.

Buck had raced after another Asp, the latter flown by Colonel Wilma Deering. He kept thinking of Wilma in that exact way—not as the beautiful blonde over whom he had become openly enamored, but what she was at this moment—an experienced pilot who was extremely skilled at flying her space bucket in a vacuum. The Earth was far below, a sphere of gleaming blue and white thirty thousand miles away. In their testing ground in space, the Asps weighed but a fraction of their Earth weight. Buck reminded himself that was in terms of weight, not mass. Up here, once they'd achieved orbit at just under five thousand miles per hour, they were weightless.

He knew he must become as familiar with these new forces and skills as he was flying a jet fighter in the atmosphere far below. Weight was a relative term. It existed only when superior forces acted upon a falling object. A man sitting on a chair on Earth's surface was able, through the rigidity and strength of that chair, to overcome the entire gravitational pull of the planet beneath him.

Anything and everything above the Earth always obeyed the inescapable pull of gravity. If you weren't balanced in orbit, with the proper speed, height, and altitude measured against the surface of the Earth beneath you, you could be in a crazy lopsided orbit, like a yo-yo on the end of a ridiculously long string, or you might find yourself beginning that long fall toward the theoretical center of the planet, which is how gravity drew you down. Once you slammed into the atmosphere at eighteen to twenty-three thousand miles an hour, unless your ship was in the perfect position to deflect the heat from friction away from you, you found out about gravity really fast. Hitting the atmosphere at five to seven miles a second was like driving a car into a cement wall at about four hundred miles an hour.

While you were up here, you were weightless, but you could never get rid of the mass of your ship, and that meant a real ballet of thrusters, reaction, counterreaction, and the finesse of a seal balancing a thin rubber ball on the end of its nose.

During an earthquake.

In a howling wind.

And Buck was flying like a very clumsy seal.

His hands and feet moved from one side of his cockpit to the other in a blur, trying to execute the right moves at the right time. Patting your head and rubbing your stomach in a circular motion while riding a unicycle was child's play by comparison.

Buck had flown airplanes and he'd flown helicopters. The latter, he came to believe with almost religious fervor when he was still a neophyte, was like an optical illusion with sound effects. His first several times, he had flown like a drunk, trying to control his training chopper as he would an airplane. At the end of a disastrously bad training day, his instructor had approached him. "Rogers," he'd said, "you're the prince of the skies in an airplane—you know, those things with fixed wings. A chopper has wings that go round and round; we call them rotors. We also have a tail rotor to compensate for torque and the clumsiness of new chopper pilots. You are doing bad things with all of them.

You know why you'll never earn your wings in one of these things? Because you have only two hands, that's why. You need *three* hands, plus both feet, to fly one of these. So tomorrow morning, when we risk our lives again, I expect to see you on the ramp with three arms, three hands, and a whole new attitude. You read me, sky chump?"

"Yes, sir. Three arms, three hands, and three feet."

"What's the extra foot for?"

"As soon as I get the hang of this, it's to kick your butt as hard as I can."

"That's something I'll never have to worry about, Rogers. You're hopeless."

It took time and it took all the stubbornness he had, which was a great deal, but in time he became very good indeed. He mastered the skittish helicopter and won those wings to go with his others. After helicopters, he flew vertical takeoff Harrier jets until he'd mastered those as well, until finally he could fly just about anything with wings, from hang gliders to immense 747 jetliners.

But that, he was being reminded every second, was another world, another time. This was battling it out with another space fighter. Fortunately for Buck, these were training sessions, in which the student was supposed to make every mistake in the book and then learn how to correct them.

* * * * *

He watched Wilma's Asp far ahead of him, tracked her as a target in his HUD display, and finally saw a chance to fire a photon beam that would hit the other fighter and light it up like a pinball machine but inflict no damage. He snapped off three fast shots. Each flashed briefly, aimed into empty space. Wilma's Asp was a will-o'-the-wisp. Her fighter skidded and rolled wildly and performed impossible gyrations at Wilma's hands. As fast as Buck fired his attitude thrusters, adjusting the Inertron field to tighten his turns, the stubby space fighter skidded wildly out from beneath him.

"If this were the real thing," Wilma jeered over her radio at him, "you'd be turning on a slow spit with a hot fire beneath you. Get with it. I'm going to come after you now. The book says you can't fly a pursuit curve in zero-g and a vacuum, but the guy who wrote the book has never been up here. Keep in mind that if you overcontrol or make gross corrections, you'll be a dead duck. All right, buddy boy, here I come!"

He watched their relative positions on his computer display, projecting the widest variation possible of Wilma's maneuvers. Relative to Earth below—you always had to have a relative position to conceive of up or down—Wilma would come after him in a classic diving, curving attack. It was the classic rule that the machine that had the height advantage in an opening gambit of a fight, especially if it had greater power or thrust, had the advantage, and Wilma had those on her side. Buck fairly banged his fist against the computer, getting an immediate readout as to what maneuvers would keep him out from under the guns of the opposing Asp.

It didn't look good. Wilma held every advantage, and she was playing it to the hilt. A kill seemed right in her bag.

Buck smiled, then broke out into a laugh. He forgot his radios were on active throughout the engagement. "What's so funny, flyboy? Or is that your way of admitting defeat? You've got six or seven seconds, Buck, no matter what evasion you take, before I lock you into my sights. Then it's bye-bye, baby."

Buck's laugh dwindled to a chuckle. He was suddenly too busy to laugh. There's always a new maneuver, or a twist on an old gambit, in the book of every pilot ever born. When he saw the computer readout that might just as well have read "YOU'RE A DEAD DUCK, ROGERS," he knew he had to dig into his bag of tricks.

"Computer—" He stopped, cutting off the radio so he wouldn't transmit into the open to Wilma. "Computer, display area of escape or evasion from attacking Asp."

The screen flashed through a series of colors and numbers. The answer came in a limited block of space with another discouraging reply from the electronic brain: "YOU ARE DEAD."

We'll see about that. . . .

"Computer, using full-range photon beams for the attacking Asp fighter, display maximum killing range."

One mile! That was practically slingshot range, like tossing pennies into a bucket. Great!

"One more question, computer. What's the longitudinal rate

of roll of this buggy? Nose over tail, and figuring no use from main thruster. Compute at maximum flip rate to end with a sight lock for our photon beams set at maximum range effectiveness."

"Nose over tail, employing nose-up, tail-down thrusters, one point six seconds."

"Whew! That kind of acceleration is going to knock me cold." He thought furiously for a moment. "Computer! Set up that maneuver when I press automode. Complete the end-over-end through one hundred eighty degrees under computer control. I'll be off the controls at that time. When the flip maneuver is completed, what will be the bearing on my photon beams relative to the other Asp fighter?"

"Within three seconds of completion of flip maneuver, the opposing spacecraft will be six degrees, closing for a direct line of sight and fire."

"Great. As soon as the opposing Asp comes into line of sight and fire, fire three bursts of photon beams. If necessary, make whatever corrections you need and then fire off those three blasts." He thought for a moment. "Repeat and confirm."

The computer voice repeated his instructions exactly.

"Computer, the attacking fighter is on a trailing pursuit curve. How long before it is in position to fire at us?"

"Seven point three seconds."

"Execute my orders when it is five seconds from firing angle and I go into automode."

Just over two seconds. An old memory had flashed through his mind. It was a highly complex maneuver by German fighter pilots in the Second World War called the Luftwaffe Stomp, used mostly by their best pilots. When they were being pursued in a steep climb, they timed their distance carefully. With an opposing Mustang or Spitfire in pursuit, still out of firing range, the German pilot would move his controls swiftly and violently, spinning the Messerschmitt about its axis, virtually swinging around with the nose ripping to the left. In seconds, the Messerschmitt would reverse its position, with its nose—and weapons—now pointing downward at the pursuing enemy. In its climb, its maneuverability restricted, the enemy plane would fly right into the gunsights of the German pilot. One good burst of machine guns and cannons and it was all over. The hunted had become the hunter. One more victory mark to be added to the tail of the Messerschmitt.

They didn't teach that maneuver in the American or British fighter pilot training schools, and they sure weren't teaching it now. . . .

Buck took a deep breath, tensed his body, and stabbed the automode button.

Tiny tongues of flame spat upward from the nose and downward from the tail. Forward speed never changed, but in the sudden whirling-dervish maneuver, the Asp reversed direction.

Before Wilma could fully realize what Buck had done, trying desperately to get out of a situation she had never before encountered, the photon beams lit up her fighter with their deadly glow.

Wilma slumped in her harness. How had he done that? She was wiped out through some crazy maneuver she hadn't yet figured out.

Buck flipped his radio on. His voice sounded groggy, as if he were emerging from a g-induced blackout, but there was no mistaking the triumph in that voice.

"Tag, baby. You're dead."

She came around in a skidding wide turn to join up with Buck in formation. There was no more weaving or juking; the mock battle was over, and she was the loser. She punched in formation automode; the computer would hold position with Buck.

"Just how in God's name did you do *that?*" she exclaimed. "I had you in a box. There wasn't any way for you to get out." She cut herself short. "Obviously there *was* a way. This time you be the teacher, Mister."

"Buy me a drink when we land?"

"Done!"

* * * * *

Buck's boyhood dream came true three weeks later. After his mastery of Wilma's attacking Asp spacefighter, Commodore Kane judged Buck ready for fast-paced indoctrination in spatial navigation and the piloting of larger spacecraft. He met with Buck, Wilma, and Admiral Frank Bemis, who was the lead commander of very heavy spacecraft—floating fortresses, really—employed for deep forays through the solar system and especially as a cruising battlewagon in the asteroid belt to protect Amerigo Federation mining activities. The great VHS—Very Heavy

Spacecraft—were all too few and far between.

"You can compare them to the biggest and heaviest nuclear aircraft carriers of your time," Bemis explained. "One of your big carriers had a crew of more than five thousand highly skilled people, everything from pilots to navigators, ordnance teams to cooks, doctors, launch crews. But I'm sure you know that system by heart. According to your records, you were an exchange pilot from the Air Force for a while with your navy. Right?"

"Yes, sir. We kept up a complementary exchange so we'd all be familiar with what our other people were doing."

"Any cats?"

"Yes, sir. Twenty catapult launches, ten fighters and ten bombers."

"Hooks?"

Buck nodded, a wry look on his face. "Ten landings with hook snatch. I didn't like a one of them, especially three at night, one in a bad storm. It was really an iffy proposition."

"All that will help. The comparison between our Truman class space heavies and your carriers is pretty accurate. We only have seven in our entire space fleet. We try never to land them on a planetary or moon surface. Down there they'd be open targets."

"Like our carriers in drydock," Buck offered.

"Precisely. Now, you'll spend some time cramming in astronavigation. It's really an extension of your own stellar navigation in night flight over Earth, but you'll need to know more about orbital mechanics. Then there's docking an Asp or other fighter, or even a heavy scout, aboard one of our Trumans. My own vessel is the Truman, and Kane, here, has recommended both you and Wilma for duty aboard her. She's a fine craft. One more thing. The Mongols don't have more than four of their own heavies left. These vessels are just too massive and too costly to keep producing them. Losing one is like losing a major battle when you factor in the investment, not only in pilots and air crews but in an entire staff of five thousand. If we were to lose two or three Trumans, the whole balance of power between us and the Mongols, who are very strong on Mars and expanding their numbers through the asteroid belt, would be drastically altered. I want to be sure you and Colonel Deering understand that the safety of the VHS craft has the most important priority in all our combat. If it's a matter of losing your life and preventing the loss of a Truman heavy, we expect you to not only risk your life but to yield it to the better good."

"One life for five thousand," Wilma said. "Sounds reasonable to me."

"Are either of you two history buffs of the Second World War?" Bemis asked. "I expect Brigadier Rogers would be the most likely candidate."

"Yes, sir, I am. It was one of my majors when I went through the Air Force Academy."

"Do you remember the Battle of Midway in the summer of 1942?"

"Yes, sir. We considered it the pivotal point of the Pacific War."

"It was," Bemis replied, "and the lessons of that battle are applicable today. Your navy—our navy—was outnumbered and outgunned. But you tell me what happened, Rogers."

"We lost one carrier, a hell of a lot of planes and crews, and Midway was torn up pretty bad, but—"

"But?" Bemis prompted.

"We sank four Japanese carriers. They lost hundreds of planes and thousands of men, but their biggest loss was more than three hundred of their most skilled and combat-experienced pilots. That battle broke the back of the Japanese navy and turned the tide of the whole Pacific War."

"Neatly summarized," Bemis complimented him. "Now, use the term space dreadnoughts instead of super carriers, and conceivably we might find ourselves in the same position. Pilots like you and Deering are our best defense against just that happening. We could lose not only this world but a hell of a lot more than that." Bemis glanced at his watch. "Got a meeting. Big pow-wow." He rose to his feet and shook hands with Buck and Wilma.

"Welcome aboard. See you two in the great beyond."

* * * * *

Three weeks later Buck and Wilma found themselves in the second-pilot seats of a light battle cruiser ready to launch from the great spaceport spread across the Pennsylvania hills. Buck had always thought of leaving Earth as a fiery, thundering rocket blast in a wild vertical ascent. The last thing he'd expected was a smooth elevator ride.

Speedboat was an unexpected name for a space battle cruiser, but she had been so christened. More heavy fighter than a massive spacecraft, *Speedboat* was studded with ray weapons, beam weapons, batteries of missiles, and generators that spewed forth both nuclear radiation and fierce sprays of electromagnetic radiation that could jangle the brains of any crew of an enemy vessel that got too close to it.

Commander Regina Blackwell directed the battle orders for *Speedboat* missions. She commanded rather than flying herself. From her command seat, she overlooked and directed the actions of her pilots. Seated up front, viewing the world and space through a heavily armored glassite bow and a long bank of video screens that enabled vision in all quadrants were Arny Serold and Mel Cosgrove. Buck and Wilma sat in command seats behind and higher than those of the pilots, with duplicate controls. They were to watch, learn, and advance steadily but slowly into their own piloting of the cruiser. The spacecraft, with its crew of sixty-two men and women, sat in a huge cradle deep in the rolling hills of the Pennsylvania countryside. Buried deep underground were antigrav generators and microwave-beam energy lifters.

They watched Serold order the Inertron strips around *Speedboat* activated to lighten the ship to perhaps ten percent of its normal weight. "Initiate antigrav," Serold ordered.

"Antigrav on," confirmed Cosgrove. "Lifting beams on line and ready."

Commander Blackwell leaned forward. "This is a shakedown cruise. *Speedboat* has been in dock for a month for refitting, maintenance, and some new weaponry. We'll do the lunar flight and landing, do a recheck of everything, and then take her out for a maximum speed run. We'll do that angling sunward. Wilma and Buck, you'll have a chance then to take the controls and get the feel of her."

"Commander, we didn't get a complete briefing on the propulsion system. What's the main drive?" asked Buck.

"Variable nozzle."

"Like some sort of super afterburner?"

Blackwell's expression showed her surprise and pleasure. "Very well put, Rogers. That's it exactly."

"Have you gone to max drive with her yet?"

"Only once. We slipped down well below the plane of the ecliptic, away from any visuals the Mongol ships could use to track us. To cover what we were doing, we generated a gravity fabric weave—"

"I'm over my head, Commander."

"Sorry. It's a disrupter that creates a brief but very intense gravitational effect in a confined area. It warps all electromagnetic variation in the area, so light gets garbled, just like any optic or electromagnetic system. We fuzz up any attempt to track us."

"Then you went to max?" asked Wilma.

"Just that one time. We let her run until we had one million miles per hour. Any faster than that during starting and our drive would have brought on excessive g-loads. Once we reached the one million mark, we opened her up to a steady four-g acceleration." Blackwell leaned back and smiled. "We eased off the power at fourteen million."

Buck's eyes widened. "Miles per hour?"

"At max drive, we were maybe five minutes from Earth to the sun, although we never did that. The idea was to find out through an actual flight drive test what we could really do. If we figured horsepower at that speed, it would be in the trillions. That was enough. The Mongols don't have anything like *Speedboat*, but then this is our only on-line ship like this. Amerigo could build four dreadnoughts for what this baby cost."

"Ready for lift," came the call from the pilot.

"Commence liftoff," Blackwell said curtly. She was all business now, her conversation with Buck and Wilma put aside completely.

* * * * *

Inertron energy diminished the huge ship's weight. The cradles of thick coils, open at the top, surrounded the ship and fed anti-grav power to the entire structure. Weight-wise, *Speedboat* was now very close to the levitating ability of an ancient dirigible, yet she still hung solidly in the anti-grav coils. The idea now was to raise the ship in a smooth, direct ascent until *Speedboat* was out of the atmosphere. Here the microwave energy beams came into play. Powered by huge underground generators, the system fed a repulsive power to receiving points all along the hull of the cruiser. Microwave power—really an immense radar current—can boil water explosively in seconds or, directed against living creatures, including man, explode their bodily liquids and turn their skin, intestines, all internal organs, and the brain to mush. But beamed tightly and absorbed by the receivers along the hull of *Speedboat*, the microwave energy exerted a powerful upward lift to the cruiser. With almost magical levitation, silently except for the deep thrumming sound of the generators and receivers and the voices of the flight crew on the control deck, *Speedboat* seemed to hang in midair unmoving. It was amazingly like departing from Earth in a blimp or a helium balloon, which Buck had done many times.

You do not move . . . the Earth recedes beneath you, ever so gently, everything within view diminishing in size, faster and faster, until you're aware that you are high above Earth and accelerating steadily. It was nothing like the Asp fighters, which employed these same systems on a lesser scale for liftoff, then became blazing upward-streaking meteors as their main drives cut in.

"Commander," came Arny Serold's voice. "Two zero miles to diminished microwave beam."

"Acknowledged," Blackwell answered. "Bring up the aft thrusters. Three-g acceleration, angled ascent ten degrees."

"Confirmed," Serold replied, the numbers appearing magically on his heads-up display before his eyes.

"We'll fly a curving ascent steadily from propulsion start," Commander Blackwell explained. "You already know there's no such thing as a straight line in space. Everything is curved; everything warps to gravity."

"Everything is falling around something else, from pebbles to entire galaxies," Buck added.

"Precisely. So if we wanted to climb straight out to the moon, we'd be off in the boondocks somewhere. We follow a path dictated by both centrifugal force, from propulsion, and gravity, and we balance neatly between the two. The computers, which do our astronavigation for us, keep us automatically on track. On this kind of trip, the human crew performs as watchdogs over the computer pilots."

"Do we get a bone if we do a good job?" Buck smiled.

"If you're real good at it. Speaking of bones, let me ask you something that's often a bone of contention."

"Go ahead."

"To leave the Earth we had to ascend, to go up."

"Okay."

"So up we go. But without changing attitude, if we care not to, when we reach the moon for a landing, we're going down. When did the shift take place?"

Buck laughed. "You're not going to catch me on that one! You're always going up or down, but only relative to what particular surface you choose to measure from."

"The brigadier gets his bone," the commander said with a smile.

"What I still find hard to believe," Buck said, shifting topics, "is that it takes us only a few hours to reach the moon. Back in the old Apollo days—"

"When you people flew those strange space-going Toonerville trolley antiques," Wilma teased.

"I know, I know," Buck admitted, "but everything in those days had to take into account available energy. We had so much fuel and energy in the bank, and that was it. You'd leave Earth at seven miles a second, cut power, and you'd have to drift the rest of the way to the moon, slowing down the whole time."

"I understand you've flown the Asp fighter?" Commander Blackwell said.

"Yes, sir," Buck replied. "But Colonel Deering—"

"Keep the names short, please. Every second could count in battle."

"Yes, sir. Wilma's the old hand with the fighters."

"She's more than that. She has six years of combat behind her, and that makes her one of the best." She studied Buck. "I understand you took her down in your last training session."

"Lucky break," Buck demurred.

"No way," Wilma broke in. "He did some of the damnedest flying I've ever seen. One moment I had him dead to rights, and the next second I was glowing from nose to tail with photon spray. If he'd been using the disintegrator ray, my ship would have been junk."

"You'll have to tell me about that maneuver sometime, but not now. Your question first. We have a modified thermonuclear generator and a variable force field for thrust. The thermo system is pretty standard, but we don't use anything like a reactor or those atomic piston jobs so many other ships have. We feed a wire—it's about two inches thick—of lithium hydride mixed with a quark entrapment. The wire feeds into the thrust chamber, where it's bombarded by a subatomic disrupter. In that chamber, the stuff undergoes a constant, very powerful detonation. This is ejected from the aft thrusters—we have the same thrusters forward, as well—at tremendous velocity. For maximum drive, we use a magnetic bottle to squeeze down the orifice for thrust ejection."

"Is that variable?"

"Until we're nine-tenths of the way there, when lunar gravity becomes dominant and starts drawing us in, accelerating all the time."

"That's that moment when you stop going up and start going down," Buck announced.

"Hey, not bad for a space cadet."

"If we worked propulsion all the way, without inducing several g-loads, how long would it take to reach the moon in this tub?"

"Two or three hours. Certainly not three or four days. We'd thrust all the way out, then decelerate a short distance in. It's all a matter of playing the energy like a violin. We've got so much power now, and almost limitless fuel supply with the new drive, that fuel and time constraints are old history."

"Our probes to Mars under the best conditions took about eight months," Buck noted. "How long with *Speedboat?*"

"If you wanted to get there as fast as possible?"

"Uh-huh."

"Measure the trip in hours. But we'd really be hauling through both acceleration and deceleration."

"I like the new way best," Buck admitted. "The old way, you had to drift like a cork in a gravity stream, losing speed almost all the way."

"Welcome to the future, Brigadier Rogers."

* * * * *

Buck watched, fascinated, as the computer drew them in toward their landing moonport. Even from far out in space, he saw clearly the five-starred landing grid, marked by dazzling strobes. The flight crew worked quietly and efficiently, one pilot always with his hand on the thruster controls in case of an autopilot screwup. It didn't happen. Everything went as scheduled. They used forward thrusters to decelerate and level off in relation to the lunar surface, and the power grids broadcast their microwave beams to steady the ship. Inertron activation came next, and they worked the antigrav system and energy beams with exquisite control as *Speedboat* lowered magically to the landing port. The cruiser settled neatly into her landing cradle.

Buck stayed glued to the observation bow, looking at the long line of huge domes beneath which the permanent lunar personal lived, worked, farmed and maintained a major mining operation. The surface of the moon was rich in helium 3, a rare atomic isotope a thousand times more efficient in thermonuclear reactors than any other fuel, which produced gobs of energy without any radioactive or toxic waste byproducts.

Off to his right ran the long maglev and electrical propulsion systems for firing loads of helium 3 in sealed containers off the moon. Why waste tons of fuel when electric drivers would do the job at a fraction of the cost in energy and money? The bulk carriers, like sealed railroad cars, accelerated to tremendous speed along the lunar surface. Suspended above the energy rails, they never had to contend with direct friction, and in the vacuum of the lunar surface, they whipped into high speed. The upward-angled rails shot the precious materials off into space in a curving line earthward. There they were snared by microwave beams, decelerated by an antigrav force beam, and lowered gently directly to the main energy plants scattered throughout fortified centers of Amerigo. In an unwritten agreement between the Han and Amerigo leaders, neither side interfered with the other's fuel source deliveries. It was one small step in working together instead of battling each other at every turn.

"Unfortunately," as Commander Regina Blackwell observed, "it's more of a sop than any real attempt to work out our differences. But when you're starving for calm and peace, a sop is better than nothing."

Her words were prophetic.

Blackwell had mentioned the great asteroid orbiting their home planet, but outward bound from Earth, Buck had seen no sign of anything that spanned a diameter of eighty miles and weighed trillions of tons. Ancient lunar flights required first entering Earth orbit, checking all flight parameters, and then igniting upper rocket stages for the final thrust to the moon. *Speedboat* just went up and away.

Seeing the dim glow of the asteroid from the Earth's surface at night hadn't made much impression on Buck. The night sky was a constant sparkling and splashing of colors as satellites and spacecraft left or returned to Earth. Now he had the chance and the time to find out just how ominous was that dark body that had become a second moon of his home planet.

Wilma took him to the high observation control center of the lunar city. Buck had direct telescopic observation of the object to see the lights and constant activity on its surface, as well as the jets of flame from ships working in the area. On the computer holo display were all the numbers relating to distance, size, makeup, content, and purpose of what the Han and Mongols called *Luo Wengui*, in honor of the ancient White Horse Tibetans, a lesser band of natives in the Mongol mountain country known to be their fiercest warriors.

"It's virtually a civilization unto itself. The only gravity it has is from its own mass. It's obviously in free-fall orbit about the Earth," Wilma said.

"It's Mongol?"

"Brought here about two hundred years ago at tremendous expense—and loss of life as well—by what's known as the Great Asian Trio—Han, Mongol and Japanese. They used mass drivers, including funneled thermonuclear explosions, to break it free of its orbit in the asteroid belt. When it neared Earth, they went into a steady deceleration, swung it into an elliptical orbit, and then slowly circularized the orbit until it was geosynchronous."

"That would be over twenty-two thousand miles?"

"Close enough. It's been there all this time. They use it as a way station for ships leaving for Mars and the asteroid zone or farther out. It's got communications systems for all their countries, a crazy kind of comsat. Nobody needs something like that."

"Then—why?"

"Buck, it's the ultimate Sword of Damocles. Installed within the asteroid itself are explosive mass drivers to decelerate that thing if they ever wanted to do that. If the balance of power ever swung completely to our side, this is their guarantee of bringing all conflict to an end. The Japanese call it the ultimate samurai sword. It would kill everybody if they ever broke it free of orbit and rammed it downward into the planet. It would destroy every last vestige of civilization."

"I don't get it," Buck objected. "Why doesn't Amerigo hit it first? We've got bombs powerful enough to blow that thing into little chunks."

Wilma shook her head. "The big threat is that the Mongols might decelerate it out of orbit, then drive it downward. A finale to end the world, so to speak. If they detect an all-out attack on the asteroid, that might just trigger that kind of reaction. But let's say we did what you suggested. All the pieces, large and small, would mostly remain in orbit, except that so much debris would be thrown out that the Earth would be subjected to a massive wave of meteorite strikes. It would be like slinging hydrogen bombs at one another." Wilma shook her head. "No, there's got to be some other way. In the meantime, the asteroid is a death star to all of us on Earth, while the main contest goes on far from here, on Mars and in the asteroid zone. They've discovered elements in that zone the likes of which we never imagined." Wilma paused. "Buck," she said seriously, "it would even open the door to star flight."

There was no need to answer that remark. It was left unspoken by Wilma, but the secret drive of the Tiger Men and the Golden People of Mars might also hold the keys to faster-than-light travel through space.

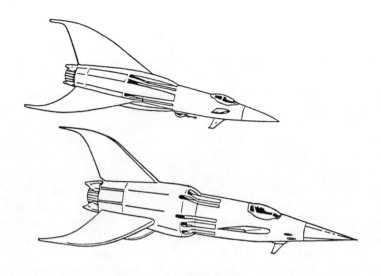

Chapter 21

Buck's time on the moon proved to be distressingly brief. He and Wilma were called to a security communications center deep within the lunar base that connected directly by ultra-high microwave frequency to Amerigo headquarters in Niagara. They looked about them to see Commander Regina Blackwell, the *Speedboat* flight crew, and several strangers. It didn't take more than one look to realize that these men and women weren't space pilots. Their gear, weapons, and even their individual stance told volumes about them.

The last time Buck had encountered such a group was when he had been assigned as a forward coordinator to a combination team of SEALS and Air Commandos in a lightning-strike blow at a hidden Syrian encampment in Central America. They went in from the air and from beneath the ocean surface, and in a devastating strike, the special warfare teams decimated the Syrian defenders. Like most such battles of this kind, neither government made official comment about the event.

Now gathered here on the moon were the team leaders of such a strike force. There was no question that they were being assembled, along with *Speedboat* and her complement of Asp fighters, for an important mission. Where, how, what, and when were questions Buck and Wilma would find out at the briefing.

It didn't take long. The microwave-beam signals from Earth came alive on large flat television screens for data display and holographic projections from Niagara. Buck and Wilma nudged one another as they recognized Commodore Kevin "Killer" Kane and Admiral Frank Bemis, the latter the commander of the Very Heavy Spacecraft Fleet, the dreadnoughts of Amerigo's space force. There were other faces not known to them, but it would all come together in the next several minutes.

Vice President Charlotte Hasafi appeared in a hologram in the room's center. She turned slowly, surveying everyone gathered in the briefing room and giving them the opportunity to see her clearly. "Ladies and gentlemen, I am not part of your briefing, but I will present a review of circumstances and give you some background that will place your special mission in perspective. For those of you who already know what we face, please be patient. There are others to whom much of this information will be completely new."

As she spoke, her form disappeared, to be replaced by scenes of Earth floating in space. Then this, too, faded away and Venus came into view.

"Let me get right to the main issue we face, which often is obscured by both coincidence and deliberate obfuscation. In the very long run for our nation, even for our planet, our great hope is that one day we shall be able to terraform the planet Venus and make it a hospitable habitat, a new world for all mankind. That is a goal not shared equally by all governments on Earth. We are bound by conflicts that have drained the national energies of many peoples. Time is starting to run out.

"No doubt most of you have accepted the planet Mars as the next major world for us. But at its best, Mars is limited in what it provides and even more so in what it can support. The planetary data are known to us all—lack of solar radiation for heat, lack of atmospheric protection against subatomic particles, a weak gravity to retain atmosphere. Much smaller than Earth, Mars still encompasses a land area as great as that of Earth, but it is all frigid desert. So for now, put Mars aside in your thinking. It is a stopgap world which one day we may be able to transform to meet future needs. The operative word is 'may.'

"Venus is our great hope. Those of you familiar with the debit side of Venus are aware of its searing temperatures, its crushing atmosphere, its slow rotation. It's a lifeless world, thick with poisonous gases in the atmosphere. In many respects, the fledgling Earth was in much the same condition. Unfortunately, we do not have billions of years to wait for nature to redress Venus's negative aspects. We must act on our own.

"That program is already under way. It is undertaken at great risk, because we expended energy, manpower, and material for Venus that stripped our military strength on Mars. For two centuries, we have poured algae into the Venusian atmosphere to feed on carbon dioxide and introduce water vapor into the upper atmosphere. It has not yet rained on Venus, but we have achieved breaks in the upper clouds, and the percentage of moisture has climbed from virtually zero to several percent. Oxygen surely will follow.

"All this, however, is not enough. Venus is cursed with a slow rotation that brought on its devastating greenhouse effect of an atmosphere a hundred times more dense than that of Earth, and a surface temperature averaging nine hundred degrees.

"The only way we can terraform Venus into a world that will safely harbor mankind is to speed up its rotation from the present Venusian day of 243 Earth days. It is retrograde in rotation, which presents no problem except that we must speed up that rotation by more than two hundred and forty times. That will give us severe turbulence in the atmosphere, but it will also establish an Earthlike weather engine on that planet. That will be the beginning.

"As yet, we do not have the capability to apply the enormous power to make this possible. The Tiger Men of Mars *do* have that capability. Their enormous energy drivers are sufficient for the task at hand. That is the immediate problem. The Tiger Men cooperate with the Mongol forces. Having survived their own catastrophe when their sun was about to explode, the Tiger Men are harsh realists. They will side with the winners in the conflict between us and the Mongols. If we reverse that situation, they will lean toward cooperation with us.

"I will now reveal what some of you know from your own experience, but many of you do not. Most of the minor battles and conflicts in recent years on Earth and the moon, and even throughout the mining outposts in the asteroid zone, have been controlled engagements, quite limited in scope. We have been content with this situation because it has drawn attention away from our plans for Venus, and the Mongols, with the Tiger Men as their allies, know that they alone possess the energy drivers for the stupendous task of speeding up the Venusian rotation.

"Neither we nor the Mongols have major forces on Mars, but what is there is very powerful. The space dreadnoughts of Amerigo are closely matched with those of the Mongols. Where we have an edge is in our smaller, swifter, more maneuverable fighters, and the *Speedboat* light cruiser with its tremendous speed. The Mongols feel secure behind their defenses and big guns. They are stolid, and they have for too long a time let down their guard. They regard us with contempt as a fighting force.

"We must change all that. The battle must be swift and decisive. We must give no quarter to the enemy. His destruction or surrender is the least we can accept. We know what the Tiger Men will do when the fighting is over, and that is to side with the victors. None of us know if they will fight alongside the Mongols. They are a race much older than we, and they consider the conflicts of war to be irresponsible.

"But they are aware we have all banished the use of nuclear weapons. We are not seeking the destruction of Mars, but the sapping of Mongol strength and their current position of superiority. Remember this: The Mongols have an inheritance of survival in fierce and harsh environments. The Gobi Desert has long been their testing ground.

"But in their contempt for the forces of Amerigo, they have forgotten that we, too, emerged from great battles in desert lands. We fought the American Indians across vast plains, through the Great Painted Desert, through Monument Valley, and up and down Death Valley. We fought battles in the Mexican deserts. We powered our way through North Africa in the second great world war, demonstrated a swift killing machine in the Gulf War, and shattered the Iranian strongholds wherever we found them. The Antarctic expeditions witnessed our triumphs, and in the frozen deserts of Canada, we held superior Mongol forces to a standstill. There is no shortage of courage or skill on our part. Mars is one more desert. I expect all of you to carry on a long tradition of meeting the enemy and either forcing his capitulation or bringing on his destruction.

"May God be with you in your endeavors."

In a blink of an eye, the holographic image vanished.

* * * * *

The assembled crews separated to pair off with other men and women with whom they would serve as teams to engage the enemy. Buck had already met with Commander Regina Blackwell of the swift cruiser *Speedboat*.

"Commander, I understand we have twenty-two Asp fighters on board, and that you plan to send these out to engage the Mongol Zhang fighters in pairs."

Blackwell nodded. "What's your point, Rogers?"

"I believe, based on past experience and new maneuvers Colonel Deering and I have developed, that it would be far more effective if we engaged the enemy in an open or running fight not with two Asps, but with a finger-four formation. It provides greater firepower, breakaway maneuvering room, and protection from Tail-End Charlie for the rest of the group."

Blackwell leaned back in her chair. "Rogers, some of what you say might make sense if I could only figure out what the devil you're talking about. Now, cut to the quick and update me."

"Yes, sir," Buck said, grinning. "It's more like postdate than update. There was a time in the Second World War when Germany and England were battling it out in the air over the English Channel and England itself. The Germans mostly flew the Emil, their Messerschmitt Me-109E, against what was considered the best fighter plane of its day, the British Spitfire.

"The British were stubborn. They fought in large groups of fighters, unwieldy and clumsy. There was a German fighter pilot, one of their high-ranking generals and also a top ace, who broke tradition. He introduced the finger four, a formation of two fighters in a flight, two flights to a formation. They hit the British with this new tactic, and the Germans clobbered the British pilots. Both planes were excellent, like our Asps and the Mongol Zhangs. Sir, there's an old proven rule of battle: *Never fight the other man's fight.* You'll get your butt waxed every time you do,

255

because you've given the advantage to the enemy.

"I've been studying Zhang maneuvers and systems and talked to all the crews I could, including Wilma, here. The way they describe the Zhang pilots, they're wide open, suckers for a finger-four formation, especially since the last pilot in that formation is always ready to knock off a pursuing fighter. He protects the formation. It works."

"Have you tried out this scheme with anyone but Deering?"

"Yes, sir. We teamed up with that brother-and-sister combo, Mari and Adrian Sceptre. They're experienced, natural pilots, and they don't have enough sense to be scared when they should be. Their whole philosophy is attack. We've practiced the finger four against formations of up to sixteen Asps, playing the part of the Mongols, shooting with photon rays to register hit scores."

"And . . . ?"

Wilma spoke up for the first time. "Sir, we blitzed the hell out of them. We scored eleven direct hits—they would have been kills had we used the hard lasers or the disintegrator beams."

"How many of your four did you lose?"

"One, sir. And that would have been damaged, not destroyed."

Blackwell rubbed her chin, poring over every bit of what she'd heard. *Speedboat* had enough Asps to free eight fighters from their regular patrols and scout attack formations of three Asps in a group.

"How long will it take to train the rest of the Asp pilots?"

"I hope I haven't stepped on any toes, sir, but they've all flown several missions using this formation. In two or three days, they'll be as good as any I've seen. You have some really fine fighter jocks aboard."

Blackwell smiled. "My toes are fine, Rogers, but you did bypass command structure."

"Sir, you've been tied up day and night."

"I know very well what I've been doing, Rogers. Your actions are understandable, even commendable. Proceed with your program, but let there be no interference with the escort missions to protect the heavier ships."

"Yes, *sir!*" Buck and Wilma chorused.

"Dismissed," Blackwell said curtly, but her demeanor was warm.

"Uh, sir . . . one more thing?" Buck asked, treading lightly.

"Rogers, what the blue blazes do you want now?"

"Sir, I've been meeting with your ordnance lead teams."

"Get with it, Rogers! Are you trying to talk the Mongols into a stupor?"

"No, sir. But I have a request that must have your approval."

"Keep it short and sweet, Mister."

Buck meant to keep it that way. He had discovered a serious flaw in the offensive armament of both sides, and he wanted to make changes in his teams of Asp fighters before they sortied out to Mars. "I'd like to modify the armament on the Asps. I have some ideas about improving our firepower. I've met with Dave Swigert, your chief ordnance man, and—"

"I know who he is," Blackwell interrupted, her brow furrowed. "What's your point?"

Swigert agrees with my changes, sir."

"Rogers, I haven't time to go into that kind of detail. But Swigert has served with me for twelve years, and he's the best ordnance man in the business. If he agrees with you, go ahead. You've got my permission. *Carte blanche*. But don't bother me with any more questions or requests! *Dismissed!*"

* * * * *

Buck grinned as he and Wilma rode a fast subsurface electric railcar to the main workshop of the Armstrong lunar base. "I never thought you'd get around to asking her," Wilma said.

"Like everyone else, there's a doorway into the mind," Buck answered. "The finger-four formation really caught her attention. Blackwell's an old fighter pilot."

"I didn't know that," Wilma told him.

"I found out everything I could about her, at least as far as her combat record was concerned. She took some heavy losses in big melees with the Asps against the Zhangs. I watched her face closely. If she'd have understood that kind of formation a long time ago, Wilma, many of her closest friends, including her husband, would be alive today. But they're not. So she went back in her mind to those days when they were getting the hell kicked out of them. Any suggestions to redress old wrongs were welcome. So was my recommendation."

"But . . . you never did explain to her what you and Dave Swigert are planning."

"I didn't have to. One step after another. Even if she didn't have full confidence in my ideas about weapons, she trusts Swigert completely. So if he goes along with me on this, she'll back it all the way. Hey, we're almost there. Swigert will be waiting for us in the weapons modification center."

* * * * *

Dave Swigert looked up from the innards of a disintegrator beam cannon, his dark, bushy eyebrows and thick mustache contrasting with the gleaming glass and artanium and plastic materials of the space weapon. An unlit cigar stub jutted from his lips. A big man with thick arms and a bull neck, he had the fingers and touch of a surgeon, but you had to see the man work to realize his magical dexterity with complicated mechanisms.

Buck and Wilma stood by the workstand. Swigert didn't say a word or even look up, but they knew he was aware of their presence. Courtesy in the midst of delicate adjustments was virtually impossible, and they were all aware of that fact of life. Finally Swigert rose slowly, holding a hand pressed against his back. "This leaning over is gonna kill me someday," he grumbled. "Do me, will ya?"

"Take the position, hotrock," Buck told him. Swigert stepped away from the table and stood straight up, arms half-raised, as Buck moved in close, face-to-face, then wrapped his arms about Swigert's lower back, adjusting his fists until his knuckles pressed against the other man's backbone. "Now!" Buck shouted, and before Swigert could change position, Buck tightened his grip to almost a crushing hold. The *craaack-pop!* of bones jostled back into place brought a gasp of pain to Swigert, and then a smile creased his face. "You shoulda been a doctor," he told Buck. "I feel terrific. No pain."

"The sawbones would give you pills," Buck told him.

"Or a few shots in your tender spots," Wilma offered.

"Or two weeks of total bed rest," groused Swigert. "Okay, Ace, did the Dragon Lady buy your program?"

"She did. I just wonder if we have the time to get it fabricated, tested, and installed in the next six days."

"Miracles take time. Fortunately, since you took your big sleep, we got miracles by the bucket. I ran your description back to Niagara Central. The computers there in the big gun department have the scoop on just about everything ever made that was designed to go bang when you pull the trigger. We wanted the Madsen Mark Nine, right?"

"That's it."

"They had everything, right down to the alloys, assembly, operation—hell, everything, including cutting metal and parts and putting it all together. How many do you want, soldier boy?"

"Eight Asps, two Madsens per fighter. That's sixteen."

"Hey, Wilma, give your buddy a cigar. He can count." Swigert scowled at Buck. "How many spares?"

"Let's go for four. We'll take them aboard *Speedboat* and have them ready. What about ammo?"

"No sweat. That also was in the computers. They've already gone past first metal cutting and they're into assembly. It'll take three days to finish everything, one day to transfer the stuff here from Earth, one day to install and test. That gives you three days more before we shove off for the big red ball in the sky."

"The what?" Wilma asked.

"Mars," Swigert said casually. "If you don't like red, color it orange. The scoop we've been getting down makes it looks like the Big One is finally at hand."

"It is," Buck confirmed. "You heard Hasafi."

"Sure did. I like the old girl. If she could, she'd be right with us flying one of these things. By the way, does Blackwell know what we're doing?"

"She's busy. She didn't ask. Whatever is okay with you got the thumbs up from her."

"There's gonna be a lot of surprised people out there," Swigert said.

"Let's hope so," Buck told him. "Especially in the Zhangs and the big stuff."

"We've been so buried in disintegrator rays and lasers and guided torpedoes that no one's had time to go back into the history books." Swigert clapped a beefy hand on Buck's shoulder. "Sometimes it pays to dredge up the cavemen from the past. Like you," he added.

"One more thing, Jack."

"Which is?"

"Except for the Asp crews and the armorers, let's keep what we're doing quiet. The fewer who know about this, the less chance there is for the Mongols to find out what we're doing."

"Ain't no Mongols here," Swigert reminded him.

"Sure, but the walls have ears."

"You've got a suspicious mind."

"Absolutely. Are you telling me we haven't any skunks in the woodpile?" Buck asked.

"Who? Me?" Swigert held a hand over his heart. "I'm just an innocent babe. But you're right. Okay, we'll stay under wraps as much as we can. If the Mongols get word of our little caper before we tie into each other, we'll know it didn't come from us. Now get outta here and let me get back to work. I'll make the first test flight with you six days from now."

"Done."

They reached Mars cloaked in an enormous force field that concealed them from the Mongol radar and other detectors. Six separate formations deployed toward Mars, spreading out into a wide flanking approach that had the Mongols convinced the Amerigo forces were plain crazy to waltz right into the firepower of the Mongol spacecraft and surface weaponry.

The force fields worked for only two days before they began to fade. At that point, accelerated laser beams were cutting through the diffusion fields and focusing clearly on the incoming Amerigo fleets.

Or so they thought. Admiral Frank Bemis had four of the massive dreadnoughts to engage the Mongol heavy spacecraft. Outnumbered seven to four, it seemed Bemis was placing his ships and their crews in severe jeopardy. He counted on the Mongol concept of battle—engage, fight, kill, destroy. Finesse simply wasn't in their plan for battle.

Their very aggressiveness was the Achilles Heel of the Mongols. Bemis had planned carefully and with enormous effort for this titanic battle, leaving nothing to chance and counting on the strange psychology of the Mongols.

"They should have stayed on horseback," he told his crews. "That's how they fight best. Cloaks and ruses simply aren't their game."

Instead of merely four, *eleven* great Amerigo dreadnoughts steadily approached Mars. Four ships were those of the Bemis force. The remaining seven were huge inflatable replicas of the dreadnoughts. In the vacuum of space, covered with steel mesh fabric and blown up to full size, the hollow "dreadnoughts" were enormous decoys with enough weapons aboard to fire intermittently. Their low-powered thrusters propelled what were virtually space balloons directly at the waiting Mongol force.

Firing steadily, the eleven ships closed on the Mongol line. They were met with withering firepower from Admiral Yesulai, whose crews cheered lustily as one after another of the dreadnoughts burst into flames. Little did they suspect that the fires were set off by a distant microwave command from the real ships commanded by Bemis. At the height of the battle, sixteen Asp fighters in a flying wedge attacked from the opposite side of the Mongol line. It had all the earmarks of a perfect double-sided attack, cutting the Mongol fleet in half.

Within twenty minutes, seven decoy dreadnoughts floated helplessly in space, burning furiously. At the height of their cheering, the Mongols spun their big guns around to cut down the attacking Asps. No one had ever seen the nuclear-powered fighters flying such insane approach paths, whipping from side to side and up and down. It should have been obvious to the Mongols that no human being, no matter how well protected, could withstand the crushing g-forces of such violent maneuvers.

The Mongols began to discover this when their own Zhang fighters gave pursuit. Pilot after pilot lapsed into unconsciousness as he tried to lock on to the erratic and senseless flying of the Asps. As the Asps rushed in against the Mongol dreadnoughts, their disintegrator and laser rays firing ineffectively, they closed the distance swiftly.

The disintegrator rays were virtually useless against the massive armored shields and the defensive force fields of the Mongol dreadnoughts. The rays first had to penetrate the defending force field, losing much of their energy to make it through the dense hulls. By the time the rays struck the thick armor of a dreadnought, they lacked the power to disrupt the molecular bonds of the metal alloy hulls and penetrate to the ship's interior. Yet the effect was frightening, for even the best-constructed vessel could suffer an unexpected breach to be further exploited by the attacking Americans.

* * * * *

"Buck, it's working! We're getting through!" Wilma's voice carried excitedly to Buck in his Asp. Before him loomed the huge bulk of a Mongol dreadnought, its hull and flanks alive with the sparkling, deadly blasts of defending weapons. Off to his left, slightly behind him, an Asp was suddenly transformed from a sleek space fighter to a blazing tangle of junk, the victim of a direct hit by a defending heavy disintegrator pulse.

Aboard the Mongol heavies, alarms sounded constantly. The big ships of the line were still exchanging fire with Admiral Bemis's four dreadnoughts. The Asp fighters were somehow evading and getting through the defending Zhang formations.

Yet the battle's outcome was far from decided. "Wilma! Send in your remote now! Full throttle, and set the computer to a hard, curving approach. Make it from below."

"Roger, Buck . . ." Wilma eased off on her power to make sure she wouldn't lose consciousness. She switched her controls to remote, cutting out her own maneuvering ability for several seconds. When she moved her controls now, the response came from an unmanned Asp fighter, crammed with high explosives and deadly pyroxin, a chemical that splashed wildly and burned any material it touched.

There was no one aboard the Asp. Obeying its electronic controls from Wilma's fighter, the Asp rocketed in at top speed, ignoring multiple hits from defending guns. A withering blast smashed the cockpit section, destroying the control systems.

But it was too late. Unmanned, uncontrolled, hurtling forward from its own momentum, the pilotless Asp smashed into the dreadnought's hull, breaching the three outer layers, covering a large section of the hull with the intensely burning pyroxin.

"Dead hit!" Wilma shouted, her voice carrying to all the other manned Asps.

"Iminez! Massey!" Buck sang out. "We've got a hull breach! Follow it up with max speed attacks! *Go!*"

One robot-controlled Asp made it in, striking directly where the first ship had blasted into the dreadnought's hull. Flames exploded within the Mongol ship, severing control lines and systems. Slowly the huge vessel began to spin about its own axis, out of control.

"Go after that ship!" Buck ordered. Four fighters went in in tight formation, targeting their disintegrator beams on the hull breach. Two more manned Asps came apart under heavy defensive fire, but the remaining two poured a steady stream of disintegrator beams and laser fire into the heavy vessel. Great sections of the hull were cracking, splitting open, revealing intense flames within.

"Break! Break!" Every Asp pilot heard the frantic warning as a swarm of Zhang fighters, until now confused by the wild gyrations of the Amerigo ships, raced in for the kill.

"This is Asp Leader," Buck called calmly. "Lead fighters, go in as close as possible to the damaged areas of that battlewagon, decelerate, and make a tight turn around that thing. Stay as close as possible to the hull. They can't hit you that close in, and the Zhangs can't fire for fear of hitting their own ship. All hands, ignore the dreadnought. Take evasive action."

He moved his own fighter in tight, almost scraping the surface of the great battlewagon as he came under and up, slower now. Wilma stayed glued to his side and behind him in perfect wingman formation. Buck glanced behind him. It was working. The Zhang fighters stayed in hot pursuit, but most had stopped firing. They were too close, and they were in peril from the very ship they were defending, whose gunners were firing at anything moving.

"Force Two, Force Two! Do you read Asp Leader?"

"Got you, Leader."

"We're coming up and around. Come in with the finger four. Make all attacks in formation. Do not break your finger-four formations. Move in fast, *now.*"

Buck's fighters swept up, around, and above the stricken dreadnought. As they came into sight of the attacking Zhangs, the Mongol fighters rushed in for the kill. Right behind them, at maximum speed, came the remaining Asps, firing from maximum range. Brilliant fire beams alerted the Zhang crews. They broke off to the right, starting a wide circling turn that would enable them to make a firing pass at Buck's force, then continue coming around to meet the second group of Asp pilots answering Buck's call.

It was time to use the Madsens, weapons that had been resurrected from wars fought hundreds of years before.

Both the Asps and the Zhangs had energy shields to ward off most of the strikes from the beamed weapons. To be effective the rays and lasers had to hold their fire for several seconds in one spot to break down those defenses. That rarely happened.

Now, however, three Zhang fighters were torn open as if by invisible knives. The Asp fighters splitting into formation strikes were firing weapons that had not been used in eons—Madsen 23-mm cannons, firing a mixture of depleted uranium slugs to punch open their targets, followed by explosive incendiaries that erupted within the Zhang fighters.

Buck and Wilma came around tight and went through a wide formation barrel roll, flashing through the energy beams aimed at them. They dove directly at the approaching Zhangs, firing steadily with their ancient Madsens.

Within twenty seconds, half the attacking Mongol fighters were in flames or blown out of the sky.

"Break off and re-form," Buck ordered. "Get away from that battlewagon. Here comes *Speedboat*. . . ."

Blackwell brought in *Speedboat* like an avenging angel. The giant ship was faster than any in the Mongol fleet, spearheaded by two finger-four formations of Asp fighters. "Ignore that first Mongol battlewagon. It's already coming apart at the seams. Escort fighters, move in against the second ship. It's hurt but still fighting. Let's finish it off."

The Asps went in in perfect formation, firing their cannons in a blistering stream against the second battlewagon. Explosions pounded the hull, breaching the defensive armor.

"Fighters, break off," came the cool voice of Regina Blackwell. "Take up covering escort position."

The attack went smoothly, quickly, precisely as ordered. The approach was clear now, and the huge ship maintained high speed. *Speedboat* launched four rocket-powered missiles, each a vacuum torpedo with a massive warhead of armor-piercing alloy. As each torpedo sliced into the hull, the incendiaries erupted, sending fire sheets raging through the ship. One torpedo took out the main controls, while another blasted into the drive section. Two torps missed, but Blackwell had the heavy ship right where she wanted it. Four more torps flashed in; three found their mark. The aft section of the Mongol battlewagon split apart, swinging around to expose the interior of the dreadnought to vacuum. A shower of debris and human bodies erupted into space.

"*Speedboat*, this is command," came the voice of Admiral Bemis. "Break off contact with the enemy. We'll finish off the other two ships. It's four to two in our favor now. . . ."

They heard Buck's voice. "Asp Leader here. The enemy battlewagons are breaking off engagement. They're thrusting at full power, outbound from Mars."

"Roger, Asp Leader. *Speedboat*, recommend you pursue, maintaining distance for safety. Launch your torps as opportunity provides."

"Yes, sir," Blackwell replied. "*Speedboat* in pursuit."

"Asp Leader, do you read me?" called Bemis.

"I read you loud and clear, sir," Buck answered.

"Commence Phase Three immediately. We've got a break. Ludendorff is already on the surface of the southern hemisphere. He's down in a heavy dust storm, but it's providing cover for his forces. The storm is moving across Mars. Let's take advantage of that weather. Seidman is coming in with the equipment and vehicle carriers. You will rendezvous with him and follow his orders. Confirm, over."

"Asp Leader. Message received. Breaking off engagement and initiating descent. Over and out."

Buck paused a moment, then went to open line. "Asp Leader to all fighters. Wolf Squadron, you're coming down with us. Take up flanking positions three quadrants. All other fighters maintain escort for our heavies. Remain in touch with *Speedboat* and meet her requirements. Squadron leaders, confirm. Over."

One by one they called in. Wolf Squadron came streaking up into escort formation. The other Asps maintained their finger-four formations and sped off at full speed to rendezvous with the heavy battlewagons commanded by Admiral Bemis.

"All squadron leaders. Let's get down and dirty. On my mark, *go!*"

They dived planetward, Mars growing swiftly before their eyes as they plunged for the surface. Buck saw the dust storm roiling the southern half of the planet. It was moving steadily northward. It was a lucky break. If they could reach their rendezvous point just ahead of the storm, while they still had good visibility, they would descend into a deep ravine, three miles wide, that sliced the surface in a north-westerly direction.

From here on, it was going to be a bare-knuckles battle.

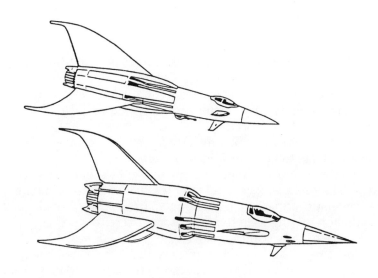

Chapter 22

To minimize the time spent in their drop to the planet, they descended to the Martian surface in a nearly vertical dive. The Asp fighters went down at reduced power, falling with gravity to reduce propulsion emissions and confuse Mongol radar and laser finders. Nose to tail, they would appear on a scope as a single long line, which didn't fit any recognition pattern locked into the Mongol computers. Dust enveloped them in orange haze as they slid into the boiling dust storm making its way across the planet.

Timing and keeping the Mongols guessing were critical factors now. Immersed in the dust, the Asps fired needle-shaped probes outward through an arc of three hundred and sixty degrees, creating the image of a wide host of craft flying downward. The EM decoys reflected full-size Amerigo spacecraft. Four miles high, one Asp triggered a following force field that gave the appearance of an entire fleet descending. Then two more decoys were fired to the north and south to give the appearance of three separate fleets descending.

"Wilma, confirm your surface scan to see if it matches our computer graphs for the landing area," Buck called.

"We're right on target, Leader," she called back. She rattled off latitude and longitude coordinates, knowing full well that they were being monitored by the Mongol and Tiger Men defenses. What the enemy didn't know is that the coordinates were false and would be converted into proper coordinates by a preset computer code. In the Asp fighters, nav consoles showed the pilots that their course was right on target. They were flying blind now, their Inertron generators kicking in with increasing power to slow their descent.

"Leader from Two," Wilma called. "We just crossed the Blue Smokies. Time to visit the bourbon plant."

The nav computer immediately presented their true coordinates. They had just crossed over a ridge of mountains; at the eastern end of the ridge, a smoking volcano spewed thick smoke into the air, mixing with the dust storm to create an electrostatic nightmare for any scanning devices.

Now they descended slowly, spreading out close enough to the surface for their radar to penetrate the dust and give them a true reading. "Dead Man's Gulch straight ahead," Buck called to his fighters. Let the Mongols pick up their transmissions. They couldn't make heads or tails from their coded speech.

Dead Man's Gulch widened out as its sides decreased in height until the Asps lowered gently into the middle of the great cleft in the Martian surface. Many thousands of years before, a river had coursed violently through this area, washing away topsoil and rocks and leaving behind a level surface at the bottom of the ravine. Ten miles ahead of their landing, the western slope of the ravine had collapsed, leaving a steep but navigable ramp for ground vehicles to traverse. If treads or wheels couldn't handle the slope, the vehicles awaiting them here under Big Mike Seidman could always use rocket booster engines or grapples to lock into the higher elevations. On the ground, Buck ordered three Asps to maintain immediate takeoff readiness. He donned powerful glasses that pierced the dust as if it were merely a slight fog. Arrayed along one wall of the ravine were multi-manned vehicles for skimming along over the Martian surface as well as an astonishing convoy of tracked and wheeled vehicles, armed with a formidable array of weapons.

Buck met immediately with Seidman. Gone were the stars that indicated his rank as a Field Marshal. Instead, he wore desert fatigues, electronic boots, and carried enough personal firepower to take on an armored column single-handed.

They shook hands. "Hell of a job you did upstairs," Seidman

greeted him warmly. "Between you and the rest of the group, you've got them hopelessly confused."

"Thanks," Buck acknowledged, "but save it for everyone on the team. They played ball like they'd been doing this for years."

"We tested that finger-four formation of yours on the ground. It works just as well for ground armor, especially in dust like this."

Buck admired the array of hardware in the ravine. "Tell me, Field Marshall—"

"The name's Mike. No rank from here on."

"Got it. How did you ever get all this stuff in here? I'd have thought you'd stand out like a Christmas tree."

"Near Mongol headquarters there's a serious underground fault. It leads right through the center of the Tiger Men as well. We put a cyclonic disrupter—that thing that keeps bursting every few minutes for several hours—right down the hole. The damn thing hit a soft spot, and they had one very neat and angry volcanic eruption on their hands. They were too busy taking care of that to notice us. We also planted a couple of exploding decoys on the Phobos moon to further divert their attention, and here we are."

"How far to the Cydonia Plain?" Buck asked.

"A hundred and six miles as the crow flies, if a crow could fly through this dust. We've already mapped out the best course to follow, but it could get pretty nasty the closer we get to that monolith of the face. The Mongols and Tiger Men have been moving up their power generators. They'll gravlift them to their big ships for transport to Venus. At least that's the way we've got it figured. They're armed to the teeth in that area. It's a funny thing, though. They must figure we shot our wad out in space, because they don't seem worried about anybody tackling them on the ground."

"That makes sense from their viewpoint," Buck said. "After all, they're the big boys here. We're interlopers and outgunned."

"We'll see about that." Seidman grinned.

"Do we have wind generators to keep this dust storm perking and keep us under cover?" Buck asked. "From out there in space, it looks as if the storm covers the whole bottom half of Mars. There's some kind of thermal effect involved, so even the infrared scanners are confused."

"We won't need to help nature with the dust storm, Buck. For a planet with an onionskin atmosphere, that's a hell of a wind blowing this stuff."

Buck adjusted his breathing helmet. "There's enough nitrogen in the atmosphere to measure between four and seven pounds per square inch. That's like mountaintops on Earth."

"Yeah, sure," Mike Seidman said tiredly. "And when's the last time you encountered a dust storm atop Mount McKinley? Look, we'll have time to jabber all we want when this is over. Right now let's get our people on the road."

"Wait one minute, Mike. We sent up those new oxygen systems. I hope they got here in time."

Seidman looked puzzled for a moment. "I haven't seen anything different from what we've always had, Buck."

"You wouldn't. You know Captain Ardala Valmar?"

"The lady sea dragon? Sure I do. She's a hell of an officer."

"Ardala developed a new nasal insert," Buck explained. "It's oxygen in solid form, tremendously compressed. Whenever any gas passes over it, it releases pure O two. You stick a container in each nostril—"

"Just what we need when we sneeze."

"Mike, stay with me on this. The thing releases oxygen according to the inhalation process. Each of these things is about half an inch long. The chemical catalyst in the gadget releases normal oxygen flow for about ten hours. When you don't need it, it simply permits ambient oxygen to pass through it. My point is, we don't need the masks and systems as long as we have these available."

Seidman rubbed his chin, thinking hard. "It would give us a real advantage over the Mongols. The Golden People and the Tiger Men have adapted to local temperatures and air pressure. When we wear the masks, they look down on us as some sort of weaklings. Seeing us without all that crud will give them some food for thought. It also ought to drive the Mongols nuts. I'll check. You make sure your people are in their assigned vehicles. In the meantime, I want to talk to that Japanese guy who just landed."

"Who is it?" Buck felt a cold chill down his back.

Seidman tapped a scroll. "Name is Takashi Inoyue. Apparently he's spent a lot of time with old Benjamin Barney in special ops."

"Mike, what is he doing here on Mars?"

"It's all a surprise to me, Buck. We got a coded message from Black Barney with some strange story about Inoyue having information about a major subterranean water source here on Mars. According to the scuttlebutt, there's even a deep underground river ten, maybe fifteen miles beneath the surface, and—"

Buck couldn't remain silent. "Hold on, Mike. How could Inoyue know about that?"

Seidman shrugged. "There could be a renegade among the Tiger Men—you know, someone gets ticked off with his own people and sells out to us if we promise to make him the big cheese after we clean their clocks. It could be anything. Besides, I've got more important things to worry about than some water source. That comes later. Right now, we've got to keep the Mongols from throwing us off the planet. Got it?"

"Got it," Buck said. But there were holes in the story. He would have to talk with Dawn Noriega and Wilma. Together, with their special talents, they might be able to figure out what in blazes was going on here.

"Forget about Inoyue, Buck. First things first. We've got to get these troops up to the Cydonia Plain. Aren't you the one who told the story about the Tiger Men's plans to help the Mongols transport some huge power drives to Venus?"

"I sure was. Still am," Buck answered.

"And we're supposed to stop them before they can get them off-planet?"

"That's the idea."

"Then let's get with it. I've heard some disturbing reports that the Mongols have some heavy antigrav equipment to lift those things and get them sunward."

Buck nodded. "Right on, Mike. The way I look at it, we'll use ground vehicles as far as we can with our combat troops and weapons to the Cydonia Plain. We won't really know what's going on there until we can eyeball the whole thing ourselves."

"What about the new jetpack flybelts?"

"They're limited in range and endurance," Buck explained. "We won't use those until we're close in and see what we're up against."

"Good enough. Let's get this show on the road."

271

BUCK ROGERS

* * * * *

Things didn't work out quite the way they planned. The dust storm increased in intensity, blanketing the world about them with thick dust that began to choke up their ground vehicles. They were groping their way along slowly. The lead vehicles, towing huge tank trucks, sprayed cryogenic mist ahead of the convoy. The super-cold gas formed the dust into clumps that fell slowly to the surface, clearing visibility somewhat.

Wilma drove a half-track with Buck at her side. A navigator behind them tried to match the aerial photos they had with the computer maps of the Martian surface. Their visibility was poor at best.

"Buck, this is foolhardy," Wilma told him, her face grim. "As soon as we can see a few hundred feet in front of us, the wind shifts and we're blindfolded again. The ground is shifting beneath us. The ground we're traveling over consists of nothing more than deep dust pits. Six vehicles have already slipped down those slopes. We got the crews out of two that couldn't be recovered, but we lost one entire crew. They're trying to get them out now."

"We can't wait for them," Buck said coldly. He had a pained but stubborn expression on his face. "The longer we take to get to Cydonia, the more likely we are to come under attack. What about the sonar systems?"

"They're not reliable in this dust. We're getting bouncebacks from thick concentrations of dust. It's almost impossible to tell what's dust and what's the side of this ravine. Then we have all that down-sloping of sand that's taking boulders with it. The cryogenic fog that clumps this stuff works only for a short distance. We're barely crawling."

"And at any minute we could go right over a ravine we don't even know is there," Buck said sourly. "Get me Seidman."

"Mike here. That you, Buck?"

"Affirmative. Look, Mike, you know what we're fighting out here, and—"

"I know. I recommend you take a scout force and go out with the new jetpacks. You can spread out, maneuver easily, and you can carry those assault rifles. They'll work against whatever we run into. Be on the lookout for some enemy flying scouts. I've got

Dawn Noriega up here, and she's sensing something in the air, but she can't tell what it is."

"Stand by, Mike."

Buck turned to Wilma. "Relax. Let go, woman. See what you can pick up."

Wilma placed her hands on each side of her head, closing her eyes. "Confusion . . . darkness. I get a feeling of . . . of something rapacious. Never felt that before. Ask Mari to come forward."

Wilma and Mari sat close together, heads touching, trying to receive whatever emotions were being broadcast from what lay ahead. "Buck, tell Noriega that Mari and I are sensing the same thing. The thoughts, or whatever they are, are almost primeval. It's more like instinct than thought, but they definitely are airborne."

Buck relayed the message. "Buck, Noriega here. They're right. No coherent thoughts. The only image I'm picking up is . . . well, biting and eating."

"That makes a hell of a lot of sense," Buck said with open sarcasm. "Mike, I recommend you keep Noriega with you, scanning for anything she can pick up. I'll take Wilma, Mari, and Adrian, plus two complete assault crews. Those new belts should work well here."

The belts had been modified for Martian surface operations. On Mars, everyone weighed only thirty-eight percent of Earth weight. The Inertron strips were nearly three times more effective. They could be used for hovering as well as slow flight, but each belt had a pack of neutrium fuel on a slowly unwinding spool. In the small thrust chamber of the jetpack, the neutrium was bombarded with a ruby laser and instantly converted to tremendous heat and pressure. The pressure was ejected from twin nozzles that gave the wearer the ability to fly swiftly and maneuver as quickly as the wearer could twist his or her shoulders.

An added advantage was that it left their hands free for using assault rifles. The newer rifles were several times the power of the older weapons, using both laser beams and projectiles, smaller versions of the Madsen cannon Buck had mounted in the Asp fighters. Each shell had a lesser primer charge to reduce recoil, but as soon as the round left the rifle, a microrocket flashed for tremendous punching power, laser beams and projectiles hitting in staccato fashion.

It took two hours after leaving the convoy for the fourteen members of Buck's team to reach the edge of the Cydonia Plain. They stayed close to the surface whenever dust conditions permitted. They knew their exact positions from the GPS transponders each man and woman wore as part of his or her equipment. These sent out signals picked up by Amerigo ships off-planet. Their position was triangulated and flashed back to the individual wearer, so that they knew at a glance where they were within thirty feet of their location at any time.

They flew over rilles and deep ravines, went around sudden abutments and volcanic domes, closing the distance steadily. Suddenly Wilma flew alongside Buck, signaling him to come closer. Speaking with the nostril oxygen cylinders gave their voices a dull sound, but the lip mikes accommodated the change.

"Mari and I are sensing those strange feelings again," she said. "I don't like it, Buck. It's almost as if we were reading the instincts of an animal rather than the thoughts of a person."

He stared at her, then switched to open line for his team. "Everyone, lock and load, safeties off. Be ready to open fire at any moment. It looks as though we've got some predatory company coming our way, both on the ground and in the air. If you see *anything* out ahead of you, kill it."

Wilma looked confused. "What was that all about?" But even as she asked the question, she readied her Q-Seven-Six rifle for open fire.

"Your feelings are confused, but you and Mari have been smack on, Wilma. Those thoughts you're getting? You felt they were primeval. They are! We've had reports that the Martians brought with them some of their own creatures. These are big reptiles, adapted to the light Martian gravity. Seidman told me about them. They're called sandscoopers. They fly fast and low, furrowing the ground with their lower jaws and teeth, and snap up anything they catch."

"*That's* what's out ahead of us?" she asked, her eyes wide.

"And not far at that!" he shouted, bringing up his rifle and firing three short bursts.

Wilma just had time to look up to see a vicious winged animal with both fur and feathers, a razor-toothed beak, and powerful wings whipping dust as it bore down on them, squawking hideously. Buck's laser fire started an fire burning in the chest of the creature, and the explosive shell that followed blew it apart. Blood and airborne flesh showered outward through the dust.

"Here comes another one!" Wilma shouted, firing. Two down.

Two more came at them from straight on, then they veered to one side, slowing as if they were sniffing the air. Abruptly they swung to the left, razor beaks open, wings folded as they dived for the ground.

"Blood scent!" Buck shouted. "There's so little game here, they can smell blood like a shark does back on Earth. We've just sprayed blood and guts all over the ground. It's mealtime for them! They're not interested in something that might fly away when there's a meal ticket waiting on the ground. Rogers to forward team; did you guys read me?"

A chorus answered him, all in the affirmative. Doug Millford was flying left point and called in. "Buck, you don't need to kill them! Just let some blood out on the ground and it's like a homing beacon for the others. They go in for the kill immediately. We've got a bunch fighting right now, tearing each other apart. It's like a pack of vultures after a dead horse."

"All hands, you heard Millford. Kill a couple of them, then climb up, and let's all go to maximum drive. Okay—let's do it!"

They raced ahead, the GPS locators keeping them on track. Wilma sounded a warning to Buck. "The sonar's changing. There are some kind of high structures ahead."

"That's their Cydonia station. Everyone—descend right to the deck. Stay low! There's a ridge ahead. I want everyone on the ground there. Keep low until we can check out what's waiting for us. Descend immediately."

They landed on the upslope leading to the ravine top. Buck and Millford went up the slope, hugging the ground, while the rest of the team stayed with weapons at the ready. Buck knew that the stopping of their forward motion would let the spaceborne fleet know where they were, and the same information would be passed on to Seidman, who was coming up fast behind them.

Through binoculars, Buck looked out over a flat plain extending into the distance. He spotted six great spacecraft through the now-diminishing dust storm. "Cargo carriers, from the looks of them," Millford said. "I've seen them before. Light armament, strong antigrav lifters, and they can set down almost anywhere. But I don't understand what they're doing here."

Buck focused on the eastern slope of the Great Face. Huge doorways had rolled to the side, revealing an enormous tunnel leading into the famed Face of Cydonia. "You see it?" Buck asked Millford.

"The damn thing is *hollow!*" Millford exclaimed. "That explains a lot, doesn't it? My guess is it leads to a major subterranean chamber."

Buck agreed. "See those long cylinders? Energy transformers. That's what they're getting ready to move to Venus. Keep a close watch for us. I'm going to record a compression message and get off a burst transmission to Admiral Bemis. He'll get it to Kane. But there's something funny going on down there. I don't like it."

"I sensed something odd, too," Millford agreed. "Look at the firepower they've got spread out down there. Heavy weapons teams, surface vehicles, even a squadron of Zhang fighters. It looks like they're ready for a full-scale ground assault. It's too much to keep tied up like this when we're beating their brains out in space."

Wilma and Mari edged closer to them. Both women were obviously in pain; Buck recognized the sign of fierce headaches. They were picking up something mental from down below.

"Something is wrong here, Buck," Wilma blurted out. "Mari's getting the same feelings. It's as if this is a facade. They *want* us to see what's here and report it to our fleet."

"That doesn't make sense," Buck said warily.

"Buck, Wilma and I together can pick up much more than either of us can alone. And we're getting the same signs. Down below, those people are doing their best to get a message to us. It's crazy, but that's what's happening. Can you reach Noriega? If she's getting the same readings, what we're getting is some kind of deliberate deception."

Seidman got Dawn Noriega on the line. "Whatever you're seeing down there is real," she confirmed. "But there's a lot of joking around and wisecracking among those people. That is definitely *not* like the Mongols. That's all I can get, but Wilma and Mari are right."

"Is that heavy stuff supposed to go to Venus?" Buck asked.

"Yes. But we can't tell what it's for when it gets there."

Buck leaned back against the slope. "The women are right. Something stinks down there. I've never known a Mongol who had a funnybone. You heard Noriega. Laughter! That's a crock, and yet . . ."

"I know," Millford said. "She's never wrong about what she reads. Not only that, but—"

Even through the thin air, they heard the wail of sirens from far below. "Uh-oh," Buck said. "School's out. Notify Seidman immediately."

"He's way ahead of us. Noriega's on the line for you."

"Dawn, Rogers here. Make it quick, lady. They're onto us. We'll have company any moment now."

"Maybe more than you expect," she said immediately. "From what I've been able to make out of the jumble I'm getting, the Tiger Men are insisting they take you people on in a death battle. Something about the Mongols being heavy-handed, even acting in a superior fashion. So the Tigers are going to run with the ball. But, Buck, this is a different game. The Tigers have genetic mutations of some very nasty animals they brought with them from their home world. I have mental images of them—bigger than rhinos and very heavily armored, like living steel plates on their hides. They've got spiked horns and—"

"How are they used?"

"Saddles and riders, but—wait! I'm detecting that these creatures are combinations of animals and machines. Extra protection for their vital systems, that sort of thing. They're stupid, and they use enhanced neuronic flow to their brains. If you knock out the rider—he's heavily armored as well—the dumb brutes will probably keep charging at you without knowing why."

"Thanks, Dawn. We can see them now. They're moving out. And you're right. They look like tanks."

"Buck, don't be misled. They're not that clumsy, and they're as fast as a racehorse. Don't judge their speed by their size or their shape. They'll be on you before—"

"Later. They're starting toward us right now. Damn, they're fast!"

The attack came in a long line. Tiger Men, their eyes blazing, stood in their saddle stirrups and fired ray guns, urging on the strange armored animals with their wicked horns. Their legs pounded along the ground like thunder, rolling closer and closer. Buck's ground troops fired steadily. Their laser beams heated up the armor plate, but only momentarily. Behind each splash of light came a rocket-propelled 23-mm cannon shell, armor piercing and accelerated under full force into the beasts' bodies. Several faltered and went down to their knees, but they forced themselves back up and continued the attack.

"Get the riders!" Buck shouted into his radio. "Hit them with the cannon shells!" That worked only for a few moments as force shields went up before the saddles and riders, rendering the lasers useless and diminishing the penetrating power of the Madsen shells.

"They're getting too close," Wilma said nervously, voicing what they all knew.

"Aim for their eyes," Buck ordered. "Three men against one rhino, rapid fire."

The volley slowed down the thundering attack. Several of the beasts, their eyes torn open by the exploding shells, wheeled about wildly, blinded and in pain, the urgings of their riders useless. But still more came on, approaching the edge of the slope leading upward to Buck's comrades.

"Everybody be ready to retreat using your jetpacks, on my order. Go down the ravine and take cover behind the first turn you come to!"

"Hold them off just a few more moments," Millford called. He reached behind him to his pack and removed a strange weapon with coils along the barrel. "It's a vibratory spanner," he explained quickly to Buck. "See that area the rhinos have to pass through to get to us?"

"Yes, but—"

Millford fired, not at the attackers, but at the sloping ground in front of them. He swept his strange weapon from side to side slowly. Dust boiled up and the ground seemed to slump. "It's a molecular disrupter. It doesn't do much against armor shields, but it's what every farmer dreams about! That ground is now a dust pit at least thirty feet deep. They should hit it at any moment."

The herd crashed into the powdery soil. Like a herd of buffalo thundering off a high cliff, they spilled and tumbled into the soft dust, crashing to the bottom of the trench.

Buck didn't waste a moment. "Incendiaries! Fire incendiaries into that trench now!" Rifles roared, and new clips were rammed into their slots. Flames leaped from one end of the trench to the other. The beasts within, unable to climb out, were driven to madness by the searing flames. Fire roared and crackled ever higher. "Some of those Tiger Men are getting out of there!" Buck yelled. "Cut them down!"

A moment later he modified his orders. "Hit them with one Madsen explosive charge each. Just one! I want to see blood and raw meat."

Wilma and Mari shuddered at his words, but in moments they saw the wisdom of his orders. Body parts and blood sprayed across the area below them. Great winged shapes appeared immediately, the huge airborne killing machines they had encountered earlier. The blood drew them as if by magic, and they swarmed over the remains spattered across the ground. Several wounded Tiger men emerged from the blazing trench. The great flying beasts tore into them with maddened savagery.

The battle seemed endless. "Buck!" He heard Dawn Noriega's frantic call. "They're sending Zhang fighters out against us. To our right and behind there are caves. A huge overhang, and cover beneath it."

Millford pointed to the area beneath the overhanging cliff and the cave openings. "Like she said, there it is. But a fat lot of good it's going to do us when those Zhang fighters come in. They'll slow down or hover on their antigrav and just pump lasers and disintegrator rays at us in the caves. Unless those caves go back a couple of miles, we're going to be between a rock and a hard place."

"I'll explain later," Buck snapped. "Everybody, move out. Don't waste a second. Make for those caves. *Move!*"

They scrambled down the opposite side of the slope, away from the crackling flames, the stench of savaged human bodies, and the hideous cries of the winged killers. "They won't be bothering us for a while," Wilma said, glancing at the sky where the predatory birds wheeled and dived.

"Not until they're full, anyway," Buck said. "Save your breath. Run. Get into those caves."

They made it beneath the overhang, stopping just inside a cave. Their escape seemed fruitless, however. The Mongol fight-

279

ers were doing exactly what Millford had figured. They moved slowly over the ground, headed for the caves, where they would soon turn them into a shooting gallery.

"Wilma, see those boulders out in front of us?" Buck pointed to a field of huge rocks that had tumbled from the high cliff.

"When I start for them, stay low and follow me. Millford, you too. When you hit those rocks, get behind the biggest one you can find and keep low. I don't want those Zhang pilots to see us."

He glanced at the approaching Zhangs. "Listen up, everyone! Keep up a steady fire against those fighters. All I need is for you to keep them occupied for several minutes. When I give the order, cease fire and take cover as deep as you can go inside the caves."

He and Wilma, with Millford right behind them, dashed for the boulders. Ray beams whistled and hissed about them as they zigged and zagged over the sand to the rocks. On the ground, safe now, they lay on their backs. Over them, the could hear the cover fire from their own forces. As Buck hoped, the Mongol fighters slowed their approach.

Buck pointed overhead. "See that break in the cliff line?" he asked. "It's a long fault line. That cliff is barely hanging on. Mari, Adrian . . . do you read me?"

"Go ahead."

"Keep firing from where you are. Let those Zhangs come in slowly until they're directly beneath the overhang in front of the caves. Then get back in there and out of sight. Take cover wherever you can find it. Don't wait for us."

"But—"

"That's an order. Get with it!" Buck snapped.

The others did exactly as told. They fired in short bursts, slowing down the Zhangs, which floated in, levitating in the light Martian gravity, their Inertron systems keeping them afloat, rocking slightly from side to side as they fired their own weapons and were hit by the blasts from the defenders.

Finally the Mongol ships were where Buck wanted them, directly beneath the overhang.

"All hands, everybody! Get back into those caves right now. Move, move!"

Buck, Wilma, and Millford lay on their backs, shielded by boulders from the Zhangs, firing with their autorifles into the weak line of the overhead cliffs. The Madsen shells exploded in the fault, splitting the crack in the cliff ever wider. Finally they felt the ground tremble and heard a great rumbling roar.

They scrambled to their feet and ran for their lives through a gauntlet of ray beams from the Zhangs. But the Mongol firepower was off its mark. The three figures had come into view without warning and were doing some fast broken-field running. Dust showered down, then a great *crraaack!* filled the air. Buck and the others threw themselves into a cave, rolling over and over, then dashing to their feet and running deeper into the cave. The cave became a tunnel that angled sharply to the left.

"In there!" Buck shouted. "Stay close to the wall and cover your head!"

The ground spasmed around them, and dust rose in a choking cloud. The sound of an enormous roar filled the world about them.

Buck grinned. "Now *that's* what I call an avalanche!"

The Zhang fighters with their crews lay smashed beneath several million tons of rock and dirt.

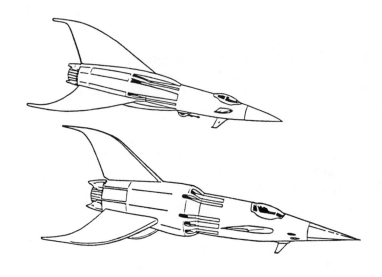

Chapter 23

Mike Seidman waited for them at their last rendezvous point. "The battle upstairs is over. Before they got their clocks thoroughly cleaned, the Mongols broke off the engagement. We've got a lot more than the standoff between us and the Mongols we hoped for when we started this fracas. You did a hell of a job at Cydonia. Headquarters is mighty pleased. We're still not certain what the Mongols have up their sleeves, but we're a lot more prepared now to handle anything they try then we were before.

"My orders are to get you aboard *Speedboat* at the first opportunity. They especially want Wilma and Noriega to be with you for a big meeting at the Niagara Orgzone. I know they want to talk about Venus, but you're more in the know about that than I am. We've got a Schirra transfer ship waiting to take you upstairs and dock with *Speedboat* for a fast run back to Earth. We've got the ships and the people to clean up what's left out here. Oh, yes, I have a message for you. It's from Regina Blackwell. She said to tell you she's got a porterhouse steak, some dark beer, and a big cigar for you—plus a quiet private room after that for you to get some shuteye on the way back home."

Buck sighed and managed a smile. He was dog-tired; he hadn't slept in three days and nights. "Blessed be the lady," he said to Big Mike. "Tell her I'll take the meal, the beer, and the sleep in that order."

Speedboat went down the gravity chute toward Earth at a rapid pace, then swung into an elliptical approach path with forward thrusters blazing to minimize their time en route. When they entered Earth's atmosphere, Buck watched Regina Blackwell handle the super-fast cruiser as if it were her own personal skycar.

"Something new has been added," he said to her as she maneuvered toward a huge waterfall off the top of a new rectangular building at the edge of Niagara.

"Looks are deceiving," she answered with a smile. *Speedboat* moved slowly into the waterfall. The world disappeared behind a hissing, foaming cascade of water. They emerged from the vertical torrent in an enormous spaceport. Regina took *Speedboat* neatly into a docking bay.

"The council is waiting for you, Wilma and Dawn. We'll be checking our ship out and refitting. You're going to be riding with us to Venus."

Buck looked at Blackwell sharply. "As great as this ship is, you're not taking her down into that hellish pit of a planet, I hope."

"Not on your life," she laughed. "Just wait until you see the bucket we've got for you."

He embraced Regina briefly and warmly. Soon he and the two women were in a tube car on their way to the council chambers.

They were surprised to see Killer Kane with the president and his staff. Buck didn't ask questions; he'd hear soon enough what was going on.

Their meeting centered around a huge oval table heaped with fruits and nuts and flavorful wine. It was obvious that Vice President Hasafi was leaning toward traditional Saudi hospitality with the fruits and nuts, with a nod to her English background for the wine. After the obligatory congratulations for the performance at Mars, the council got down to serious business.

* * * * *

"There has been a long-standing tacit agreement between this council and the Celestial Mogol," Hasafi began, "that Mars would be developed by the Mongols in concert with the Tiger Men and the Golden People, while Venus, which they consider to be virtually impossible to terraform for human habitation, would be left to us for development. The Mongols are, to say the least, a people of dark suspicions. Basically, they are untrustworthy."

She tapped a pen gently on the table, reviewing her notes. "Yet we've managed to avoid further nuclear confrontations on Earth. This was not accomplished through cooperation, a desire for peace, or anything save sheer survival. It is incredible to think that we had to resort to twentieth century savagery to implement the ancient MAD program. No offense, Brigadier Rogers, but the truth is inescapable."

"Madam Vice President," Buck spoke quickly, "I take no offense or find any fault with what you say. The concept of MAD—Mutually Assured Destruction—between the United States and the Soviet Union was all that separated the world from nuclear devastation. There's no point in burning down your neighbor's home if the fire also consumes you and your family."

"Spoken with great clarity. I appreciate that, Rogers. Yet we are riven with disturbing news about Mongol interest in Venus. It is, shall we say, almost senseless. They are pouring immense energy and material into transforming Mars. Even if they are successful, it must be ongoing in its application because of planetary characteristics with which we are all familiar. It should relieve them to know we are concentrating on Venus. Yet we have just engaged in a fierce and costly engagement in space and on Mars as if the Mongols believe we intended to throw them off the planet for our own purposes."

She glanced at the other council members, who nodded briefly, and she continued. "Commodore Kane may shed some light on this puzzle, but he also brings confusion. It is almost certain there is a great underground river within Mars. That fact, coupled with the polar ice caps, means the Mongols have real promise in Martian development."

"Madam, are we working in concert with the Mongols in their plans for Mars?" Buck asked.

She appeared startled at the question. "Heaven forbid! It would be a pact with a scorpion, or perhaps the devil," she added.

"Then why was Takashi Inoyue involved with the Tiger Men in explorations for such an underground river?"

"Commodore Kane can answer that question. Commodore?"

"Rogers, that's a two-way street. The Mongols are hardly experts in underground waterways. And despite their long tenure on Mars, neither the Tiger Men nor the Golden People are any better. Inoyue is an expert. He can survive underwater operations longer than any man I know. We spent a lot of time in special operations, with the SEALS and other groups."

"I'm sorry," Buck said, "but I still don't understand why he's helping the Mongols and others."

"He's charting the details of below-ground water flow. Source, quantity, how long it may keep flowing, that sort of thing. These are details the Mongols desperately need to know. It can only enhance their desire to make Mars their next dominant world. No doubt they'll have problems with the Tigers and the Goldens. But right now he's a hero to them."

"May I ask what this assistance does for us, sir? I don't mean to be impertinent, Commodore," Buck stressed, "but why should we help the enemy?"

Kane leaned back in his seat and smiled.

"With what Takashi is doing, we'll know everything the Mongols and their allies know about the subterranean water system. If events should ever bring us to have to fight for our benefit on Mars, we'll know as much as they do. That makes them pretty damned vulnerable."

Buck sat quietly. He hadn't liked this whole arrangement from the beginning. Valuable data or not, it smacked to him of the same kind of appeasement he remembered all too well from the history of his own time. But Kane had spoken for them all, and he had little more than ancient history and his own opinions to offer. Best to keep his silence.

Hasafi looked to Dawn and Wilma. "We know that you, Dawn, are telepathic, and that Wilma is an empath. Isn't there a third crew member with Wilma's receptivity?"

"Yes, sir," Kane answered for Noriega. "Her presence was not requested here for this meeting. She is at work servicing Blackwell's ship. If you want—"

Hasafi gestured for silence. "It won't be necessary, Commodore." She turned back to Dawn and Wilma.

"Let's put aside the Mongol plans for Mars, at least for now," Hasafi instructed. "Both of you play critical roles in our plans. Using your special talents, did you pick up any messages, thoughts, images, or plans of the Mongols as they relate to Venus? Let me go on for a moment. We have Brigadier Rogers's reports on the energy machines he witnessed on the Plain of Cydonia, and he is convinced they are destined for Venus. The general agreement is that the Mongols will leave Venus to us. His report disturbs me greatly. Can you add anything to what he has said?"

"It is highly disturbing," Dawn replied. "I believe Wilma Deering agrees with what I felt." Wilma nodded, and Dawn went on.

"There were many images relating to Venus and its rotation, Madam Vice-President. Some thoughts were clouded and hazy, as if an attempt was being made to prevent the Mongols in command from, well, broadcasting mentally is as good a phrase as any. We are both in agreement that the energy drivers are destined for Venus. We do not know why. Wilma functioned as a passive receiver while I attempted to increase the images of what is planned by the Mongols for the future. We both received feelings of great intent."

"It is my impression," Wilma stepped in, "and I must emphasize that this is strictly a feeling, that a great sham is under way."

"And that is the impression you both received?"

"Yes, ma'am," they said unison.

Buck leaned forward. "May I interrupt? There's something else that I find disturbing."

For the first time, President Grenvil Logan joined the discussion. "By all means, Brigadier."

"This may not relate to what Dawn and Wilma have reported, or even what I saw personally at Cydonia. But something is very much out of whack, and when something is awry or it doesn't fit the scheme of things, that bothers me. There's something else I picked up on our return to Earth from Mars in *Speedboat*. Commander Blackwell used a cloaking device when we approached Earth. That's pretty automatic because of possible Mongol monitoring of our space traffic. As we came into our elliptical path and then began thrusting for de-orbit, we encountered an unexpected anomaly in the gravitational fields we use for accurate approach."

"Do you know what that anomaly was?" Logan queried.

"Yes, sir. It took quite a while for the computers to come up with the answer, because we didn't know what to ask. The variation in the gravitation fields is being caused by the asteroid the Mongols placed in orbit some time ago. Anything eighty miles in diameter, even at an orbital height of eighty thousand miles, is going to exert its effect on both the Earth and the moon. But that effect has long been calculated, and it's known right down to the last decimal point. Recently, however, it has shifted."

"How?" Kane shot at Buck.

"The automatic approach was rejected by the flight computer," Buck answered. "Commander Blackwell, of course, has recorded all the details. You can study her report if you wish."

"Just the answer, if you have it, please," Kane said sharply.

"Mongolium—the asteroid—is increasing its distance from Earth."

Logan turned to Kane. "There's always been some subatomic spray from the power systems aboard that thing, Kane. But has it changed in any way?"

"Less than one percent. It's within the longtime parameters," Kane replied.

Logan made an immediate decision. "I want that asteroid monitored constantly for all parameters—subatomic spray, velocity, any further increase in orbital path or perigee—anything."

"Yes, sir."

"But there's something more immediate and important to consider. I do not like one bit this sudden increase in Mongol interest in Venus. I like even less what Rogers found at Cydonia. I want Venus scanned with high-energy radar, lasers, thyronic probes. Send robot ships out there. Cover the damned planet from one end to the other. If there's even the slightest change in its patterns, I want it reported immediately. And I want every watchdog system we have to keep tabs on the movement of Mongol ships sunward. Rogers, you said they were amassing powerful energy drive systems?"

"Yes, sir."

"The kind that generate power over long periods?"

287

"Yes, sir. Immense power. It's either subatomic or gravitic systems linked to thermonuclear generators. It's big, Mr. President."

"Could it affect conditions on Venus?"

"There's enough energy there, over a period of months, to affect rotation speed."

Logan turned to Killer Kane. "I want direct personal observation on Venus. I want men and ships sent down into that hellhole. The remote systems won't be enough to tell us what the devil is going on down there, and I don't like it. My own sixth sense tells me something is going on. Brigadier Rogers?"

"Yes, sir."

"You turned in a sterling performance aboard *Io*. You've had some background in underwater research, haven't you?"

"Yes, sir."

"Deep?"

"Yes, sir."

"Think carefully before you answer me now, Brigadier. Would you be willing to take a ship down to the Venusian surface? Word of your exploits has spread throughout our fleets, and you can have your pick of the best we have to go with you. By God, I'd go with you myself, but—" He shrugged. "I've often wished I had become a sailor instead of being stuck in this blasted presidency."

Buck smiled. "I can understand that, sir."

"You'll take the assignment, then?"

"Yes, sir."

"Kane, will you go with him?"

"Why not? He's a good-luck charm, that one is," Kane boomed.

"That special battle cruiser we're building for a future Venus expedition," Logan asked. "When will it be ready?"

"Now, sir," Kane said immediately.

"That will be your vessel, Brigadier Rogers. You'll have a crew of no more than ten. It's no pleasure yacht, but it's a bundle of trouble for anything that gets in its way. You may have the honor of naming your new vessel, Rogers."

"You can't beat the original, Mr. President. We'll call her *Nautilus*."

"Highly appropriate." Logan's palm slapped the table. "You

get under way in four days. You'll have to work day and night with your crew to get ready."

"We'll be ready," Buck promised.

* * * * *

Nautilus was shaped like a huge oval, a football shape with various protuberances jutting from its massive hull. In reality, *Nautilus* was a six-hulled vessel along its outer shells. Between each hull, cryogenic generators kept up a steady flow of super-cold gas and liquid to dissipate the terrible heat of the Venusian atmosphere. Even the portholes maintained this powerful temperature control, making *Nautilus* a floating ice-box in what amounted to a boiling lava pit. Jutting outward at various positions were giant steel blades, a feature that Buck had insisted on. "If we encounter opposition from the Mongols or anyone else in that hellhole atmosphere, using standard weapons is going to be a dicey proposition. Explosive charges can be tricky to control because of the natural pressure of fifteen hundred pounds per square inch at the surface. I also want a ram installed in the nose. It may go all the way back to the times of fleets of ancient Greece, but ramming an enemy vessel at high speed in such an atmosphere could put it out of business faster than anything else."

He gathered his crew. He chose Commander Regina Blackwell from *Speedboat*, and Ardala Valmar from *Io*. No one could handle a big submersible with more skill than Valmar, and no one knew Mongol spacecraft better than Blackwell.

Wilma Deering and Dawn Noriega were essential to the mission. No one could foretell what they might pick up from Mongols or other people on Venus. Black Barney and Killer Kane were a formidable team in any conflict. Doug Millford had proved his worth with Buck on the Plain of Cydonia. Big Mike Seidman could fill in at almost any position and, if necessary, could leave *Nautilus* in an armored cryogenic suit to attend to any repairs of the submarine. Doc Huer was the last of the crew, as necessary for his medical skills as for his experience and wisdom.

"Our liftoff from Earth will follow standard operation," Buck told his crew in a final briefing. "I want Regina on the controls throughout flight until we enter the Venusian atmosphere, then Ardala takes the helm. Kane and Barney are to oversee all operations. Wilma and Dawn, you'll monitor systems, and several times each duty period you'll retire to one of the external viewports to see what you may be able to pick up telepathically. Seidman is responsible for the ship and its propulsion system. Doc, in addition to being our sawbones, I want you to handle communications and data recording of all systems. Millford will be my alter ego for whatever comes up, and he's ready to take over any armament system from anybody else as needed.

"There's an old expression that best fits this moment. Let's shove off."

* * * * *

They lifted off in standard antigrav fashion, boosted by the microwave beams. For the outbound—sunward—portion of the flight, they had attached a nuclear booster for added speed, to be jettisoned when it was no longer needed. During departure from Earth, Admiral Frank Bemis launched fourteen more spacecraft to mask their flight. With seven ships firing nuclear boosters at full power, spraying enormous clouds of subatomic particles and neutron fog into vacuum, it was impossible to track any one ship. Amidst the cover from the other ships, *Nautilus* was launched sunward. Regina Blackwell took them perilously close to the sun in a huge, looping arc. Any other ship save *Nautilus*, with its cryogenic-layered protection, would have heated to lethal limits. But Blackwell skimmed the edge of danger, and as they came looping around the sun, she jettisoned the nuclear booster. Halfway to Venus on the backside of the loop, she sent the booster off at a tangent into open space. Not blocked by any planet, the booster exploded in a titanic blast. The gravity warp of the blast and the flood of gamma, X-ray, and neutron radiation could hardly be missed by the Mongols.

"They've lost another ship to a failed propulsion system," was the conclusion in Mongol headquarters. "Good riddance."

* * * * *

"The best way to get deep into Venus's atmosphere," Regina Blackwell explained, "is to go in fast, like a meteor. The visible radiation will be picked up by Mongol outpost sensors."

"You want us to be picked up?" Doc Huer asked, not really believing what he'd heard.

"Almost, Doc, but not quite!" Regina told him. "Just before we reach the upper atmosphere, we'll encase *Nautilus* in an expandable envelope of magnesium. Friction with the atmosphere will turn the envelope into a raging fireball visible halfway across the solar system. When we decelerate, we'll jettison the envelope, the radiation and glare will completely cover our presence, and we'll drop into the Venusian atmosphere at a controlled speed. I advise all of you to tighten your belts and harness. This is going to be one wild ride."

"Recommendation," said Killer Kane.

"Please," Blackwell acknowledged.

"Before you jettison the mag cover, activate a maximum force shield for added protection. This atmosphere isn't like space. It has areas of thick gases, and we may run into the upshot of one or more volcanic eruptions. I'd hate to collide with a few thousand tons of rock, even in this bucket. The force field will handle anything out of the ordinary until we decelerate to safe maneuvering speed."

"Excellent suggestion, Barney. Thank you. Will you attend to the field?"

He laughed. "My hand's already on the controls, Commander."

Forty miles above the surface of Venus, they plunged into the clouds of sulfuric acid and carbon dioxide. At this height, the Venusian winds blew fiercely, and even within the massive armored hull of *Nautilus* they could feel the autopilot correcting for wind gusts. Strapped and harnessed into g-seats, they watched the temperature needles rising steadily and felt deceleration as they plunged downward. Blackwell's command came quietly but firmly. "Ten seconds to envelope expansion." The seconds seemed to tick away slowly, but right on time there was a dull boom as cryogenic gases blew an outer magnesium hull about the spacecraft. Almost immediately fire raged around the decelerating vessel.

"Rogers," Doc Huer called out. "You ever go through this kind of maneuver before?"

To his surprise, Buck nodded. "Once. That was enough."

The crew looked at him in surprise. "When was that?" Huer asked.

"A very long time ago. I was about twelve years old. They used this same maneuver in a movie called *2010* to decelerate a Russian spacecraft going into orbit around Jupiter."

"Did it work?"

"It worked," Buck said with a grin.

Suddenly an enormous shock wave slammed against the hull and the electrical meters spiked. "Lightning," Blackwell announced. "We're a lightning rod for all sorts of electrical activity. We'll get hit plenty of times on the way down."

At ten miles up, they were the center of an electrical maelstrom, with lightning flashing all about them. Barney cut loose the magnesium envelope. It fell behind them rapidly, blazing, attracting its own lightning strikes.

"Six miles to landing," Kane announced. "Recommend bringing in the antigrav lift and activating Inertron bands. We're decelerating rapidly."

"External temperatures are diminishing," Seidman called out as he studied his instruments. "We're just under Mach One and still slowing."

"Velocity is down to just under one hundred miles per hour," announced Barney. "Hydrojets coming on line in fifteen seconds."

Then they were cruising at slow speed, decelerating with the antigrav units. *Nautilus* rocked and pitched from powerful lightning strikes. "The outside wind is down to less than forty miles per hour," announced Ardala Valmar. The crew was working together like a fine watch.

"Thirty-degree right turn," Buck ordered. "We've got a volcanic eruption dead ahead. Sensors picking up heavy objects lofting in from below."

Nautilus veered gently to the right, then resumed course. They were using radar, lasers, cryogenic scanners—everything possible to maintain their preset course based on radar-imaging charts of the surface.

"Skin and internal temps holding," Barney announced. "All cryogenic systems working perfectly."

Outside the outer skin, the temperature was already nearly two thousand degrees. "Confirm pressure," Blackwell called.

"Fourteen hundred psi," Barney answered. "Just as advertised."

"We're getting some visibility now," Buck announced. "Height above surface is only three hundred feet. I'll put the scanners on the holos."

They looked upon a scene that might have been a painting of Hades. Everything was a murky orange, the sun a dim light barely able to penetrate the thick clouds above.

"Full power to the lights," Blackwell ordered.

"Lights coming on," Barney announced.

A battery of superxenon halogens speared the orange murk, intense light beams reflecting from the strange atmosphere as if it were a fog bank, revealing scaly rocks and slag all along the surface.

Seidman's voice boomed in their headsets. "Listen up, everybody. I'm picking up metallic objects ahead of us."

"We'd better slow down until we know what the devil is out there," Doc Huer recommended.

"No way, Doc," Buck said. "In this atmosphere, we're a submarine. "We've got to keep moving. We're negative buoyancy, like an aircraft. If we drop speed, we'll sink like an overloaded sub."

"Barney, what do you make of what's in front of us?" Valmar questioned.

Barney kept his eyes moving from the visual holos to his instruments.

Barney delayed his answer. "I'm setting up the holo imaging with full screening for ambient conditions. You'll be able to see outside if you're wearing the informax goggles, but everything on the holoscreen will be in three dimensions. Get ready for a shock." He paused again. "Buck, arm all weapons systems. Kane, get on the missile batteries. Millford, man the intercept systems. Seidman, you and Doc get into your armor suits and be ready for surface excursion. Check in with me, everybody. Blackwell, if I call for power, give me everything this bucket has. Valmar, you support Blackwell. Noriega and Deering, see what you can pick up."

They executed Barney's orders, then looked at the holoscreen with disbelief.

Before them spread a Mongol encampment. They saw three spherical vessels on the ground, with men moving about in armor suits, and several tracked vehicles, but what really commanded their attention was a huge thermonuclear power station, assembled in orbit and then maglev lowered to the surface. Thick cables ran from the station to a series of huge tubular banks, burrowed at low sloping angles into the ground.

"Barney, have they detected us yet?" Blackwell asked. Everyone was ready for any emergency.

"No," Barney replied. "Stand easy, everyone. I killed all lights and thrusters when I first detected the camp, and I've got a cryogenic fog drifting across the entire area. To the Mongols, we're nothing more than a cold spot in this crazy atmosphere. But it may not stay like this for very long."

Ardala Valmar turned to Dawn and Wilma. "Anything?" she asked.

"Pictures . . . muddled scenes," Wilma answered. "Something spinning. Huge, planet-sized, spinning like mad. It feels wrong somehow."

"Dawn, how about you?"

"Someone is thinking about . . . the future. I have a hazy picture of a new great city amidst mountains, but everything is surrounded by water. Cold . . . blizzard . . . Japanese."

"*Japanese?*" Barney blurted out. "That doesn't make any sense!"

"The images fade in and out. Someone, or a group, is thinking of a great victory, a new world order . . . then it fades again."

Barney turned to Buck. "Hey, I know the Japanese. The only people who hate them more than the Mongols are the Han, and I *know* they won't work with the Japanese. Dawn, any idea of where this place is you're imaging?"

"Islands . . . winter . . . mountains and water. That's all I can make out."

"Work on that puzzle later," Blackwell said in a no-nonsense tone. "Look sharp. See those floating spheres? They're armored, and you can see the rocket launchers. The warheads are probably set to explode at a distance of at least one mile from the spheres. That would create enough overpressure to damage *Nautilus* and let them survive the shock. What they don't know is that we could take a dozen of those kinds of warheads and not even quiver."

"But they could be crazy and fire something to penetrate our hulls," Buck snapped. "Those things are manned, and we've got weapons to penetrate any kind of armor. Seidman! Set up the Madsens for high penetration only. We don't need incendiaries here, we just want to hole those things and let this atmosphere do the rest."

He watched the spheres approaching, three of them in a **V** formation, closing steadily. Then it hit him. They were floaters, like rubber rafts being pushed slowly on a lake, while *Nautilus* could maneuver like a wolf chasing sheep.

"Full ahead!" Buck commanded. "Gunners, fire when the target is in range. Everyone hang on. We're going to ram that sphere on the right. In five seconds, I want a spray of xenon flares to blind their sensors and tracking devices."

Five seconds later the missile array went out, sparkling and burning fiercely. The Mongol crews were caught by surprise. Even their pilots reacting clumsily, the spheres bobbing about like corks in a turbulent stream. A fusillade of Madsen cannon shells ripped into the lead sphere, cracking it open like an enormous walnut. Instantly metal folded inward, powerful armor plating twisting and splitting like shards of glass. A dull boom sounded over the distant cannonading of incessant lightning strikes as the sphere imploded to a mashed pile of junk.

"Hard right!" yelled Barney. "Missiles coming dead on! Hard right and climb!"

Buck didn't answer as he maneuvered *Nautilus* under full power. Her thrusters powered the great spacecraft upward, an enormous teardrop shape seeming to leap into the murky orange sky. At the same time, Buck rolled out of the climb, still under power, and dove directly at the target sphere. Without orders, both Kane and Blackwell fired a spray of missiles to confuse their target. The sphere started up, dropped like a stone, then bobbed to the right. Buck went in at reduced power, and an enormous magsteel ram sliced into the sphere like a hot poker into a ball of butter. As the metal yielded, poisonous atmosphere under enormous pressure ripped into the sphere. There was the sound of another implosion as Buck reversed thrust and pulled away from the mortally wounded sphere.

"Everybody fire steadily at that third sphere. Fire a brace of seeker homers. They'll probably launch some heavy torps at us, and we may not be able to withstand a direct hit." Even as *Nautilus* launched counter-torp rockets that would race against the incoming missiles from the last sphere, Buck sped forward, the belly of *Nautilus* scraping rocks. Mongol missiles sped overhead, lacing the orange sky with trails of fire, only to finally exhaust their fuel and impact with the distant ground and explode harmlessly.

Buck dismissed the spheres from his attention. Ahead of *Nautilus* reared a high, steep cliff. Weapons turrets studded the cliff face.

Barney spoke directly to Killer Kane. "This installation isn't even supposed to be here! What the hell is going on?"

Kane laughed. "No time for questions, old friend. Rogers! You see those turrets? They're missile launchers, and there's too many of them for us. If you've got a plan, use it now!"

"The best defense . . ." Buck started.

Kane finished it for him: ". . . is a good offense, so let's let them have a full blast and then get out of here."

"You heard the man," Buck confirmed. "I want every weapon we have to fire immediately against that cliff. Torps, missiles, Madsens on full autofire. Kick off every xenon blinder we have as well. As soon as we've let everything loose, hang on. We're getting out of here. Valmar! Blackwell! As soon as we launch our weapons, I want full thrust, maximum possible climb, curving ascent. I'll be doing some weaving and S-turning on the way up. Fire lightning xenon flares to our port and starboard and let them float down. They won't be able to track us. *Fire!*"

Buck just had time to see one of their missiles, followed by a stream of exploding Madsen cannon shells, rip into one of the enormous cylindrical tubes. From everything he had learned of such energy mass drivers, the tube should have been studded with transformers that would accelerate the energy charge as it went through the tube and deep into the mountain into which it was fixed.

The transformers were there, visible only for seconds as the side of the cliff collapsed under the withering firepower.

A tremendous shock slammed into *Nautilus*. "We've taken a

torp," Doc Huer said calmly. "Heavy damage. Cryogenic protection systems are falling off line."

"Overdrive, *now!*" Buck shouted to Valmar and Blackwell. A blast of nuclear fire well behind him slammed him back in his seat, crushing him against his backrest. He tasted blood as his teeth bit into his lower lip, and he was barely able to move as *Nautilus* accelerated quickly. Behind them, through the holoscope, he saw explosions where they had been only moments before.

They climbed at a breathless pace, the nose section blazing from friction, heat seeping into the crew compartment. They were taking five, then seven, then twelve times the force of gravity. Several of the crew were already unconscious, blood streaming from nose and ears. They couldn't take this much longer. Suddenly a dazzling light appeared before them. The sun!

"Out of atmosphere!" Blackwell announced.

"Decelerate to five-g max," Buck ordered, trying to save his crew. Racing away from Venus, maintaining the punishing acceleration of five times gravity force, speed building up swiftly to dangerous limits, Buck instantly changed their acceleration and course. He took direct command of their power now, reducing acceleration to three g's. "Fire off trail decoys," he ordered. "Let them track the dummies."

Blazing torps with subatomic spray and xenon superflares burst in a curving line away from *Nautilus*'s course.

"Buck, you read me? This is Doc."

"Go ahead."

"You realize we're in an orbital curve that's taking us straight toward the sun. Pretty soon this thing is going to pass a million miles an hour when we start being pulled in by solar gravity."

"Right, Doc."

"They had some light cruisers out here we didn't see on the way in," Doc went on. "You have them on your scope?"

"Got 'em, Doc," Buck said, his voice deceptively calm.

"They may be able to outspeed us, Buck," Doc said.

"Rogers," Kane added, "I hope to Hades you know what you're doing. This bucket ain't no spacefighter. Any Asp or Zhang can run circles around us. We're in a submarine. Will you please keep that in mind?"

"Yep," Buck laughed. "That's why we're going to play Wile E. Coyote."

His words were met with a chorus of "*What?*"

"Make sense, will you?" Blackwell said sharply.

"When you can't outfight them and you can't run away from them, you vanish," Buck laughed. "Or at least they think you've vanished. Even better, they might believe you've been destroyed. Seidman, prepare to launch dummy ship."

"Ready," came the answer.

"Then let her go," Buck ordered.

A long cylinder sped away from *Nautilus*. Immediately Buck cut power, impelled by their speed alone, leaving no exhaust trail. Behind them, a metal-coated duplicate of *Nautilus*, a rigid balloon, expanded into the same size and sensor readings as *Nautilus*.

"We're close enough to the sun now that we'll be accelerating steadily," Buck told his crew. "So is that dummy ship. Any moment now it should trail a false exhaust they can't miss with their sensors. They'll be within firing range soon, and I want them to hit the dummy. When they do, the impact will set off the high intensity flares, and at the same time, it will emit signals of the ship breaking up, pieces going out in all directions."

"And what will we be doing all this time?" Seidman asked.

"We're headed straight for Mercury. Look at your screens."

Behind them, missiles slammed into the duplicate *Nautilus*, setting off violent explosions. Buck closed on Mercury, running without power. Nevertheless, their rate of closure was frightening. At the last possible safe moment, Buck played his next card. "Full rad shields!" he ordered. An intense energy shield surrounded *Nautilus* to ward off the powerful radiations streaming outward from the sun.

"This close in," he said aloud, as much to himself as to his crew, "we're blanketed by Mercury's disc, and solar radiation is making hash of the Mongols' sensors. They can't see or detect us . . . so they'll believe that dummy was us."

He worked the controls as if he were in a fierce race around a pylon course. Crater walls seemed to leap out at them. Buck slammed the controls in full reverse thrust, decelerating almost to a hover, bringing in the Inertron and antigrav fields. *Nautilus* went down like a helicopter, slowing steadily.

"We're not taking any chances," he announced. *Nautilus* rounded the curve of the planet into sunside as Buck lowered the ship into a deep crater, shielded from the sun by towering walls. They felt the hull touch rock. "Shut her down!" he barked. "Life-support systems only!"

Nautilus lay like a great shark at the crater bottom, shrouded in darkness.

High above, three Mongol battle cruisers raced by, unaware that they were passing directly over the *Nautilus*.

Two hours later, sensors sweeping space in all directions, Buck lifted *Nautilus* slowly. "Blackwell, as soon as we're clear of high solar radiation, get off a subspace message to Admiral Bemis. Have him send in a heavy force to clean up any Mongol spacecraft they can find. No quarter is to be given."

"You've got it," she answered, sealing the doom of the remaining Mongol battle fleet.

* * * * *

Buck was stage center as the group met with the Amerigo High Council. "We have all studied your report," President Logan began. "We've also seen the reports of the crew of your vessel, *Nautilus*. You have all performed in a most exemplary manner, and we are grateful." Logan stacked papers neatly before him.

"Our study of these documents, as well as viewing the videoholos and instrument readings, tells us a great deal. But by their necessary impersonal nature, they leave much unsaid or explained. We know that events witnessed and judged by some crew members will produce different conclusions on the part of fellow crew members." Buck and the others nodded.

"It is our desire that this meeting be conducted in a completely informal manner. Do not stand on diplomacy or even courtesy. Please feel free to interrupt whenever you have something to offer you judge vital. Consider this session a debriefing for all of us. For the remainder of this session, no rank or protocol should interfere with what we need to know. Brigadier Rogers, please proceed."

"My report differs somewhat from the others, as you have already noted," Buck began. "We saw the same events, but what we judged, as you point out, was obviously affected by what background knowledge some of us might have, which others lacked.

"Unless I am otherwise corrected, I believe I understand what the Mongols—in concert with the Tiger Men of Mars—have not only been planning but have also actually begun. They have been more than devious, with the destruction of this country, and even all of Earth, as one of their primary goals."

He paused to let his words sink in. The council remained silent, but from their facial expressions and uncomfortable shifting in their seats, Buck could tell just how much of a bombshell he had set off in their midst.

He worked his way slowly through the events on Venus with *Nautilus*, then paused as he described the huge cliff face studded with weapons, and especially the huge energy drives being built deeply into the surface of the planet. He then described how one of the huge cylindrical energy tubes had been sliced open by his weapons.

"This energy system," he said slowly, "has been described to me, and I believe this conviction is held by most of us in Amerigo, as cooperation by the Mongols in speeding up the rotation of Venus. This is being done to eliminate the greenhouse effect and to initiate an Earthlike weather engine system on that planet. The intended goal is a rotational period of twenty-one to twenty-six hours to accommodate that goal."

He took a deep breath. "I know what I have to say now will not go over easily with you, because it contradicts your own convictions and your belief in the integrity and honesty of others, especially the Mongols."

He held up his left hand with two fingers extended. "Two things reveal to me, and perhaps others, what the Mongols and Tiger Men *really* are doing. I'm aware there is a so-called gentleman's agreement about terraforming Mars for the Mongols and Venus for our Federation and our allies. The agreement is a farce. The word of the Mongols is no better or worse today than it has been ever since they began destroying other cultures in their passion for conquest. They will do *anything* to achieve their goals.

"So they have pretended to cooperate with you in a long-term agreement. In reality, you have been snookered."

Logan and the other members of the council looked puzzled.

"Snookered?" Logan repeated. "I don't understand that term."

"It means," Dawn Noriega offered, "the Mongols have lied about every agreement they have made with us."

Murmuring began on the dais. Buck moved quickly to cut it off and drive home his point. "The Mongols and their Tiger Men allies have been conducting an enormous charade. We have helped them search for water resources on Mars, among other things. We even sent Takashi Inoyue, perhaps our world's leading authority on subterranean water sources, to assure Mars a plentiful water supply for many years to come."

"And they have agreed," broke in Vice-President Hasafi, "to assist us in accelerating the rotation of Venus. Brigadier Rogers, do you really think we have been unaware of the great power station the Mongols have placed on Venus? Remember, we helped design, build, and install it."

"May I ask," Buck spoke slowly, "how many power-drive generating installations were built by Amerigo and the Mongols on Venus?"

"Three, Brigadier."

"If you please, Madam. Buck turned to Dawn and Wilma. "Report."

Wilma stood tall before the council, joined by Dawn Noriega. "At Brigadier Rogers's orders, we spent considerable time while in the Venusian atmosphere attempting to pick up images, thought pictures, or any other information on Mongol activity on Venus. We confirmed the three stations."

"Then what is your point?" Hasafi asked, impatient.

"Madam Vice-President," Wilma intoned, an ominous note in her voice, "Dawn Noriega and I located sixteen such energy installations on the planet, thirteen of which are not on any of our charts, nor is there any record anywhere in our intelligence data banks of their existence."

Stunned silence followed her words. "Colonel Deering, we're talking here about hunches, aren't we? I mean, a psychic message, perhaps, but—"

Dawn Noriega stepped forward. Her voice was as icy as her

facial glare. "Madam, we are not psychics, we are not witches, and we are not magicians. We have been given an ability to receive extremely low-frequency radio waves generated both by planetary bodies and the human brain. There is nothing mysterious about what we can receive, no more than a great opera singer achieves her spectacular voice through being blessed physiologically rather than by means of magic."

"I meant no offense," Hasafi said quietly.

"None taken, Madam. May I also point out that in the sensor recordings of *Nautilus* as we traversed the Venusian atmosphere, there will be readings of power sources and other radiations not indigenous to the planet? They are artificial and unmistakable, and they may easily be confirmed as to their exact locations."

"Admiral Kane, will you stand for confirmation on what we have just been told?" asked President Logan.

"Done, sir," Kane boomed.

"Kane, damn it," Logan said in frustration, "how the devil did they lift that much mass on their own to Venus! We never picked up anything of that size departing Earth, and there's nothing on Mars—"

"But there is, sir," Buck interrupted.

"What? How?"

"For all the time the Tiger Men and the Golden People have been on Mars, they have concealed the ships that brought them here—spacecraft, gravity warps, and other systems that make our best equipment almost antiques. Those energy drives were taken piecemeal from Earth to Mars," Buck explained, "and there they were assembled. Then, cloaked in gravity warp, the Tiger Men transferred them to Venus and placed them deep beneath the surface in a position both to warp space-time and to accelerate the rotation."

"Wait," Hasafi said hurriedly. "What does space-time warp have to do with all this?"

Buck couldn't help but smile. "They will warp space and create a gravity well directly in the path of the revolution of Venus about the sun. Venus will follow natural law and begin to fall into that gravitational well. As fast as it does so, the attractor will continue to move ahead of Venus. It's just like falling down a deep well—there's always more room to keep falling."

"The why of all this," Logan complained, "still eludes me."

"Sir," Buck said slowly, "it's simple. The Mongols have made their pact with the Tiger Men to terraform Mars. When that world once again flourishes, with a spacegrav warp to retain atmosphere and water vapor, then the Mongols will be at the mercy of the Tiger Men, who are desperate for food-stuffs to meet their needs. When Mars reflects their home world, the Mongols will be turned into slaves. Mental pressure alone will accomplish what physical force could never do to the Mongols, who would rather die than be enslaved. But they will be, from a distance, lobotomized and made helpless slaves."

"But not until Mars is ready?" Logan persisted.

"Yes, sir."

"Do you mind if I ask you a few questions in rapid order, Rogers?"

"At your service, Mr. President."

"I'm trying to fit all the pieces together, so bear with me." Buck nodded.

"Why have the Mongols assisted us in planning an increase in Venus's rotation?"

"To render the planet uninhabitable for Earthmen."

"That sounds . . . forgive me, Rogers, but it sounds crazy, insane!"

"Yes, sir, it does."

"How does helping us accomplish *that?*"

"Doctor Huer is, among other things, a mathematical genius and what we used to call a computer whiz. Working with Admiral Kane, they computed the increase in rotational speed of Venus from the mass energy drivers as well as that space-time gravity warp, the deep well I detailed a few moments ago.

"We need a Venusian rotational speed close to that of Earth to begin the terraforming process, Mr. President. But when full power is applied to the gravity warp and the mass drivers, Venus will act like a planet gone mad, with a rotational speed of approximately two hundred and forty rotations per Earth day, or ten times faster than we have on Earth. The result will be quakes, slides, and explosive volcanic action, with no hope of achieving Earthlike conditions."

"And they believe we would simply stand by and let this happen?"

"Hardly, sir. That's where Mongolium enters in."

"The asteroid?"

"Yes, sir. Mongolium is in a state of orbital change. It will go out another twenty or thirty thousand miles, and when the Mongols are fully established on Mars, they'll be ready to destroy Earth—and us. They are quite willing to wipe out this planet if they can become the masters with the Tiger Men of Mars."

"How will they use—"

"Mongolium will be turned in its path, then accelerated rapidly until it is on a direct collision course with Earth. Most of the Mongols—the rulers, anyway—will be gone from Earth by then, along with perhaps a half-million Japanese specialists and scientists. At that time, they will hurl the asteroid, which has a mass of billions of tons, into Earth with a collision speed of ninety thousand miles an hour. The impact will fracture Earth like a piece of clay dropped on a tile floor from great height. The planet will be shattered. Presto—no more competition from Amerigo or anyone else. Earth will be gone forever."

"That's pure madness!"

"That it is, sir."

"Admiral Kane, this seems to be in your line. In the absence of Admiral Bemis, I ask you what we can do about that asteroid?"

"Blowing it up, where it is now, won't help," Kane said brusquely.

"Why not?" asked Hasafi.

"We'd need an enormous quantity of thermonuclear bombs to even try to break it up. Since the asteroid is still populated, and the Mongols haven't started it back yet, we'd simply be inviting another thermonuclear war. And even if we did break it up, there would be a lethal rain of huge meteorites on Earth that might be just as devastating as a war."

"If we had the Martian gravity warp—I mean, the Tiger Men and their means of creating a gravity well—we could keep it accelerating away from Earth," Logan said.

"But we don't have that, Mr. President," Kane reminded him. "And I doubt if we have much influence with the Tiger Men. They've been in the Mongol camp a long time. But first things first. What can we do about the asteroid?"

"I have an idea," Buck offered.

"By all means, let's have it!" the president said, nearly shouting.

"There's one science Amerigo has that exceeds anything else," Buck noted. "That's your mastery of cryogenics, on either a small or mass scale."

"Are you proposing we freeze them out, Buck?" Kane asked sarcastically. "What bloody good would that do?"

"It's a better idea than you think, Admiral, especially if we tie it in with some other powerful threats. We're a long way from helpless."

"What kind of threats, Brigadier?" asked Hasafi.

"First, Mongolium is occupied. It still must be controlled as to direction and velocity, and finally starting back to Earth. That means a working crew, enormous machinery. Complex machinery. I've studied the orbital mechanics of that thing—with a lot of help from Doc Huer, let me add. In a few days, it will have enough velocity, if it's not decelerated, to leave the orbital planes of Earth and our moon. It will fly north of the plane of the ecliptic and go into an orbit that won't come closer to Earth than a few million miles—the kind of orbit that will be stable for a few million years, anyway."

"How do we put them into deep-freeze?" asked Logan.

"With your lifting systems—antigrav and beamed power—we could send a few million tons of ice into the asteroid. Even a few big comets would tear them up. As fast as water struck that chunk of rock, impact friction would shower it out across the surface and into any ports or openings. It would also sublimate instantly into ice. It would be a deep freeze that would knock out their machinery."

"There's a problem," Logan said.

They turned to the president. "The Mongols won't just stand by and do nothing. We'll have a fight on our hands."

"Use thermonuclear weapons," Buck said.

They stared at him in disbelief.

"Are you mad?" Hasafi said icily. "Hasn't the history of this planet gotten through to you? Thermonukes have poisoned our world. They—"

"Madam, I never said to *explode* them. I said to *use* them."

"You have an ingenious way about you, Rogers. Please don't stop now. Obviously you have thought this through."

"Yes, Ma'm, I have. The Mongols are failures as diplomats. Force is the only thing they understand. They know what thermos can do. But there's one group that is absolutely terrified of hydrogen bombs, especially those in the gigaton range. A few of them exploded on Mars will wreck its future completely."

"Are you proposing we bombard Mars with hydrogen bombs?"

"Never," Buck said emphatically.

"Then what *are* you proposing?"

"We place several huge bombs in orbit about Mars. We land ships in all critical areas of Mars—ravines, underground chasms with water, in the polar icecaps. We let the Tiger Men know that unless they change their tune, we'll set off the bombs, and it's good-bye Mars, Tiger Men, and the Golden People."

"You're talking about risking everything on a bluff?" exclaimed Logan.

"Sir, are you familiar with the name von Clausewitz?"

"I am not, Rogers."

"He was one of the greatest political and military thinkers of all time. Von Clausewitz specialized in simple answers to complex questions. Let me ask you one, sir. What is war?"

"I beg your pardon?"

"What is war?"

"Why, war is an attempt to destroy your enemy and—"

"Let me save you time, sir. War is an expression of political failure, nothing more, nothing less. When you cannot function politically, your failure—at least in our history—is war."

"You are not through making your point?"

"No, sir. One more question. What is the ultimate goal of war?"

"To destroy the enemy's ability to fight, obviously."

"No, sir. That's utterly wasteful. It is to make the enemy change his mind. No more, no less. If he is convinced he cannot win, then he will stop fighting in order to survive. If he is convinced of that *before* he starts to fight, you have won your war without a single shot fired. That is why, I must add, you need not have a single actual bomb placed on Mars. If we act boldly, the threat will be perceived as real. The Tiger Men know our history and know we are perfectly capable of acting like madmen, lobbing hydrogen bombs about and all. And the natural consequence to follow is that they must strip the Mongols of power, or they will bring down upon them the wrath of our bombs."

"And if they find out it's a bluff?"

"Sir, no one plays that kind of chicken. One mistake and you lose the game. The Tiger Men are anything but stupid. The risk is too great for them to take." Buck laughed. "Besides, they consider the Mongols little better than savage brutes, utterly without redeeming value."

"You are certain of their attitude?"

"Absolutely. They have had a spy in our midst for years. He travels back and forth between Earth and Mars. He plans for his country eventually to rule Mars. His people are utterly ruthless in eliminating all competition."

"*We have a spy in our camp?*"

"More a traitor than a spy, but, yes."

"Who?" Barney shouted, his face a mask of rage.

"Takashi Inoyue."

Icy silence met his statement. Then Kane spoke in a cold, measured tone. "*Mister* Rogers, you're talking about a man whose courage is unquestionable, a man who fought alongside me for years. *For* Amerigo."

"Admiral, every word you say is true. But all this time, he has served another master—the old samurai warrior clan of Japan. Many years ago, he was planted in our midst, serving faithfully, but always doing what he could to reestablish Japan as a major power. Now they have yielded Earth to us, just so long as they become a dominant power on Mars. Inoyue is there to increase the power of the Mongolians, to use everything he could to keep track of our ships in space and on Mars and Venus. Did it ever strike you as unusual that, even with full cloaking and all the ruses we could think of, the Mongols were always present in force to engage us? They always knew we were coming and what our plans were."

"Good God, man, how can you ignore what the Mongols did to his wife? Beating, rape, torture, and slow death!"

"He set up his own wife to convince you of his undying loyalty to us."

"He set her up?"

"Perfectly acceptable behavior for a samurai. What is good for the empire is always acceptable. All will be evened out in heaven."

"Start giving me facts, Buck. And I want *proof*."

"Inoyue made a mistake on the mission aboard *Io*. I didn't catch it at first. Until the *Io* mission, he had spent all his time with you. Is that correct?"

"Yes, it is."

"And when he wasn't with you?"

"He was on missions we sent him to fulfill."

"Especially in South America?"

"Why—why, yes," Barney faltered. "What of it?"

"While he was following your orders, Admiral, he was also cozying up with the Chileans and the Mongols."

"How do you know that?"

"Without anyone on our team saying anything to him, he knew too much about Dawn Noriega, her telepathic powers, how she could communicate with sea life, and how she'd struck up such an extraordinary relationship with the Atlanteans.

"He also told us he was returning *sub rosa* to Japan to help develop new systems to be used against the Han and the Mongols. What he was really doing was passing on to the Mongols our communications codes and other data, which helped them to always be one leg up on us. Then miraculously, just before we left for Mars, who shows up to accompany us but Takashi Inoyue? How could he have known the exact time and date, without being in touch with us, unless he was using Mongol equipment to monitor our frequencies? There was no other way.

"Then he made one very big mistake—a slip of the tongue, perhaps. As we were ready to shove off for Mars, he told us that he had been back to Chile to learn more about the aliens. Dawn Noriega had queried the Chileans *from our base in Amerigo*. She didn't have to leave to find out, and you can't tap a telepathic line.

"We knew he'd been back in Japan, but he was always hush-hush about exactly what he was doing there. For someone as sharp as Inoyue, that sent up a red flag. If he remained in Japan, we might never have suspected him. But we found his name in a Mongol code message we intercepted, and it was from Vladivostok. Unless he was working with the Mongols, he could never have gotten through one of the most heavily defended ports in the world.

"I spoke of this to Dawn, and she began to come up with some disturbing images from Inoyue. He was supposed to have been lost in searching out underground rivers on Mars, but one of the images Dawn picked up was of Japanese lettering carved into a wall of an underground lake. It was a marker, a guide. Inoyue had it all mapped out already, and he'd never been lost. But it explained his long absences from us. Even you didn't see that, Admiral. Yet when we were moving across Mars and ready to lift off from the planet, we got bushwhacked, right in the middle of a dust storm covering the whole planet! They were monitoring our frequencies the whole time, courtesy of Inoyue.

"There was—is—one more test. The Japanese used secret agents on a long-term basis. They would plant their people in a foreign land for years. They were part of the local community, a fifth column, so to speak. Then, when Japanese forces made their moves, they always had amazing knowledge of defenses and how to get through them. By now it was getting obvious we had some kind of agent on our hands." Buck shook his head. "There was one phrase that kept repeating in my brain. It wouldn't go away, and the more I heard it, the more I was convinced I was right."

"And what was that phrase, Rogers?" Logan asked.

Standing to his right, Dawn Noriega was visibly shaken as scenes of violent death, fire, and destruction reached out to her from Rogers.

Buck took a deep breath and looked directly at Black Barney.

"Remember Pearl Harbor," Buck said.

*   *   *   *   *

"I'm still not convinced," Black Barney said stubbornly. "You don't hang a man on circumstantial evidence, no matter how strong it seems."

"Admiral, when you were a SEAL and with Special Forces, including sabotage missions behind the Mongol lines, you and your men always had a recognition signal, an expression, a physical move that was ingrained deeply into your subconscious."

"That we did. In fact, it was so deeply implanted in our subconscious that we could never use or make the signal unless it was being used as a code."

"In other words, Admiral, you couldn't practice that signal or just casually demonstrate it to someone, could you?"

"Absolutely not."

"Tell me, Barney, what was that code with the SEALS?"

Barney started to speak. A moment later, face flushed, muscles quivering, he leaned against the wall for support.

"I *can't*," he gasped. "If ever I break the code without good reason, it's like a blow to the heart. I can't say it, Buck. I'd die first after the conditioning we went through."

"Did the enemy, especially the Mongols, use the same system?"

Barney nodded.

"If someone used that code on you, did you respond automatically, without thinking?"

"We did. It was pure reflex. We couldn't do anything else."

"Then if I'm right about Inoyue, wouldn't he have been trained the same way?"

"Absolutely."

"Do you know the secret Mongol sign of recognition among their agents?"

Barney shook his head. "Not by a long shot. Not that we haven't tried, but we never got it."

"Barney, did you know that back in my time I was assigned to Intelligence?"

"Yes, I knew that."

"Did you also know that I spent time on Sakhalin Island, well north of Japan and a major Russian base, with full Mongol security forces guarding the missile-launching complexes?"

"No, I didn't know *that*."

"Again I ask you: If the code is given to a hypnotically controlled agent, he must reply, as trained, from his subconscious?"

"Yes."

"No doubts?"

"What are you getting at, Buck?"

"Takashi Inoyue is here, working in a comm center. I'd like to have him come up here with everyone watching."

"Why?"

"You'll see soon enough."

Inoyue appeared soon, curious but relaxed. "Takashi, will you please stand over here, facing me?" Buck asked.

The Japanese nodded and did as requested. He and Buck stood face-to-face.

"Takashi, I wish to demonstrate to our friends here an old Tibetan greeting. It dates back to when the Mongols first invaded China, from 1260 to 1368 A.D. There were few people on this planet at this time who had the courtesy or culture of Tibetan society. They would even greet one another in a ceremonial way."

They watched, astounded, as Buck moved his head forward, stuck out his tongue, and held his palms open at his waist.

Without thinking, reacting to Buck's strange movements, Inoyue performed a mirror-image movement of hands and body. His face whitened and he reeled back as if struck by a physical blow.

"Seize him!" Buck ordered. Dawn Noriega was already prepared, a pistol in one hand. She fired, and a thin, snakelike steel cord lashed out, swinging around and around Inoyue, pinning his arms helplessly to his body. "Give him another," Buck prompted. "The legs this time." Another shot, and Inoyue collapsed to the floor, fully awake, unharmed but helpless.

Buck turned to the group. "The ceremonial greeting you just witnessed was originated by Zhunche Liang of the First Mongolian Cavalry. He was a brilliant strategist, and he developed a fifth column against all his enemies.

"The greeting is ritual, a sign of great courtesy. The tongue is extended, exposed to show its natural color, for if it were black, that would be a sign that this person speaks evil and poisons all whom he meets. The open hands at the waist prove the absence of weapons. The greeting has been in existence, unchanged, for many generations. Only the men and women of the Secret Society ever know it."

Buck turned to President Logan. "Now that we can close the leak in our security and keep the Tiger Men guessing, we may have a good shot at a future in which we can learn to live with each other."

"I'm amazed, Rogers," the president said slowly. "Amazed and grateful . . . I am in awe at your determination to follow through on your hunches and beliefs. Is there any similar greeting from your post we can teach our own people?"

"Sure," Buck said, but he wasn't smiling.

"Remember Pearl Harbor."

POOR old Jules Verne! He took a look into the future and all he saw was the possibilities of the Airplane and the Submarine. The real facts of science—the tremendous advances in invention which were to include such amazing devices as the jumping belt, interplanetary rocket ships, the rocket pistol, inertron and all the other amazing developments of the twenty-fifth century—which Buck Rogers herein describes—Jules overlooked them all.

Now listen to Buck Rogers.

Buck Rogers

By PHIL NOWLAN *and* DICK CALKINS

* *

I, BUCK ROGERS, am the only man alive, so far as I know, whose normal span of life has been spread over a period of five centuries!

I was just twenty years old when the great World War of 1914–18 ended and I was mustered out of the Air Service where I had served for eighteen months on the battle fronts of France as a Pursuit Pilot. Soon after returning home I got a job surveying the low levels of an abandoned mine located near a great city. Deep in this mine, I was cut off from return by a cave-in, and succumbed to a curious and unidentified radio-active gas I had descended to study. I sank into a state of suspended animation in which I was "preserved" in all my youth and vigor until, five hundred years later, some shifting of strata once more let air into the ancient workings— and I awoke.

I had no idea, at first, that I had been unconscious for more than a few hours. But when I staggered up out of the mine a shock awaited me. Gone was every handiwork of man that should have met my eyes, swallowed up in a forest obviously centuries old, though the contours of the valley and the hills opposite were familiar.

I shall pass over the days of mental agony that I spent in the attempt to grasp the meaning of it all, days in which only the necessity of improvising crude traps and clubs with which to secure food preserved me from insanity, and begin with my first glimpse of a Twenty-fifth Century American.

A TWENTY-FIFTH CENTURY AMERICAN

I saw her first through a portion of woodland where the trees were thinly scattered, with dense forest beyond, from which she had just emerged. Overjoyed at the prospect of human companionship at last, I was about to shout, but something in her tense, alert attitude warned me.

She was clad in rather close-fitting garments. Around her waist was a broad belt, and above it, across her shoulders, a sort of pack, of about the proportions of a knapsack. She wore gauntlet gloves and a helmet.

She was backing cautiously away from the denser section of the forest, step by step, when suddenly there came a vivid flash and a detonation like that of a hand grenade some distance to the left of her. She threw up an arm and staggered a bit, in a queer gliding way.

Then recovering, she retreated more rapidly toward me. At every few steps she would raise her arm and, it seemed, merely point here and there into the forest with a curious type of pistol, from the muzzle of which there was no flash nor detonation. But wherever she pointed there was a terrific explosion deep among the trees.

After firing several times she turned quickly toward me, and leaped desperately, and to my amazement, literally sailed through the air, between the scattered trees for a distance of fully ninety feet; though at no time during this jump did she rise higher than about twelve feet off the ground.

But as she completed her leap her foot caught on a projecting root and she sprawled gently forward. I say "gently" for she did not crash down as I would have done, but slid in a weightless sort of way, though when she finally collided with the trunk of a great tree, she seemed to have plenty of *horizontal momentum*. For a moment I stood gaping in amaze-

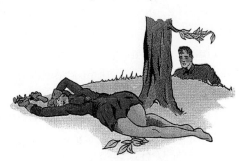

SHE FELL SLOWLY TO EARTH

ment. Then, seeing that blood oozed from beneath the tight little helmet, I ran to her, and got another shock; for as I exerted myself to lift her I staggered back and nearly fell, quite unprepared for the lightness of her. She weighed only a few pounds, perhaps 4 or 5.

For a moment I busied myself trying to stanch the flow of blood. But her wound was slight and she was more dazed than hurt. Then I thought of her pursuers, who by this time must have come up within shooting distance. I heard no sound, however.

THE PURSUIT

I took the weapon from her grasp and examined it hastily. It was not unlike the automatic to which I was accustomed. With fumbling fingers I reloaded it with fresh ammunition from her belt, for I heard, not far away, the sound of voices, followed almost immediately by a series of explosions around us.

Crouching behind a tree, I watched, accustoming myself to the balance of the weapon.

"THE EVIL FACE"

Then I saw a movement in the branches of a tree. The face and shoulders of a man emerged. It was an evil face, and it had murder in it.

That decided me. I raised the gun and fired. My aim was bad for there was no kick at all to the weapon, and I struck the trunk of the tree several feet below the girl's pursuer. But it blew him from his perch like a crumpled bit of paper. And he *floated* to the ground like some limp thing lowered gently by an invisible hand. The tree, its trunk blown apart by the explosion, crashed down.

Then I saw another one of them. He was starting one of those amazing leaps from one tree to another, about forty feet away. Again I fired. This time I scored a direct hit, and the fellow completely vanished in the explosion, blown to atoms.

How many more of them were there I don't know, but this must have been too much for them, for shortly afterward

I heard them swishing and crashing away through the tree tops.

I now turned my attention to my newly found companion, and observed, as I carried her lightly to the nearby stream, that she was gloriously young and beautiful, and that her apparent lack of weight was due to the lifting power of the strange device strapped across her shoulders; for though slender, she was well developed, and there was firm strength in her lithe young body.

She moaned softly as I gently removed the close fitting little helmet, and there were orange-gold glints of fire in her hair where the little beams of sunlight, filtering through the forest foliage, fell upon it.

Her injury was really trifling, though the blow had stunned her. Still holding her lightly in my arm, I washed away the blood with water from the stream. At the refreshing touch she moved a bit, and half opened her eyes, and looked at me, it seemed, without the full realization of consciousness. Then she sighed and relaxed. "Thanks," she murmured. "That f-feels good. I'll—I'll be all right in a moment." And unconsciously she snuggled a bit closer in my arm.

THE AWAKENING

Then I felt her body stiffen, and she was looking at me with wide, startled blue eyes. For a moment she was as one paralyzed with amazement. Then, in one sudden whirl of violent motion she had torn herself from me and landed some ten feet away facing me in tense, alert hostility. In her hand was the gun, which I had put back in her holster, and there was no doubt about her readiness to squeeze the trigger had I made

the least nervous movement.

"Raise your hands!" she commanded in a cold, hard little voice. And I reached for the sky without argument. "You're one of them," she accused. "And I'm taking you in. Where are the others?"

I tried to grin, but fear it was a sickly effort, for the gun in her hand looked businesslike, and the blue of her eyes was as cold as ice now. "You mean the man who—who attacked you?" I asked. "No, I'm not one of them. In fact I think I disposed of a couple of them for you—with your gun, which you see I gave back to you."

"RAISE YOUR HANDS!"

At this she seemed less sure of herself; but no less suspicious. "Put down your hands if you want to," she conceded. "But at the first break . . ." There was a wealth of meaning in the unfinished sentence.

"Now then," she said, advancing a step, "Who are you? What are you doing here?"

"My name is Buck Rogers," I replied. "And I'm not doing anything much except trying to keep alive with the little game I can catch around here."

"Your clothing is strange," she mused, looking me over from head to foot. "There's something queer about all this.

There lies that outlaw over there. You must have captured him, because I didn't. All I remember is making a big leap, catching my foot in something, and then—I saw stars!"

I explained exactly what happened while she gazed straight into my eyes, her glance never wavering.

"I believe you," she said finally, and after a moment's hesitation, put away her gun. She took a single easy "step," covering the entire distance between us, and said simply; "Thanks for saving my life. Now what's the rest of the story?"

There was no way out of it. I couldn't invent a yarn successfully to fit conditions in a day and age of which I knew nothing, and I certainly did not expect the girl to believe that I was centuries older than she. But I had to take a chance.

SHE LISTENED INCREDULOUSLY

She listened patiently; scornfully incredulous at first, but with more tolerance and growing amazement as I went on. And when I had finished she looked thoughtfully at me for some time.

WILMA

"That's all very hard to believe," she said at length, "but I do believe you, Buck Rogers." She held out her hand. "I am Wilma Deering, of the East Central Org, and I'm just finishing my turn at air patrol."

"Air patrol?" I queried. "But you have no plane here, have you? I don't see how you could use one in this forest."

For a moment she looked puzzled, then laughed. "A plane? Oh yes. Wasn't that what they used to call the old-fashioned airships centuries ago?

BUCK USING JUMPING BELT

"No, I haven't one here, but we have aircraft of many types and all are greatly superior to those in use in the ancient civilization you knew. You don't need them when you have a jumping belt"; she indicated the pack across her shoulders; "unless you're going a long distance. What I mean is, I'm on patrol or guard duty to give warning—with rockets—in case any raiding aircraft of the Red Mongols come this way. But come Buck," she added in a most friendly manner. "We must return at once to the city. And I promise you some amazing sights if the knowledge we have of life as it was lived here five hundred years ago—back in the 1930's—is true. Great scientific marvels have been brought about since then."

Quickly we stripped the jumping belt from the fallen outlaw. Adjusting it properly on my shoulders, Wilma showed me how to leap with it. My efforts were crude but soon I caught the knack of it, and, although I could not match Wilma for speed or distance, we made rapid progress and at last came in sight of a city so amazing in its magnitude and seeming complexity that my astonishment was boundless.

CONQUEST OF GRAVITY

I found myself in a world in which gravity had been conquered by means of truly marvellous inventions. Science had accomplished wonders.

The mysteries of the jumping belt were explained. It was made of *inertron*, a synthetic element of great *reverse weight* which falls *away* from the center of the Earth instead of *toward* it, and which counterbalances all but a few pounds of the wearer's weight. I learned to leap great heights and distances with that pleasant and effortless ease that made aircraft and other vehicles in the 25th Century unnecessary, and indeed undesirable, for personal transportation, except where speed or protection from the weather was required, or where crowded conditions precluded the use of the jumping belt.

It was a strange sensation at first, to give a little hop that normally would carry me twelve inches off the ground, and shoot into the air some twenty or thirty feet, to drift down and land again almost as lightly as a feather. Or to give a great shove against the ground, and soar sixty or seventy feet upward.

But for *speed leaping* I found it was necessary to cultivate a certain delicate instinct of balance. I felt very much as I had when, as a boy, I ran alongside a horse, letting the animal pull me as I took great, leaping steps. In short, I found that although weight apparently had vanished, *momentum remained* and if I hit anything while shooting forward horizontally, I hit it hard.

It was for this reason that the use of jumping belts in cities, useful as they might have been in leaping to the upper stories of buildings or the upper levels of the vast moving sidewalks, was generally prohibited. The temptation to make speed with them was too great. Too many serious accidents had been caused by those who leaped into crowded places with uncontrollable momentum. But to soar across the country, in great easy leaps of sixty to ninety feet or more at the speed of an ice-skater, was delightful.

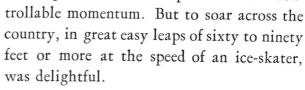

WOMEN SOLDIERS

It was, perhaps, all the more delightful to me because my instructor in the art of leaping was *Wilma Deering*, that slender, blue-eyed, golden-haired, high-spirited young *soldier-girl*

WILMA

who was destined to be my companion and capable assistant in so many astounding adventures in this marvelous universe.

Equality of the sexes had been one of the developments brought about during five centuries. It was part of the education of all young girls to spend a certain amount of time in *military service* as well as in various industrial and mechanical activities. Naturally, most of them stayed in the kind of service to which they were best fitted (and the mechanical conveniences of the age made them practically as efficient as men in nearly all lines) unless they married. Then they adopted home-making as their career, and were subject to call for military or other service only in case of emergency.

Wilma, who had self-reliance, fearlessness and stamina, even beyond the high average of her 25th Century sisters, had naturally remained in the military service, for which her talents eminently fitted her, and into this same service I naturally gravitated.

WEAPONS OF THE 25TH CENTURY

The weapons and equipment of the military service were most interesting to me. Men and girls wore close-fitting uniforms of a *synthetically fabricated material*, not a woven cloth, that had the consistency of soft leather and yet was most difficult to cut or tear. For service in cold climates, uniform cloth was *electronically* treated to radiate inward a continuous glow of heat, while the outside surface was heat resistant. For warm climates the cloth was given a spongy texture for aeration, and a high ratio of heat conductivity.

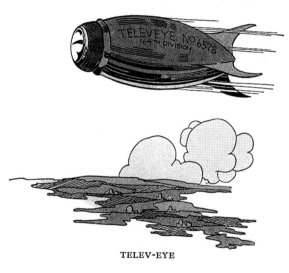

TELEV-EYE

The jumping belt was, of course, a part of the regular equipment, as was the close-fitting helmet, of the same material as the uniforms, into which were built the tiny receivers of the individual radiophone sets that enabled an officer to give commands to his entire force, scattered over an area miles in extent, or to converse with a single scout individually from a distance.

Of the weapons, the *rocket pistol* was the nearest thing to the firearms of the 20th Century, I knew. It was very much like an old automatic, except that its magazine was much larger, and the propelling charge was in a tiny cartridge case that travelled *with* the highly explosive bullet instead of remaining in the pistol, giving flatter trajectory and greater range. And some of these bullets had explosive power equal to artillery shells of the 20th Century.

There were, of course, *rocket guns;* great squat cannon from which leaped self-propelling shells capable of shattering an area of a mile or more in radius.

The *telev-eye,* used either as a weapon of destruction or for scouting, was an aerial torpedo, its weight eliminated by inertron counterbalancing, radio-controlled, with a great "eye" or lens, behind which was located a television transmitter that relayed back to its operator, who was safely entrenched miles in the rear, the picture which this "eye" picked up. Once the telev-eye picked up a fugitive aircraft, that ship was doomed, for no ship could outmaneuver or out-speed these terrible projectiles of destruction, which were so small that they could seldom be hit by enemy guns.

Another most efficient weapon for short range work was the *paralysis gun.* This was a pistol, from which flashed a faintly visible, crackling beam of energy vibrations that temporarily paralyzed certain brain centers. A person hit by this ray instantly dropped rigid and paralyzed, to remain that way for minutes

PARALYSIS GUN

or hours, and then recover with no worse effects than a bad headache.

But to me one of the most amazing weapons of the 25th Century was the *lightning gun.* This wasn't really a gun at all, though it was called such from its general appearance. It was an electronic generator and projector. From it flashed forth an invisible beam of carrier-wave oscillations along which could be sent a stupendous electrical charge. Its use was against aircraft. It was only necessary to focus the beam on the unsuspecting target, and then flash along it an electrical charge of opposite polarity to that in the clouds. When that ship later neared a cloud, it was struck by lightning. Obviously great care had to be taken in the operation of the lightning gun, or the gun itself

LIGHTNING GUN

might pull a bolt down from the clouds. It could only be used under certain atmospheric conditions. Batteries of these lightning guns were stationed at strategic points over the country and along the sea coast, co-ordinated to "fire" all at once, in groups, or singly, as necessity required.

AMAZING CITIES

I entered into the life of the 25th Century with a mighty zest. On every hand were marvels almost unbelievable. Cities of towering pinnacles. Others that had been roofed over with great domes of *metalloglass*, a transparent product with a strength greater than steel. And still others that were in reality one single great building, spreading for miles, with mazes of thoroughfares, internal corridors and external galleries, along which shot automatically controlled *floating cars*.

The lift in these cars was furnished by an over-balance of inertron, but the *cosmo-magnetic* grip of the guide rails embedded in the pavements held them down to within twelve inches of the ground. One had only to enter one of these cars, locate his destination as to avenue, cross-corridor and level on the triple dial and then relax. An amazingly

25TH CENTURY CITY

complex system of car and power-house controls guided the vehicle promptly and safely by the shortest available route to the recorded destination.

But I never ceased to wonder at the amazing number of these marvels whose real beginnings, back in the 20th Century, I could actually recall.

Radio? It was basically and fundamentally woven into the whole fabric and structure of the 25th Century civilization. But *such* radio! Radio that embraced myriad types and varieties of *electronic, sub-electronic, infra-magnetic* and *cosmic* oscillations. Matter could be formed out of force with it. And even as the 20th Century scientists conceived and executed great scientific advances, so the 25th Century scientists to an even greater extent developed new, *synthetic elements* of strange properties, not existing naturally in any part of the universe. Inertron, for instance, was one of these. It had weight; but its weight caused it to fall *up* instead of *down*.

RED MONGOL TERROR

However, despite the development of five vivid centuries of scientific achievement, man's own social and moral progress still lagged behind the progress of his creations. True, the average was far higher than it had been in the 20th Century, but there were on the face of the globe races whose advance in material civilization had been accompanied by moral and spiritual decay.

There were, for instance, the terrible *Red Mongols*, cruel, greedy and unbelievably ruthless, who for a time, all too long, utterly crushed a large part of humanity in a slavery frightful to contemplate.

In their great battle craft, sliding across the sky as though riding on columns of scintillating light, they drove like a scourge over all North America, with their terrible *disintegrator rays* blasting men and entire cities into n o t h i n g n e s s. Where these beams fell, matter simply ceased to exist, and an instantaneous flicker was sufficient to gash the

RED MONGOL WITH DISINTEGRATOR RAY MACHINE

landscape with channels and canals sometimes a hundred or more feet deep and leave iridescent, vitreous scars where soft earth had been before.

The disintegrator ray, however, became one of the most useful tools of 25th Century civilization in small projector form, with which tunnels could be bored and automatically finished with a hard vitreous surface with amazing rapidity, or with which refuse could be most economically destroyed, either by use of the hand machines or permanent installations.

Wilma and I saw service in the war against these cruel Red Mongols and played an exciting part in the many fierce battles with them.

KILLER KANE AND ARDALA

But even among the more advanced races criminals still existed, and it was the destiny of Wilma and myself to frustrate 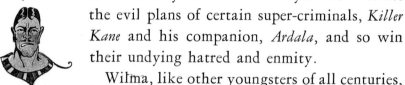 the evil plans of certain super-criminals, *Killer Kane* and his companion, *Ardala*, and so win their undying hatred and enmity.

Wilma, like other youngsters of all centuries, had had her dreams, and unfortunately these

KILLER KANE

had centered lightly at one time on a man who then had an unblemished reputation for integrity and ability, but she had broken with him instantly when she realized the potential evil that lay beneath his vivid personality. This man was Killer Kane.

My coming and the interest Wilma showed in me had fanned Kane's smouldering resentment into a seething flame of hate. He later plunged into a criminal career of such utter daring and magnificent proportions as to be unequalled in the annals of two centuries. And though the beautiful, sleek adventuress, Ardala, was his constant and capable partner in crime, Kane never forgave nor forgot the wound to his vanity nor his consuming passion for revenge.

And Ardala, though giving Killer Kane all the affection and loyalty of which her fierce, deceitful, feline nature was capable, suffered constantly the pangs of burning jealousy, and in consequence matched his hatred of Wilma and me with an enmity for us no less deadly because of her subtle talents.

Throughout the Earth, and even beyond, into the vast voids of space, and

KILLER KANE AND ARDALA

other strange planets, Wilma's struggle and mine with Killer Kane and Ardala was fated to continue.

CONTROL OF SPACE SHIPS

For interplanetary travel *was* an accomplished fact in the 25th Century. Even back in 1933 aviation engineers constructed a craft to fly the *stratosphere*, that upper section of the Earth's atmosphere in which the air is too rare for breathing, and from which its density declines gradually to the vacuum of interplanetary space.

The first *space ships* in which we, Wilma and I, feeling infinitely less than microscopic, dared the immensity of outer void, were rocket propelled. In a vacuum, whirling fan blades are futile for propulsion, for there is nothing for the blade to pull or push against. But the rocket, so to speak, provides "air" against which to push. The blazing gas, roaring out of the rocket tube, piles up against that which was emitted the preceding instant, and has not yet had time to expand to extreme rarefaction. The reaction of this piling up shoves the ship ahead. And since there is no air friction in space to retard the ship a

ROCKET SHIP

single impulse would give it a momentum that would continue forever, or until it was altered by some such event as entering the gravitational field of some planet, or colliding with a planetoid. Such speed, however, would be very slow, and the enormous distances to be covered in space made it imperative to attain speeds undreamed of in the antiquated days of 1933—five hundred years in the dim past.

INTERPLANETARY NAVIGATION

But with a continuous blast such as these ships used, they roared away from Earth at constantly accelerating speed. A rate of acceleration somewhat less than that of a falling body on Earth (and even back in 1933 experiences of aviators and parachute jumpers had proved the human system can stand the acceleration of gravity) but which constantly continued for even a few hours produced terrific speed.

And as the space ship was so constructed that its *bow* was its *top*, and its *stern* the *base*, this *upward acceleration* had the effect of pressing its passengers *downward* against its decks with something not far from equivalent to the force of gravity. At the half-way mark the ship, now floating through space at frightful speed, was gently swung about by small side-blasts, steadied with its *base* pointed in the direction of travel. And so for the second half of the journey the main blasts acted to *decelerate* the ship gradually, and at the same rate as the former acceleration. This deceleration substituted for gravity in the same way, and by the time the ship arrived at its planet of destination a few days, or a few months later, its speed was so reduced that it could safely enter the atmosphere and ride down on its rocket blast to a gentle landing.

The controls of these space ships had been so carefully worked out by the scientific engineers—and the ships themselves so nicely balanced that a crew of two men—or girls for that matter—could easily operate one of the gigantic crafts.

OLD DOCTOR HUER—SCIENTIST EXTRAORDINARY

But this conquest of vast distances had not been possible until Old Doctor Huer, foremost scientist of the 25th Century, with whom Wilma and I were associated in many adventures, had invented a method of creating *matter in gaseous form from the energy impulses of sunlight and cosmic rays*, with sufficient speed and in sufficient quantity to serve as rocket fuel. For no ship could hold enough rocket fuel for an entire interplanetary trip. It had to be derived from some outside source en route.

DR. HUER

NON-RECOIL ENERGY

Huer, an amazing man for his age (I knew him to be over seventy), an indefatigable scientist and an irrepressible adventurer, also invented and developed the practical application of *non-recoil energy*, or as it was sometimes called, "*one-way energy*," by which a man might literally "lift himself by his bootstraps."

The non-recoil energy tube was a small affair, resembling an ancient electric flashlight. It emitted a beam of energy which acted with controllable "push" against anything at which it was directed, but without any recoil whatever against the user. The principle was not dissimilar to that of shock and rebound absorbers on ancient automobiles or the recoil devices of ancient cannons, but it was a matter of carefully balanced electronic and sub-cosmic energy control rather than one of mechanical construction.

Curiously, a man might hold one of these tubes pointed upward in one hand, and placing his other hand over the projector lens, rise on it as though holding on to a strap.

Force tubes, of course, had been known for a long time, but in these the push was equal at both ends of the tube. They were, as a matter of fact, almost identical with the powerful *repeller rays* on which the dreaded air-raiding ships of the Red Mongols rode, beams of faint light that pushed downward with terrific force against the ground, and upward with equal force against the keel of the ship generating them. The Mongols maneuvered

their ships by the simple method of altering the slant of these rays. Slanted astern, they drove the ship forward, and vice versa.

Huer's non-recoil energy, of course, had innumerable applications. It was ideal motive power for all kinds of vehicles, aircraft and space ships. And in *industry* it had a thousand applications.

ECONOMY OF LABOR

Had we not been plunged by circumstances, and the deadly hatred of Killer Kane and Ardala, into one desperate adventure after another, we could have found a never-ending interest in the adroit uses to which this convenient power of Dr. Huer's was put in the daily industrial life of the people. I had seen men punch holes in the hardest steel with a device little larger than a screwdriver, and with no more effort than a housewife might use in cutting biscuits out of a slab of dough.

COMMUNITY KITCHENS

There was very little home cooking, however, in the 25th Century. At least not in the cities; and only a small percentage of the population was required to run the *farms*.

A marvelous system of conveyors led from the *community kitchens* to every apartment. One could order his meal a la carte or table d'hote. In due course a wall panel would slide back, and a "floating table" would ease gently into the room, safely balanced on "*lifters*" of inertron, with everything in readiness. It required but the pressure of a finger to guide this to any part of the room where one chose to sit, and anchor it by lowering the counterbalancing weights underneath it. When hunger was satisfied, it only remained to push the table back and close the panel on it. The kitchens themselves were mazes of ingenious devices for handling the food and dishes, which for mechanical considerations were square rather than round.

MECHANICAL CHEF

SYNTHETIC FOOD

But I never could cultivate a taste for certain of the foods that were the product of synthetic laboratories. For by this time less than half of all foodstuffs came from the farms. Men had learned to create the most nourishing of foods from minerals alone, by a process of disintegration and electronic recombination into complicated organic substances easily assimilated by the human system.

VANISHED FARMS AND ROADS

Indeed, most of the land was no longer under cultivation, for an area of a few miles radius around each city was all that was needed for agricultural purposes, so much of the bulk food was produced synthetically. In consequence the *forests* were growing again, and vast sections that had been highly farmed in the old days were now stretches of woodland and prairie untouched by the hand of man, for even freight was not carried by rail, and there was no use for *roads*, although over the beauty of this wilderness the *air routes* hummed with the swift passage of freight and passenger traffic from one center of population to another, and occasionally outing parties or forest patrols could be seen leaping lightly over hill and dale with the aid of their jumping belts.

THE RED PLANET

But my interests were not confined to Earth. Stranger still than this world of the 25th Century were those other worlds to which my adventures carried me.

Mars, with its clear sparkling air, its cloudless skies and its pale, greenish yellow sunshine, its vast red deserts and great canals, many of them ten to twenty miles wide, sweeping in straight lines and immense curves, to form fascinating patterns when seen from the upper air levels; its peculiar beasts, its occasional jagged mountain ranges of crystal-clear quartz, and its amazing people, so like those of Earth in most respects, but so unlike them in certain of the customs and mental reactions.

MOONS OF SATURN

The *Moons of Saturn*, a little galaxy of worlds, some larger and some smaller than our dead, airless moon of Earth, were so close together that they appeared (from the inner ones) like great pale discs sliding perpetually in confusing orbits across a blue-grey dome. And *Saturn* itself, always an amazing sight as it filled half the sky with its great rings looped around it. On these worlds I never knew whether to call it night or day, for the reflected light from Saturn was almost as great, although soft and diffuse, as the hard, clear light from the distant sun; and that from the other moons was much like the light of Saturn itself.

THE LIQUID-AIR OCEANS OF JUPITER

Jupiter, another amazing planet, where men lived on vast plateaus that were in reality the tops of mountain ranges *thousands of miles* above the valleys, in the mysterious depths of which the blue air liquefied under a pressure almost too great for the mind of man to comprehend. No Jovian had ever plumbed the depths of those valleys. No craft *could* descend into them more than

JOVIAN INTERCONTINENTAL FLYER

a fraction of the way. No material existed in the universe of which a vessel could be made that would not crush like an eggshell under that super-pressure. So Jovian life was confined to the mountain tops that were continents surrounded by "seas" of air, across which the intercontinental flyers flashed on their weary journeys; for the distances were vast. Jupiter has a diameter about ten times that of Earth, and many an intrepid explorer has been lost thereon.

THE EROS MYSTERY

Then there was *Eros*, the cigar-shaped planetoid that swung end over end in an orbit beyond that of Mars, and on, and *in* which Wilma and I found things that staggered and shattered our imaginations.

ATLANTIS, THE CITY UNDER THE SEA

But there were wonders on Earth too, undreamed of back in the 20th Century, even though hints of them remained in old forgotten legends. The legend of *Atlantis*, for instance, the city and continent that sank beneath the sea in prehistoric times, and of whose original inhabitants many of the Caucasian races are descendants.

Atlantis still existed, under the ocean, inhabited by men who through the countless ages had become amphibian, who were equally at home in the artificially ventilated corridors and chambers of their submarine city, or in the water of the sea surrounding it, who had a civilization no less advanced, but strangely different from that of Earth's land races, from whom they had been living apart for eons.

It was Wilma and I who "discovered" Atlantis. It was there that one of our most desperate struggles with Killer Kane and Ardala occurred. Far beneath the surface of the Atlantic, these two super-criminals succeeded in balking our every move. However, it was we who finally succeeded in—but that is a story in itself.

THE ASTERITES

And there were the *Asterites*, tiny men not more than a foot tall, who came from outer space, and began with deadly determination their campaign of conquest and destruction of the planet Earth. And it was Wilma and I who bore the brunt of their first attack, with consequences that could not have been foreseen.

ASTERITE AND WILMA

AND SO, it was among such surroundings and events as the foregoing that Buck Rogers, the lithe, sinewy, 20th Century youth who by a strange trick of fate jumped the time gap from the 20th to the 25th Century, and Wilma, that dashing, fearless lovely girl of the new day, lived and loved and struggled, both joyously and mightily, to overcome the evil that not only for the World, but for the Universe, was personified in the ruthlessly bitter, magnificent wickedness of Killer Kane, and the evil that lay in the heart of Ardala.